Sow the Wind

Book One of the
At the Edge of Promises Series

Chris Burgess

Copyright © 2024 Chris Burgess

The moral right of the author has been asserted.

Apart from any fair dealing for the purposes of research or private study, or criticism or review, as permitted under the Copyright, Designs and Patents Act 1988, this publication may only be reproduced, stored or transmitted, in any form or by any means, with the prior permission in writing of the publishers, or in the case of reprographic reproduction in accordance with the terms of licences issued by the Copyright Licensing Agency. Enquiries concerning reproduction outside those terms should be sent to the publishers.

This is a work of fiction. Names, characters, businesses, places, events and incidents are either the products of the author's imagination or used in a fictitious manner. Any resemblance to actual persons, living or dead, or actual events is purely coincidental.

Troubador Publishing Ltd
Unit E2 Airfield Business Park,
Harrison Road, Market Harborough,
Leicestershire. LE16 7UL
Tel: 0116 2792299
Email: books@troubador.co.uk
Web: www.troubador.co.uk

ISBN 978 1805143 260

British Library Cataloguing in Publication Data.
A catalogue record for this book is available from the British Library.

Printed and bound in Great Britain by 4edge Limited
Typeset in 12pt Adobe Jenson Pro by Troubador Publishing Ltd, Leicester, UK

For Sarah, Michael and Joe

"You are as like the forming of God as ever people were… you are at the edge of promises and prophecies."

Oliver Cromwell

"For they have sown the wind, and they shall reap the whirlwind."
Hosea 8:7

1

(Breda, The Dutch Republic, 1637)

Why wouldn't they get off his chest? He was struggling to breathe with the weight. A dead man? Wounded? When they had needed darkness to cover their advance, the full moon bathed them in light. *Curse it!* Now, when he needed to push the man off him, he couldn't see anything in the pitch dark. *Now the clouds are here*, he thought bitterly. *Where were you an hour ago?!*

He was on his back in the dust and found he couldn't move his arms. He tried to wriggle from under the weight but couldn't move at all. Damn, but it was hot. He was sweating in his leather coat and cuirass, and he could feel liquid pooling against his back. He remembered taking a blow like a hammer to the steel of his breastplate but nothing after that. He must have passed out. Even now he felt nauseous and only just on the right side of consciousness.

He could hear shouts and some screams, but only faintly. He must be surrounded by his men. Veterans from his father's tercio. *Surely they can't all have fallen. Someone will drag me back to our lines.* These men didn't run from the enemy, particularly from heathen English dogs. But no hands were laid on him. No one was rolling the pinning weight off him and lifting him under his arms. The sounds he had heard had grown fainter and silence had fallen. He was alone. Alone in the dark.

He strained to lift his head so he could see his situation better. Pain lanced across his chest and his head felt it would split in two. He clenched his jaw with the effort and managed to lift his head, fighting the weight of his helmet, just enough to see down his chest. There was nothing. Not even the distant glow of the besiegers' campfires. Just blackness. With a sudden jolt of horror, he realised he couldn't see.

A low moan escaped him as panic rose in his throat, but he clamped his mouth shut. Rodrigo, first son of the Duke of Dénia, did not cry out. He would not cry out. No! What he would do was try to move. To move back towards the protection of the trees they had left only a while before. No chance now to take the outer defences with all hope of surprise gone. They would regroup and try again, this time without the damned moon to betray them.

He found he could raise his hips slightly, which surprised him, given the dead weight he felt constricting his chest. Breathing was becoming even more difficult, and he felt himself drifting towards unconsciousness again. He tried to roll, waiting for both the relief and the pain of the body lying across him shifting, but he felt nothing. He arched his back and found that if he dug his heels into the dirt, he could move slightly along his length, even if his arms were seemingly no help. The pain was intense and again he had to clamp his teeth together to strangle a cry, but now it was clear there was nothing lying across him. Perhaps the weight he felt was from the steel of his cuirass, buckled in deflecting the lead musket ball. He had to protect his dignity, but he also knew there may be godless English mercenaries just waiting to finish him off and loot him of his armour and his precious sword. The blade, the finest Toledo steel, was not

(Breda, The Dutch Republic, 1637)

feeling too precious at the moment as his movement caused the jewelled pommel to stick into his gut, worming under the lower rim of his cuirass. If he could only manage a few paces, perhaps some of his men would notice him and drag him to safety. He braced himself for the rush of pain and struggled to move again.

Over the next five minutes he travelled the equivalent of ten steps, flopping along like a beached tuna, his breath rasping in his throat, sweat drenching him. The constriction on his chest was getting worse and he finally realised that the pooling liquid in his cuirass wasn't only sweat. His hopes were in retreat. He thought he could manage just one more effort. This time, instead of the same packed earth beneath him, he felt the edge of a slope and, without the use of his arms to steady himself, he rolled helplessly downhill. One, two revolutions, and he came to a stop. There was a faint splash and his legs were immediately soaked up to the top of his thighs. He felt coarse reeds pressing against his face, but he had no leverage to move his head away.

He stared up into the night sky with his sightless eyes, but he knew where he had come to rest. Not towards the safety of the trees, but into the ditch at the foot of the rampart, right under the eyes of the English. The closeness of the summer evening with the strain of his efforts to move were cooking him. A very slight breeze touched his skin and he thought it the most delicious thing. He thought of standing in his father's castle, the old Venetian fortress above the bay. Palm trees swaying slightly in the breeze off the sea in the spring when he had pleaded with his father to allow him to go on campaign. To follow in his father's footsteps and win glory in this righteous war against the heathens in Flanders. This was not how he had thought it would end. And Rodrigo of Dénia now assumed this was the end.

A peace settled over him and he summoned prayers to his mind, mumbling quietly in the darkness. The attack had been foolhardy, but surely none could doubt his bravery. His father would understand. The Cardinal-Infante would understand. He had done his best. There was no shame.

He could feel a rising tide in his chest and he felt the panic again. He took a huge gasping breath and knew there wouldn't be another one. In the blackness, right in the middle, he could see a pinprick of light. As he fought despairingly for air, the circle grew larger. Was he moving towards the light, or was it coming for him? *It's coming for me*, was Rodrigo's last thought. His straining muscles relaxed. His mind was a blank slate. Whatever had animated his limbs and had driven him across that open ground to the rampart, and had taken his thoughts back to his home, had now departed.

2

(Breda, The Dutch Republic, 1637)

Richard Farrell wiped the sweat from his forehead and cursed the sun. The heat was relentless and for the third time in a few minutes, he stared over at his commanding officer, willing him to call a break. To allow him and the rest of them some relief from their labour and some shade.

He had never dreamed of glory. As a young boy he had played with a wooden sword, leading charges or defending the breach to his last breath. He had been honoured by his king and brought despair to his enemies. A soldier, a captain, a hero. But he had never considered life as a soldier and yet, at the age of fifteen, here he was.

The weapon he held now was not famous, but he had learnt that it was the one that soldiers most commonly wield. And he was doing what soldiers mostly do. Digging. Day in and day out. Digging trenches. Sometimes, to break the monotony, he dug latrines. But mainly trenches. And as he stood in today's trench, barely able to peer over the hard-baked lip of brown earth at the flat, blasted landscape, he contemplated again how things never quite work out how you hope they will.

He had arrived on the continent from England early in the new year and he had been camped outside Breda, in the Low Countries, since July. It was now late August and after months of icy winter temperatures, followed by weeks of wet weather and strangely high winds, the weather had turned hot. As one of the youngest and newest recruits in the band of English mercenaries, he was rewarded with the most prized tasks. Digging latrines and digging trenches. The well-fed, rosy-cheeked teenager was now a lean digging machine. Three months of basic rations, never-ending labour and scorching weather had hardened muscles and sinews and thinned his face. The plump cheeks of childhood, sustained by the fertile soil of East Anglia, were burnt brown, although now red with exertion. He had aged two years in six months but had seen little action, only the foul and bloody aftermath.

His company was attached to one of four English regiments supporting the army of Frederick Henry, Prince of Orange and Stadtholder of the Dutch Republic. The Dutch had been fighting the Spanish for decades, more recently in alliance with the French, and Richard knew that close by were battalions of French troops and mercenaries, and on the far side of the city, many Scottish soldiers stood, or more likely were digging, alongside the Dutch regular troops. He also now knew that the attempt to take Breda had not been the main aim of the campaign. The Stadtholder was supposed to be attacking Dunkirk to secure access for the army to Flanders, but the contrary winds had delayed the assembling of his force and they were late starting. He had feinted towards the port, which had drawn foot and horse out of Breda to support the imperial troops in Dunkirk, but then Frederick had marched rapidly, with cavalry in advance, and had caught the Breda defences by surprise. They did not gain the gates but had driven off all the cattle in the surrounding fields, leaving the defenders short of provisions.

(Breda, The Dutch Republic, 1637)

Richard had caught up with the army, along with half a dozen other would-be soldiers from Suffolk and Essex here, at Breda. They had come into the English camp, after wandering around the perimeter of the siege asking in vain for the whereabouts of the contingent of their countrymen. They had been met with sullen silence and incomprehension from the Dutch, hysterical laughter, insults and kicks up the backside from the hardened Scottish mercenaries, and a professional level of disdain from the French. As he met up with the English, Richard had felt defeated even before he had stood toe to toe with any imperial troops. The only Imperials he had met were dead, and not about to test his courage and martial skill.

The countryside around Breda, what he could see of it from the trench, bore witness to the fact that this was just another in a line of military actions in the area. Famously, it had held out against the Spanish for eleven months, before being surrendered to Spinola. Now, only twelve years later, the Dutch were trying to win it back. The tramping of men, the quartering of horses, the felling of thousands of trees for shelters, trenches, mines, and for fires, had left the flat, green, fertile land a desolation of brown mud, now slowly hardening under the newly arrived summer sun.

When they had arrived in camp, the company's captain, Browne, had welcomed the boys with four pieces of information. The first three were practical and logistical. "This is where you sleep. This is where you eat. That is where you shit. Do not mix any of these up." The fourth would change the course of his life, although he was not to know it at the time.

"...And this is Master Roger DeLacey. You are now his... I hesitate to use the word 'responsibility' so, whatever you want to call it. He has survived campaigning for nearly ten years.

He was at Lützen, where Gustavus Adolphus met his fate. He was at Nördlingen. This means he knows something of the conduct of war and campaigning, although God knows that not many would want to pry into his mind to find out what that is. Master DeLacey is not a God-fearing man, but listen to him. Learn from him. Do as he says and you may also live long enough to be damned as surely as he will be."

Richard and his companions eyed the man pointed out by Browne, one of about thirty other mercenary soldiers scattered around the inside and outside of the barn, all looking for some shade and relief from the midday sun. He sat, leaning against the shaded wall of the ruined barn, knees drawn up, long brown leather coat draped around his shoulders and black, broad-brimmed hat shading his face.

Browne shouldered his baldric and scabbarded weapon. "Show them what it is to be valued members of our company, DeLacey."

The man pushed back his hat allowing a view of a weathered face and regarded Browne steadily with a hint of a smile animating the corners of his mouth. "As you say, Captain. But from the looks of them I would say that will be a lifetime's work. Mind you, their lifetimes may not be as long and as fulfilling as they may currently hope." He smiled more broadly. "I expect these additional responsibilities will be recognised in my pay, eh, Captain? Fair's fair, and you *are* a godly man, and one to keep his word."

Browne ignored this. "Take them to see our new Spanish neighbours. And take spades. Our new friends need to learn some of the basic arts of soldiering, and we need to do something about the smell!" There was some further, rather grim, laughter from those in earshot. "And DeLacey?" This as DeLacey was struggling to his feet.

"Captain?"

(Breda, The Dutch Republic, 1637)

"Try not to lose any like you did the last lot. As you say, we will need all the bodies we can get in the next few weeks. I have no doubt."

"Yes, Captain. But that was unlucky. You have to say so. As God as my witness, the silly fucker did say he could swim…" The hard London accent jarred among the rural tones of the other soldiers. There was an explosion of laughter from some of the other mercenaries lounging against the walls of the barn, but others looked on with disdain. Browne shook his head in mock despair, muttering that God would never knowingly be a witness to anything DeLacey did. He left them to it, striding out into the heat of the day for a conference with other company captains and their commanders.

"Right, gentlemen. Find a home for your belongings, grab a spade – they're outside – and meet me here in ten minutes. At least you country fuckers should know how to dig. There is space inside, at the far end – as far away from me as possible. And don't worry about your possessions. We may be mercenaries, but we are not thieves." Some looks were exchanged among the other soldiers around them. "Well, mostly…"

3

(North-West England)

She came down from the rocks two hours after dawn. It was midsummer's day, and already the sun was climbing up into a cloudless blue sky and starting to warm her face. She had seldom felt so... complete. She had no better word for it. She felt so aware of all that was happening around her. The pale lemon of the early light washing across the silver-white bark of a stand of birch trees, creating long shadows across the heather and gorse, glowing yellow. Early-rising bees braved the cool air to drift lazily from the flower heads, on overlapping shifts with the grazing rabbits which infested the undergrowth of copse and moor alike. The world around her hummed with existence and she felt it all like the flow of a slow-moving river over her skin.

She jumped from one clump of grass to another, avoiding the peaty bogs and occasional pools of dark water, looking like tar pits from a forgotten time. And the pools were ancient. Left behind by the heavy rains of weeks ago, now shrinking and concentrating their essence under the summer sun, they would never quite disappear entirely. Refreshed by rain, they retained their secrets in the deep black mud under the surface. But the knee-high tussocks of reeds, tiny green lances with their coarse banners, provided reliable footing and she would not fall victim.

The mud around the pools was stippled with hoof prints. Smaller ones from sheep and roe deer, larger ones from fallow and red deer. She thought back to last night and being woken in the moonlight by the soft sounds of the herd cropping the grass between heather, gorse and bracken. Soft ripping sounds, low grunts and coughs, but otherwise silent. Passing like ghosts through the birch, the moonlight causing the dappling on the flanks of the fallow deer to shine like stars, captive in their coats. She had struggled to return to sleep after that, excited by the prospect of the midsummer dawn and drawn to concentrate on the faintly discernible vibration she could detect with her ear pressed tight to the rock, still warm from the sun, when all else was utterly silent. She always marvelled at this, that the rocks too seemed alive, but no matter how she focused and channelled, she could never connect with them in the same way.

Before sleep, she had stood in the last light of the setting sun of midsummer's eve, washing her body with the red light as if it were water. Lathering the rays and smoothing them across her skin, open to the light. She said her words, a soft low chant that went with the sun's last moments. Words she had learned from no one, that she had created over time, honed and perfected until she was happy. They would change again, she was sure. As she studied. As she learned.

She had also spoken words to the rabbit she had snared. Stroking its head and ears to calm it. Holding it up above her head in her hidden place among the rocks, so it saw the sun finally disappear, even after her own last glimpse. Then, gently, but with a quick strength, she had twisted its neck, her eyes tightly shut and body entirely still, as she focused on its final second of life. Gutted, carefully skinned, spitted over her small fire, well shielded by the surrounding gritstone, it had made a feast. She had accompanied it with bilberries which grew in multitudes on the moorland, mushrooms and water from the pool. When she lay down on the warm rock, with her pack roll under her head, she was filled.

She had greeted the new sun in the same way, coating all of her skin with the fragile, hazy pink light of the start of the longest day. Her favourite day. Her magic day. One of the few days away from life. When she had time to watch, to learn and to think of nothing else but her questions. She knew her rite changed nothing. But it made her feel good, and it *felt* right, so maybe it did change things after all. She had placed the rabbit's innards some distance from where she had slept, on a small area of sand and mica. Now, as the sun gave enough light, she had lain down and carefully watched the ants swarming over the small pile, the bluebottle flies droning in circles to a landing.

With the rabbit pelt wrapped in leaves in her pack, with a dozen others, now she could stride on across already-yellowing grass, the awkward footing of the upland marsh behind her. Above, she heard the whistling of a kite, descending from its early morning thermal to investigate what the ants and flies were so industriously attending to. She ate up the ground quickly, and in half an hour, she walked up a narrow fold in the ground alongside a stream, ice cold over the rocks. A dipper greeted her, bobbing politely at the point where the cleft opened out into a small basin, and where the stream fell over the brink of the pool and exited the hollow. On the grassy bank, at eye level, on the far side of the water she saw the red-brown coat and black-tipped tail of a stoat disappearing into the bracken, ceding the water rights to her. It would watch and return when she was gone, before heading home.

The pool was filled by a trickle of a waterfall, coming from a height roughly twice hers. She had never known it dry up, or produce a torrent even after the heaviest weather. In some way it felt sacred to her, like the rocks, which the local people called the Roaches. They were to her an essence. A concentration of their kind. The Roaches were more rock than other rocks. 'Stone' was too small a word. The pool was so perfect in shape, so unfailing in flow, so consistently icy cold, so dependable. It was like the goddess of pools. Sun and rock and water – she knew her answers were bound up in all of this. She was close to an understanding. Life. Death. Life again. The moment of transition between the two.

She filled her water bottle. She lay on the grassy bank as the sun's direct light started to find its way over the lip of the folded ground and turned the stream of water into a sparkling string of light. She closed her eyes and started to review her knowledge. A skylark's bubbling song, mingling with the voice of the stream, provided accompaniment.

The stoat, by now thoroughly fed up with waiting, skirted a wide loop around her motionlessness and made do with a smaller and less perfect pool, lower down the little valley.

4

(England, The Hague and the Dutch Republic, 1637)

Richard followed his companions to the far end of the barn and found an empty space which, from the smell of it, had been much used during the hours of darkness when members of the company did not want to risk the uneven footing around the latrines. His companions were laying out their packs and what bedding they had, some attempting to hide any valuables in folds, pockets or crannies in the barn wall.

They had become quite a close-knit bunch over the previous weeks, sharing hardship, pooling their limited money and looking out for each other. He was closest to Will Fletcher, from the village which neighboured his own. Will was the son of a tenanted farmer, as were most of his other companions. They had never been close friends but had met on regular occasions at fairs and markets, as their fathers had sometimes conducted business together. It had been Will who had first raised the idea of soldiering. Richard had dismissed this initially, but as the months had passed, and he approached his fifteenth birthday, he had begun to think more and more about his future and was struggling to see his place in the world.

By contrast, Richard's family had a small manor close to Godmanchester, within a mile of the Great Ouse, and farmed the fertile flood plain, along with a handful of tenants whose families had lived on the modest estate for generations. Richard had enjoyed a stable, happy and carefree childhood. He had two older brothers and a younger sister. John was ten years older than Richard and was already taking on much of the business of running the estate from his father, whose age was catching up with him. Lionel, only a year or two younger than John, had entered the Church and, through his father's influence, was leading a congregation in a village about twenty miles to the north. Where John was hardworking, calm and patient, Lionel was fiery and intense. Richard knew he was more like Lionel. Both had strong views on what was fair and right, and this, combined with very short tempers, meant that he clashed with his brother often, John stepping in as peacemaker before his father stepped in with the birch.

Closest to him in age was Angelica. She was the light in the family's life, which seemed to Richard a balancing of the fact that their mother had died in her delivery. His father had named her his angel. She had a love of pretty much everything and everyone in the world, and an unselfish and unquestioning adoration of her family. Richard felt that it was almost as if she had in some way absorbed the life of her mother – such was the way she was bursting with joy and energy, like a small sun warming their world. Richard loved her above all else, and they were inseparable as they grew up together.

It was after speaking with Will that he had started to feel an increasing restlessness. He looked at himself and saw just a burden to his family. He helped out with the labouring on the estate, learning to supervise as well as bending his own back, but he knew he would never have any real say in how things were managed. He would not inherit. His free time was spent improving his riding at which, despite his young age, he was already highly accomplished. He was a good shot with his father's matchlock and pistols, although powder and ball were expensive, and he could not practise as much as he wished. But where was it all leading him? He was in the way. He was a plough looking for a field. An axe without logs to chop.

So, in early January of 1637, with no other plan that inspired him, and no particular passion for the calling, Richard started his campaign to persuade his father of the merit of becoming a soldier. If he was expecting a long and difficult process, he was disappointed. In fact, he was rather surprised, and not a little hurt, at how receptive his father was to the idea. Richard suspected that his father shared his own uncertainty as to what he was going to do with his life and had concluded that this may indeed be one way to solve the challenge of 'what to do about Richard'. Both agreed that Richard's future did not lie in the Church. His father was a religious man, but no more or less than anyone else in the area. Richard did not possess Lionel's passion and dedication for the Puritanism that was widespread in their area. The debate seemed to be more about how they should proceed than whether he should go at all.

With no wars abroad and comparative peace at home, the army was small and opportunities for any kind of military career seemed challenging. However, his father's time in the local militia had left him with a few contacts among those men who had gone on to make a living in soldiering. One of these, Matthew Bray, had been in the village at Christmas, and his father had met him by chance in the Blue Boar. Bray had returned from the Low Countries where he had been serving with a regiment attached to Goring's forces, supporting England's Dutch allies in their endless war with the Spanish. Bray was something of a local celebrity. A well-travelled man, he had the aura of a hard sort who had seen more war and horror in fifteen years soldiering on the continent than all the inhabitants of Richard's village in their lifetimes combined. They had spoken at length, catching up on Bray's stories, and Richard's father responding with news of local events, and what could be read from the occasional political pamphlets that made their way out to the countryside from London.

So, when he raised the subject of soldiering with his father, the immediate action was to find and consult with Bray. Unsurprisingly, they found him by the fire in the tavern, absorbing as much of the fire's heat as possible to fend off what was a particularly cold January day. Bray had listened with a bored indifference to their questions, but in the end, after enjoying copious amounts of the Blue Boar's hospitality, had offered Richard, and friend Will, the chance to join his own unit. In fact, it soon emerged that one of the reasons he had stayed in the area for several months was to find new recruits to bolster the regiment's numbers, and Richard reflected that they could have saved time, and the expense of the ale, if this offer had just been made at the start of the conversation. He had no doubt that his father was very aware of this too but had felt it a price worth paying.

Richard and Will were to rendezvous with Bray's sergeant, a man called Price, at Lowestoft, from where a boat would take them across to The Hague. They would wait there for Bray and other small contingents of recruits and then would march to join the main army. Richard had listened with growing concern at the speed with which events were unfurling. He had imagined in his mind a prolonged period of farewells with his family and the opportunity to impress his friends with his daring. But in the end, it had been a rushed two days getting together his gear, polishing his father's old sword and saying tearful goodbyes to his family.

Saying goodbye to Angelica was particularly upsetting. She could not understand his need to go and his apparent determination to leave her behind. With his growing apprehension about the journey and what awaited him in Flanders, this heart-breaking separation, and an overwhelming feeling of guilt that came with it, had rather taken the edge off the excitement of starting on his new path. He wondered again at the motivation for his decision and found nothing other than boredom and a lack of alternatives. That would have to do for now, but it seemed precious little to hold on to.

And as the days passed, Richard had come to realise that things seldom seemed to work out quite as planned. He arrived in The Hague with Sergeant Price and ten other recruits after a stormy winter crossing that left him feeling turned inside out. He had never known that the human body could contain fluid in such inexhaustible supply. Even when this had all been dispersed across the pitching deck, he had not been allowed to die quietly but was forced repeatedly to try to catapult his stomach to join the bile. His only consolation on reaching the dock was the knowledge that his sickness had distracted from the sheer terror of their small ship's passage through – it seemed, rather than over – the watery mountains.

Even as he was recovering from this ordeal, and as they waited for the arrival of other parties for the gathering of recruits, he was hit by a real blow. The first group to follow them across the North Sea brought the news that after years of facing the risks of campaigning across the Low Countries and beyond, Major Matthew Bray had slipped on the wet dock in Felixstowe and fallen between the dock and the ship's side. The weight of his cuirass and other equipment had taken him straight to the bottom, and his body had not been recovered for several hours with the change in the tide.

With the loss of Bray, he felt cut adrift, with little connection with his former life. His glittering, romantic career as a soldier was stuck in the silt of Felixstowe and showing no sign of buoyancy. He leaned more and more on his growing friendship with Will, who had borne the news with what he was discovering was typical stoicism.

He was also concerned at the lack of respect he was being shown by Sergeant Price. Bray had assured his father that he would be considered as a junior officer, albeit in need of significant training, befitting his position as a member of the minor gentry. But Price treated him just as he did all the others, that is with utter contempt and quick violence. It seemed Bray had omitted to communicate his special status, and Price was not one to be reasoned with. Once the ship had left the quay his winning smile had disappeared like the sun going behind a snow-laden cloud, and as far as Richard could see, it wasn't going to shine out again before hell had frozen over. Looking back, he marvelled at the effort it must have taken for Price to contort his facial muscles into anything remotely resembling a cheery demeanour.

Even Price had not tried to drill them during the crossing as the deck was never horizontal for more than a few seconds, but he had successfully instilled into them hunger, pain, frustration and of course fear – all the key components of a life in the military. Now they were on dry land, albeit covered in snow or muddy sludge, he had them up at first light, marching endlessly, and trying to teach them the rudiments of fighting through mock combat with wooden weapons. This seemed to involve Price mocking their attempts at combat while beating them senseless with the wooden weapons. Also, Richard was becoming convinced that Price was not a truly godly man. He seemed to know all the whorehouses in The Hague and Rotterdam – and there were quite a few – and would place two or three of the new recruits on guard outside the establishments to warn him if the local police put in an appearance.

While Richard was mainly cold, hungry and nursing bruises, most of the other boys were stoic about the physical conditions but horrified at the ungodly behaviour of Price. Raised in good Puritan families, the swearing, whoring and drinking carried out by this one man in a month was more than they had observed in their lifetimes, and they genuinely feared for the contamination of their souls from the man's mere proximity. Richard knew he was getting a flavour of real army life, but things that tasted like this wouldn't have been fed to a dog back at home.

With Bray gone, Richard was becoming increasingly in favour of seeking a boat back to England, but Will persuaded him to persevere. Will, as politely as he could, given the difference in their status, had emphasised his commitment to 'making something of himself'. Richard had not registered the unspoken accusation that his own motivation was more romantic than pragmatic, and that this dose of the real world would not deter a 'real' soldier.

Eventually, towards the end of March, Sergeant Price's group had been joined by enough other boys to justify a march to join the main body of the army. One of these groups came with a captain, who assumed command of what was now a unit of sixty. Having assembled them all in rough ranks, much to the frustration of Price's troop, he commended Price for 'whipping these boys into shape' and awarded him a day's leave to spend as he wished. Price turned and looked over his shoulder at the boys assembled behind him and… a miracle! The clouds parted, the sun appeared again and a contented leer spread across his face.

5

(Breda, August 1637)

Back out in the furnace of the August afternoon, DeLacey led the troop of lads south-east, away from Breda. The flat countryside was a baked, dead wilderness. Breda had been besieged several times as the tide of the seemingly never-ending wars washed repeatedly across it. There were few trees, most having been felled for fuel, or for building encampments, trenches and mines. Grass had been trampled by thousands of men and horses, and the dominant colour of the landscape was a depressing grey-brown. It felt a million miles away from the fertile countryside of the fenlands, and Richard reflected, yet again, that things seldom seemed to go as planned.

It had taken a scarcely believable four months to march from The Hague, the journey punctuated by long, boring halts as they met up with other parties of English and Dutch soldiers and linked up with supply trains. Finally, they had caught up with the main body of the Stadtholder's army. Then, within a few days' journey from Breda, he and a number of the other new recruits had been sent to steal supplies from local farms, or 'foraging' as their officers had called it. In a sudden, wild summer storm they had lost their way and become separated from their company. When they had stumbled into the mercenary camp, Captain Browne had spotted them and taken ownership, to replace, he had said, men lost in a skirmish with the Spanish a day earlier. Browne had told them he would square this with the colonel and that they were now 'his'. Richard never knew if he had done this, but looking back he doubted it.

In his dirty linen shirt, woollen breeches and disintegrating boots, Richard could already feel the sweat forming around his hat band and starting to drip between his shoulder blades. The temporary relief of the barn's shade was a memory, and the lads, spades over shoulders, trudged after DeLacey.

After a few minutes they could see a small rise in the otherwise flat fields – some kind of earthen rampart. One or two figures could be seen slowly pacing along it, backwards and forwards, muskets over shoulders.

"Outer defences. Rampart and ditch," DeLacey informed them over his shoulder.

"I thought we was the ones doin' the siegin'," offered one of the other lads.

"Cardinale-Infante tried to relieve the city when we first arrived, but he was pushed off. His main body has moved on, but he left some horse and foot to keep us occupied, and to attack supply lines. Not enough to cause us real hurt, but just in case we got bored like... So we dug this as a back door. Well, when I say *we* dug it, it was a bloody army of farmers and peasants that ol' Frederick, Prince o'fucking Orange, brought with 'im that dug it. There were thousands of 'em and by God but they finished this ditch in a few days. The Spanish keep comin' to give it a knock, all friendly-like. Usually at night. Hadn't seen 'em for over a week, but we had guests last night. And that's why you lot are out here with me now."

They were now walking up on to the top of the chest-high

(Breda, August 1637)

rampart, the nearest sentry slowly strolling to meet them. His hat was the only shade offered for half a mile, and in a slightly rusted steel cuirass and leather jerkin, he was scarlet in the face with sweat dripping off the end of his nose.

"You the relief?" he said, looking doubtfully at the spade-armed group of lads.

"Aye," said DeLacey. "And burials. You head back, friend, we got it now. Send some other buggers out here in three hours." Some of the Puritan boys winced at the language. The man just nodded in gratitude.

"And Edward?" nodding his head in the direction of the other sentry a hundred yards to his left.

"Aye. Him too."

The mercenary slithered down the loose, dusty slope of the rampart, shouting over to his companion, who waved across and started heading back to the camp around the barn. DeLacey was left on the rampart with Richard, Will and the five others, and now they looked out over the land beyond it. At their feet, the ground fell steeply away to the bottom of the ditch created by the digging of the rampart. Despite the heat, there was filthy water of indeterminate depth with weeds, reeds and ragged bushes clinging to the edge, undisturbed here by the movement of men. On the far side of the ditch the land stretched away, flat but with the glint of a larger body of water in the distance and small stands of beech and birch trees, even a hint of grass.

"That's water from the River Marck. The Dutchies dammed the river and diverted it into the ditch. Very helpful of them. Helps keep out the Spanish, and it's deep in places. Deeper than it looks. Like the captain said, we lost one in there a few days ago."

It was the ground just below them that caught their attention. The outward slope of the rampart and the land immediately beyond the water. A dozen or so black mounds stood out starkly from the grey-brown dust. The ones across the ditch were serving as perches for crows and ravens, but all of them hummed and pulsed like living things.

"Right, lads. This should keep you busy. Two of you for sentries, five for digging. You two on the left," DeLacey's head nodded in the direction of two of the boys, Godfrey and Walter, "post yourselves one hundred good paces in that direction. When you get there, one of you walk away from us for one hundred paces, the other walk back to us. When you have done that, walk back to meet each other. Go on. Push off."

Walter looked confused. "But what do you want us to do when we have done that?"

DeLacey looked equally confused. "Well, you do it again, don't you!"

"Oh. Right you are." A pause. "And then?"

DeLacey rolled his eyes and walked over to Walter. Before anyone knew what was happening he had cuffed Walter heavily around the head with his leather gauntlet. "Do you mock me, boy?! Do I strike you as someone who likes to say things more than once?!" he bellowed into Walter's surprised face. He put his hands on Walter's shoulders, spun him around and shoved him off along the rampart, giving him a savage kick up the arse to get him moving. He turned to Godfrey who had very sensibly backed off a few paces.

"Are we clear, sir?"

"Very clear! Could not be any clearer! We are watching out for Spanish, right?"

"God give me strength! If you see anything at all, you come running back to tell me immediately and tell your idiot friend to fight them to the death. His death, that is…!"

He watched them jog off into the heat haze, slowly shaking

his head. He turned back to the others. "Right, boys. I count about a dozen of the poor sods. So two large holes should do it. You'll have to drag these ones," nodding at the black heaving lumps on the slope of the rampart below them, "to the other side. And make the holes at least twenty paces from the ditch."

It took Richard a few moments to understand what was being asked of him. He had been staring wide-eyed at the seething masses throughout DeLacey's ranting and was still unsure what it was he was looking at. Subconsciously his brain had made the correct identification, but somehow he could not quite accept the picture as real. Then he felt a soft thump between his shoulder blades and Will's quiet voice in his ear.

"Come on, Rich. Let's get this over with. We would want someone to do this for us if we were in their place." Richard nodded, still staring. Still unmoving. Will raised his voice to carry to the other boys. "You lot start digging, Rich and I will bring these ones over."

DeLacey could see the shock and horror on their faces and clearly decided brusqueness was the right way to go. "Come on! The poor fuckers can't bury themselves. Keep your gloves on if you have them, and if you have scarves or anything else like that, tie them around your faces like this." He dragged his scruffy black cravat up over his nose and mouth so just his eyes showed. "All the good stuff has been taken, but if you see anything you fancy on them, you can help yourself. If you have the stomach for it. They don't need it now. But that don't mean you treat 'em with disrespect!" And as the three in the digging party set off slowly down the slope: "And be careful crossing the ditch! We never found the one we lost in there."

"You comin'?" Will was looking back over his shoulder as he headed towards the first mound. Richard nodded, pulling his scarf up over his face, wishing he could use it as a blindfold. As they approached the body, and Richard could no longer deny to himself that this is what it was, the black flies rose in a sluggish wave from the end nearest to them, like a black shroud being pulled back to enable identification. Both boys immediately swung around and vomited violently.

During the night, foxes and stray dogs had been busy, and the crows had followed them at first light. The corpse had lost both eyes, and the skin, almost pure white but blotched with black and purple underneath, was heavily lacerated, with chunks of flesh missing from arms, face and thighs. The belly was slashed open and large strings of intestine showed through. As well as the animal scavengers, humans had also been busy. The man's boots and jacket were gone, and he had no armour, weapons, pack, jewellery or other belongings.

"Picked clean," came DeLacey's voice from behind them, but softly and without the aggressive edge from before. "Come on, lads. One at the head and one to take the feet. Keep him face up or all his guts will come out."

The flies, which had settled back to work after the first disturbance, rose again and formed a stubborn cloud around Will and Richard as they bent to their work. His own stomach still heaving, he tried to hold his breath to avoid the terrible stench. He tried to carry the body without looking at it, eyes wildly trying to find some point to fix on. He looked at Will and saw him staring wide-eyed back at him but nodding to indicate they should lift together.

"One. Two. Three!"

As they lifted, struggling under the weight, Richard saw how the man died. In addition to the gaping black holes of his wasted eyes, a third hole in his cheek marked the entry of the ball and, as his head lifted from the ground, Richard saw that it had taken most of the back of his skull off. He fought for control of his stomach and failed, vomiting this time into his scarf and then over the corpse, but managing to maintain his grip.

(Breda, August 1637)

He had seen death before, what with sicknesses and fevers, as well as old age, carrying off villagers from the village, but he had not been close to this type of violent, savage death. It was hard to believe the awkwardly shaped thing that he and Will struggled to haul down the slope had once been a human. A person full of life – feeling, loving. Living. This 'thing' was entirely devoid of any spark. There was now no clue as to the type of person that it had once been, in fact it was hard to see how this lump of meat could have ever existed in the same way as he, Richard, did. It was missing... something. The man's soul, he guessed. Gone to be with God – or as the man was undoubtedly Catholic, his soul was in the other place? His brother Lionel could have talked to him about these things. Reassured him of the life to come. But this somehow felt different. Not a triumphant victory of the saved, but sad. Desolate. Lonely. Wasteful.

The more he tried to hold Will's gaze, the more he stared into the man's face. His mind flipped the face into his own, and he imagined himself being lugged to an unmarked pit like the carcass of diseased livestock. And then worse. The face rotated through a sequence of his brothers and father. His sister, Angelica – God, no! And then thinking of his dead mother, who he could not in honesty remember, but his mind fashioned an image in any case. He could feel himself losing grip of himself, not physically this time, but getting lost in whirling thoughts and emotions like water cascading through the gates of a sluice.

"Rich. Rich! RICH!" Will's voice cut through, damming the torrent of confusion.

Richard looked up sharply. Looked around, not at first entirely sure where he was. He looked back up the slope and saw DeLacey staring back, a strange, slightly puzzled, concerned look on his face. He saw the other lads, spades in hand, looking back over the ditch at him, one of them laughing at his gormless expression, but the others perhaps also sharing some of his obvious shock and discomfort.

"Sorry, Will." Then quietly, "Let's get moving."

"C'mon, boys. Sooner started, sooner finished," shouted DeLacey. "Put your backs into it!"

An hour later and the bodies were covered over, marked only by the darker brown of the freshly dug ground – the richer, more fertile earth from beneath the dry, dusty topsoil leaving a sign that would itself soon fade under the hot sun. DeLacey called them back up the slope, the lads damp below the waist from repeatedly wading the ditch. Initially this had been a pleasant cooling, but the boys were now starting to smell badly as the heat raised steam from the ditch water.

With some effort, DeLacey managed to retrieve the two sentries, Walter only realising that he was not being given a friendly wave when DeLacey drew his sword and mimed a decapitation. Once he was back in shouting range, Walter was left in little doubt about DeLacey's message and also, to his complete surprise, learned new information about his parents, and his sexual relationships with various farmyard animals.

"Right. You two," nodding at Will and Richard, "sentries. The rest of you back to the barn and try to clean some of that muck off your breeches or the men will think you shat yourselves at the sight of dead Spaniards."

With uncomfortable looks exchanged between them, the five headed off through the haze.

"You two – what are your names?"

"Richard Farrell."

"Will Fletcher."

"Right, Master Farrell and Master Fletcher. As before, one hundred paces out along the wall and then split. You will be relieved in two hours. Roughly. Maybe."

(Breda, August 1637)

"And you, sir? Where will you be?" Richard asked nervously. Even though they were less than ten minutes from the barn and the company of well-armed, seasoned mercenaries lounging in the shade, the rampart felt isolated and vulnerable. The time spent with the recently deceased was still fresh in his mind.

"Are you mad, boy? I'm off to rest after my exertions. A highly trained military man such as myself needs to rest so he can perform at the highest level. You two fuck off and guard me while I sleep. Such clever and brave lads as yourselves can surely guarantee our safety."

Will and Richard shared a look which DeLacey did not miss. "Not resting from the digging. That's for you young and sprightly stalwarts." He stood in front of Richard and stared into his eyes from a few inches away. "Who do you think put the extra eyehole in that fucker's face? I've been up all night, boy!"

Richard and Will set off along the top of the rampart as DeLacey strolled back to camp. Richard noticed that their shadows were gradually angling up the rampart and starting to lag behind them, a welcome sign that the sun was finally making its way nearer to the horizon, although, if anything, the temperature in their personal oven seemed even more extreme and the atmosphere was getting more oppressive.

They counted out a hundred paces, and Richard offered to take the line away from camp and, from his point of view, further away from the Spanish dead. As he turned to start his pacing, Will stopped him. A hand on his shoulder.

"You OK? You went a bit, I don't know, odd."

"Yes. I'm fine. And thanks, Will. Really. I guess all this…" he shrugged as he looked around, "…this… I am just taking a while to understand it."

"Nothing to understand, is there? It is what it is. Is this not what you expected, Rich? This is soldiering. It will feel a lot better when we get paid, although God knows when that will be!"

"Will Fletcher! Do you blaspheme?!" Richard laughed. Perhaps for the first time in weeks. "What would your mother say!"

Will also blurted out a laugh. "You're right." He grinned. "I think that Master DeLacey is a bad influence on me!" They both exploded in laughter – a reaction to the horror. When recovered, they trudged off in opposite directions, one toward the sun, the other with his back to it.

*

Richard turned and the low sun blinded him. Again. Every time he forgot. Through the light, he could just make out the dark outline of Will moving back towards him at a slow, steady pace. He looked out over the ditch, and the angled light helped him to pick out the trees, water and even a few farm buildings in the distance, things that the earlier heat haze had largely hidden. Nothing was moving. Any farmer still in the area would have tried to sell or move his animals away weeks ago before they were 'foraged' in the name of their Stadtholder, Frederick.

He glanced back the other way, towards the camp around the barn, and was rewarded with the sight of three figures slowly making their way towards them. He waved at Will and pointed. Will acknowledged with a wave of his own. Richard had been passing the time tossing pebbles at targets down in the ditch as he walked along, and now he turned and threw the remaining handful towards a floating piece of fence post in the murky water. A woody 'thunk', some splashing misses, but also a clear metallic 'clank'. Richard stopped dead and peered down into the water. Just beyond the wood, wedged into the bank of the ditch and under some weeds, he could now see a glint of something floating on, or just below, the surface.

Why didn't I see that before? Must be the changing slant of the sun that had now illuminated the ditch more clearly. He shouted to Will but headed down the slope before waiting to see if Will had heard or reacted. He could definitely now see that the metal was a cuirass, or at least the backplate of a cuirass. Maybe the day would yield something more valuable than nightmares; a cuirass would be a substantial addition to his meagre collection of equipment, and his personal safety.

Without hesitation he waded again into the filthy ditch and surged across towards what it was now clear was a body, snagged on some branches sticking out from the muddy bank. He pushed back the submerged legs and grabbed the top rim of the metal armour. He yanked back and freed the body of its entanglement, the body coming free but also heading rapidly for the bottom of the ditch. Richard called out involuntarily and hauled back harder, almost losing his footing in the slippery silt. He could see long black hair waving under the rear rim of a steel helmet as he pulled the corpse back towards the 'safe' side of the ditch.

Keeping hold of the rim of the cuirass he attempted to drag the body out on to the muddy slope, but the sodden clothing and dead weight caused him to slip onto his arse, water lapping around his waist. "Shit!"

"Rich! What is it? Oh! Wait! Let me give you a hand." Will joined him at the water's edge, panting from his run along the rampart. They grabbed the body under its armpits, one on each side, and digging their heels in, slid the body out of the water in one heave until it lay on the slope with just the boots still in the water. They rolled him over onto his back.

Unlike the bodies on the dry land, this one was relatively undisturbed by scavengers and flies. The face of a young man, in his late twenties, looked back up at them. His eyes were misty, like Richard had once seen on a blind man in his village, but otherwise he was intact. His cause of death was clear, though: a neat round hole punched through his polished steel cuirass. The young man's face seemed inexpressibly sad. He had seen death coming and had faced it alone, in a filthy ditch, in a foreign country. This time Richard felt like weeping, not vomiting.

Judging from his dress, it also seemed clear that this man had been in command of the raid. The cuirass had engraving and rims in brass, and this was matched on the morion helmet, two red feathers from the crown lying sopping across the man's face. A padded red-leather surcoat, stained black with his blood, projected from under the steel, and baggy red breeches were tucked into the top of expensive-looking, leather knee-high boots. The face was framed by shoulder-length black hair, plastered to his cheeks by the ditch water and tangled in the neatly trimmed beard.

An empty leather pistol holster sat on the man's hip, but what drew Richard's attention was the hilt of the sword hanging from a fine, lace-edged baldric. An intricate basket, of what looked like silver, protected the grip, and a small red gem set in the end of the pommel flashed and sparkled in the lowering sun. Richard, who was nearest, reached out and tugged at the hilt, smoothly drawing a slim foot of glinting steel. Some engraving was visible and Richard, completely forgetting the dead carcass the sword was attached to, leaned in closer to be able to study it better. This blade was as removed from the old lump of metal that he carried, as a racehorse from his father's pair of plough horses.

Will, always the practical one, was searching through the man's small leather satchel. He whooped as he held up a fistful of coins. "Rich! Look!"

"What you got, boys?" came a voice from above them.

(Breda, August 1637)

"What you found then?" DeLacey turned and called down the slope to the other two lads who were with him. "You two wait there a while. And keep your eyes open. There could be danger and I don't want to put you in harm's way!"

Then he started down the slope towards them.

"Damn him," muttered Richard. "Quick, Will, hide that money in your breeches."

"Master DeLacey sir. I think he's some kind of lord or duke or somethin'," called Richard, seeing out of the corner of his eye Will's hand slowly moving behind his back, feeling for a pocket. "We must have missed 'im before 'cos he was stuck under the water."

DeLacey slid to a halt in front of him and looked down at the body. "Aye. Some kinda grandee. Actual Spanish as well, not one of their Walloons or Italians like are held up in there." He jerked his thumb over his shoulder in the direction of the city. "Pretty armour." He looked down. "And very nice boots. I could do with some boots!"

Will and Richard exchanged looks at each other and at their own boots, both pairs of which looked significantly sorrier than DeLacey's.

"Er, how does this work, Master DeLacey sir? 'Cos we *did* find him and drag him out."

"What do you mean, boy?" DeLacey was already going through the man's possessions as Will had done, minutes before.

"Well. His things. His armour, boots and…" he paused, trying to appear nonchalant, "…his sword. They are Will's and mine, ain't they? Bein' as how we found 'im."

DeLacey was busy dragging the body around so he could get at the straps on the cuirass. He nodded at Will. "Give me a hand liftin' 'im, won't yer. So I can drag this baldric over 'is head. Sword looks a good one."

"Yes. That's what I mean, sir…" said Richard, getting a bit desperate, he couldn't help himself, "…and I would like it. My own is no good and…"

DeLacey straightened up and looked from one to the other. He spat expertly between them into the dusty earth. "I'll tell you how this works, boy. We strip him. We carry this lot back to the camp. You want the sword?" Richard nodded, not knowing what was coming next. "What about you, Fletcher? It's Fletcher, ain't it? Do you want to keep them coins you stuck down your waistband as your share, or have you got your eyes on somethin' else?" Will flinched and looked helplessly at Richard.

"Er. I dunno, sir. I mean yes, I want to keep 'em, but is that my share? We don't know how this works."

"Well, lads. Here's my thoughts on the matter. I could just take it all, as your commanding officer. Or I can take a cut, as your commanding officer. Or we can also think about the men back at the barn who actually did the fightin' last night. Seems like they got a claim too, as it's unlikely either of you bastards put a ball in 'is lordship here. What do you recommend?"

Will and Richard looked at each other again. Was this some kind of a test? Was this where they proved their manliness by standing up to DeLacey? What he said did seem reasonable, but Richard felt that their digging of the graves and carrying of corpses, and patrolling in the worst of the day's heat, also merited something more. He was exhausted, mentally and physically, hungry, thirsty and he felt a long way from home. He was at breaking point, and he *really* wanted the sword. He came to a decision, swallowed hard and with a slightly quavering voice said, "How about we three pick one thing each, and then divide up the rest with the others?" He looked across at Will for support.

(Breda, August 1637)

Will nodded vigorously. "That seems fair. I'll give back the coins – they're easier to divide. You could have the boots, Master DeLacey sir! You said as how you liked 'em. Me, I'd like a bit more protection if we're going to be fighting soon. Could I take the breastplate thing? What about you, Rich?"

DeLacey smiled, but Richard felt it was not a comforting type of smile. "I know what your friend here wants. He's got 'is eyes on that yard of Toledo steel, 'aven't you, boy?" The smile disappeared like a snuffed-out candle. "So, you think I'm going to be happy with a pair of boots against the value of that plate, and the pretty sword? Do you think I was born yesterday?" He took a half-pace forward and lifted his left hand to rest on the hilt of his own sword.

Richard felt himself almost fainting. The heat and hunger and shock of the first brush with violent death had taken him to the edge. He didn't really feel in command of his senses but heard himself say, with a surprisingly steady voice, "I don't think that, sir, but I do think it is a fair suggestion." He looked at Will. "If Will is happy with me takin' the sword." Will just stared back, mouth slightly open in surprise and worry.

There was a long silence when DeLacey stared at Richard from just a long stride distant. Richard could hear a skylark trilling somewhere high in the air above them, a counterpoint to the dirt, death and ugly tension in the space that he occupied. DeLacey's eyes were hard, cold. But then his gaze softened slightly and his face wrinkled into a smile, twisting the old scars into changing patterns. "You know what, boys? Today I'm feelin' good. I've eaten – afraid you missed the mutton – I've slept in the shade, and some of the boys foraged a barrel of something that could possibly be apple cider. Most important, after our little party with the Spanish last night, I can still cast a shadow, and that's always good news. And now you tell me I've got a new pair of boots. Well, thank you, boys!"

He slapped Will on the shoulder but kept his eyes on Richard. The warmth of his smile had not quite reached his eyes yet.

"But let me make a suggestion now. I'll take your deal. We give the loot to the captain. That way the dividing up is his responsibility and we can't be accused of having favourites – good way to make enemies in a mercenary company," Will and Richard both nodded, but then, "...but I will take the boots, the plate and the Toledo steel. Just to look after 'em for you both while we are in camp."

That unexpected twist was like an abrupt slap across the face to Richard and, before he knew it, he was flaming angry. His father would have recognised the wild temper that erupted when Richard felt pushed over the brink. All the tension of the day erupted in him, uncontrollable, and he rode the tide. His already sunburnt face darkened with uncontrollable rage and he hissed at DeLacey, spraying him with saliva, "You dirty thief! Like we will ever see them again... I found him! I dragged him out. The sword is mi..." DeLacey's leather-gauntleted right fist, propelled by a strong, straight arm, caught Richard flat on the nose which immediately burst in a shower of blood droplets. Richard took a rapid step back, caught his heel on the body of the dead Spaniard and crashed backwards into the mud, head inches from the water. His fall created a fan of red mist which was shot through by the light of the reddening sun. Richard's scrambled brain registered this as a strangely beautiful thing.

Will's gaze followed Richard's fall, but when his eyes snapped back to DeLacey, a nine-inch, razor-sharp poignard was at his Adam's apple, with DeLacey's cold blue-grey eyes staring into his between the knuckles of his hand, shaded under the wide brim of his hat. "Got somethin' to say, Master Fletcher?"

With an eye still on Will, he stuck a hand towards Richard. "Get up, Farrell."

(BREDA, AUGUST 1637)

When Richard was vertical again, blood was leaking quickly from his broken nose, off his chin and down his dirty linen shirt. Now he felt the pain, a throbbing, intense ache oozing through the fingers he pressed to his face. DeLacey grabbed him by the bloody shirt front and hauled him closer. "How long do you think you would hang on to those pretty things in that company?" He jerked his head in the direction of the camp. "Not called mercenaries for nothin'. They wouldn't think twice about relievin' you of them things. But I think they would ponder a while before takin' 'em off me, don't you?" He shook Richard hard, causing another small spray of blood. "Don't you, Master Farrell?"

Richard nodded, only just hanging on to consciousness. "Was that a 'yes' or did I break yer neck?"

"'Uss," Richard managed. "Yes, sir," from Will.

"If you leave the company on your feet, come to me and they're yours. If you leave in a shroud, then they's mine. Call it a keeper's fee. But if either of you ever question my word again, I promise you it will be the last time you do. I may be many things, boys, and some of them I ain't that proud of, but if I give my word on somethin', it stays given. Now strip the guy and wrap up your pretty things in his shirt and breeches so it's not obvious what we got. I'm tryin' these boots on!"

Ten minutes later and it was done. The corpse was stripped, dignity preserved by the linen underclothes that were now his only remaining possessions. Richard, who had just about managed to stem the bleeding from his nose, wondered at this. In the end, whose dignity was it they were protecting? More about their own perhaps. Having stripped the body of everything valuable, leaving him covered by his underclothes was somehow symbolic. Something to show they themselves were civilised, and not just like the crows that pick the body after they were gone back to the camp.

Except this was not what happened. As they followed DeLacey back up the slope to the top of the rampart, DeLacey with the makeshift sack over his shoulder, he looked back at them. "What the fuck do you two think you are doing? Bury the bastard. Other side of the ditch. Then you come back to camp."

The other two boys from their party, who had been waiting anxiously on the blind side of the rampart, looked up in horror at Richard's smashed face and bloodstained shirt. "See, lads," DeLacey called back over his shoulder as he trudged back towards the camp, "I told you it was dangerous. No need to thank me for keeping you safe."

6

(North-West England)

The mid-summer sun was well past its zenith and was starting to lose a little of its warmth. A few small clouds had started to drift across what had been, up to that point, a perfect cloudless sky. She was making her way down the Black Brook, keeping close to the water, shielded from sight in the narrow fold through which the water gurgled and bubbled. She crossed frequently, sometimes from rock to rock, sometimes pressing her toes into the black earthy bottom and feeling the grip of the icy water.

Here and there, where the flow was slow, marsh marigolds clung, daringly holding their vibrant yellow over the clear water, insects accepting the offer to swing precariously over the current. There was no clear path, and she navigated through clumps of the brown-green-yellow of reeds and coarse grass, cropped short by sheep and deer. Skylarks had been her companions all day long, but these were now drowned out as a rowdy flock of rooks swept low over the moor, heading for the woods and down towards the valley of the River Dane.

Half an hour later she stepped into the cool of the trees – ash, beech and birch – and she struck off from the water, now angling up the steeper sides of the valley. She could hear the harsh, grating sounds of the rookery above her, and detoured slightly, not wanting to collect their offerings in her hair. In the early evening the wood was alive with bird song, and the sun laid the long shadows of the trees across the ferns and wildflowers around her feet.

Perspiring slightly, she reached her goal. A narrow cleft in the side of the valley, guarded by mossy gritstone stacks. Pausing for a moment in the undergrowth opposite this entrance, she watched and listened intently. Satisfied, she moved quickly across a small clearing and through the gap, about four feet in width but four times her height. She hopped lightly from stone to stone in the dim light, avoiding the thick black mud that covered the floor of the chasm. The cleft was open at the top, with the walls rising vertically. Water dripped through ferns perched on small balconies, glowing brightly at the top of the walls where they caught the sun's slanting golden light. After a few yards, the floor dropped quickly down to the left before rising again and turning right.

It was cold in the narrow space, like a church entered on a hot day, and her skin puckered and dimpled. Only at noon at this time of year did the sun ever penetrate to the floor of the chasm, but now, just a few hours after midday, there was no memory of its warmth in the damp air. At the lowest point, there was a substantial pool that spanned the space, now nearly ten feet in width. It was black, and still, reflecting the strip of daylight high above. The edges were occasionally disturbed by drips from the surrounding walls, erasing the image of the outside world. She bypassed the water, clinging to the algae-slicked rock, holding onto the tough stalks and fronds of ferns. Now she followed a line of stepping stones that had been placed who knew how long ago, and this path started to rise with the contour of the valley side, rising to meet the rock walls and exiting back in to the world of light and warmth through a stand of birch.

(North-West England)

Just at the point where the incline began there was a fold in the rock. This was invisible from almost every angle due to the contours of the cleft. Dripping ferns also camouflaged the narrow fissure, but she had found it long ago. Taking care not to leave footprints, she hopped from a stepping stone on to a small ledge in the wall itself and carefully worked her way into the gap, just a foot above the mud. By the time she had wriggled through she was damp from the walls and vegetation, but she emerged into an almost perfectly circular cave, open at the top where leaves could be seen fluttering in the sun. A few years ago, a seed had landed in a small crack in the rock and, well watered, and with just sufficient light, had taken hold. Now a beech sapling was clamped to the vertical surface twenty feet up, its young crown projecting through the gap.

She waited a few moments to let her eyes become accustomed to the deeper gloom and then laid her pack roll down on a platform of dry rock which sat above the ubiquitous mud, sheltered from dripping water by an overhang. With the lateness of the day, she knew she had to move quickly and she surveyed a number of other items already carefully stored here. She stripped to her linen undergarments, shivering slightly, and pulled a leather roll from a crevice in the dry rock wall. Unrolling this she pulled out and dressed in her everyday clothing: cream-coloured petticoat, black waistcoat, buff skirt and cloak, and her coif. She put her woollen stockings and mules into her bag; she would need to carry these over the mud of the cleft before she cleaned her bare feet and put them on. The clumsy shoes were not made for climbing around on wet rock faces.

An hour later she was on the path that followed the River Dane along the wooded valley to the hamlet of Wincle, where she had her small wood-built hut. She moved quickly, her large pack roll across her shoulders. Dusk was approaching and the sounds of the woods around her were slowly fading as the birds started to think about roosting. The noise of the river was a constant companion, changing as the depth increased and decreased, or width narrowed and widened, shifting its voice over sand, mud or stones.

After a while, at the edge of hearing, she started to pick up another sound. It became the steady tread of hooves on the path behind, now again quickening to a trot where the trees and undergrowth allowed. She also heard the lighter, busy noises of dogs. Two, perhaps three. She thought about stepping off the path and hiding. There were plenty of good places for it. But she knew the dogs would get her scent and then she would have to explain her concealment.

She was now only a few hundred yards from the village and the path skirted the edge of the flood plain where the trees had been felled to allow for the grazing of cattle. As the noises suggested the horseman was nearly upon her, she stepped off the path into the edge of the trees, leaving the open grass for horse and dogs to run.

Less than a minute later the dogs, two beautiful brindled greyhounds, burst from the trees and shot across the cropped grass of the floodplain in pursuit of a rabbit that they had flushed. It jinked to right and left, having the advantage of agility but lacking the full-on speed of its pursuers. Every time it gained a few yards from its manoeuvres, the greyhounds also ate up the distance immediately. Silent, tongues lolling, utterly focused on the rear quarters of their prey. The rabbit was desperately trying to regain the heavy cover of the woods, but the slightly larger dog was almost on it, jaws opening to make the final grab. It jerked left, evading capture by inches, but ran straight across the path of the other hound, the female, which took it across its haunches. Teeth sank into flesh and the rabbit screamed, rear legs limp but front end still squirming for freedom. The bigger dog, the male, ended its agony, biting through the neck and pulling the animal into two pieces. There was a shower of blood and entrails as the female shook its portion of rabbit and both dogs set to feasting, seemingly oblivious of her presence.

She watched quietly, waiting for the horseman to appear, and he came out of the trees at a trot. She kept very still, her eyes down, hoping to be seen as an unremarkable part of the scenery in the fading light. She hoped the rider's eyes would be fixed on the dogs and their successful hunt. She thought her hope had been fulfilled as he turned off the path and down onto the grassy meadow towards the dogs.

As he moved away from her, she raised her head. He still had not seen her. "Cassius! Dido! Here! To me! Here! Leave that now! Come here!" His deep voice boomed and the dogs obeyed immediately, dropping the remnants of the rabbit and trotting across the grass towards him, heads and shoulders smeared with blood, tongues lolling. "Look at you both. How can I take you back to the Hall like this?" He slid down from his saddle and she could see he was proud of his animals. He pulled a cloth from behind his saddle and tried to clean the worst of the blood from them as they squirmed and tried to pull away. He spoke quietly to them, rubbing behind their ears, but it was when he stood up to remount his horse that he looked across the saddle and saw her.

He was clearly surprised, seeing her still and quiet in the edge of the trees on the far side of the path. Taking the reins in his hands he walked the horse back to the path, the dogs at his heels. As he approached, she could see that he was a tall man, with shoulder-length wavy brown hair and neatly trimmed goatee beard and slim moustache. He had a neutral, unreadable expression on his long face, which made her slightly nervous, although she maintained her calm exterior.

She thought him to be in his thirties. Strong, assured. Now she could see the hilt of a long dagger under his calf-length riding cloak, and the flash of white lace at his collar.

"Good evening, mistress. My apologies. I did not see you standing there. I hope my hounds did not startle you. They are ruthless with rabbits but are softer than butter with people." He laughed suddenly. "As you can see!" The bitch was licking her hand and Cassius was sniffing excitedly around her pack roll. "Come here, dogs. Leave the poor woman alone."

"Thank you, sir. They did not frighten me. They are beautiful creatures. So… elegant. So… skilled." Now she was down on one knee stroking Dido and tickling Cassius under his chin.

"Well, clearly they have taken to you. I am not sure that they will come home with me now." His voice was warm, and he smiled, but his eyes remained cautious. "You are broad at a late hour. Are you far from home, Mistress…?"

She ignored his fishing for her name. "No, Your Lordship. Thank you, sir, but I am just making for the village by the bridge. My home is just ten minutes away. And I think your dogs are interested in my pack, not me. I have rabbit skins for the market tomorrow, and herbs for drying. It must smell very fine to a hound."

He smiled again, clearly noting her reluctance to give him her name. "Well, please allow me to escort you to the bridge at least. I am bound for Swythamley Hall where I am staying for a day or two. My name is Brereton, Sir William Brereton. Please, would you walk with me?"

She relaxed as she became more confident that his intentions were genuine. She smiled in return. "Thank you, sir. I have much to do before the morning and must hurry, but it is reassuring to have company as the dark comes."

They walked along the path, now just broad enough for them to walk side by side, with the horse, an impressive black stallion, content to pace behind them. The dogs made the most of the last of the light, chasing each other madly across the grass. In minutes they were at the Dane Bridge and climbing a steep bank that took them up onto its arch. "Well, mistress, where is your home?"

"There, sir. The last on the right. Two minutes away." She pointed through the gloom up the hill. "Thank you, Sir William, for your escort and your kind words. I will have a story for my neighbours in the morning."

"Perhaps we will meet tomorrow as I will be travelling home and will most likely make my way through the market. Take care, although I can see you are already properly cautious. You still have not given me your name. That is well, but I counsel you to try to make sure you are safely home before nightfall, even when the night is at its shortest." She nodded her agreement. He made a small bow, mounted his horse and set off in the direction of Swythamley Hall. She stood a few moments in the road, watching him disappear. She had been careless. Foolish.

And now she had a long night ahead to prepare for the market. She reached her small hut, lit a candle and set to work.

*

Little more than two miles away, in his bedroom at Swythamley Hall, Sir William Brereton sat with his feet on the hearth of the fire and reflected on recent events. Yesterday he had met with a number of prominent local landowners, and former fellow Members of Parliament, to discuss happenings in the country. He was a deeply devout man and was aware of the unease around, and indeed open criticism of, the King's moves to introduce his new prayer book in Scotland. Concerns about what that might mean for England, together with Charles's continuing opposition to summoning Parliament and the imposition of the damnable tax of ship money, was trying the patience of his loyal subjects. *Always more taxes!* Now he learned that another former Parliamentarian, John Hampden from Buckinghamshire, was contemplating resisting the tax. Making a principled stand.

He wondered, as he looked into the fire, where this was heading, and what role God intended for him. There must be more he could do? He tried to lead a godly life. He tried to encourage others to follow his example. He supported those preachers whose charisma, fire and eloquence outshone his own. But there must be something greater – something bigger that he could embrace to demonstrate his love of his Saviour and Lord.

Charles was King by God's will, but why did he persist with such apparent high-handedness? Why did he not squash forever the rumours of his sympathy for Catholicism? Why did he always seem set against the views of those he had the duty to rule? He recoiled from the idea that he may one day have to side against his King!

But through all the confusion of his mind, one image kept burning through the obscuring mist. The face of the woman on the path. Mistress… who? Although she had hardly spoken, he had felt her intelligence. More astute than the common folk. And she had been beautiful. No. Beautiful was not the right word. She had an unearthly quality to her. Fey. Wavy brown hair tucked inexpertly under her coif, high cheekbones, her skin browned by the sun, and hazel eyes, he thought, although in the poor light he could not be entirely sure of their colour. She had a slight look of the Barbary Coast to her. But out alone at that time? Returning from where? There had been no mention of a husband at home. She was a mystery. He felt a compulsion to find out more about her. To confirm to himself what colour her eyes really were, if nothing else. He felt somehow that was important.

For a while, the picture of her in his mind's eye pushed high politics and religious turmoil from his mind. He forced himself to picture his wife and admonished himself for weakness, but he thought more about the market at the Dane Bridge on the morrow and how his plans were flexible enough for a visit.

7

(Breda, August 1637)

Richard lay awake. The heat of the day had refused to leave the barn, the humidity packing the space like stuffing in a cushion. But the oppression, and the aching pulse of his broken nose, were only the backdrop to the whirling chaos of his reflections on the day just passed. His own stupidity in losing his temper. Again. His guilt at potentially putting Will in danger through his actions. And the risk that he may have soured their relationship with DeLacey who, from short conversations with some of the other men, was clearly an admired, but intimidating, figure in the company.

But the picture that rotated into focus most in his mind was that of the ruined face of the corpse he and Will had first carried. He no longer felt shocked by the gore, or the horror of the flies. It was not the presence of these things, but rather the absence of another. A lacking. An emptiness. Once he had belatedly realised that the black, seething mounds were bodies, the picture from the rampart, with the stagnant ditch water and the parched land beyond, was a vision of hell. Not the hell of the sermons in the village chapel, all fire, redness and shrieking demons tormenting hordes of the damned. But

(Breda, August 1637)

a noiseless, desolate, bleak, interminable, forgotten place. An emptiness, an absence of life, emotion or feeling.

The corpse itself, staring mutely through its veil of black flies at the flat grey-white of the sky, echoed that blankness. The animated, warm, vigorous body that had left the Spanish camp was now no more than a pile of rotting meat.

The soul. Richard clung to the thought. What he saw was no longer a man, because a man was not his physical body. The body was just the candle wax. The thing that provided light, and warmth, and purpose, was the flame. Without the flame – the soul of man – the body was just undelivered fertiliser.

The man's soul is with God, Richard thought, and that was comforting. But his brother Lionel had unpleasant things to say about Catholics. The war in which he was embroiled was as much about the struggle between Catholic and the godly, as it was about power and territory. The relentless march of the counter-reformation, feared across Protestant countries, including his own. How could Man ever know enough of the mind of God to know which was the right way to worship? The right way to be. To live.

And what was a soul anyway? Did all living creatures have a soul? Cows, and dogs and horses? They too exhibited the same 'loss' when they died. So, what had departed from them? Were there heavens and hells for good horses and bad ones? Did badly behaved dogs suffer torment in some afterlife? He scoffed at that, but in so many ways these creatures seemed little different to him, at this fundamental level.

Richard had never given any serious thoughts to these things and wished now he had paid more attention in church, and to his older brother. Lionel had such a certainty about these things and that must be consoling, but try as he could, no explanations presented themselves to him. The only recurring thought, his only certainty from his own observation, was that the rotting bodies of the Spanish they had buried today seemed to have very little to do with the glory of God. No trace of heaven was on them, no triumphant release. Just possible futures that had stretched ahead of them, now ended. Empty. Finished. Gone.

These thoughts swept around in his head like the great flocks of starlings in the dusk over the flat land around his village. But they would not settle onto the fields or roost in the trees, but mesmerised him with differing, shifting, shapes and forms. But always coming back to form that blank, ruined face.

He resolved in the hours before dawn, as the temperature finally started to bring more comfort, that he would not end in that way. Not for as long as he could prevent it. He could not think of himself as a coward, but he would not throw his life away. And then he thought again about DeLacey – the man who had found a way to survive in this world of war – and he came to a decision.

*

Just after dawn, Richard was crouched on his haunches beside the sleeping DeLacey. It was still quiet, with few men up and about. He had been there nearly two minutes before he reached out a hand and gently shook DeLacey's shoulder. "Master DeLacey? Sir?"

"Fuck off." A grunt from under the hat brim.

"Please, Master DeLacey. I wanted to apologise for yesterday. It was wrong of me."

"Accepted. Now fuck off."

"I had not seen men dead, not like that, before and… and… and I think that, and the heat, I was not myself. I am truly sorry for causing offence."

"That may be so, Fletcher, but it is also true that you knew what you wanted when you saw it and were prepared to face me down for it." He pushed the brim of his hat up and Richard could see one eye looking at him unblinkingly. "At least until your nose got broke."

"It's Farrell, sir, and yes, I know. I am sorry for all of that. Master DeLacey sir, could I ask two things of you. I know I am in no position to do so after yesterday…" he added hurriedly as the other eye also came into view, looking none too friendly, "…but perhaps I can also do something for you in return?"

"You can fuck off, that's what you can do…" came the low, gravelly response.

"Yes, yes I will… go away, but can I please speak?"

"Ask."

"The sword you are holding in safekeeping for me, for which you have my thanks…" he added hurriedly again, "…I do not know how to use it, at least not how a sword like that should be used. I have no doubt a man such as you is an expert at fencing. Would you teach me properly? The training we had before we arrived here, and since then, was…"

"Shit?"

"Not helpful."

"And?"

"And, like I said, the sight of the dead Spanish. I have decided. I do not wish to die as they did. There did not seem to be much… glory in it. Not for them, anyhow…"

"Expect they thought the same at the end…"

"Yes. But you, Master DeLacey, the captain said you had been soldiering for ten years. You are not dead. But also, you are respected. The other men seem to look up to you."

"Nothing gets past you, does it? It's difficult to look up to a dead man, boy, 'cos they're usually six feet below the ground."

"Yes. But what I mean is, sir, you have found a way to stay alive yet are clearly not a craven. You have fought, but you have survived. You have found a way that works."

"For God's sake, Fletcher, what is it you want so I can go back to sleep!"

"It's Farrell. Sorry. I want to learn from you. When I signed up to come here, I had dreams of being… I don't know, a hero, I suppose. But now I just want to be alive. I want to go to heaven, of course. Be with God an' all that. But just not yet. Can you teach me to be like you? To stay alive? I am sure I will learn soldiering now we are here at the fighting, but I expect that will just teach me ways to get killed more quickly."

There was a long silence.

"I am not a coward. I know I must fight, and I will, but I think you know ways of doin' that and not gettin' killed."

Another long silence.

"Master DeLacey? Sir?" Richard thought he had gone back to sleep. *Damn the man!*

"I'm waiting."

"Sir?"

"You said there was something in this for me?"

"Oh, yes. My pay, sir. It would be yours. Half of it. For a year. So, the longer I stay alive, the more you get." Richard felt proud of this idea. "It's what my father would call an incentive."

Richard could see no expression in the deep shadow under the hat. "I'll think on it a while. But there was somethin' else you promised to do."

"What was that?"

"You promised to fuck off, Fletcher, and let me sleep. That's something you can do now."

As it turned out, DeLacey did not get any more sleep. About ten minutes later Captain Browne strode into the barn, rousing the men. Richard could hear men stirring outside where Browne had already done his rounds. He looked like he was in his best uniform, such as it was, with breastplate polished and a red sash across his chest. His helmet was held under one arm; a white feather had been found to add glamour.

"C'mon! Hurry, lads. Let's look our best for our colonel! Inspection in fifteen minutes. Today we find out our part in the plan for attacking the city. Let's look the part. Get them up and ready, DeLacey!"

DeLacey was not protesting. Richard, who was now studying his hoped-to-be mentor, noted that he was soon up, tidying his bed and other possessions and then haranguing the men around him to hurry. Helping to adjust belts, plate, hats and ushering the men out into the early morning. He caught Richard's eye and the faintest of smiles touched the scarred face. Richard also noted that the men listened to him and hurried along under his friendly, and not-so-friendly, encouragement. Whatever rank he held, and Richard still did not know what this was, seemed irrelevant. The other mercenaries reacted with surprisingly few audible profanities.

Richard managed to work his way through the bustle of activity to be close to DeLacey. He again caught his eye and raised a questioning eyebrow. "First lesson. Browne is a good man, if sometimes a little pious for my taste. He will do his best for us. If we help him get right with darling George Goring, then it may go better for all of us."

Richard nodded. "Who is Goring?"

"Colonel George Goring. Regular army. Ambitious arsehole. Foolhardy with the lives of others and, to be fair, with his own as well sometimes. Bit of a drinker and apparently fond of other men's wives, so maybe he is not so bad after all." A wink at Richard's shocked expression. "He's not really our commander, but we are attached to his regiment. But he's set on glory to gain advancement – which is dangerous for us. He sees greatness for himself. But Browne knows his man. I think he has a good plan – and I may have added a few o' me own thoughts into that too." Another wink. "Now round up your mates and stand together right at the front if you can. Goring wants to review 'is brave troops."

The men were pulled up into ten ranks of approximately twenty men. Richard, and his companions from their march, were at the right-hand end of the front row looking conspicuously unthreatening. Others on the front row, those wanting to be seen and recognised, stood tall, chests out. More than one was quietly praying. DeLacey stood in the middle of the front rank, looking every inch the enthusiastic soldier.

The enthusiasm lessened the further back in the ranks, with those at the rear only just managing to avoid openly slouching, eyes downcast, more carelessly dressed and armed. Richard, who had never seen the company of mercenaries drawn up together before, also thought that despite this, he would not want to be facing these men. What they lacked in fervour, they made up for in cold menace.

It was clear all the English troops were under review that morning. Looking to east and west, Richard could see blocks of men drawn up in formation. Small forests of sixteen-foot-long pikes held at attention caught the eye, here and there along the line.

From his position in the front rank, Richard could see a small body of horsemen trotting towards them. Browne jogged his horse out to meet them and then joined the party, riding at the front next to a tallish individual who, even at this distance, Richard could see was grandly attired. They were followed by a number of mounted officers, all with red sashes similar to Browne's. The exception was a particularly dashing officer in a long blue coat, whose hat was embellished with long blue and white feathers.

(Breda, August 1637)

As they got to about thirty yards distant, DeLacey suddenly took off his own broad-brimmed hat and waved it in large circles above his head. "Hurrah for Colonel Goring! God save the King!" He turned and gave those behind him a stern look. The enthusiasts in the front rank soon took up the cheer, and by the time the party arrived in front of DeLacey, the company were all in full voice and making an impressive noise. They reined in their horses in a cloud of dust that rather spoiled their splendid arrival. Browne signalled for quiet, although he was clearly pleased at the reception the men had provided.

Richard could now see the grand figure talking with Browne and assumed this was Goring. He could also see why the man was popular with the ladies. He was the epitome of gallant. Polished black armour, edged and engraved in silver, with an immaculate white lace collar extending over the top six inches, below his goateed chin. Shoulder-length brown hair framed his face, exhibiting slightly prominent eyes either side of a longish nose. His expression was haughty and disdainful. A face used to command.

Richard was close enough to catch some of the conversation.

"…now in position. Frederick Henry is now ready to start preparations for assault. We will not have a long siege, sir. By God we will not wait around. They have under 3,000 men in the city. We are nearer 24,000. We will be focusing on what they call the Ginneken Gate and, as you know, this is on our side of the city.

"I know yours is an irregular company, Captain, but they will be valuable in what is to come. What is their status?" Goring was looking past Browne at the men and could not help noticing the newest recruits, Richard and his companions, who did not look the most impressive fighting men. The disdainful expression deepened. Richard could hear Goring clearly. He had a naturally loud voice and was facing straight towards him.

Browne, however, had his back to him and was more quietly spoken. "...Spanish raid two nights ago..." Richard strained to hear. "...building numbers. Training not complete... new recruits..."

Now they had moved off slowly in an easterly direction and he could hear nothing more, although Goring and Browne were in deep conversation. Behind them, the blue-coated officer followed and Richard saw Goring turn in his saddle to also introduce him to Browne. Blue-coat raised his hat, bowing extravagantly from the waist to Browne, who looked half amused, half impressed.

The group then halted again. There was pointing towards the city, nodding, more handshaking, and they moved on to the next body of infantry, with Browne peeling away and trotting back towards them. He pulled up in front of the men. DeLacey took a half-step forward, clear of the ranks. "What's it to be, Captain?"

"Men!" Browne raised his voice so he could be heard at the back. "We have been given the honour of digging!"

There were some strangled cheers, quickly hissed into silence, but most of the men smiled broadly, slapping each other on the back.

"We are to start immediately. We will dig a covered trench towards the hornwork in front of us..." he half turned in his saddle to point, "...in coordination with our friends, the French." Some laughter through the ranks. "Stand ready. We will organise parties while the engineers mark out the line of our trench. The French are digging just to the west of us, aimin' for the same goal, and so the pride of England, and of Colonel Goring, is at stake here. We all know what we need to do!"

(Breda, August 1637)

DeLacey shouted back, "Finish second. Gallantly, with honour and dignity!" Great laughter among the men and even a smile from Browne.

"Officers to me, please," called Browne, and the men dispersed, in search of breakfast and to use the latrines before the heat of the morning made it an almost suicidal pursuit.

8

(Breda, August–September 1637)

It was heading towards the end of August and the mercenaries had been digging the trench for over three weeks. After a period of spectacular thunderstorms which had broken the heat and humidity, the weather was cooler. Sunny days were fewer and rain more frequent, and the trenches were a few inches deep in water. Richard's back, shoulders and arms, which had ached constantly for the first week, had now learned the task and were hardened and better able to cope. His mind too was much more focused.

After some humiliating badgering, DeLacey had eventually accepted his offer and had been schooling not just himself, but also Will, in the better use of the weapons they had. This included the Toledo rapier, but DeLacey had insisted he must also learn how to work with his father's heavier militia blade, as the rapier was unsuited to a pitched battle. It had quickly become clear that, of the two, Richard was the better shot with a matchlock, having had an opportunity to learn from his father and practise on the manor farm. He was also lighter on his feet and quicker with a blade. However, the moment they put one of the company's pikes into Will's hands, it was clear he was a natural. Although only a year older than Richard, he

(Breda, August–September 1637)

already had a far larger frame, and the weeks of hard labour had only enhanced this. DeLacey also perceived that Will's stoic temperament, calmness and stubbornness were well suited to the pike phalanx. He had told Browne, and they had been assigned respectively to the musketeer and pike groups within the company.

So while Richard practised his fencing with DeLacey, who was the best swordsman Richard had ever seen, DeLacey had also found one of the other men to drill Will with the pike. Three or four times a week they would work, and Richard was amazed at the amount of time they spent on footwork, posture and positioning of the hands. But he could also see a huge difference in his own skill levels from when they had started at the end of July.

DeLacey also tried to instil in both boys the way a mercenary company operated. He explained why the backbreaking job of digging had been so welcomed by the men. "If we are digging the trench, they will consider us too exhausted to be first to attempt the walls. We will need to rest and others will take on that glorious task – poor bastards. We might be in the third, or maybe fourth, wave and, by that time, if our glorious leaders know their business, we can stroll into town and see what goods are on offer."

Richard and Will learnt what they came to call 'the DeLacey Doctrine'.

Fight bravely when you have to, but explore all other possibilities first.

If you have to fight, make sure someone important sees you do it (and remind them of it later).

Always help out your fellows if they are in difficulty (and remind them of it later) – unless they are idiots intent on getting themselves and others killed unnecessarily.

Always stand behind a larger man.

Never be first to do anything – except collecting your pay.

Don't talk religion or politics – family, wine, women and money are safest.

Never steal from your comrades – unless it is definitely worth the risk of being caught.

They also gradually felt themselves becoming an accepted part of the company and no longer raw recruits. DeLacey showed them how unexpected acts of help and support could win friends and which of the men they should avoid. They recognised the cliques – the old soldiers (which included DeLacey and other veterans), the Puritans, the hotheads intent on glory (not too many in Browne's company), the strong and weak. They learnt to respect the softly spoken Captain Browne, mirroring the respect that DeLacey showed him. They saw how he tried to manoeuvre his boys into completing the safest tasks, but those which were highly visible to the commanding officers. How he secured good provisions and billeting, and how he maintained good relations with fellow commanders, no matter the nationality.

Richard had been particularly impressed when Jean de Sête, 'Monsieur Bluecoat' from Colonel Goring's party, had happened upon one of their training sessions. He was shocked to find that de Sête knew DeLacey and that they had shared a few drunken nights in The Hague. De Sête was aide de camp to Hercule Girard, Baron de Charnacé, the French ambassador to the Stadtholder, and formerly one of the King's musketeers, his personal guards. He was now acting as liaison between the French and English digging parties and regularly called on Browne. Richard was delighted beyond words when de Sête had complimented him on his fencing style and had asked to take a closer look at his blade, nodding appreciatively at the workmanship and balance. He had some pointers for Will too, again about footwork, but also advice on using a

(Breda, August–September 1637)

long knife when the pike is dropped or fighting becomes close quarters. Even Richard and Will had heard of Roi Louis's musketeers, and DeLacey ribbed them for days about their open mouths and wide eyes. "Followed him around like dogs after a bitch in heat," he laughed, bringing some of the other soldiers to hysterics with his impressions of the boys.

The trenches were at least six feet deep and angled in to the hornworks – the water-surrounded fortifications outside the main city walls – from the east. They were lined with timber and roofed to protect the diggers and the assault troops from imperial sharpshooters on the walls of the hornworks. Occasionally there would be musket and artillery fire aimed their way, but the line identified by the engineers, making use of the few hollows and contours, helped to shield Richard's company. It would be only in the final twenty yards or so that the enemy would be able to enfilade their position. Then the heavy wooden shielding would be vital. They knew that activities on other sides of Breda were intended to draw attention from what was to be the main assault, and the defenders' lack of men, and perhaps ammunition, meant that there was no concerted fire aimed in their direction.

As they approached this mark, the digging switched to night-time. As well as being safer, it was also cooler, and progress accelerated.

On 27 August, as they were getting so close they could start to recognise some of the faces on the walls ahead of them, cheers were heard to the south-east, and word came that the French had completed their trench and were forming earthworks to protect the assault troops which would start moving up. That night they were visited by Colonel Goring and Captain Monck, who Richard recognised from the party which had accompanied Goring during the review. Disappointed that he had been beaten to readiness by the French, Goring informed

Browne that despite this, the English would be first to make the assault.

He ordered the trench to be finished the following day at whatever cost and called for the immediate making of fascines – great bundles of sticks, lashed together with rope – that would be used to span the moat to enable the assault on the hornworks. Nearly all Browne's company were tasked with the digging, working at almost double the tempo of previous days, with quick changeovers of digging parties as room for working was limited. Those not digging were put to work making the fascines. These would be sunk into the moat to create a makeshift bridge, allowing the troops to reach the walls of the hornwork for scaling or mining, and also to provide some protection to the attackers. Browne also deployed a dozen of the best shots in the company to act as sharpshooters, lying in the dark and firing to keep the heads of the defenders' own musketeers down.

Richard had started to raise a hand to volunteer for this duty, knowing he was a good shot himself, and thinking he was at a good distance from the enemy to be facing much danger. But DeLacey, standing behind him, clamped his arm to his side. "Unless of course you have changed your mind about a glorious death, boy. The flash from your musket in the dark makes you a clearer target than if you were stood up firing in full sunlight. Your choice of course…"

The trench was finished before ten the following morning and earth was raised at the end to further protect the troops that would be forming for the assault. Browne assembled the company again, this time to announce that their pay would be distributed, according to contract, once the assault was completed. This, he added, was just to ensure that no one decided that they would rather miss the excitement of the battle to come. They were, after all, mercenary soldiers.

(BREDA, AUGUST–SEPTEMBER 1637)

*

By the first day of September, preparations for crossing the moat were complete. As dusk fell, word came that Colonel Goring was offering a sizeable reward for men to start the process of laying the fascines into the moat. This would be right under the muzzles of the Spanish muskets and cannon, and so the reward was significant. Richard and Will had learned enough by now not to raise an arm for this task.

With DeLacey and about thirty other men, they crouched near the end of the trench, their task to shuttle the fascines forward to those who would be doing the actual laying of the bundles. With them, to Richard's surprise, were not just Browne, but also Colonel Goring himself and a party of English gentry who had become his companions, wishing to see action and to share the glory. DeLacey elbowed him in the ribs and nodded his head at one particularly exotic-looking member of the party. "See the prick with all the feathers? That's Prince Rupert, Count Palatine of the Rhine, and nephew to our King. Don't be fooled by the garb – he's not much older than you but has been fighting for years. Has no fear apparently. That usually translates as no brains, but he has survived so far so maybe stupid *and* lucky..."

They watched in silence as the first six men hooked their arms through the ropes holding together the first of the fascines and made ready to climb the end of the trench. With a final prayer, and stirring personal address from Goring, and after slaps on the back and words of encouragement from the mixture of hardened soldiers and eager gentlemen, the six pulled themselves up the slope. As soon as the first made it to the top of the ladders, the first shots were heard. The thick bundles of wood were providing reasonable protection as they emerged into the field of fire onto the lip of the moat and were lost from view. Richard heard shouts in English, more distant ones in another language, splashes and then the first screams. A body pitched back down the slope, bouncing off the ladders to land on its back. The top half of the man's head had been shot off by the heavy musket ball and the more fastidious members of Goring's party took a rapid step back, frantically trying not to slip in the mud of the trench.

After no more than three minutes, a single soldier was sliding rapidly back down the ladders, still clinging to the bundle. "Well?" came Goring's urgent voice as Browne also came forward to crouch next to his man, a man Richard recognised as Walker from their own company.

Walker shook his head, as if trying to clear his thoughts, and did a quick check to reassure himself he had not been hit. "T'others are done for. The Spanish know their work, even in't' dark. Lots of 'em on that wall. Gi'us some water." This to Browne, ignoring Goring. A flask was passed to him. "They was 'it as soon as they sank the sticks in't' moat. I would 'ave been too if I'd done t'same."

"Yes, man, but there is no point carrying the fascines up there if you are going to bring them back down, is there? That is not going to earn you the gold." Goring looked hard at Walker, looking like he would like to shoot the man himself.

"No, sir," said Browne. "But if I may, p'rhaps we can send up squads with thicker bundles to help protect them as are layin' the bridge?"

Goring considered this for a moment and nodded. "Right, Captain. Just as you say. Proceed, but do so quickly. If we are to complete this before dawn, we must push on rapidly."

Another group of volunteers, fifteen this time, attempted the moat. As Browne had foreseen, the tactic of shielding the layers of the fascines with heavier, denser bundles was working, but there was still a stream of injured coming back, including two of the original six who had been feared dead. A line of replacements waited to continue the work, faces betraying mixed emotions of dread, enthusiasm and eagerness for the promised reward. Resistance from the walls ebbed and flowed as ammunition would run low, troops were rotated and the targets were more or less effectively shielded. They knew that the French were also attempting to bridge the moat and defenders were being pulled in different directions to try to stem the work.

Gradually the moat was being bridged and progress was reported to the impatient Goring. He was either pacing up and down the trench, shepherded by his staff to keep him as sheltered from fire as possible, or encouraging those bringing up more fascines. He urged the men up the ladders, commiserated with the wounded and kicked the slackers. By the early hours of the morning, the English barrier was only some fifteen feet from the far side of the moat, but the volunteers were more and more exposed to the fire of the defenders. Little progress was now being made in the steady concentration of musketry and other missiles.

Throughout the night, Will and Richard carried and heaved the awkward bundles of wood and sticks. They helped to carry the wounded away from the moat and brought up water and other supplies for the exhausted workers. The atmosphere was frenzied, the night itself hoarse with the sounds of pain, excitement, encouragement and rage. In a moment of relative quiet, during a pause in the activity as more materials were being brought up the trench, Will sagged against the wooden boards of the trench, arms around his knees, chin on his elbow. Exhausted, his shoulder-length fair hair plastered with sweat against his tanned forehead, he watched his companions trying to find water and food. He reflected on the change in his life from just a year ago. From preparing the harvest with his family and friends, to preparing an attack on the walls of a foreign city, held by some of the best troops ever seen across Europe. He felt differently about himself too. Here, his stoicism and quiet demeanour were admired. His steadiness, and his willingness to take on arduous work with no complaint, were making him a popular companion, whereas at home the villagers teased him as dour, and maybe a little slow. His quiet good nature taken advantage of. He liked what he was becoming and, despite the chaos and fury around him, felt almost peaceful. This feeling of being comfortable with himself also gave him the confidence to be more engaged in conversations with the other men. To contribute thoughts and ideas, and to find these were considered, not just ignored or dismissed.

By contrast, he had seen Richard go through huge emotional highs and lows. After the nose-crunching encounter with DeLacey, where he thought Richard had blown any chance for the two of them to get on within the company, his friend had gone into a downward spiral of gloom and despair. He knew that this was to do with the shame of losing his temper again, but also he had seen the profound effect that the confrontation with death had had. In the weeks following, the effort of the trench digging, together with weapon sessions with DeLacey, had brought a sharper focus to Richard. A concentration on both building his strength and skills, yes, but also periods of distance, when his mind seemed engaged in some deep enquiry – staring into the distance, moving his lips like a child in church pretending to sing. These moments always left Richard troubled. Whatever it was he was wrestling with, he did not seem able to resolve it. Although they had not known each other well when they set off from home, they had grown close. Will was concerned that his rather changeable friend could get them both into deep trouble, but he also could not help feeling like an older brother, worrying for his wayward sibling.

Will glanced to his left where Richard was talking quietly with DeLacey. That was also strange. Why was DeLacey taking such an interest in Richard? He knew about the agreement they had come to over Richard's pay (and he had made sure that he, Will, had made no such promise!), but this was closer – beyond a financial agreement. Not exactly a father-son thing. He could never see DeLacey as a father figure. More like an interesting uncle who visited now and again after adventures in exotic parts of the world. DeLacey clearly saw something in Richard that intrigued him, or he was playing some sort of game that Will could not fathom. Will had respect for DeLacey, despite the foulmouthed banter that clattered against the armour of his own church-learned morals. But as self-appointed older brother, he would be watching.

And as he looked up, he realised that he too was being watched. On the other side of the trench, back against the boarding, was Captain Monck. Will recognised him, as he had been prominent all night, rallying the volunteers and supervising the musketeers. He has holding a flask which may have contained water, or more probably wine, and was observing Will over the rim as he drank. He was a powerful man, not overly tall, but broad and seemingly well used to the charged atmosphere around him. His face betrayed no emotion, his black eyes unwavering in their scrutiny. "Don't recognise you, boy. Are you one of Browne's company?"

"Aye, Captain. New recruit, sir."

"You been on the dam yet? Volunteered?"

"No, sir. Been hauling the bundles up to the end of the trench all night."

"I see. How old are you, boy?"

"Sixteen, sir."

"When the time comes, when we mine the walls and must force the breach, will you do your duty? Or will you still be carrying wood?" There was no change in tone. No actual accusation, but Will felt like he had been slapped. But Will could also keep a close rein on his emotions, locking his expression to blankness and keeping his voice level. "I will do my duty as my captain commands, sir. You need have no fear of that."

The slightest hint of a smile at Monck's mouth failed to warm the granite of the rest of his face. "I am glad to hear it. Where are you from?"

"Near Huntingdon, sir."

"Farmer?"

"Yes, sir."

"So why are you here, in the Low Countries, fighting imperial troops, instead of preparing your harvest?"

"I came for adventure. For excitement, I s'pose. In the beginning, anyway."

Again, the slight twisting of the heavy lips. "Enough excitement here for you, boy? If there is not enough adventure, think of the honour, sir. Of duty. Service to your King, and service to God."

Will looked back at Monck, saying nothing. At that moment Goring and his entourage swept by, heading for the business end of the trench to inspect progress. When Will looked back to Monck, he realised he had gone, attaching himself to the back of the party. He thought about the unexpected encounter. He knew what Monck was doing, trying to wind him up to fight. He knew he didn't need the encouragement. Unlike Richard, he didn't buy so much of DeLacey's doctrine. He wanted to fight. He wanted to win. He still wanted the glory. Because when he went home, he wanted to be recognised, admired, even slightly feared. Not the slow ploughboy, but on equal terms with those of higher birth and, if he admitted it to himself, equal to Richard.

With so little work needed to complete the bridging of the moat, Browne's men could see Goring's frustration at the halt in progress. He called for more musketeers to suppress the murderous sharpshooting from the wall. This appeared to help and as dawn approached, he made a renewed offer of 250 guilders per man to those brave enough to complete the work.

With this added incentive to bravery, and with the massed English musket fire keeping heads down on the wall, four men risked the dam and, by mid-morning, had won their reward. Word spread along the trench that the work was finally done and a bridge sixty feet long and fifteen feet wide had reached the base of the hornworks wall. Cheering was heard from further back down the trench, and Richard and Will were treated to the sight of Prince Frederick Henry himself passing their company to inspect the work. From their position they could see but not hear the congratulations lavished on Goring by the Stadtholder, and the clear message of urgency to start mining the walls of the hornwork.

But the day would be bittersweet for Goring. The head of engineers sent over the bridge to assess how best to lay the mine complained that the bridge was too unsafe. Further work was carried out to strengthen it. When this was complete, to the consternation of those around him, Colonel George Goring himself accompanied the miner over the fascine bridge to see for himself. Driven by pride and impatience, it seemed he was not going to delay any further and risk their glory being snatched by the French at the last. But as he made his way back over the bridge, a musket ball from above evaded the screening and clipped his lower leg. He was carried down the ladders and into the trench where the wound was immediately examined. The colonel was then whisked back down the trench on a stretcher followed by his bleating entourage.

Further setbacks followed. Thirty minutes later the body of the chief miner was also carried past Richard, half his head shot away, and news reached Browne, from de Sête, that Ambassador Charnacé had been decapitated by a cannon ball and the French had stopped work out of respect.

A Lieutenant Colonel Hollis assumed temporary command and announced to the regular soldiers, Browne's company and the engineers at the head of the trench that no further action would take place that day. Half the musketeers providing suppressing fire were stood down and the rest of the day was spent making preparations for the assault. Browne's men were relieved of duty and made their way back to the barn area to rest, eat and sleep.

9

(Breda, September 1637)

That was the last Richard saw of the trench for several days. They learnt that the French had completed their dam the following day, and now troops and artillery were being marshalled ready for attack. Browne told the assembled company that they would be supporting the attack indirectly, providing covering fire from forward positions, and helping the engineers to maintain the head of the trench and carry forward supplies and ammunition after the breach had been made. There was general satisfaction with this and the mood among the men was good. The attack was set for 7 September. They would move up the night before.

During these days Richard and Will had further sessions with DeLacey, who had become more talkative with them. They learnt that, despite appearance to the contrary, he was from an old aristocratic family and his ancestors had come from Normandy with William the Conqueror. They had been a powerful force at the courts of kings and queens through the ages and had estates in north Kent and in Berkshire, close to Reading. His grandfather had 'pissed it all away' gambling, drinking and whoring. He had died in a duel and left his own father nothing but debt and humiliation. His father had gone into military service and distinguished himself there, being knighted for his valour. He, DeLacey, had inherited the martial skills from his father but the less attractive character traits of his grandfather. The life of a mercenary seemed to suit him perfectly and he saw himself as carrying out a valuable social function – redistributing the money he earned, and the booty he 'collected' from the powerful, to whores, taverns and guesthouses across Europe. "Always thinking of those less fortunate. That's me."

Will was struck powerfully by DeLacey's classless outlook. He had descended from one of the truly elite families to this day-to-day existence. He saw that the respect of the men came from acknowledgement of his military skill and how he conducted himself, not his ancestry, although he was sure this was not widely known. DeLacey seemed to accept all men equally, as if all started on the same level. He formed his opinions on the basis of how a man behaved with his fellow men, on personal merit, rather than bloodline. He saw that he treated himself and Richard equally, making nothing of the elevated status of Richard's family, modest though it was.

But he knew that DeLacey was unusual in this. He had never met anyone else who shared this outlook and although Richard was his closest friend, even from him he felt he could sometimes detect a separation. Unspoken and subtle, but it was there, and it burned in him. And, increasingly, he felt that this feeling, this passion, this growing sense of inequity, must be a message to him from God. *All men are created equal in His image? Not in the world I know!*

He found himself talking with the men of the company who followed a more puritanical faith. He was lost, and frankly not interested in their discussions of popery, idolatry and other details of the right and wrong ways to worship, but

(Breda, September 1637)

was drawn by the *idea* of simple faith, without trappings of wealth and power. No showy extravagance of gold plate, silver crosses and elaborate altars, to put the ordinary folk in awe. This made sense to him. A man should be valued for what he did, not who his parents were, or what title he inherited. When he returned to England, if he survived this war, he would learn more about Parliament and think more on these wrongs and how they could be righted. For now, he would keep his thoughts to himself.

*

It was the evening before the assault on the hornwork. The mines were set and Browne's company was preparing to move up the trench to support the attack. Richard was strapping on a leather cuirass and hooking his father's militia sword, now with an edge unrecognisably sharp, onto his baldric. He had been detailed to provide covering musket fire for the assault, and the sword would be an encumbrance, but he didn't want to die wishing he had taken it.

As the company made its way up the trench, he fell in beside Will. He noticed he was wearing the embellished steel cuirass they had taken from the dead Spanish grandee and had also found a steel helmet. He was carrying his pike. As they were only supposed to be supporting the attack this seemed unnecessary.

But the thing that he noticed most was his state of agitation. He was breathing heavily and seemed restless, constantly checking straps, putting on and taking off his helmet to adjust it.

"Will. What is it? Are you OK? This should be easy for us tonight; we are not really involved."

No response. Will took his dagger from the sheath at his

back and wiped the blade on his sleeve and examined it before replacing it.

"Will!"

He jolted like he had been slapped. "What? What's wrong?"

"That's what I'm asking you. Why are you like…" he paused, indicating the pike, the cuirass, "…this? You are not really involved. You are not even with the muskets tonight."

Richard took an involuntary step back as Will loomed over him, anger in his face. He had never seen his friend like this; it was a different person in front of him. "Good God, Will! What is it? What have I done?"

Will put his hand to his face and took a long, slow breath. "Sorry." He put a heavy gauntleted hand on Richard's shoulder. "I think I am just excited at the thought of an actual fight after all this waiting. Y'know, dig and practise. Dig and practise. I don't want to let anyone down is all."

"Will, you never let anyone down." Richard breathed a sigh of relief as his friend re-emerged from wherever he had been. "Look, relax, Will. DeLacey's view is that the art of soldiering is avoiding fighting whenever you can." Richard smiled, hoping this was something they could both laugh at.

But Will's face hardened. Not rage now, but perhaps something colder. "Yes, that's DeLacey's view. Taken him a long way, ain't it? Seems he has no thought o' duty. Of what's right. I'm not like 'im, Rich." He paused and looked at the ground. "So, maybe I'm not so much like you."

Richard stared at him. Somehow this was worse than the fury. Where had this come from? Why was he saying all this now?

Will's expression softened again. "Rich. I'm your friend. Hope to always be so. But I am different from you. You know that. Born into a different life to you. For me there is more

(Breda, September 1637)

to this than the money. Or excitement. A laugh. Surviving another day. What's it for? I reckon if you are going to risk your life it has to mean something more than that. I'm not sure what that is, but I'm thinking more on it."

Richard was still staring. Now open-mouthed. "Fuck me, Will Fletcher. That's more than you've said in six months. It's those dodgy apples, isn't it? You've been poisoned!"

"You should not blaspheme, Rich," Will said quietly. Then, realising how this sounded coming from his mouth, he laughed. It seemed that all his inner tension had found an escape. "Forgive me, Rich. I am all recovered."

The company was on the move. He slapped his friend on the back, forgetting the steel and immediately regretting it. "Let's talk on this more, Will. See you after the attack. Perhaps we can have an ale on it?"

"Yes, Rich. And… good luck tonight. I think we will all need some." And with this slightly puzzling response Will pushed himself up the line of men. Richard stood and watched the tip of his pike disappear up ahead.

Although they seemed to have parted well enough, he was shaken by the exchange. He came to realise how much he leant upon Will's friendship and turned over in his mind his words and what they might mean. DeLacey was a valuable companion, but not a friend. He did not want to lose that. He collected his musket, supply of powder and ball, and strolled slowly after him, deep in his thoughts.

*

As it turned out, the company waited at the base of the assault trench for several hours. It was well after midnight when the order came to move, and many had to be woken. The leading men were a few hundred metres from the head of the trench when there came a sudden torrent of fire from the walls of the hornwork accompanied by loud cries and the sounds of many men on the move. Richard sensed, rather than saw, an answering surge from the bodies ahead of him. DeLacey hissed into his ear, "Sounds like the Spanish are sallying out, trying to dislodge the mines and bridge!" Answering musketry was heard, and now the first sounds of steel on steel and the screams of the injured and dying. A shout from ahead of them: "Browne! Captain Browne! Get your men ready. Wait for the call!"

Word was passed down from the front. "Get ready. Get ready." Some in whispers. Some in steady, experienced voices. Some, like Richard, with a slight crack in their voice, betraying the fear, excitement, anticipation and dread. Powder was checked, topped up. Unloaded weapons were quickly loaded. Swords loosened in scabbards. Richard almost laughed to himself. *Where is Will? Where is the big lump to stand behind just when you need him?* He paused. *Actually, where is Will?*

"Muskets to the front!" Browne's shout funnelled down the trench. "Now!"

DeLacey slapped Richard on the back. "Off you go, son. Head down. Nothing foolish. If you get a shot, make it count. I'll just wait here. Never been good with one of those..." He smiled encouragingly at Richard, who knew full well that DeLacey was one of the best shots in the company.

He pushed his way up the trench, along with twenty or so others. Right at the front of the company, he still could not see much of what was happening. But he had found Will. Crouching against the wall of the trench, a few feet from the captain, he was gripping his pike with an intensity that made the leather of his gauntlets creak. In the torchlight, Richard could see his jaw muscles squirming as he ground his teeth together. His eyes were unblinking, staring up the trench,

(BREDA, SEPTEMBER 1637)

but unfocused. He seemed in a bit of a dream-like state and, suddenly, Richard felt a cold fear for his friend.

"Three lines, lads." There was just enough room for six of them to stand shoulder to shoulder where the trench broadened out. Richard, with his careful training, made for the rear rank, picking the largest man to stand behind. "Front ranks, kneel," shouted Browne. *Shit! There goes that part of my plan...* He felt very exposed.

"Wait for the order to fire. We do not know who is coming out of the smoke first. We do NOT want to hit our own. Pikes! Behind. Two ranks!" From the corner of his eye Richard saw Will fall in behind them with other pikemen. He was right behind him and leant forward to whisper in his ear, "Don't worry, Rich. I've got you if they come."

Richard turned his head, and caught the hard, cold, determined look in his friend's eyes. "Yes," he said, "I know. I know you have." He paused. Turned again. "Do you want to swap positions?"

Will laughed. "I'm happy here, thanks. If I stood in front of you, you'd more likely hit me with that thing. Don't forget, I've seen you shoot!" They both laughed this time. Richard felt calmer, more in control. The urge to find the latrines waned and he found his awareness of the surroundings, and his concentration on the job in hand, strengthen. *This is it. In ten minutes, I could be dead. I may never see my family again.* He pictured his sister being given the news. Her tears. Her loss. Without him there to comfort her. The cause of her pain. *Bollocks. I'm going to survive this. Let the fuckers come!*

But they didn't come. There was a terrific detonation to the right, above their heads, followed immediately by a sound like a gale through trees. The screams. "The drake," Will shouted. "They're clearing the walls." The canister seemed to do its job. The firing from the hornworks stopped and the sounds of battle ahead of them gradually receded. Then cheers. English cheering.

The men around him visibly relaxed. Shoulders sagged. Chins sank forward onto chests. Long held breaths were released. The sally had been stopped. They had not been needed. The order to stand down was passed down the line. *Thank God*, thought Richard.

He and Will sat shoulder to shoulder against the wall of the trench. As it was reported, the action had been very limited. No more than twenty or so English, led by Monck, had been involved in the melee and they had held the imperial troops at the far end of the fascine bridge. The musketry and the grapeshot had kept the defenders pinned so that they could not get enough of their numbers down the walls to spoil the mine. The dead and the injured were carried past them, one endlessly screaming his pain, knee shattered by a musket ball, ends of bone grinding together. Face and neck wounds from the shove of pikes, no noise from the nearly dead, or those deep in shock. A trail of blood left down the middle of the trench, soon lost in the pools of muddy water.

The assault was confirmed for the morning and, once again, the Stadtholder himself would be there to witness the assault. *Oh, three cheers for William!* thought Richard. He slept, his head on his friend's shoulder, dreaming of the faces of the casualties from the fight coming past him, endlessly repeating, looking blankly at the stars, or silently looking to him for help. Answers he could not give them. Help he could not offer.

*

He was woken before dawn. The company was stirring, preparing. Richard had watched Monck rally the assault troops. These were just thirty hand-picked men, a mix of

(Breda, September 1637)

pikes and muskets. With him were captains Abrahall and Hammond, commanding a further forty pikemen and twenty musketeers, as well as a swarm of what DeLacey dismissively described as 'gentlemen volunteers'. "Here for the glory. Here to make their names or bravely die in the attempt." He paused, hand on his heart, striking a pose. "The silly bastards."

"What a way you have with words, Master DeLacey," said Captain Browne who was passing just at that moment.

"I'm a poet, Captain. You know that. I get right to the truth of a thing."

An hour passed before a commotion further down the trench signalled the arrival of Frederick Henry, with his entourage. There was scarcely room along the trench for him to pass through. There was an increase in musket fire from the English lines as they strove to keep the heads of the defenders down – doing what they could to ensure the supreme commander's safety.

Frederick had a swift conversation with the captains who would be leading the assault and then headed smartly back down the trench away from Richard and the assembled men. They were to attack immediately, as soon as the mine was blown. Browne's men were reserves, to follow up the successful assault with other regular troops. Or to cover a retreat.

Richard's calmness from the day before had deserted him again and he felt sick. *This is the life you chose, you idiot. No one forced you to come here.* Somehow, that didn't help. He thought again of Will. His friend was more concerned about letting people down. He was worried about his own skin. *Why are you here?*

They formed up in lines, two men deep, on either side of the trench, leaving space for others to either advance or retreat through their company. Richard was opposite Will, DeLacey further back and out of his field of vision. He and Will were about ten ranks from the front of the company where Browne stood. He wished he was in the rear rank so he could lean against the wall of the trench. His legs felt weak and his palm sweated on the wood of the musket. He repeatedly eased his sword a few inches out of the scabbard to keep it loose, until the man next to him elbowed him, irritated by the rhythmic clank of the steel. The air in the trench was starting to reek as men used it as a latrine. A little way back down the trench, one of the men vomited, a result of fear and the fetid air. Not that his actions helped… Richard recognised Walter, one of the lads who had arrived with him and Will. He caught his eye, smiled and nodded encouragingly, despite the fact that he was close to doing the same.

Richard looked to his left, straining to see past Browne to the assembled assault troops. Now he could hear Monck's voice raised in a final exhortation for courage and honour. He could not see him, or hear the words themselves, but it was punctuated by cheers and shouts from the men. He heard a resounding "Amen" and seconds later the ground shook beneath his feet. A split second later there was an incredible roar as the mine exploded and a mushroom-shaped cloud of soil, rock and dust was lifted into the air. Seconds later, another detonation shook him as the French mine was also fired.

While the dust was still hanging in the air, mingled with the grey smoke from the explosive, Monck was leading his men over the fascine bridge to what Richard assumed must be an enormous breach. Men flooded after him, a thicket of pikes waving as the running men struggled to keep control of the sixteen-foot weapons.

As he strained to see more, peering around his neighbour as they all struggled to see what was happening, there was a shout, and grabbing hands, and in his peripheral vision he saw Will surge forward between the lines of men. Just as Browne

(BREDA, SEPTEMBER 1637)

was turning to see the cause of the disturbance, Will sidestepped his blindside and was gone, his bulk blocking out the view of events ahead.

"Will! No!" Way too late, he knew. Suddenly he had control of his legs again, and without thinking he too was on the move, shouldering his way forward. "I'll bring him back, Captain!" he shouted at Browne as he too dodged past, not waiting for an answer. *What am I doing? This isn't in the fucking doctrine! And how am I going to bring him back even if I can catch him... Will, you stupid, stupid bastard! You're going to get yourself killed! You're going to get ME killed! Shit. Shit. Shit. Shit*, he panted as he ran along the trench after the assault troops.

He climbed the end of the trench, sensing Browne's company and other soldiers moving up behind him to prepare to reinforce those who had challenged at the breach. But he was by now many yards ahead of them. He reached the near end of the fascine bridge and was staggered at the sight before him. It was difficult to take in the huge aperture in the hornwork wall, as he needed to watch his footing on the crossing. He glimpsed Will ahead of him, scrambling up the rubble to the breach, already overtaking the laggards in Abrahall and Hammond's commands. And there were bodies, some moving feebly in the dust and ruined stonework, and others crouching behind larger pieces of masonry, unable or unwilling to push on through the breach. Clearly those arriving first had met the full force of the imperial volley and these men were trying to rediscover the courage needed to get moving again.

Richard could now hear the shouts, screams and occasional musket fire coming from beyond the ruined wall. As he reached the far side of the moat and looked up the slope, Will had disappeared into the smoke and dust cloud. There was no point calling to him over the din of the fight, so Richard saved his breath and poured up the incline. In seconds he gained the brink and came upon a line of bodies, dead and wounded, neatly arrayed along the line of the wall. The remnants of the stonework were sprayed with blood, and the dusty ground was readily soaking up more, with splinters of bone and the contents of split heads and punctured guts adding to the gory artwork.

He dragged his horrified, wide-eyed gaze up and looked down into the hornwork, into the chaos beyond. The imperial troops were massed in a tight formation. He could see musketeers frantically trying to reload, preparing for another volley, surrounded by a body of pikemen. These were heavily engaged by the English pikemen, with a group of around thirty English musketeers away to the left trying to enfilade their phalanx. Richard could see immediately that the English were heavily outnumbered but were nevertheless pressing home the attack. Right in the centre he could see Monck in his black enamelled armour, pushing frantically at the steel heads of the enemy pikes with his sword and free hand, trying to force his way into sword range where the pikes would become a useless liability. With a start he saw Will careering down the slope, heading for Monck. Cursing, he followed him down and vaulted one of the gentlemen volunteers who was trying to rise, despite a smashed shoulder. Any thought of his own safety had vanished; he had to protect Will, so he could then kill him himself for his rash stupidity.

A disciplined volley from the English cut into the enemy formation, and pikes swayed and fell like trees in a strong wind. This was not a Spanish regiment; they lacked the discipline and were struggling to deliver a meaningful response from their own muskets. But the pikes were steady and unyielding, and the English struggled to break through. Looking up from his feet, Richard could see Will arrive at the back of the English pike formation, weapon held vertically. He shouldered his way

(Breda, September 1637)

forward, straining to get to the front. *God above, has he got a death wish?!*

Richard stopped. From his slightly elevated position he could see through the patches of dust and smoke. Monck had found a gap in the line and had pushed through, followed by a half-dozen of his men. He was engaging an imperial officer hand to hand, crushed in between bodies and the heavy wooden pike shafts. He clearly saw an imperial musketeer, behind the officer, finish loading and raise his weapon to aim at Monck, who was conspicuous by his bravery and distinctive armour. The distance was only a few yards. Unless there was misfire, he couldn't miss. A shout from behind warned Monck of his predicament and as he half turned to face the danger, trying at the same time to fend off his opponent, an English pike flew inches past his left ear. Not shoved but thrown with tremendous force. It sailed past the imperial officer and struck the musketeer in the middle of his face as he tried to parry it with the musket, throwing him backwards off his feet, his musket discharging as he fell. Without looking for the source of his deliverance he turned back to his foe and, strengthened by his reprieve, quickly cut him down through the angle of neck and shoulder, a carotid fountain splashing across his face and those around him. Half turning to the body of men behind him, Monck bellowed, "For God, and for Goring!" and flung himself into the mass of the enemy. Those in the immediate area were clearly stunned by the fury of the assault and, at precisely that moment, there was a cry to the left and French soldiers were pouring through the breach their own mine had wrought.

The imperial formation was crumbling. Soldiers at the rear were making their escape, heading to a narrow bridge over the moat that separated the hornworks from the main city walls. Those at the front started to sense they were being abandoned and started backing, trying to maintain discipline while disengaging. Now they were being pressed from three sides as French and English musket fire continued to take its toll.

As the enemy broke and ran, Richard could see those English who had been most heavily involved in the hand-to-hand fighting collapse in exhaustion to the ground. Monck was among them. Frantically scanning the area in front of him, he saw Will, also on his knees, holding his right hand to the side of his face. He started towards him, and as he got closer realised there was blood pulsing between his fingers, his face deathly pale. He was just twenty yards away when he saw one of the imperial soldiers rise from a pile of bodies and lurch towards him, long dagger in his raised right hand. No time to reach Will, who raised his left arm to fend off his attacker. Instinctively, he raised the musket, half aimed and fired. The ball caught the man in the thigh, shattering the femur in a spectacular path of destruction. The man was spun around on his good leg as he corkscrewed to the ground, mouth open in silent agony.

Richard lurched past Will and swung the musket over his shoulder by the barrel to bring it crashing down on the injured man's head. Once. Twice. The man fell back on the second impact and didn't move again. At that same instant, Richard felt a jolt, like the blast of heat when an oven door is swung open. He felt it sweep through him and then gone in an instant. But it left him feeling strangely elated. And strong. *Never felt so strong!* He flung down the musket and swept out his father's sword. *His* sword now! *Where are the bastards? There must be more of them!* He felt a rage, a berserk fury that went way beyond anything he had felt before.

He swung back to Will and saw a man leaning over his stricken friend. He raised his sword over his head and, with

(Breda, September 1637)

two hands, prepared for a massive down-stroke that would have split the man's head like a turnip. Will saw him over the man's shoulder; his eyes went wide in shock. "No!" he shrieked. At the last moment, as the blade was descending, Richard caught the shout and, not able to divert the stroke, locked his arm muscles and the edge hovered, trembling, an inch above the man's black, thinning hair. The head slowly turned, and the body shifted, and Richard was looking into the eyes of Monck. He now saw the black armour, the unreadable gaze. Richard, in turn sank to his knees. The strength he had felt, the power in him, gone. Vanishing into the dirt like water spilled from a bucket. "Sorry. Oh God, so sorry," he gasped. "I thought you were…" Monck looked steadily into his eyes. "I know. And now I must thank your friend twice." He turned back to Will, now ignoring Richard, who slowly got back to his feet and retrieved his musket.

Monck was speaking to Will. "It was you? With the pike? I have never seen anything like that – thrown with such strength. My thanks, sir!" He peeled Will's hand from his face and studied the deep gash that had split the skin along his cheekbone. "The ball that was meant for me did this, I think. Make sure you wash it. With boiled water. It will require a stitch or two." He paused and looked more carefully at Will. "Do I know you? You were not in my company. Why are you here, now?"

Will managed a twisted smile. "The other day. You asked me, sir, if I was ready to do my duty. Forgive me but I didn't like the suggestion that I might not be. I wanted to prove it. To you, and I think to myself."

"The farm boy. Am I right?"

"Yes, sir."

"Come and see me when you are recovered. You might want to thank your friend here, as he just as clearly saved you, as you did me." He stood, looked again at Richard with a flat, blank expression, swivelled on his heel and jogged off in the direction of the continuing fight.

Will looked up at Richard, looked him deep in the eyes, and nodded. Richard, suddenly exhausted himself, nodded back, feeling the strength of feeling behind the gesture. He was drained of emotion, of words. He sank down next to Will, tore a strip of cloth from his shirt and pressed it firmly to the wound on Will's cheek. "Hold it here. Can you walk?"

Will nodded. Just as Richard was levering himself to his feet, he became aware that Browne's company was passing them, following behind the advancing figure of Monck. They could only ever have been a few minutes behind him and Will. Browne jogged past and gave them both a look that suggested he felt they had taken leave of their senses. Moments later DeLacey stopped next to them. "You both alright?"

"Yes. Will needs to get this seen to but yes, we are OK." Richard expected some withering, sarcastic, blasphemy-laden reply, but there was just a nod of acknowledgement and "Take him back down the trench. Rest. Get him to eat something." Genuine concern on his face, then replaced by something grimmer as he nodded again and turned to follow Browne. Over his shoulder: "Save something for me, you mad fuckers!"

10

(North-West England)

The market was centred on the Dane Bridge, a graceful single stone-built span, providing a crossing of the river. The settlement at Wincle had existed around the bridge for hundreds of years, as the bridge carried the important trading route between Leek and nearby Macclesfield. The Hollow Way, it was called, as the countless feet and hooves of centuries had worn a sunken lane, flanked by trees and hedgerows. In high summer it was a tunnel through beech, oak and ash. In the autumn it had a carpet of brown, red and gold. In the winter and spring, it was ankle-deep, oozing mud. These days, wool, salt and iron passed along the Hollow Way and over the water, and this traffic, together with traders, farmers, craftsmen and ordinary folk from the surrounding areas of Swythamley, Allgreave and Wildboarclough, and some even from Sutton and Langley, made the monthly Wincle market an important local event.

Pens of sheep and cows occupied the floodplain of the river. Cages of poultry lined the sides of the bridge itself. The stalls of butchers hung with meat. There were trout from the river, the stallholder fighting a losing battle against the flies and the growing warmth of the day. And there was a stall set up with barrels of local ale. The red-faced, red-nosed, corpulent owner was doing a roaring trade even at mid-morning, in turn beaming at his customers and backhanding the young lad and girl doing the serving for being too slow or spilling too much as they tried to meet his demands to work quicker.

But much of the business was being done around simpler setups. Rugs or cloth laid on the ground with the products of local people and craftsmen. Vegetables and early fruit. Freshly baked bread and cheeses. Clothing, shoes or items for the household such as pots, or carved wooden bowls and implements. Her leather roll was on the edge of this section of the market. She sat on a small wooden stool behind her goods – piles of scraped and cleaned rabbit skins, simple rabbit skin mittens and muffs, and bunches of dried herbs. She also advertised her skills as a seamstress and spent much of the day working on repairs that market-goers would bring to her. But mainly she was hoping to see one of the visiting tradesmen who would buy her rabbit skins. This was where she would make most of her money. The skins were used for lining cloaks, hats and gloves, and she could nearly always find a buyer as Macclesfield was becoming a centre for making such things.

She was working on some stitching on a linen shirt when she noticed a pair of boots stop at the edge of her mat. The owner of the boots coughed to gain her attention, and she looked up. Disappointment, and apprehension. Not a trader to buy her rabbit skins, but an admirer of her own.

"Mornin', mistress. Gonna be a warm 'un."

"Mornin', Samuel. Reckon you're right. You brought some stock along today?" Samuel Brassey already looked very warm. His curly black hair was plastered to his forehead with sweat and his face was bright red. She could also see that he had come to her by way of the ale stall and that he had fought a terrible battle with his shyness to be standing here, talking to her. He shifted his weight slightly from foot to foot and looked like he would rather be somewhere else. Samuel was a tenant farmer in Wildboarclough, helping his older brother's family raise cattle on the lower ground by the river, and sheep higher up the hills. It was a good-sized parcel of land and the Brasseys were considered to be doing well.

She liked Samuel, although they had hardly spoken previously. He was quiet, hard-working, kind with his animals with whom he would rather spend his time. It was unusual to see him at market. Normally his brother and sister-in-law would transact the business and he would stay on the land. He had become even more withdrawn following the loss of his wife. She had passed within months of the wedding from an illness, and he had all but disappeared from public life after that. Two years had passed, roughly the time she had arrived in the village.

"Aye. Some ewes, and some chickens." She could see his brother and sister-in-law watching from the other side of the road, occasionally speaking quietly to each other. Her heart sank as she had a terrible premonition of what was to come.

He cleared his throat. He looked intently at the toes of his boots. Looked at her, right into her eyes, but chose the boots to address his words to. "I have seen you before, Mistress Hume. Once or twice. I was wondering, me now being alone, and you also alone, if…" there was a long silence; he looked up again and this time managed to hold her gaze, "…if you might walk with me, later. After the market. Afore I take for home. I would be honoured." He pulled nervously at his full, thick beard. Courtship was swift in these isolated communities.

She knew she had to be quick and firm to finish this, but not to destroy him, and not to antagonise his family. She spoke quietly, so no others nearby could hear her reply. "Samuel. It is I who am honoured. I hear that you are a good man, and I am deeply sorry for the loss you suffered. If things were different, perhaps we might talk further, but it would be unseemly for me to walk with you. You must know that I am wed, Samuel. My husband is soldiering in Flanders and… Well, it would be wrong of me. You must see that?"

He didn't look surprised by her answer, expression hardly changing. He half looked back over his shoulder towards his family and seemed to take encouragement from that. He squared his shoulders. "Aye, mistress. I had heard you was wed. My Alice passed two year gone. Your husband ain't been seen for two year. Ain't no one here has seen him. Ain't it time for you to say he has fallen in the wars? Ain't it time now for you to think o' yerself, and move on, like?"

"Samuel, what you say is true. He has been gone from me for what seems an eternity. Maybe he has fallen, but I have no word of it. If I marry again, and he be still living, God would damn me. All these here would condemn me. I am truly sorry, Samuel, but I cannot walk with you."

He stood in front of her, knuckles showing white on the shepherd's stick he carried. But, she sensed, almost in relief. She smiled and softened her eyes. "Samuel. Perhaps you should rejoin your brother and Mistress Brassey. I am sure they will have need of you with the stock."

He gave her a slightly unfocused stare, then nodded briskly and walked away. She watched him go, picking his way between buyers and sellers to find his brother. She pretended to return to her mending but watched his meeting with his brother and sister-in-law. She knew now that her time was up. She would need to move on again. Not far perhaps, but away from this village. She did not want to become a talked-about person. She did not want to be noticed.

She cursed quietly to herself; the conversation among the Brasseys was not going well. Older brother Henry had spun Sam around and, planting two hands in the middle of his back, shoved him back towards her. He grabbed his arm and was marching him through the throng, one or two people stopping to look at their progress. Mary Brassey followed in their wake, a determined expression set on her thin face.

The trio came to a halt at the edge of her mat. Henry Brassey, half a head taller than his younger brother, was otherwise very similar to Samuel. Thick, black, curly hair and beard. But the similarity ended there. His dark eyes flamed with anger, his face also red – from ale, from the warmth of the sun, but mainly from rage. Mary leaned around him to get a better look, her small mouth compressed into a thin, white line. Pale blue eyes disdainful, cold, bitter.

"You turned 'im away. My brother. *You*, turned *him*, away." His voice was low, menacing.

"Good mornin', Master Brassey. Mistress Brassey. Samuel. A warm day." She smiled and squinted up at the sun. "And goin' to get hotter."

"Aye. It is goin' to get hotter." No smile in return from Henry. Sam looked at his boots again, an agony of embarrassment on his face. "Who are *you* to turn *him* away?" He pointed at her with his blackthorn stick, point only about a foot from her face.

"As I explained to your brother, Master Brassey, I am a married woman. That's who I am to turn him away. It is godly to do so. Do you not agree?"

His volume raised fractionally. "Married? Really? No one round here has seen no husband of yours."

"As I said to Samuel, he is at war, in Flanders. He has been gone these three years. I do miss him terrible."

"You see, Henry. 'Tis as I said. Let us go. There is no good in this." Samuel tugged his brother's elbow and turned to go, but Henry shook him off.

"You get back here. This woman insults our family and you would let it slide? Mistress…" he turned back to her, "…Hume here thinks that she, in her state and with her reputation, can refuse my brother. I don't think so."

"If you think so little of me, sir, why do you pursue me so? I would have thought that the last thing you would want is any family connection to one such as me. Let it go, sir. I cannot do what you ask and keep with God."

"Don't play pious with us," Mary hissed. "Seldom seen you in chapel. 'Tis not natural and 'tis probably not legal! And we would not be here if Samuel was not so taken with you. It is time for him to wed again and he will entertain none but you in his heart. Despite what we have counselled, believe me!"

She faced Samuel. "I am truly sorry, Samuel. I thank you for the honour you do me with your thoughts. But I cannot help you in this. It is my fate, and the Lord's will, that I await my John. Even if I must wait my lifetime."

Henry again: "But he needs to marry again. It is important to… to us. To him…" He faltered and Mary dug him in the ribs with her elbow. This roused his anger again. "It is heartless of you to refuse him. And I say you lie about your husband. D'you hear me, woman, you lie!" With that he took a threatening step onto the mat, muddy boot crushing bundles of pungent rosemary. He towered over her and for a moment she thought he was going to strike her with the stick. She leaned back sharply to avoid him and fell backward off her stool onto the grass.

She was, however, fully in control. She saw that they were attracting the attention of a number of people and she knew that any foolish reaction on her part would just create a bigger scene. Better to let the energy dissipate. Better to stay where she was on the ground and say nothing. What more could they do here in the centre of the market?

The woman next to her, another seamstress, had cried, "For shame", as she fell, and was up on her feet remonstrating with Mary Brassey, and Samuel was trying to pull Henry away. Henry, perhaps realising he gone too far, just stood frozen to the spot and stared down at her, lying on her back. At that moment a potentially recoverable situation tipped over. A deep voice boomed from behind the Brasseys. "What is the meaning of this?! Let me through there!" From her vantage point she could not see the speaker, but to her horror she recognised the voice.

At that moment, the Brasseys parted and Sir William Brereton strode between them, Samuel to his right, Henry and Mary to his left. He looked down at her, scarcely believing what he saw. He reached down and offered her his hand. He gently pulled her to her feet and, once vertical, she took two large steps backward, trying to distance herself from the group. Brereton then spun around to face Henry who also backed off a pace. "What, sir, do you mean by this behaviour? You struck her?! You struck a defenceless woman. My God, sir, are you an animal?"

"Sir. Your Lordship! I did not strike her. I may have startled her is all, moved a bit quick, like." He stuttered, frantically trying to understand what was happening. The man was clearly gentry, but no one Henry had seen before.

"He did not strike me, Sir William; it is how he described. I lost my balance and fell. It was silly of me. I think perhaps the warmth of the sun and the excitement of the day..." She let the sentence trail off. She was desperate for the situation to defuse, not escalate. She noticed Samuel had already swung round and was striding off, pushing his way roughly through the crowd. Sir William did not see him go. He focused on Henry, left hand resting lightly on the hilt of his sword, now clearly visible, gripping a riding cane in his right hand.

"Then, sir, I think you owe this lady an apology at the very least. And when you have apologised to her, and to my satisfaction, you should leave as quickly as you can. I do not wish to see your face here again today." He took a half-step forward, all the while staring fixedly into Henry's face.

Sir William? Must be Sir William Brereton. God above! Why is he here? "Of course, Sir William. Of course." He turned to her, and he felt the embarrassment, loss of dignity and, above all, rage rise in him again at the sight of her. He gritted his teeth. "Mistress Hume. I meant no harm. I acted foolish. Please accept my apology." He did his best to keep his voice level, but his emotion was plain to those around him. His eyes flashed a look of pure hatred and fury.

She did not want to give Sir William any excuse to prolong this nightmare, so she replied quickly, before he could intervene again. "You are very gracious, sir. Of course I accept." She nodded at him, and to Sir William, "My thanks, sir. T'was just a misunderstanding. All is well now."

Henry nodded back and went to go, but Mary Brassey was not so easily cowed. "You should know, Sir William, about this woman. Do not be hasty in your judgement of my husband. There are many consider it strange for a woman of her age to live alone. She claims a husband, but none has ever seen 'im. To wander the countryside and moor by herself. At all hours." Mary looked at her. "Oh yes, dear. I seen yer, and it ain't natural for a woman." She turned back to Sir William. "There are many says she does unnatural things." Her voice dropped to little more than a whisper as she looked him in the eye. There was suddenly silence all around them. "There are some say… she be a witch…"

And there it was. The word. The woman next to her exclaimed angrily, "Mary Brassey! There is none that say that but you. And while *she* may not know why you are so keen for Samuel to marry, we all do! Keep your accusations to yourself."

"And you keep your opinions to yourself, you are little better than her!" Mary hissed.

"No such thing as witches, you stupid…"

"Stop this NOW!" Sir William shouted. He turned on Mary, breathing hard. "Are you making a formal accusation? Are you? Because if you are, and it is found that this is a malicious accusation with no foundation, you will face the law yourself! Well? What do you say?"

Mary faced him and did not falter under his angry gaze. "I will say nothing more, sir. I have no desire to make a *formal* charge of witchcraft. Not at this time." She did not need to. Mary knew, as she herself did, that Mary had already said enough, and said it loud enough. "Come, Henry, let us see to the stock and let Sir William enjoy his day amongst the commonfolk." And they were gone, disappearing through the muttering crowd that had gathered around them.

Sir William now turned to her. "Are you quite alright, mistress? Mistress Hume did I hear?" He had a look of concern, and something a little more worrying. She recognised it at once. *Curiosity*. Oh, damn Mary Brassey to hell!

"Quite well, Sir William. My thanks for your help, and to you, mistress." She turned to her right and held the seamstress's hands in hers. "My thanks for your words to help a stranger."

"Oh, but she is a wicked one that Mary Brassey. Take no heed of her. All 'holier than thou', she is. They need to marry Samuel off to get their hands on the plot of land next to theirs. It is a condition of the tenancy – only to be let to families of husband and wife. They are just using poor Samuel. Although I too had heard he was sweet on you, dear." She winked, and then stood watching Sir William and her, waiting to see what further entertainment might arise. The most exciting market day she could remember since them pigs got out and ran amok through the stalls.

Sir William smiled at her. "So you are like Penelope, awaiting the return of her Odysseus."

"Sir?" she replied, a puzzled look on her face. She was *not* going to step into that obvious trap.

"Never mind," he smiled again. "Well, I hope you will not suffer from those fools again. I will be back through this area again in a month or so; I will perhaps check that you have not witnessed any retaliation. Good day, ladies." He tipped his hat to them both, and with a slightly lingering look in her direction, he turned on his heel.

"Well, Mistress Hume!" said the woman. "I shall get you a stick so you can beat them off. Samuel is a good man, but I think Sir William is the one for you!" She laughed. "And if he ain't good enough for you, pass him on to me, I haven't had… well, you know. It's been a while, let's say." She blushed scarlet and clapped her hand to her mouth as she realised what she had said. "Oh my. My big mouth."

She laughed in turn. "Never mind, mistress, I was thinking the same. We both need to do penance."

Over the heads of the crowd, she saw Sir William ride off on the black horse. His carriage followed behind, and she smiled as she saw the dogs looking out of the window, tongues lolling. They wound off up the hill towards distant Macclesfield and the flat land of the plain. An hour later, Henry and Mary Brassey were driving their stock back to Wildboarclough. Soon after that, she packed up her goods and said another thank you, and a farewell, to her new friend.

It was around two in the morning when she left the cottage with her prized possessions, her savings and some practical items. She moved quietly up the hill and by dawn was several miles away from the village.

(NORTH-WEST ENGLAND)

It was around six in the morning that they found Samuel Brassey, swinging gently from the stonework of the Dane Bridge, the issue of his marriage now resolved.

11

(Breda, September–October 1637)

Having helped Will back to the camp, Richard had made his way back to the wall, feeling he may still have duties to fulfil. He joined a line of regular soldiers doing the same, but before he had even got as far as the fascine bridge, he met Browne's men coming back down the trench. Many of them acknowledged him with a nod and a smile, and he found DeLacey towards the back of the line, talking quietly with Browne. They parted, Browne heading back to speak to some of the other officers, and DeLacey, looking up, saw Richard.

He beckoned him over, an unreadable look on his face. They slumped down and put their backs to the trench wall. "Well, that went better than anyone expected. Except, of course, them that died, or got themselves shot to bits," said DeLacey. "Abrahall and his men managed to take the bridge to the city that the bastards were retreating across. Got there just as they were going to fire the cannon that would have cleared it… He saved many. An unusually brave man. Unusual in that he is a brave man who is still alive!"

"Like Will?"

DeLacey frowned, took out his dagger and started to prod

at the ground between his feet. "Not so sure about brave. Are you? Do you know why he did it?"

Richard relayed their earlier conversation. He expected a joke, a sneer, but DeLacey's frown deepened. "Sounds like your friend is becoming politic. I hear there is a growing number in England who feel in a similar way. Particularly in your part of the country. Can't see it myself. Them that has will keep and do everything they can to stop them that wants from gettin'. You start questioning the rights of them with property and where do you stop? He'll be after King Charlie, demanding a share of the crown jewels!"

Richard laughed. Then DeLacey half turned to Will. "Look, son, my readin' is that now the hornwork is ours, the Imperials won't last long. Wouldn't be surprised if they give it up in the next few days. We outnumber them and they know full well that now we can bring up more guns and fire straight into the city as we want. It's just a matter of time and they are not stupid. Live to fight another day and all that. You thought about what you're going to do next?"

Richard looked puzzled. "How do you mean? I guess I'll go wherever Browne takes us next."

"Well. Campaigning season will start to wind down soon as autumn comes on. Browne's company will start to disband, wait for next spring. Some will go home for the harvest. What will you do? Go home too?"

"I don't know. Hadn't thought about it. I need to speak to Will." Richard really hadn't given it a thought. He felt exhausted, but still half in the battle, while DeLacey seemed to have moved on without hesitation. Richard guessed he had seen many such days. And then he remembered, and was shocked, really shocked, that he had not thought about it until that moment. "Master DeLacey. I killed a man. I shot him and then broke his skull with my musket while he was lying on the ground. While he was looking up at me. I killed him. He's dead."

A short laugh. "That *is* what you are paid for, son." DeLacey saw the fragile look on Richard's face and his look changed. "Look, son, you might have killed before today, when you were firing up at the walls. That didn't seem to bother you? This is a war. People die. It could have been you. Or Will. Or, God above, it could have been me! Think of that untold tragedy!" He laughed. "I'm not saying you should enjoy it…" Richard started at that. *Is that what I felt? Enjoyment? It wasn't like that.* "…but you need to get used to it. If you are going to be a soldier, this is going to happen a lot – unless your luck runs out and they get you first. And I thought that was why you were paying me to teach you? Or did I miss something?"

"No." He paused, thinking about what he could say to DeLacey. Trying to put into words how he had felt. *Is it like that for everyone? The strength, the fury, the feeling of power…* He decided he would keep that to himself for now. He looked at DeLacey. "No, Master DeLacey. You are right. As always." Time to change the subject. "So, what will you do?"

"Well. I am going to Amsterdam." Richard nodded. He had heard a lot about the place in the weeks since he arrived. "Lots of merchants there. Rich families, lots of property, lots of goods, lots of money. People like that need protection, and who better to supply it than a battle-hardened veteran who forced the breach at Breda and helped the Dutchies recapture their city. They should be prepared to show some gratitude!" He paused. "Look, son. Do you want to come along? Maybe Will too?" Richard saw a look on his face he had never encountered before. DeLacey actually looked embarrassed, awkward.

"Us? With you? Why?"

(Breda, September–October 1637)

More awkwardness. Silence. Silence so long Richard even turned his head to make sure DeLacey hadn't fallen asleep. So quiet Richard could barely hear him. "I had a wife, Richard. Her name was Rose. I had a son. Benedict. I had a daughter. Elizabeth. We called her Bess. Bessie." He scratched and jabbed hard at the floor of the trench with his dagger. "They are dead, Richard. All of them. Plague took 'em. In two weeks, all of them, gone. And I was not with them. I was…" he paused, "…away. I never saw them before they were gone. I do not even know for sure where they are buried. Somewhere east of London town." He cleared his throat and Richard didn't dare turn his head to look at him. He sat rigidly still, hardly breathing, feeling like any movement or interruption would be a kind of disaster. A betrayal. The shouts and clatter of soldiers moving up and down the trench seemed miles away, unreal. They were in some small cell of quiet, prisoners of this sudden tide of emotion. Richard wondered how DeLacey was going to get them out, because he didn't know what to say, or do.

"And sometimes I think I see something of myself in you. I too have a temper, as you know. You are brave, you can fight when you have to. But you also have a brain. You are good company. I think that maybe my boy might have been a bit like you. It is too late for me. It is too late for him. But you can do something with your life. You have your own family. Father and mother, brothers and sisters. I don't want to be your father, but maybe I can help you – while you are away from them. I have very little purpose in my life now and it would please me to do so. This is… difficult for me, Richard, but the offer is there. I ask you to think on it." Now he turned, eyes moist with unshed tears, somehow daring Richard to laugh at this openness. His need. "When I saw you go after Will, I thought that I might be too late. So many of the new lads fall in their first action. So I wanted to tell you this now."

Richard was stunned. He had never seen any hint of this in DeLacey. Coming so quickly after the recent violence and horror of the fight, he was not sure his brain was joining up all of the pieces correctly. He couldn't hold DeLacey's gaze but spoke slowly and carefully. He desperately didn't want to say the wrong thing, so kept his words to a minimum. "Actually, my mother is dead. She left the world as my little sister joined it. I am very sorry for your loss. I am sorry I don't have better words. You do me an honour in sharing this with me. I think you have not shared this often. There is much to think about, but I must get back to Will. I will talk to him, and I will think carefully on your suggestion. I promise you an answer soon." He rose to his feet. DeLacey stayed seated but looked up at him.

"You have an old head on young shoulders, boy. My thanks for your answer. Think on it. We have some time, and I will not pursue you on this." He put his head down again and was lost in his thoughts as Richard left him.

*

A month later, Richard was on a horse making his way to Amsterdam across the flat, featureless fields of the Low Countries. In front of him, DeLacey rolled in his saddle, evidently nearly asleep after saying farewell to Breda with several cups of local cider as they had eaten their fill at a tavern near the north gate.

It had all happened much as DeLacey had predicted. A few days after the English and French breakthroughs, the Scottish had also made a breach. A fortnight later, the Dutch had captured further fortifications and, after negotiations of surrender, the whole imperial garrison had marched out of Breda with their weapons and colours, and they had marched in.

(BREDA, SEPTEMBER–OCTOBER 1637)

Will had recovered from his wound, but even with some skilled stitching from one of Browne's men, he bore an ugly scar across his right cheekbone to his ear. He had sat stoically through the process, staring into the fire the man had used to cleanse the needle, and he escaped any infection. The red of the wound was fading to brown, and the stitches were out. He and Richard had laughed about how which of Richard's broken nose or Will's scar was more likely to appeal to the ladies. To the ribald amusement of those nearby, DeLacey had chipped in that the only ladies they were ever likely to encounter would only be interested in the size of their purses, not their faces.

He had spoken to Will about DeLacey's offer and what they should do about it. He didn't pass on everything he had been told; it didn't feel right to do so. He knew immediately that Will would not go for it. "I am signing as a regular. I spoke to Captain Monck and he will vouch for me. He is a good man, Rich. I could follow a man like that. I don't want to be a bodyguard for some rich Dutchman. I have met people here who think like me, Rich. I feel like maybe we can make some kind of change. Make life better for ordinary people. I'm sorry, Rich, it's just how I see it."

They had parted as friends and as he jogged along on his horse, Richard thought that if Will survived his fights to come, he would become a most formidable man. He now knew that he had seriously underestimated his friend, and while he did not understand all he said, he respected his passion and that he had some kind of purpose in his life. He had no plan. Just an uncertain future in the company of a man he did not fully understand but with whom he now felt some kind of bond. When Browne had shaken his hand and asked if he would be back in the spring, Richard had no answer.

The Toledo rapier sat on his hip, and his wages had been paid. Browne's men had been awarded a bonus by the grateful

Stadtholder for their part in securing the breach. DeLacey had not taken Richard's money. Said he had never intended to. Richard was not so sure.

The autumn afternoon sun was still able to warm his back, and the falling leaves were starting to coat the muddy lane, horses' hooves pushing them down into the muck. He thought of home and his family busy with the harvest. He wasn't ready for that yet. Maybe he just needed to wait and see what Amsterdam could bring. Wait and see. That was a plan at least. And anyway, things seldom worked out as he had planned.

He now definitely heard a snore from in front of him. Richard smiled, quietly caught up with DeLacey and slapped his horse smartly on the rump with his leather glove. The horse, which was also almost asleep, leapt forward with DeLacey desperately grabbing for the reins. Richard laughed and laughed. This would do for now...

12

(Amsterdam, January 1639)

Richard eased his legs down off the table top and massaged the muscles of his thighs and calves, illustrating painfully to him that he had been sitting comfortably by the tavern fire for too long. He arched his back and pushed his thumbs up and down his spine, under his leather coat, to ease the stiffness. Had he actually fallen asleep? The tavern was still busy, but there was space now to move around. People were gradually shifting out through the door into the piercing cold of the January night.

Here and there, hopeful whores wandered through the thinning crowd, trying to tempt customers to linger just a while longer, but they were fighting a losing battle and it seemed their hearts were not really in it, not on any level. He saw Anna dragging a fat, balding man in an expensive-looking waistcoat towards the stairs with grim determination, one hand on his lapel, the other with a handful of the front of his breeches. But as he put one foot on the bottom step, he suddenly cleared his head and batted her off with the back of his hand. As she released her grip both fell on their arses, struggling to get up – he trying to drag his considerable mass upwards using a convenient chair, she fighting the effects of the considerable volume of gin that had been donated to her over the course of a busy evening by appreciative patrons.

Richard, sensitive to the potential for anger arising from loss of dignity and loss of earnings, quickly stepped between them and hoisted the portly burgher to his feet, swinging him around to face the tavern door as he did so. He guided him past the door, collecting the man's voluminous, fur-trimmed robe from the back of his chair as he went past, and steered him into the street. The man thanked him, eyes having difficulty in focusing on Richard's face, turned away quickly and vomited long and loud across the doorstep of the tavern. Richard took a long stride over it and stepped back into the hot, smoke-laden din, slamming the door. The tavernkeeper caught his eye and nodded his thanks as Richard returned to his seat near the fire.

Another hour or so and he made his way upstairs to his lodging, just down the hall from where the girls did their work. Klaas had pushed a few small coins into his hand and he exchanged one of these for a glass of gin which he took upstairs with him. He had always hated this time of year. The revelry of the Christmas period, and the high spirits and optimism of the New Year were gone, and the bitter, grey-black winter ruled. While he knew there would be a return of the sun's warmth, and the long evenings of summer, spring always seemed such a fragile prospect and, for now, melancholy was his king, and his god.

He lay fully clothed on the straw mattress, under a thick woollen blanket, and looked at the patterns the damp had stained into the ceiling, like maps of islands with complicated coastlines drawn on parchment. He imagined the excitement of exploring the bays and inlets, going ashore for adventure, having a life with some purpose and stimulation. Abruptly, he recalled his affinity with the ocean on his crossing from

England to the Low Countries, and his enthusiasm sank without trace. *Shit! Is there nothing more than this for me? This wasn't what I had in mind when I left home.* He took a swallow of the fiery gin and slammed the empty glass down on the floor, his eyes filling with tears of frustration and disappointment. The sharp noise elicited a scuffling in the far corner of the room as the resident rat ran for the gap in the plaster. Richard swept up the glass again and hurled it with all his strength at the direction of the sound as he roared his impotent rage. The thick glass shattered on the floor and embedded the soft plaster with shrapnel shards.

He shrugged off his coat and sank back onto the mattress, pulling the blanket back in place. *And where is Roger? He has been gone for weeks, scouting down towards Breda, trying to pick up news of Browne and the company. He should be back.* He hated to admit it, but despite the fact that DeLacey and he were increasingly close, he would not put it past him to weigh up the effort of returning to Amsterdam to collect his 'friend' Richard and find it more expedient to sign up and forget his surrogate son.

There was a soft knock at his door, introducing a soft voice. "Risch? You alright, Risch? I come in?" It was Cornelia from the room next to his.

"Yes, I am fine, Cornelia. Please. Come in."

She had arrived at the tavern about six months ago, around the same time as Richard, orphaned by a combination of the war and a fever taking her mother. In a stampede of townsfolk trying to escape rumour of a Spanish incursion, she had become separated from her brother and found herself alone, vulnerable, and with nowhere to go. She had been begging outside the front door for days and no matter how many times Klaas chased her off, she kept coming back. He had finally caught her and, taking a good look at her for the first time, saw not a pest but an investment opportunity. Ever the businessman he worked to secure the deal, feeding her up with stews of beef and barley and letting her wash away the filth of Amsterdam's gutters. Shrewdly he had let her stay, sharing a room with two of his working girls, but not pressing her to work. She had said she was sixteen and, cleaned up, she was very pretty with jet-black hair in ringlets, blue eyes and a small gap between her front teeth, the result of a punch in the face by an unsympathetic city scout. This gave her a look of innocence and a slight whistle when pronouncing certain words, which always made Richard smile.

After a month, Klaas had pointed out to her that she could perhaps think of a way to show her gratitude. No, he didn't mean by cleaning or waitressing. She was already popular with his customers, making the place look prettier. Perhaps she could make his customers even more welcome? He had smiled and asked her to think on it. Two days later he had been more direct. Would she wish to revert to her former begging? With Amsterdam booming with trade, money was flowing through his tavern. She could earn an easy living, with roof and board. She just had to contribute to the commercial enterprise more energetically than she had done. Two days later he had kicked her out, throwing her few possessions after her, and he had waited.

Two hours later she had come back, eyes red with tears, and had pleaded with Klaas to take her back. He was all smiles and hearty laughing. Why, of course! A misunderstanding was all it was. She could have her old room back. Oh yes, and of course she could start her new career that night. Richard had to admit that after that she had settled in very quickly and seemed to have found a kind of peace with the work. Of all Klaas's 'girls', she was closest to him in age and they became friends. He looked forward to seeing her, and they would talk,

(Amsterdam, January 1639)

him with his few words of Dutch, and trying to teach her some English.

He pulled himself up on his bed and put his back against the wall as she came around the door, closing it softly behind her. She was wearing a long linen nightdress, almost to the floor, and he thought her hair was down around her shoulders, although he struggled to see anything with the cloudy sky obscuring the moon beyond the window. With her arms wrapped around her for warmth, she tiptoed across the boards and got on the bed next to him. He flipped the blanket over her and she leant against him, putting her head on his shoulder and holding his arm.

"You call out," she whispered. "You alright?"

He stared straight ahead into the darkness "Yes, Cornelia. Just feeling sad. A bad day. And I can't see when I will have a good day again. A day when I can get away from here."

"You want to get away? Why get away?"

"This…" he waved his free hand around in the dark "…is not what I want. I do not want to be working as a tavern guard when I am twenty. I am a soldier."

"Not understand, Risch."

"This is not for me. I want more. DeLacey and I came here looking for work. To earn real money. Not the few coins I get from Klaas."

"You want more? You not like us here?"

"It's not you, or the other girls. It is not even Klaas. At least he is a fair man. There just must be… more… I can do."

"You not like me, Risch?" He heard her voice catch a little, turning her whisper low and throaty. He felt her eyes on him in the dark.

He turned his head to her and could just make out her looking up at him from under her lashes. He felt her breath on his skin, and his stomach jumped and flipped.

"Cornelia! No! Of course I like you." Now it was his voice that caught. He cleared his throat, feeling at once foolish but also a sudden, undeniable desire for her. "I like you a lot."

"Oh. Good. I hoped so, Risch." She reached with her left hand and pulled his head down towards hers. It was not Richard's first time – he lived in a tavern with a lively brothel upstairs – but it was the first time he had felt like this. The blood pounded in his head and he felt slightly sick. His body was responding quicker than he thought possible. They kissed breathlessly, and he snorted slightly as he fought for air through his nose, not wanting to break the connection but worried about showering her with phlegm. *Oh God! Don't let me mess this up.* But then he remembered who he was with and knew he was in the hands of a professional. Then, literally, he was. Her nightdress was up around her waist and things were moving to a very rapid conclusion…

13

(Amsterdam, January 1639)

Now reduced to a bloody errand boy, he thought bitterly as he trudged through the dirty snow-mud sludge on the pavement of the Damrack towards the Dam. Drips fell from the front of his broad-brimmed hat to confirm the continuing stately descent of the light shower of large, wet flakes. His shoulders were soaked where water had crept through the widening gaps in the seams of his long leather coat, and his freezing feet reminded once again that his boots were long past being functional and were now merely embarrassments. To his left, the creak and groan of some of the hundreds of vessels that populated the Amsterdam waterfrontage were accompanied by the rattle and flap of miles of rigging against the forest of masts. The whole mass of them rose and fell gently together, causing the masts to rock back and forth like trees in a stiff breeze. Richard felt slightly sick just watching them, so he kept his eyes down on the road. *As befits my status.*

He angled left across the Dam, putting De Nieuwe Kerk behind him and entering Halsteeg. As he reached the corner, the change in direction and camber of the paving, coupled with a stubborn sheet of ice left untouched by any thaw, sent him sliding. Arms waving frantically for balance, his boots gave up any attempt to find grip and enthusiastically played along, sending his legs into a dance of stiff-limbed kicking before finally sending him crashing onto his arse in the wet slush.

To add injury to injury, as he fell, the base of the oak truncheon, which helped him to keep the peace in the Saucy Sailor, impacted the cobbles and shot upwards from the loop in his belt, striking his still-descending cheekbone with terrific force. His head jerked back violently and smacked against the stone, leaving him dazed.

He tried to struggle up, but his boots betrayed him again and he landed with another thump on his coccyx. His curses were violent enough to melt the dirty snow around him. With his head splitting with pain from the two impacts, he slowly managed to regain a vertical aspect, albeit bent over, and vomited copiously. Disoriented, head throbbing, he leant heavily against the wall. *Where the hell is the tavern?* He felt the back of his head, and his hand came back damp with his blood. *Other way. Not far now.* He turned on his heel, legs still wobbling and eyes struggling to focus. He put a heel into the steaming contents of his stomach and executed the splits, ending up lying on his side.

"Have you no shame, man! Drunk at this time on the Sabbath?" His smattering of Dutch was good enough to pick up the meaning, and the disdainful tone of voice was understandable by anyone. The burgher walked on past, his chin in the air, black cloak swirling through the light flakes.

He put his head in his hands and sat for a while, waiting for his head to clear, until the cold wetness of the street seeping through his breeches prompted him to stagger unsteadily to his feet. The pain, cold, bewilderment and embarrassment made for a heady cocktail, and his anger was ignited. He swung the peacemaker with all his strength at the wall, venting a melancholy roar to the grey, glowering sky. The truncheon snapped, leaving him holding just a foot of splintered oak, in hands still vibrating from the unforgiving impact.

With this hanging limply from his right hand, he weaved his way back to the Sailor, left arm held out sideways for balance.

Those few customers and staff inside the dimly lit tavern leapt in surprise as the door crashed open, framing a black shape against the grey-white background. The person swayed, assaulted by the sudden heat of the large fire, and slowly, stiffly, fell forward onto the stone-flagged floor. It took a few moments for warm, somnolent minds to register exactly what they had witnessed and whether they, personally, would be expected to do anything about it. Then Cornelia, DeLacey and Klaas sprang towards Richard's unmoving body.

Cornelia was first there and tried unsuccessfully to roll him over, calling his name repeatedly, frantically. DeLacey shoved her to one side and held her back with his outstretched arm.

"Just wait! Let's see what has happened before we move him!" His eyes quickly took in the closing, bruised eye, the bloody handprint on his face and the nasty-looking wound on the back of his head, matting his hair to his head. He also saw the shattered truncheon lying half under his body.

He leapt up, sweeping out sword and poignard in a single fluid movement.

"Klaas! Don't let Cornelia finish him off while I am gone. Boil water and start washing the wounds, particularly the one on the back of his head. Don't move him and don't let him up. I'll be back!" And he ran through the door, turned right and his boots pounded off up Halsteeg.

Cornelia shouted a string of aggressive instructions at Klaas as she knelt and started to examine Richard more carefully. His eyes were flickering open, and he was drooling from the corner of his mouth. He tried to raise his head, but she gently pressed him back down. "Don't move, my darling. Keep still. We must see where you are wounded and wash away the dirt and blood. Oh, my poor, brave hero. How many were there? And on a Sunday! What is this city coming to? So brave to fight them off and come back to me. Roger will get them. He will make them pay!"

Richard's head felt like it was splitting open and he was only just hanging on to consciousness. He struggled to focus on her words. *Fought them off? How many? What?*

"Whaaa? Who?"

Klaas stood behind Cornelia, looking shocked at the blood. "Poor Richard. He doesn't remember what happened. Must be the blow to his head. You are right, Cornelia, he is a hero! He is *our* hero! Where is that water?" he shouted in the direction of the kitchen.

When DeLacey came back a few minutes later he found Richard sitting on a chair near the fire with Cornelia gently dabbing at his wounds with a cloth and bowl of steaming water. His sick-stained coat was over another chair and steam was rising from his drying shirt. Klaas was already serving his customers again, apparently managing to keep his concerns well under control. Richard looked very pale, apart from the swelling under his eye which was turning from red to purple and gradually closing his eye completely. DeLacey judged that he was a lot more alert than when he had lain unconscious on the tavern floor.

He pulled up another chair and straddled it, leaning his chin on his forearms as he looked at the growing lump. "Reckon you broke your cheekbone, Rich. Not much we can do about that, I'm afraid. Still, when the swelling goes down, it will be a match for your nose."

"That is not helpful, Roger," Cornelia said, frowning at him

(Amsterdam, January 1639)

sternly and concentrating on her English. "Risch is my hero. I will doctor his swelling very good. He will be handsome again soon."

"Ha! Yes! I had heard you were looking after his swelling, my dear." DeLacey's eyes twinkling above a wicked smile. "He is in good hands!"

She expertly flicked the wet cloth and caught him in the middle of the forehead. DeLacey swore ripely but held up a hand in a peace-making gesture and kept his leer. "Very naughty man you are, Roger." Cornelia couldn't help smiling in a satisfied way and went back to dabbing the blood from Richard's hair. DeLacey, looking more serious, leant forward again. "So how many were there, son? Did you see their faces? Can you tell us what happened? They were long gone when I got there."

Richard looked at him for a long time before answering. He spoke quietly – almost a whisper – the pounding pain in his head making even talking excruciating. "Two, I think. They came from behind. Just saw them at last minute. Jabbed back hard with the peacemaker and caught one in gut. He threw up down my back, the bastard, but the other one caught the back of my head."

DeLacey relayed the whispers at a louder volume to the rest of the room. And then, "Oooh. That must smart. A wound like that. What did you do?"

"…Spun round and broke the wood across first one's back. He went down. But second one jabbed me in face with his staff. The first one ran and when the other saw I was still on my feet, he followed. I made it back here, just about."

There were nods of approval and even some light applause from the half-dozen regular customers who were enthralled spectators. Cornelia swelled with pride. "My hero," she whispered into his ear. "I need to get more water," and she headed off to the kitchen with the crimson-filled bowl.

Richard was getting a little more colour into his face, partly due to the proximity to the fire, partly blushing. DeLacey leaned in closer, and he too spoke in a whisper. "Fell over, didn't you, lad? Slipped in your own sick, I'd guess. Cracked your head on the stones, eh?" He looked down at the pool on and below the chair from his soaked breeches. "Pissed yourself too perhaps." He looked back at Richard again and raised one eyebrow in enquiry.

"What? No!"

"One pair of footprints, son. No sign of a struggle. Just your tracks."

"Can't tell anything from that. You're making it up." Richard narrowed his good eye at DeLacey; the other was already closed and couldn't narrow any further. *God, my head hurts, and now this? What have I done to deserve this? Oh yes. Lying...*

"Maybe not, but then I spoke to Johanna from the brothel on the corner and she saw the whole thing. Still drying her eyes from laughing when I talked to her. Sorry, who is making what up?"

Cornelia was coming back. Richard, in a desperate whisper, said, "Please, Roger, say nothing."

DeLacey winked and smiled. He leaned back and looked up at the returning nurse. "Well, my dear. When you are done with that, he should go to bed. Even heroes need their rest, and he has earned his."

He turned back to Richard, a more serious look on his face. "And when you feel up to it, I have news from my journey. News of Browne. News of war."

*

Richard woke to the grey morning, a sky of flat slate through the peeling window frame. He was propped on his side on two

(Amsterdam, January 1639)

straw-filled pillows, and he had a moment of disorientation, panic and nausea until he remembered that he was only looking at the day through one eye. The back of his head throbbed and pulsed, and his cheekbone ached – stabbing pain when he moved his jaw. A gull swept past his window, white and grey on grey. Everything was monotone here in the winter – even the people in their Calvinist black, walking grey streets with the black water of the canals and waterways.

He heard a gentle snoring behind him and he reached back with his hand. *God, I hope that's Cornelia and not Roger*, he thought, although he was pretty certain who it was. He twisted slightly, trying to keep his head as still as possible until he was ready to ease it round in one smooth motion. He tried to find the best way to lean his head back against the plaster without squashing the bandage over his wound. It was Cornelia. Curled up under the woollen blanket with just one eye, and some black curls, visible. She was whistling slightly through the gap in her teeth and Richard thought it was the most beautiful, the most innocent thing in the world. He felt himself start to get interested in the options available, but when he shifted his position slightly to free himself from a tangle in the blanket, the pain in his head told him not to be so damned stupid.

She felt his movement and the eye opened. She slowly emerged from beneath the blanket, reluctant to leave its warmth for the frigid January air. "Risch? Are you alright? How your head is?" Her eyes were still sleepy but looked at him with a depth of concern that he could not remember seeing before. She sat across his legs, on top of the blanket, and studied the closed eye and swollen cheek. She gently prodded it with a careful finger, but he winced and jerked his head back, cracking the wound on the back of his head against the wall. He howled, and the throbbing intensified.

"Oh, Risch! I so sorry! So stupid!" She gently pulled his head forward and gestured for him to turn it away from the window so she could use the dim light to get a better look. She carefully lifted the bandage and studied the cut, which sat nicely amidst a cushion of swollen, angry, red skin. "It looks clean. But you need to be careful not to hit again." She smiled tentatively at him.

"Good idea." He spoke through gritted teeth as the tide of pain gradually ebbed. "And thanks, Neelie. For looking after me." He gave a weak smile in return.

She looked up at him from under her lashes. "I like looking after you, Risch. I have to work today, but I could look after you first. If you like?" She shifted the weight of her arse, resting on his thighs, slowly from side to side and her smile was not so tentative any longer.

"Oh, Neelie, I would like that very much, but my head is going to burst if I move an inch. Would you get me some water?"

She looked mildly disappointed but nodded and hopped off the mattress. She grabbed her shawl against the cold and stopped half out of the room, looking back over her shoulder. "I will get you some tea, Risch. It is a new thing that Klaas has got. He says it is very good."

Richard smiled and nodded, regretting the movement immediately, and watched her small, wiry form skip away, bare feet padding down the wooden planks of the landing.

Fifteen minutes later she returned, carrying a tray with water and an earthenware mug, steaming invitingly. She found DeLacey sitting on the floor with his back to the wall, just to one side of the window. "Hello, Roger. I am sorry, I have only got tea for Risch. Do you want some too?"

"Thanks, Neelie, but no. I have tried some already." He made a face at Richard. "Maybe it is a Dutch thing. It'll never

(AMSTERDAM, JANUARY 1639)

catch on in England." After Cornelia had put the tray down, DeLacey smiled at her. "Do you think I could speak to Rich in private for a while?"

"Of course, Roger. But do not tire him out. I must help Klaas now so I will see you later, Risch. Perhaps you will be feeling better." She gave him a look full of promises and headed back to her own room.

DeLacey smiled broadly at Richard. "It's nice to see young love. Did you cut a special deal? And where did you get the money to afford it if I might ask?"

Despite his throbbing head, Richard could feel the familiar anger rising. "Look, Roger, it's bad enough having to think about what she does already, without your smart remarks. I hate it. Having to share her with the fat, old bastards that Klaas calls his valued customers, as well as the sea captains and sailors who come through here. I hate it! It screws me up inside." He paused to let the ache in his head subside. "And now I am lying here wondering if you have… well, you know what I mean. I couldn't bear that. God, I wish I had the money that I could buy her out of this, before I go mad, or she gets the pox! Or both! There is nothing else in my life in this shithole to look forward to except seeing her."

"If it makes you feel any better, son, no, I haven't… you know what I mean. I like a bit more flesh and a bit more experience. You've really got it for her, haven't you."

Richard looked down at his hands resting on the blanket. "Yes," he said quietly, almost as if speaking to himself alone. "Yes, I have. I have not felt like this before about any of the other girls here. And I can't… you know what I mean, when she has just come from a customer. It doesn't seem right. I have to wait for her day off. Otherwise, well, it's difficult to get things working. And I feel so angry. I feel like it's their fault, but I know it isn't."

"Rich. I am not saying what you are doing is wrong, but remember, you are still very young. Sixteen? And living in a brothel with working girls is not like living in the normal world. And Neelie is not like a normal girl. Don't get me wrong. She is sweet, and clever, and obviously has fallen for your good looks…" He gestured at Richard's battered face. "In fact, I am talking myself into giving it a go after all…"

"Don't you dare! Don't even think about it, Roger. It would be the end for us and… a matter of honour to settle!" He half rose up on the mattress. *God, my head hurts…*

DeLacey looked back at him steadily. "First, you need to learn to appreciate humour and wit when you come across it. Second, boy, be very careful to talk about settling matters of honour. You are getting good with your blade, but not good enough yet. You really need to think before you open your mouth, or it will be the death of you one day…"

There was a long pause. Richard carefully leant his head back against the wall and looked up at the damp-blistered ceiling. "I'm sorry. You are right. I can't control my anger and it feels like it's getting worse. But I'm just so bored. And frustrated. I have no… purpose here. I can't see a future but this. It's just day after day the same thing. And that makes me angry, even though I know it is me I am angry with. Somehow that is worse. No money, no way to, I don't know, get better. To advance myself. Maybe I should just have stayed at home. Although somehow I don't think my family would approve of me being with Cornelia. And I know what you are saying, but I really feel that this is different. She is special and I can't bear her having to do what she does."

DeLacey smiled. "Well, my boy, I think I have some good news on that front. Money, action and maybe a trip home all in one go! My trip was not wasted. I didn't see Browne, but I know where he is and what he is doing. Have you heard what has been happening in Scotland?"

(AMSTERDAM, JANUARY 1639)

"It's not really been top of my mind. What has it got to do with us?" He took a careful sip of the hot, green-coloured water, trying to avoid the bits floating in it. "Oh my God! What *is* this? People drink this?" He washed out the taste with the water and spat it onto the floor.

"Well," said DeLacey, ignoring the tea's latest critic, "it seems that the Scots have got themselves all excited about the King's desire that they should all pray like the English. He has forced his new prayer book on them. They smell popery and power to the bishops. They like their Kirk and don't want anyone, even their King, telling them how to talk to God. They have all signed what they call the National Covenant – it's like an oath. So they call themselves the Covenanters. And now it's war."

Richard looked at him, open-mouthed. "What? War? With Scotland? Over a prayer book? That's madness…"

"Well, if you would go to war over a whore," a sharp, angry look from Richard, "…then why is it mad to go to war over your faith? Just because you have strayed from the path of righteousness, Richard Farrell, it doesn't mean the rest of us are lost sheep. In the end, it doesn't really matter, does it? You were happy to fight the Spanish on behalf of the Dutch for money; at least this time it's your own country and king. Well, probably…"

"What do you mean, *probably?*"

"Well, I guess we will be fighting in the King's army, but there are two sides to any war. And the pay could be better on the other side. It's worth considering… Don't you think?"

"I couldn't fight against my own country, Roger. Not just for a few shillings more. I don't understand why someone can want to kill another man over how he worships God, but I couldn't fight against my King."

"Not even if it meant you could free Cornelia from her current line of work?"

A long pause. "On the other hand, I suppose you have to be open-minded about these things. I suppose we could just find out more, and then consider our options."

DeLacey laughed grimly. "That's my boy. But the thing is, we need to do our finding out and thinking quickly. Both sides are raising troops and both are desperate to find men with experience of war. I have heard that Scots over here, those who have been fighting for the Swedes and the Dutch, are being called back to turn their recruits and militia into fighting units. Charlie-boy is doing the same. There are agents recruiting for both sides here. Now. We must act quickly to get the best deal."

"Oh God. I feel terrible. And I must look terrible. When should we go and find these men?"

"Actually, it's perfect. You look fresh from the fight. Perfect to create the impression of a hardened military man. Just don't tell them you were fighting with the cobbles and your own wooden stick! We should move tomorrow. Strap on your blade and pistols, we need to create the right impression. And make sure you clean the sick off your coat!"

"Oh, very funny. But, yes, I will be there."

"Good man. Now rest today. And I mean rest. No indulging in… you know what I mean, later on. If we get this right, you can make some money, have adventure, rescue your damsel and maybe even get a visit home. Does that not drag you out of this melancholia?"

"Yes, Roger. It does. Thank you for this news. You have saved me, I think." Despite this, Richard sighed heavily.

"That doesn't sound like I have brightened your mood."

"No, it has. Immensely. But now I will have to tell Neelie that I am going away to fight. She will take it hard."

Roger smiled broadly. "Yes, I have heard that about her."

He ran for the door as the mug of tea crashed into the wall beside his head…

(AMSTERDAM, JANUARY 1639)

*

At mid-morning the following day Richard and Roger set off for their first meeting. Roger had slipped out the previous evening and, after some discreet enquiries, had found an acquaintance of the agent acting on behalf of the Covenanters, who held the power in Scotland and were building their military strength. The 'middleman' had been at Breda and this had been helpful in securing them an opportunity to meet.

For the first time in many months Richard had the rapier attached to his baldric, partially hidden by a long cloak borrowed from Klaas. The leather coat was still too stained for a meeting in a warm tavern. With his battered face and bandaged head he looked a lot tougher and battle-hardened than he felt, but Roger was delighted with the effect it made. Both were armed with pistols and looked ready for business of any kind. They were waved off by Cornelia who wore a sad, resigned face. Richard had tried to reassure her of his intentions to return a richer man from the war, to take her away from her current existence, but she seemed to have contracted his melancholy.

They met the Covenanter agent in a nearby tavern, sitting in a dark corner scarcely warmed by the blazing fire. The man was uncannily as Richard had imagined him. Fiery red hair and beard, a crushing handshake, a passionate Presbyterian and almost impossible to understand. There was a lengthy conversation to determine that the two English mercenaries were just that, and not spies of King Charles. The fact that they fought alongside Scots at Breda was, as DeLacey had anticipated, very helpful in establishing their bonafides as unaligned soldiers. Once a measure of trust was established, they learnt that, as DeLacey had also heard, many experienced and respected Scots commanders were returning from the

German and Dutch battlefields to help build the Covenanter army. DeLacey nodded approvingly at names such as Alexander Hamilton and Sir Robert Monro.

The agent was an Edinburgh man, appropriately called Fleming. He was attached to the staff of Sir Patrick Drummond, the conservator at the Scottish staple port at Veere, south of Rotterdam. Fleming told them he was acting without Drummond's knowledge, as the man was loyal to Charles and so a traitor to the Covenanter cause. Drummond would inform the King of any movements of men or arms to Scotland and so was a major obstacle given he controlled the comings and goings of the staple port.

They discussed pay, which seemed reasonable, and logistics, which seemed more fraught and would probably involve passage on a Dutch or Swedish merchant ship to Leith, Edinburgh's port. Already Charles's navy was intercepting ships bound for Scotland and had seized muskets and other arms bound for the Covenanter army. It would not be good for them to be caught in such a manner.

They shook hands and promised to respond to Fleming's terms within three days. Fleming laughed and said that he expected they were off to see the English recruiter, unless they had already been. Mercenaries, he said, were entirely predictable because they all had but one faith. "You should know, though, boys, that this army of the King is but a rabble. They have no one of experience to lead them, except a few such as Jacob Astley. They may offer you more money, but when did the losing side ever pay their soldiers with anything except dishonour, misery and death? Fare you well and God be with you."

Outside in the cold grey of the waning afternoon, Richard shivered. His head was aching again, and the sudden change from the warm fug of the tavern to the biting wind off the

North Sea did not help. "He has a point, Roger. They seem to be the more... professional. They have the best men to lead them."

"What happened to 'I won't fight against my King'?" DeLacey sneered back. "But, yes, he does have a point. Astley is a good man, but he is one of only a few. The army has gone to shit – just a bunch of militias who only train in drinking and falling off their horses. But let's wait and see what our own true countrymen have to offer."

It took a little while to find news of the King's agent, but they tracked him down to a house right on the dockside, close to a line of warehouses with cranes and hooks and pulleys for loading both sea-going ships and river-barges. Despite the cold and darkness of late afternoon, there was still plenty of activity, with goods being loaded and unloaded endlessly. The agent was unavailable, but his staff agreed that he would see them the following evening.

They returned to the Sailor. Richard, exhausted, took to his bed. He was half relieved, and half disappointed, that Cornelia did not come to find him there. As ever, he could find no clear plan of how to proceed and, anyway, experience was showing him that any plans he did make came to nought. But he also reflected that he was more and more acting on impulse, allowing his temper to rule him, and then having to grapple with the consequences. What the hell was he doing? And what was he going to do about Cornelia?

She was the only thing in his life here in Amsterdam that he valued. He knew what he felt for her *was* love. It wasn't about feeling sorry for her – her miserable recent history and her early-grave profession. It wasn't just the 'you know what I mean', although that was certainly an activity that occupied his mind. He knew DeLacey was right. He *was* still young and had no experience of 'normal' women. But she could melt his insides just by looking at him, especially when she gazed up at him with her big dark eyes through her lashes. Just thinking about it made him weak.

But. He wanted more than this life at the Sailor. He was something. His family were something. Not nobility, not gentry, but a step up from the commonfolk. They had some property. They had respect in the community. Whatever it was, he had to find a goal for his life. At the moment, the only thing he was proud of was that a girl like Cornelia would want to be his. But the only way he could see that he could make anything of himself was through a military career. And now, finally, maybe there was a chance to move forward.

But. Moving forward meant being away from her. That in itself was bad enough, but say he did progress through the ranks? *General, let me introduce Cornelia, my darling wife. Family? Oh, formerly an orphan whore. You may have had her if you passed through Amsterdam…*

He told himself that he cared nothing about this. But he knew that part of him did. A lot.

*

He was standing on a low cliff, looking down onto a beach. He did not recognise it. It was night-time, and it was cold. The beach was of shingle, and under the light of a huge, full moon, the pebbles glistened black, as if they were wet from a recent wave. But they were like that all the way from the waves to the back of the beach. *That's strange.*

The waves were small, rolling a few yards up the beach, then hissing quietly back through the stones. He could hear the sound of some of the smaller pebbles rolling down with the receding waves. The moon reflected a glittering path of argent across the black water, arrow straight to a figure he

(Amsterdam, January 1639)

now saw standing in the middle of the curved beach. A slight figure, cloaked and hooded against the cold. Standing still, staring out across the sea.

Time passed. It seemed a long time passed. The figure – he was sure it was a woman – turned her head and looked back at him. He couldn't see her face; the cowl of her hooded cloak kept it in shadow, her back to the moonlight. She stared back at him for a long time, but he said nothing. Didn't move. She turned back to the sea.

It was now that he saw the sea more clearly. From a distance it looked like it was not composed of water, but was thick, like black oil or tar. It moved sluggishly, trying to raise waves, but its viscosity never let these get to more than a few inches high. As he watched, he could see that the line of moonlight was starting to contract, shortening towards the beach. The reason for this soon became clear. A line of black cloud was gradually moving towards the beach. Towards him and the woman below him. He assumed it was cloud, but there was no differentiation in its colour and texture. No gaps, no greys. Just solid black, stretching from horizon to horizon.

The woman had obviously seen this too and took a faltering step backwards. In a few moments the moon itself would be masked by the cloud, and all would be dark. But there was still enough light to see that the glutinous fluid of the sea was drawing back down the shingle, heading away at a rapid rate. Richard followed its motion with his gaze and then stared in horror into the middle distance. Still at quite a distance from the shore, a massive wave was building. High as a cathedral tower, it was sweeping inexorably towards them. There was a sudden flash of lightning from the black above and, by its abrupt illumination, he could see that the liquid was not black after all, but a deep crimson. The colour of blood. A sea of blood. A tidal wave of blood. His legs weakened and he collapsed to his knees.

But below him, on the beach, the woman did not move. She was transfixed by what the receding liquid had revealed, and that was now moving slowly, relentlessly, across the stones towards her. Figures. Black figures looking like shadows of humans, but solid, not flat. There were no clothes, everything was smooth and glistening black in the failing moonlight, like the stones themselves. There were hundreds of them, now raising themselves from crawling over the pebbles, to their knees, and now to their feet. They moved unhurriedly, and Richard could judge that they would reach the woman just before the enormous wave broke its weight over them all.

He shouted despairingly at her. *Run! Run! For God's sake, run!* But he himself could not move his feet. He did not know if she could hear him over the growing sound of thunder, the sound of the wave of blood reaching high into the night, and the crunch of pebbles as the creatures closed the distance to her. As one, they reached down and picked up black stones, raising them above their heads without breaking their stride. They were now close enough to see that they were not entirely featureless. There was no face, but something was writhing under the skin making their heads and bodies look like black bags of coiling snakes.

For a moment, seconds before they reach her, she turned again, the blackness of her hood pointing straight at him, slumped on his knees. Black hands gripping black stones raise above her. And fall. The cloud blacks out the moon. The wave thunders down. There is no sound.

"Jesus Christ! Oh God! Help her, help her, help me!" Richard rockets upright on the mattress. His nightshirt is drenched in sweat. He looks around frantically, the room illuminated only dimly by the curtainless window. He takes

(AMSTERDAM, JANUARY 1639)

a deep, shuddering breath. He realises he is still alone in the room. Cornelia didn't come and join him in bed. He swivels on the edge of the mattress, putting his feet on the cold boards, bruised, sore face in his hands. He breathes slowly, deeply for several minutes before getting up and walking to the window. Below him, the grey street is empty of people. He can see the tops of the masts of the ships in the Damrak, lit by pale moonlight.

He wrenches the window open, fighting rust and the swollen wood, shivering involuntarily in the heavy frost, and takes a piss out on to the cobbles, a floor below. He takes more deep breaths of the icy air, hands on the sill, before closing the pane and getting under the blanket. He does not want to sleep ever again. He lies staring at the patterns of damp on the ceiling, the exotic islands with their deeply fjorded coastlines, until the soft light of dawn hardens into a crisp, bright, sunny morning and he hears movement down in the kitchen below his room.

*

"It must have been about Neelie. I went to sleep thinking about her. No, not about that! About what she is going to do when we leave. How she will cope, and whether she will forget me and find another. My God, Roger, I have never been so scared in my life. It was horrible. Those... things. And she never moved, or called out..."

"Alright, Rich, you'll be giving me nightmares soon. It was just a dream. A fuckin' terrible dream, I'll admit. It was probably something you ate – God knows what Klaas puts in those sausages... A dream can't tell you the future 'cos the future ain't happened. It is the future, ain't it..."

They were walking towards their meeting, and it was freezing. A clear sky gave them some light to see by, but it was already getting slippery on the cobbles. Richard kept his eyes glued on the ground, concentrating entirely on staying upright. *Never again.*

"Maybe, Roger. But it still doesn't help me with Neelie. I either give up this chance to move on, to make something of my life, or I risk losing her. And no matter what you say, that dream is telling me something. I just need to know what I should do."

"Stay off Klaas's sausages. That's what you should do, son. Anyway, put that out of your head for the next hour. We need to be clear-thinking with this man." They slid along, taking baby steps on the thin veneer of ice around corners and staying a long way from the edge of the dock once they neared the appointment.

They knocked at the door of the townhouse, which had been converted into a shipping office. They were shown up a narrow, steep staircase to the first floor, and then into a room which was a mixture of office and sitting room. Comfortable, expensive-looking, leather sofas faced each other before a blazing fire, *hallelujah*! The room was dominated by a long table, covered in papers, and a line of ceiling-high cupboards whose open doors exhibited shipping manifests, samples and stationery.

They were offered tea, which was grimly declined, and gin, which was gratefully accepted, and they were left alone except for a nervous clerk, who shuffled papers around and watched them while pretending unconvincingly to work. It was ten minutes before the door reopened and a party of three joined them.

The largest and loudest spoke first. "Gentlemen! Well met. I hope you have been looked after. Please be seated." After handshakes all round, Richard and Roger sat together on the sofa with a view of the door. Opposite them were the speaker,

(AMSTERDAM, JANUARY 1639)

a round-faced florid man, richly dressed, and a more sober companion, pale and thin, with a goatee and black hair. The third man stationed himself behind the sofa where Richard and Roger were sitting, where he leant against the wall, in an alcove next to the fireplace. From there he also had a view of the street and seemed to be dividing his attention between the conversation and the comings and goings of the dockside. He could have been a relative of the mousy clerk, who had now left the room. Unremarkable. Forgettable.

Round-face beamed at them and gradually became redder of face as his proximity to the fire heated him up. "Gentlemen. Very pleased to make your acquaintance. I would say that it is good to see an Englishman again, but there are so many of us here in the United Provinces. So many." He paused and mopped his brow.

"Let me introduce myself! I am John Quarles. I am what we like to call a merchant adventurer! Formerly of London, but more recently of Delft, and now Rotterdam. I am in Amsterdam often, to trade, but currently I am here on the King's business." He nodded appreciatively when Richard and Roger responded with a well-rehearsed "God save His Majesty!"

"With me is Master Winthrop, who is attached to the staff of William Juxon, the King's treasurer." He indicated the man who shared the sofa with him, and Winthrop nodded solemnly back at them. "He is here to talk to you about financial arrangements, should that be necessary." Another nod from Winthrop, who swallowed nervously when money was mentioned.

"And behind you, keeping his eye on our safety and security, is Master Montague. And you never tell us who you work for, do you, sir?"

Richard and Roger both shifted on the sofa to get a better look at Montague, who was standing half in shadow. He was clothed mainly in black, with an utterly expressionless face, framed by collar-length, dark brown hair. His voice was quiet but had a strength to it. "I work for the King, sir. You need know no more than that." And he turned his head away from them, and the light of the fire, to renew his study of the street. *Arrogant*, thought Richard.

As they turned back to face Quarles, Richard caught Roger's eye and could see he was unnerved by Montague, particularly as he was forced to sit with his back to him. They had both seen the small pistol sticking in his waistband and Richard had no doubt this was not the only weapon he carried.

Quarles also seemed nervous of Montague, and muttered, "Just so, sir. Just so," before brightening, and addressing them directly. "You know, sirs, why we are here. The King has frustrated all peaceful options in his negotiations with these Covenanters and has been left with no choice but to act with an iron fist. Whilst he still hopes to achieve a reasonable outcome through negotiation, he believes, as we all do, that he must show the Scots he is serious, and that he is the true power in the Kingdom. This defiance against the lawful sovereign will not stand, sirs. It just will not stand!"

"Quite so, sir." Roger sat forward, looking indignant and ready for anything.

"We are looking for fighting men to support the cause. Not just any men, sir, but proven veterans. It is the King's regret that one dividend of the peace he has striven to deliver for his people is that his army is not what it should be. The Trained Bands are woefully short of numbers, and many need licking into shape. A sorry state of affairs. The county militias are no better. Gentlemen who are more used to hunting than fighting. Enthusiastic but not trained military men. Not like you, sirs. You are what we are looking for."

He paused and mopped his brow again, shuffling away from the fire and squashing Winthrop against the other arm of the sofa.

"We met a former colleague of yours. A Captain Browne. A fine God-fearing man. Anxious to help. He provided us with a list of names. Names of military men he recommended to us. Some of whom he said were sure to be found in Amsterdam, in Delft, Rotterdam or The Hague. Your names were on the list, sirs. What do you think of that?!"

"He said you were likely to be found in the brothels by the docks, Master DeLacey." Montague's quiet voice from the shadow. "What do you think of that?"

"Always had a sense of humour did Captain Browne. Salt of the earth, that man." DeLacey's face betrayed no emotion and he directed his comment at Quarles, not turning to face Montague. "Can we trouble you for a glass of that fine gin? Perhaps Master Montague could locate the bottle?"

"Certainly, sir. Not at all. Can we trouble you, please, Master Montague?"

Quarles was the senior member of the party, so Montague could hardly refuse. He moved from the wall over to the long table to retrieve the bottle, bringing him fully into the light – which had been DeLacey's intention. He walked slowly over to the sofas, a slim but wiry frame, well balanced in his movement. Richard raised his glass to be filled, looking Montague in the face, fully illuminated by the fire. Now he could see that Montague's eyes were grey, but he looked in vain for any other distinguishing marks. Just… forgettable.

DeLacey did not lift his glass towards Montague but waited for it to be filled on the table between the sofas. This required Montague to lean across Richard, and he could see quite clearly now, the pistol in the belt, but also the handle of a dagger. Montague looked him in the eye to let Richard know he had seen him studying this, but held DeLacey's stare even longer. They all knew the game.

He retired back behind them. Now he stood in the bay of the window, looking along the docks.

"Yes, well, you come highly recommended, gentlemen. Especially you, Master DeLacey. Browne spoke highly of your experience. Your steadiness under fire. Your experience of getting the best from your troops." Quarles was warming to his task.

"Your whoring. Your profanity. Your drinking. Your generally questionable morals. He mentioned those too," added Montague, eyes still fixed on the street.

"Careful, sir. Anyone would think you were not enthusiastic at the prospect of our joining your little war." DeLacey, a broad smile on his face but ice in his voice, continued to look across at Quarles.

"Well, sir, you may be right. I just find it hard to understand how an Englishman, especially one with so much to offer, is not already back in his own country looking for ways to serve his monarch. It saddens me that we have to meet in this place and be talking money." He leaned so he could get a better angle of view through the glass and then started for the door. "And now I have met you both, I fear I must leave you with my companions as business calls me elsewhere. Farewell, gentlemen." And he was gone, footsteps sounding quickly down the stairs but no sound from the front door.

Quarles visibly relaxed. "Now, sirs. To business. Take no notice of Montague. We are all traders here now. I trade cloth. You trade your singular skills. We all know about prices and negotiation. Master Winthrop will take you through our offer. It is fair and reasonable in every way." Winthrop leant forward and laid a paper on the table…

(AMSTERDAM, JANUARY 1639)

*

Half an hour later, Richard and Roger stood on the doorstep outside Quarles's office. "I don't trust that fucker an inch," growled DeLacey.

Richard, wiping a tear from the corner of his eye as he adjusted from the fireside furnace to the freezing temperature of the dockside, looked surprised. "It seemed pretty reasonable to me. More than the Scots are offering. I guess Charlie has the greater need for experienced men than the Covenanters."

"Not the fat fucker. Montague! I don't trust him as far as you could throw him. Met his type before. Knife in the back without a word, without a thought. Walk over people like they aren't there. For God, King and Country of course. No feelings. Cold. Scared the shit out of Quarles, didn't he? 'Cos Quarles knows that everything he says and does will get reported back to his mystery boss in London. Wonder why he left so quick, like. Best keep an eye open; I pushed him a bit in there. Wanted to see what would happen."

Richard shrugged. He had felt wary of the man but had dismissed him from his thoughts once he had gone. His bile had seemed directed more at Roger than himself in any case.

"Fancy a drink?" DeLacey nodded towards a tavern fifty yards down the dockside. "We need to talk this through."

"Sure. Need a piss first, though. You get the drinks in, I'm going to be brave and stand on the dockside."

"Typical, you tight bastard. Are you sure you're not Scottish? But seriously, don't fall in 'cos I ain't goin' in after you."

He walked off, and Richard turned to pick his spot. There was a large storage warehouse about fifty yards in the opposite direction. Richard thought he could wedge himself against the wall for support while he relieved himself, and headed off. He had seen the warehouse being built over the last few weeks. And one or two others on this part of the docks had gone up since he had arrived. Ships docked next to them, but the new structures meant it was not possible to see what was being loaded and unloaded from the quay.

He propped himself against the warehouse wall of rough, unfinished timber and carefully aimed over the edge of the dock wall into the blackness of the icy water. God, he was tired. Careful of the wound to the back of his skull, he leant his head against the wood and closed his eyes. Just as he was finishing, he heard faint talking and a faint clang of metal on metal coming from within the warehouse. He was faintly surprised that there was still work going on at this hour, but sometimes loading could go on through the night. But then he heard a sound he recognised well. Not just any steel on steel this time, but definitely the sound of two swords meeting, scraping and re-engaging.

He moved back slowly from the edge of the water and looked for a door to the warehouse. Nothing at this end. The large loading bay doors would be along the main face of the warehouse, wide enough to allow wagons and carts to enter the building. As he headed in that direction Richard noticed a window, just above head height, propped slightly open. There were numerous wooden crates lying around the walls of the warehouse, and he quickly dragged one over and climbed up. As he came close to the window, he could hear the sounds more clearly. Shouting. Angry voices and a panting, groaning sound. He quietly raised the window outward and leaned around the edge to peer into the dark interior.

The main doors must have been closed, as the only light was coming from the harbour side of the warehouse, open to the water. Faint, white moonlight, augmented with the golden glow of lamps burning on the ship moored alongside, lit the scene only dimly. Nevertheless, Richard could make out a group of figures, silhouetted, close to the harbour edge and the gangplank to the brig. The warehouse was full of crates, bundles, chests and piles of… what? There was a broad space between the goods from the main doors to the ship, and he could see one man, back to the ship, trying to hold off three others who were spread out in an arc in front of him, blocking his way to the main doors. All appeared to be armed. There was a darker mound on the floor behind the three assailants, which was the source of the moaning. One down, but not dead.

Richard's first thought was to run to the inn and fetch DeLacey, but he also knew that by the time they returned, what was going to happen would have happened. His second thought was just to walk away. He confessed to himself that he had also been a little stung that all the attention in the recent meeting had been on Roger, apart from a comment on his battered face. Clearly, he was seen as the junior partner. He knew he was, but he didn't want anyone else pointing this out.

He unbuckled his sword and pushed it through the window. He could see a pile of sacking below and dropped it quietly onto the heap. With a little difficulty he followed it through just as another round of combat sounded from the shipside. He crouched low and circled around behind piles of crates until he was just ten yards behind the three attackers. He could see from this position that the main doors were open, a gap of about two paces.

He could now study the men in more detail as they lapsed back into wary stalemate. The lone man seemed the most assured and professional. An easy stance, with rapier and poignard out in front of him. Although outnumbered, he gave the impression of being relaxed and in control. His back was to the light and Richard still couldn't see his face, but there was something about him that seemed familiar.

His three attackers were a different proposition. All heavily built, one wielded a wooden club, not dissimilar to the one Richard carried in the Sailor. The other two had curved, broad-bladed swords, like navy cutlasses. One limped slightly, a bloodstained gash in his breeches across his thigh hampering his movements. They were muttering to each other in Dutch, but Richard didn't have enough words to make out what was being said. But he knew they were angry, and frustrated. And wary.

Richard reached to his belt for his pistol and, at the same time, wondered why none of the four had firearms. Perhaps they didn't want the attention that a pistol shot would bring. Richard concluded that he didn't want that either, so instead of the pistol, his hand came back with his own poignard.

Trying to keep his breathing under control and quiet he edged forward. His inclination was to side with the lone man, but he had no idea of the rights or wrongs of the confrontation. In fact, he started to wonder why he had even got himself involved at all. But he knew he had to act now or walk away. He suddenly stepped out of the shadows of the crates and into the avenue between the stacked goods. He was just ten paces behind the nearest of the three men and, if he had been clear of whose side he was on, could have closed the gap and thrust between the shoulder blades, or slashed a hamstring before anyone had time to react.

But he knew he couldn't do this. So he coughed and said in his poor Dutch, "Good evening, gentlemen. Can I help anyone?"

The three all spun round and Richard took a few smart paces backwards. The lone swordsman, with the light still behind him, now had a good view of Richard, and the voice that followed now made his identity clear. "My God! Bonsoir, Monsieur Farrell. It is you, is it not? Well met, sir! Well met!

(Amsterdam, January 1639)

And yes, I would certainly appreciate your assistance. These gentlemen seem to have taken a dislike to me and although I sought to discourage them," he nodded in the direction of the fourth man, now with his back propped against a large chest, "they are persistent, and I am getting a little weary." Now he could clearly recognise Jean de Sête, 'Monsieur Bluecoat' and Richard knew which side he was on.

And so did the three attackers. The man in the middle, who seemed to be the leader, a huge man with a completely bald head, shouted something at his companions and closed in rapidly on Richard, cutlass held now in two hands. Although all Richard's attention was now focused on the man's blade, he could see the other two pressing the attack on Jean. But Christ, he was an ex-King's musketeer! He was alright. Richard was far more worried about himself.

Although he had continued his sparring with DeLacey, this was his first real action since the night the siege ended. Beating drunks or clubbing sailors who overstayed their welcome at the Sailor was one thing, this homicidal giant was quite another. He tried to relax and remember his training. At least the man was already breathing hard from his exertions taking on Jean. That was good. But he wasn't squinting out from under a bandage, with a head still sensitive to sudden movement and already starting to throb. Not so good.

But he had no time to think or plan further. Clearly the attackers were concerned that Richard's arrival might mean more were coming and they needed to finish what they had started quickly. The leader shouted over his shoulder at his men, but his dark eyes stayed fixed on Richard. Moments later came his first attack – a big step forward and an angled swing from high to low, aimed at Richard's head. He avoided that easily enough; a sharp backward step and the blade swept past his chest. He resisted a quick counter, suspecting a trap, and indeed the man recovered frighteningly quickly and the backswing threatened his knees. He parried with the rapier, feeling the jarring impact all through his right arm to his aching head. The feeling of relief dissipated immediately as the man stepped inside and his enormous left fist caught him a glancing blow on his broken cheekbone.

Richard kept his feet just but staggered back several steps. But then was airborne as the injured fourth man stuck out his leg and caught the heel of Richard's boot. All the air went out of him as he struck the floor, arms flailing. No time to recover as the man was on him in an instant, swinging at his head. Richard rolled quickly and got up onto one knee in time to see the cutlass blade accelerating towards him, this time threatening to decapitate him. He deflected the stroke up with the rapier and, as the man's momentum carried him in, half rose from the floor and hammered the nine inches of his poignard hard into his chest, the quillions thudding into the ribcage. The man plunged past him, tearing the knife's grip from Richard's hand. He crashed face down on the stone floor, made an attempt to raise himself on an elbow, and then slumped, and didn't move.

Remembering the wounded man, Richard swung round in time to see Jean de Sête casually run him through the heart, pausing to wipe the blade on the man's woollen jacket. The breathing, already laboured, slowed and stopped. Eyes turned glassy, staring at nothing, and the head lolled slowly down until chin rested on chest.

"Well met, Richard. I did not expect to see you here. Is this a fortunate coincidence, or were you too following me?"

"I, er, what?" Richard was slowly recovering his breath but stood, hands on knees, sword out at an angle. "What do you mean? Why would I be following you?" He backed towards his former adversary and rolled him over with his boot. The poignard was wedged between his ribs, and he had to put his foot on the man's chest to pull it out.

Jean started forward. "*Attention*, Richard! Ah. *Merde*. Too late." The knife came out abruptly but was followed by a fountain of arterial blood which caught Richard full in the face and left him gasping. "Ah, my friend. Let me assist you." Jean found a patterned handkerchief from inside his jacket and carefully wiped away the blood like a mother with a child covered in chocolate.

"So. It is just a happy chance that we meet? Nothing to do with our friend watching from the doorway?" He gestured with his head towards the warehouse entrance. Richard whirled round. "Oh. He is long gone now, my friend. But he was taking a keen interest in events. And I must say I was worried for a moment that you might not make it when you went for your fly in the air. But a good recovery, and a fine riposte with the knife. Congratulations. Very stylish." Jean grinned at him.

"You just stood watching?"

"Why yes! Most entertaining. I see Roger has taught you well. I can see areas for improvement – staying on your feet, rather than lying on your back perhaps – but very accomplished. And you are alive, my friend. That is always a good way to finish an encounter!"

Richard could now see the other two men lying on the warehouse floor. Jean must have despatched them with his first attack to have got to him so quickly. "So why do you ask if I was following you? Is that what happened with these…?" Richard gestured at the corpses around them. "They followed you here? Why?"

"Well, I am not sure I can tell you, Richard. I am acting for my government here and there are always those who have reasons to obstruct France's business. I saw you and Roger come out of the house of Master Quarles earlier, what was your business with him?"

"Jean. If you are not able to tell me your business, I do not think I can tell you mine." He smiled at Jean. "But if you have a moment, Roger is in the inn just a hundred paces down the dockside. Perhaps you can buy me a drink for saving your life and we can discuss our secrets in the warmth?"

"Ah, my friend. A wonderful thought! Give me fifteen minutes to conclude my business with the captain – who I now realise was not as anxious as you to come to my aid – and I will join you. In fact, help me with these and I will only be five minutes. And I will buy you two drinks because, as you rightly say, I owe you my life." He smiled in a knowing way which rather irritated Richard, as he now knew that de Sête could easily have finished the four by himself. But he took the compliment and helped Jean to heave the four bodies into the dock, after relieving them of some small coins. It was now that Richard could see more clearly what was stacked in the warehouse. Some crates were stamped with the word 'Solingen', another with 'Saltpetre', and he saw an opened box which clearly contained musket barrels.

"Richard. Will you please keep a watch at the doors, and I will be with you shortly."

He was back in a few minutes. The blow to Richard's already fractured cheekbone, and hitting his head yet again on the unforgiving Amsterdam ground, had left his head aching. Now the adrenaline had subsided he felt cold to the bone and had to sink down into a crouch. De Sête hauled him to his feet, surprisingly strong for a slimly built man, and looked at him with some concern.

"Are you OK? Can you walk? It was brave of you to get involved, particularly as you did not even know it was me you were aiding. And with your existing injuries." He smiled at

(Amsterdam, January 1639)

Richard. Again, a slightly mocking smile. "By the way, Richard, what happened to you? Your bandage? Your face?"

"Oh. Yes. I had to fight off a couple of street thieves. They took me by surprise, but in the end they wished they hadn't!" Richard blushed, hoping de Sête would not be able to see in the dark of the dockside.

"Ah yes. Now I remember. Roger told me all about it. Very funny, Richard. Very amusing!" Jean grinned from ear to ear.

"What? What did he say?" *Oh God.*

"Oh, he gave me all the details of your... hmm... struggle? Very funny. Everyone at the embassy thought it was very funny too. You are famous, my friend!" He laughed all the way to the tavern where Richard hoped DeLacey was still waiting. So he could kill him. Slowly.

*

Richard didn't kill DeLacey. He had felt too weak and dazed. They had sat and drank and talked for hours, and he had no recollection of getting back to the Saucy Sailor. He had struggled to take part in the discussion and could not remember much of the detail, but he did remember that Jean de Sête had put them onto what seemed to be a valuable opportunity. Something to lift them out of the current situation. He remembered that had been when the real drinking started, but not much else. Strange, that.

He sat on the mattress, leaning against the wall. So much to think about, what with last night's discussion and the letter from England that had been left in his room, and that he had seen on waking. A month ago, when he realised that he was going to be at the Sailor for some time, he had written a letter to his family, giving the place as his return address. And now he had a response.

The letter still lay unopened on the blanket. Somehow, he felt nervous opening it. It had been a year since his departure and he had found himself creating a story about his adventures that DeLacey would have been proud of. How was it received? Disbelief? Pride? Scorn? He surprised himself by thinking that, actually, it wasn't his father's opinion, or his older brothers' opinion that mattered most to him, but his sister Angelica's. What would she be thinking of him?

He tipped his head back and closed his eyes, his cheek quietly throbbing in time to the reopened wound on the back of his skull. *Nothing for it. Why write home if you don't dare read the reply...?*

Dearest Richard

[He recognised his oldest brother's handwriting.]

We were so happy and relieved to receive your letter. We try to follow events in the Low Countries from the newsheets and pamphlets that we can obtain, but it is not easy. God be praised that you are alive and safe in the great city of Amsterdam. You seem to be prospering, and getting onto the staff of Colonel DeLacey [a sudden promotion for Roger] *sounds like a very promising start to your career. I will pass on the news about Will Fletcher to his father, when I next see him.*

Things are very much the same as far as the estate goes. We had a reasonable harvest, but this bad winter – all we seem to get at present – makes life difficult for the villagers. We do what we can. I hope to see you before too long and I will let Lionel and Angelica add some words as we are all gathered here for Father's birthday [of course, the old man's birthday!]. *Keep yourself safe.*

John

(Amsterdam, January 1639)

On the next page, there was a change in handwriting – this time Lionel. More untidy, as if his hand and pen could not keep up with his thoughts. His writing ran at a breathless pace – the speed Lionel seemed to exist at.

Dear Brother

It was good to hear from you – even if you are lodging in an inn! Beware, Richard!

The country is proud of what our men achieved against the Spanish. The fight for the true religion is the challenge of our times and we see threats to our freedom to worship everywhere.

Of course, there are some that see even the King's own religious views as opening the door to popery, and he surrounds himself with advisers like Archbishop Laud who are swinging us towards Rome. He raises the power of bishops and now is looking to impose his views on the Presbyterians in Scotland. He has met his match there, Richard! They stand behind their covenant 'For Religion, Covenant, King and Country' and would sink Laud's liturgy! Would that men in England would take such a stand – what a day that would be!

I see it in my own parish, Richard! We are under scrutiny for our Puritan faith. The bishop sends his dogs around to monitor all we say and do. It cannot stand forever! A day will come.

God be with you, Richard. I am sorry to rant on so; it is my daily preoccupation. We all love you and wish you safely home soon when your work is done. Do not forget your prayers, brother, amidst all the excitement of your new life.

Lionel

And what would Lionel say if he knew we had been discussing joining the King's army against the Covenanters? He was also worried about Lionel's passion on the topic. The last few days had shown him that one had to be careful with words and who knew who was listening to, watching or reading things that would be better not known. Lionel must be careful.

And now Angelica's careful hand. She would be approaching womanhood and of an age to be married. He trusted his father and brothers to do right by her, but he hoped she could find happiness and not just a match that satisfied family reputation.

Dearest Richard

It was so exciting reading of your adventures. I know you write modestly to us, not wanting us to know of the dangers you face, and your heroism [Actually, dear sister, quite the opposite, he thought glumly, now rather ashamed of his inflation of his role at Breda and since. *Colonel DeLacey! Shit...*], *but I know you to be brave and honourable* [Pah!] *and not afraid to risk your life for others. We miss you, Richard! I miss you! You left so quickly it felt like I had lost you forever, but to get your letter was like you had risen again – I should not write that, Lionel would not be pleased!*

But I want to hear about your life in Amsterdam! [Boring misery!] *What are the ladies wearing?* [Not much in a brothel!] *Are the young men handsome?* [Not the three who attacked me last night!] *What is the food like – what do you eat?* [Klaas's fucking sausages!] *And of course, I want to know about your young lady, because a handsome heroic brother like mine must have fallen in love!* [Let me introduce you to my orphan whore...]

We miss you, Richard. Stay safe, be careful. But please send me more news. Write again soon. In fact, write to me now!

Angelica

(AMSTERDAM, JANUARY 1639)

There was a postscript from John on the back.

Richard. You will be wondering why no word from Father [Yes. I was]. *Unfortunately he is ill, and has been for some time. He complains of pains in his stomach and his digestion is not good. He has good spells, but we all fear for him. He sends you his love, and hopes that you are well and finding your way in life. But please be prepared, Richard. I am not sure what time he has and we are all worried for him. I will write to you again if things turn for the worse and maybe you can obtain leave to return home. He would like to see you again. He loves you, but you know him well enough to understand he finds it difficult to show it.*

John

He read the letter again. He should go home now. The news about his father troubled him. Who knew how quickly the end might come as it now seemed likely to do. He read between the lines of John's addition to the letter. Clearly John had little hope of a recovery, and John was as sensible, true and level-headed as anyone he knew.

But. The events of last night and the discussion with de Sête had excited him. Had woken him up. Like a match struck in the darkness of his melancholy and frustration. If everything could happen as they had discussed, he could be looking at a totally different future. Money, adventure, a chance to take Neelie away from the Sailor. To save her and advance himself. To find his way in life as his brothers and sisters already thought he had. To go back to England now risked losing all of that.

My God. Nothing is easy!

He amazed himself by starting to feel resentment towards his father. He had been quick enough to wave Richard off to an uncertain future and now he was trying to drag him back just as he had the chance for something. Not a guarantee maybe, but a good chance.

But this was his family. His father. His father who struggled to bring up four children without his wife for the last fifteen years. Who laboured to keep the estate running, and to do right by the tenants who relied upon him for work and housing. Could he turn his back on him as he was dying?

But what if John was wrong? What if he headed home and his father made a recovery? The resentment he was feeling now would be nothing to the betrayal he would feel then. Betrayal? Betrayed by his father not dying as predicted? *I am a shit of a son to even think this way for a moment.*

The thoughts in his head would not settle. He resolved to speak to Roger and Neelie. He often felt Neelie had more wisdom than both he and Roger combined. Neither had their own family, so that would make them objective, wouldn't it?

And what about the conversation with de Sête? His recollection of detail was hazy from the effects of his battered head and the gin, but he remembered his excitement as they had talked.

De Sête had confirmed that his role with the French Embassy in Amsterdam was not a straightforward diplomatic one. He was engaged in sourcing military equipment for his King, and he had been investigating potential supply and building contacts in the arms trade in Amsterdam, ever since Breda.

He talked of the massive movement of arms and armour through the city and how the United Provinces were one of the main hubs of the European arms industry. Amsterdam was involved in manufacture of weapons, ordnance and munitions, and other cities were similarly specialised. Richard couldn't remember it all, but The Hague was known for cannons,

(AMSTERDAM, JANUARY 1639)

Utrecht for armour and grenades, and Delft for firearms and gunpowder.

But Amsterdam was the axle of the hub. Nearly all the arms that flowed through and out of the country came through the city. From other Dutch cities but also from Hamburg, Bremen and Lubeck. Inventory was warehoused, shipments were consolidated. Finance was arranged and the deals were done. And a few powerful men, with the full backing and support of their government, were coordinating the trade.

Richard reflected that this massive industry had grown because of the constant conflict the Dutch people had faced, for decades. He thought of England and knew that there was nothing similar. Peace was not a good environment for selling the tools of war. With the confrontation starting with Scotland, both sides would be scrambling for equipment – de Sête confirmed this was already happening – and where better to turn than the Dutch.

De Sête had thrown some names around. He knew that Quarles was buying not just men for the army but weapons and armour too. In the Scottish staple port of Veere, Sir Patrick Drummond was also closely involved, but was acting for the King, informing him of the movement of material to Edinburgh. He was not trusted by the Covenanters as Fraser had told them. But it was men like Louis De Geer and his brothers-in-law, Elias and Pieter Trip, who dominated. They were not only buying, selling and manufacturing in the provinces but also setting up a thriving arms industry in Sweden. Together with financiers such as the Lampsins from Middleburg, it was these men, and other powerful industrialists and merchants like them, that were being courted by representatives of the Covenanters and the King.

Huge amounts of money were in play, and de Sête had felt that it was more likely a commercial rivalry, rather than a political motivation, that had led to his own brush with a harsher and more direct style of negotiation at the warehouse. Which all went to lend weight to his suggestion. With all this money, and this 'friction' as Jean had put it, and the emergence of two English-speaking countries as key buyers, was there not an opportunity for two experienced military men such as Roger and Richard to get involved?

He had made a lot of contacts. People who owed him favours. And now Jean felt he owed a debt to Richard for stepping into the situation at the warehouse. He could make enquiries, and then introductions. They would come with the personal recommendation of one of the finest soldiers in all of France, as he modestly described himself. "What could possibly go wrong, *mes amis?*"

It sounded to be just what he needed. He couldn't wait to act on this, but he and Roger were now in Jean's hands, and a delay would at least allow his face and head time to heal before meeting a potential employer.

But a third thought chased these two matters around his gently throbbing skull. In many ways it was the most concerning because he really didn't understand it. He had no way of even start thinking about it. As he had experienced in the assault at Breda, he had again encountered the unexplained, unexplainable surge of energy at the moment his foe had died. But this time he had sensed – he couldn't describe it as seeing – a movement, a flow of… something… from the dying body to his own. Like water spilt on a rough floor finding a channel that it can move along, it had found him. And again, he had felt the power, the strength fill him, and lift him.

When Jean had finished off the wounded man with a thrust through the heart, there had been a fainter sensation, but still he had felt… something. While Jean had concluded his business on the ship, it was as much as Richard could do

(Amsterdam, January 1639)

to stand still. He had been twitching and clenching his fists to stay quiet by the warehouse door, to control built-up tension, but gradually, he had felt the tide recede, and it had left him empty, cold, exhausted. He had needed Jean to haul him to his feet, but he could still feel the echo of it.

This occupied him more than his father's condition, more than the prospect of a new and potentially dangerous career. It had felt so good, like he had the strength of two men, but it also felt, somehow, wrong. He would not talk about this to anyone. People were burnt as witches for less. That was not the way he wanted his story to end.

*

A week passed before they heard again from de Sête. He called at the Sailor, and Richard and Roger cleared an area at the back of the tavern of a couple of sleeping drunks, so that they could have some privacy. De Sête described several meetings he had attended, mainly on his own behalf, where he had casually introduced his connection with the English mercenaries as an addendum to the discussion, and others where the access to experienced security personnel was the main topic under discussion.

He had met with representatives of the Trip family who, with Louis De Geer, had done so much to establish Amsterdam as the hub for the European arms trade, but it was his discussion with brothers Gabriel and Celio Marcelis that seemed the most promising. Their agent, Pieter Hudde, was looking for men who 'could handle themselves' for a series of shipments that were planned for the next months. He was intrigued by the prospect of hiring Englishmen, as his business was very likely to involve commerce with that country. He wanted to meet them. Tomorrow.

They valued Jean's friendship too much to buy him food at the Sailor. So they thanked him with gin, but also some reasonable French wine that Klaas had secreted away. Secreted away because he had stolen it from a drunken customer. They parted until the morning when Jean would guide them to the meeting place. Hudde was concerned about giving anything away about his business dealings, and Jean was equally concerned about his personal safety, given recent events. Richard knew this was false modesty, as he had already decided that if any man fitted the description of 'could handle himself', it was Jean de Sête.

*

The meeting had gone very well. Hudde clearly had great respect for de Sête and they had done business before. His introduction of Roger and Richard was therefore very persuasive, and Roger's backstory of violence was convincing. Jean's personal endorsement of Richard's skill and bravery offset any concerns about his youth. Richard had sensed that both Roger and Jean really wanted to say more about his still-obvious injuries, but they held their mouths, and he was grateful.

Things had moved quickly after that. They were to accompany Hudde, along with two Dutch employees, to supervise the loading of a shipment of gunpowder in The Hague, and to guard it on the trip back to Amsterdam where it was being consolidated into a larger shipment. Hudde didn't tell them where that shipment was bound. The journey back would be partly by road and partly by the newly dug canal, from The Hague, via Delft, to Leiden. At Leiden, it would be loaded onto carts to finish the journey.

The round trip would take three days, including the loading and unloading, and Richard was saying a long goodbye to

Neelie. He had spoken to both her and Roger about the letter from his family and, to his surprise, neither had encouraged him to return to his sick father's bedside. Having both lost their families in different ways, he had anticipated them insisting that family came before everything, and how could he be thinking about ignoring this last chance to see his father alive, but no. Roger, although still tragically melancholy about his wife and children, had no real love for his father. And for Neelie, who had lost her father to the war when she was still young, he was a distant memory. She couldn't remember his face, or his voice. He was just a presence and a name her mother had cried over. "Don't be foolish, Risch. Your future is here with me. Now you will have money perhaps we can be properly together. We can leave the Sailor and find our own place. We could perhaps… marry?"

He had had the same thought. *Why not?* "Let's see how this latest venture works out, my love. The pay is good, but who knows if I am any good at it? Or if Hudde will use us a second time? It is not exactly what I saw myself doing when I left home to go to war."

Nevertheless, they felt the urgent need to practise certain aspects of married life a couple of times before Richard, now exhausted, tried on the uniform that the Marcelis brothers favoured for their employees. Nothing too ostentatious – just a waistcoat of dark blue velvet, with an entwined 'G' and 'C' in gold thread on the left breast. With a white linen shirt, new black leather broad-brimmed hat and brown leather breeches he felt he looked the part. His disfigured cheek and nose gave him the look of a man harder than he himself felt, but perhaps that wasn't a bad thing. God only knew what type of encounters they might have on the road and perhaps just the look of a man would stop any attempt on their cargo. Anyway, he thought, Roger was ugly enough, and hard enough, for both of them.

He changed back into his old clothes and settled back on the mattress next to Neelie. The weather continued ice cold; the change from January to February had brought little relief. He settled down to sleep, anxious to be on his best form for the morning departure.

*

The following evening, two hours after sunset, Richard was sitting with his back to an oak tree, keeping low in the dark among a dense patch of ferns and brambles. The earth was frozen hard, and his breath hung about him in the still, freezing air. He sat on his pack to keep himself off the icy ground, and he shivered under two woollen blankets. He had wound his baldric around the lower half of his face, covering his ears and nose, but one of his eyes dripped a slow stream of tears which was gradually soaking into the supple leather across his cheek. A loaded, primed musket was balanced across his lap, his knees were drawn up towards his chest, and he kept flexing his toes and feet in his boots to stop them from seizing up in the cold.

He pictured the others at the wharf in The Hague. They must be almost finished packing the shipment on to the sledges. But they wouldn't be cold. A few hours of carefully shifting crates and barrels of gunpowder, the half-dozen brass cannon, and quantities of cannon balls, grenades and pike staves would have them working up a good sweat. Hudde said he had hired three sledges for the return trip, as the freezing weather had frozen the canal for weeks on end and transport was now limited to dragging specially adapted barges over the ice. But he wouldn't be lifting any weight himself, despite being a hugely tall and broad man, with a barrel chest and sonorous voice. They could probably have got all the material onto a single sledge if they had piled it high, but Hudde wanted to spread the weight of his valuable cargo, particularly as three of them would be riding on the sledges.

The canal, or *trekvaart*, as the Dutch called it, was intended purely for passengers, their fares maintaining the upkeep of the waterway, but the name of Marcelis, and the impressive size of Hudde's purse and personality, had persuaded the local officials that they could make an exception on this occasion. The only condition was that the sledges must travel during darkness so as not to inconvenience their usual passengers or draw attention to the fact that they had eagerly accepted Marcelis's bribes.

It would have taken them most of the daylight hours to make the journey from Amsterdam to The Hague. The Marcelis company had provided them with good horses, as well as the offer of firearms and other weaponry. Roger was already well catered for in that respect but had replenished ball and powder. Richard had selected a pair of flintlock pistols, and a good sword for use on horseback. He was leaving his rapier at the tavern. All weapons and supplies would be deducted from their wages, but at a heavy discount.

The other two guards were Jacob and Arie and had worked with Hudde before. They seemed solid, and competent, if not very talkative. They had little English, and as Roger and Richard had only basic Dutch, the conversation on the road did not flow. Pieter Hudde, however, had been involved in trading with England and Scotland all his adult life – Richard estimated he was in his forties – and had a good command of the language, as well as some French, Danish and German.

Hudde rode with Richard and Roger most of the way to Leiden, talking to them about the business, the assignment they were completing and alerting them to things to look out for. He was exceptionally careful in his planning, fully aware of the large amount of money the Marcelis brothers had staked in the shipment, and the enormous profit for successful delivery. He sent Jacob riding ahead to scout the canal paths, note anything unusual and identify places where ambushes were most likely. Although Hudde had used the route before, it had been more than three months ago, and while he stressed the likelihood of attack was low, he had clearly been disturbed by Jean's story of the warehouse, and he hinted of other 'interferences' that he, and other arms shippers, had encountered in recent months.

He also instructed Arie to set out an hour after them, to hang back and observe anyone who appeared to be following them. Roger was impressed with the thinking and Richard tried hard to absorb as much of the knowledge that Hudde was imparting as he could. They learnt that the shipment that their material would form part of, was for export. At this stage, Hudde would not say to where. The government permitted this, even encouraged it, as long as there was no risk that their own military needs could not be catered for. The provinces had been at war for so long that the government had granted extremely attractive terms to arms manufacturers, in return for guaranteed supply when needed. Artisans were provided with workshops for no charge, and later were subsidised when these workshops grew into water-powered mills. Saltpetre was provided free to gunpowder makers in Amsterdam, Rotterdam, Flushing and Hoorn. The risks for entrepreneurs with capital were lowered, and their profits soared.

Hudde had not always dealt in this trade. He had started in agricultural produce and the flower trade, but those who had invested early, like De Geer and the Marcelis brothers, had found that the return on arms and munitions was like nothing else, and they had expanded and concentrated their efforts.

(AMSTERDAM, JANUARY 1639)

Once they reached Leiden, they met again with Jacob, and compared notes on the road. All had passed uneventfully, and Jacob had already made contact with the owner from whom they were hiring wagons for the return journey. They talked about encounters with other travellers, and all of them had identified a small hamlet, hemmed in with beech and birch woods, as the most likely place where a body of men could conceal themselves.

They ate a swift meal of bread, cheese and sausage – far better than anything Klaas ever served – washed down with beer. And then to the docks, where new buildings, warehouses and a clean, bright inn jostled to be closest to the head of the canal. Coming from his village, Richard was quite used to the idea of water transport, the fens and rivers providing a convenient means of moving goods around, as well as for smugglers to hide in, but the new canal was a wonder. Arrow straight, it aimed south-west and disappeared over the horizon into a slight, frosty haze. Both sides were flattened into broad paths and they could see, about a hundred yards distant, two huge draught horses, one on each side of the icy strip, led by the jagers, wrapped up against the cold. Their breath, and that of the horses, created plumes of vapour visible even at distance, and above the noise of waiting passengers and wharf workers, they could hear the growing rumble of the runners bumping over the thick ice.

The *trekschuit* was like a long, low-roofed barge, with a few windows in the sides to allow in light. It had been raised up onto two runners that ran the length of the vessel and it constantly twitched from side to side as one horse or the other gained ground on its companion. Jacob again set off first, leading his horse down the towpath and inching past one of the giant animals towing the *trekschuit*. Then he mounted and trotted briskly away.

Hudde, Roger and Richard waited for the disembarkation of the incoming passengers. The smell of vomit coming from the opened hatch door, and the green faces of several of the travellers, attested to the jolting ride, and the operators tried to conduct a quick cleaning of the vessel before allowing the new passengers on board. A number of them looked slightly uncertainly at the ice, one rapping it hard with his walking cane, before gingerly climbing inside. A number of the ladies were holding kerchiefs to their noses, and all seemed to be reconsidering the wisdom of the journey.

Just before they were ready to depart, the Marcelis party headed off, now in single file on the narrow towpath. After an uneventful hour, they came upon Jacob, holding his horse, standing by a stone footbridge over the canal. The far side, beyond the towpath, was heavily wooded, with a narrow but well-used path heading from the bridge, through the trees and towards a distant group of buildings, pluming wood smoke into the gathering gloom of the afternoon. Jacob engaged Hudde in an intense conversation, gesturing at the bridge, the woods and the canal, in turn. Hudde translated for Roger and Richard, although they already had the gist of it. "Jacob says that if anyone wanted to disrupt our shipment, this would be the perfect place. The bridge from which to shoot down on us, or drop things on to us, and the trees as a secondary firing point and an escape route. I think he is right."

Roger agreed. "So what's your plan, master?"

"Well, that's what we hired you for. You are the military man. What is your advice?" Hudde stared down blank-faced at DeLacey who in turn looked at Richard and shrugged.

"If I was lookin' to take you on here, I wouldn't drop things onto your heads from the bridge. I would drop 'em onto the ice. If that goes, you ain't gettin' nothin' past this point, and you're sittin' targets for good men with muskets either on the bridge, or in the trees. Put a ball through the draught horse's head, and you're double fucked!"

"Yes. That would do it. As you say, we would be fucked. Jacob?" Jacob nodded seriously. "Very fucked," obviously following Roger's meaning. Hudde asked the obvious question. "So, what do we do?"

"Well. If you want to make sure of getting your cargo back to Leiden, you need to stop them holing the ice in the first place. If they know, or have guessed, your plan, they will crack the ice after the last passengers have gone, and before you arrive in the early hours with the stuff. So sometime before midnight, I guess. So why not ambush the ambushers? Leave a man hidden here, or maybe two, and they can guard the bridge. If it is just a straightforward fight, then you have hidden allies who can give the fuckers a surprise when they have a go at you. You have just got to decide how many to leave, and who."

Hudde pursed his lips, resting his bearded chin into the palm of one of his enormous black-haired hands. "I like this plan," he nodded after a few minutes' thought. "I do not want to weaken our party too much in case we have difficulties before we get to this point, so I don't want to leave two." He paused and looked at Roger carefully. "I don't want to leave Jacob or Arie, as I want them both with me. I know them. Despite de Sête's words, I don't know you yet. I think splitting you up for this plan is a good idea. If you try to trick me, at least I can kill one of you. One of you two should stay," he said quietly, looking from Roger to Richard.

All of the ride since Leiden, Richard had been thinking about riding along the ice and remembering his torrid crossing of the North Sea. He knew that within minutes of starting that twitching, jerking, rocking journey he would be throwing up helplessly. Anything, anything to avoid that feeling again. And here was his chance. To hell with any danger. He thought it pretty unlikely that anything would occur anyway. The journey had been boring and… normal. He was the man for this job. "Master Hudde. Let it be me. I am quieter, and quicker, and just as good a shot as my colleague. Leave me with two muskets, some food and an extra blanket. I will do this."

DeLacey eyed him doubtfully. "You sure, lad? If something happens, we could be miles away and you will be on your own."

Richard was thinking only of avoiding the sledge. "Of course. Nothing I can't handle."

And now here he was, chewing slowly on the remains of the sausage, trying to make it last as long as possible. Staring into the dark, ears straining to pick up the slightest sound. There was not a breath of wind, no movement of air. The bare branches and twigs of the oak and the other trees were black inky lines painted across the clear, starlit sky. A half-moon gave some pale light, and, in the chill air, he occasionally picked out voices coming from the houses at the end of the forest path and across a field, showing some lamp light through their windows a half-mile away. He could sense the distance from which the sound came and it did not worry him. It was his immediate surroundings he was focused on.

Initially he had been busy, scouting out the land around the small bridge. There were footprints in the frosty ground, but it was impossible to tell how recent on the iron-hard earth. He dismissed the ground on the far side of the canal immediately. It was flat and open. There was no cover. He focused on the bridge and the wood, trying to put himself in the shoes of any possible ambushers.

It was possible that any attackers might come along the canal towpath, but he thought it more likely they would approach through the trees, along the narrow path. He walked up and down it in the fading light, identifying places where,

(Amsterdam, January 1639)

if it were him, he would place men with muskets. He then picked a spot twenty yards back from one of these, on the left-hand side of the path, where he could hide himself in the thick ferns. He could just about see the bridge through the bare trees but cut down a few small holly bushes and ferns to give him a better view, leaving his hiding place well screened from all other sides.

He checked his two pistols and the two muskets, and loosened his heavy cavalry sabre, not wanting the metal of blade and scabbard to freeze together. He didn't want to be tugging at the hilt while someone took careful aim at his head.

He had been thorough. He had been practical. But now, four freezing hours later, he was getting desperate. He could no longer feel his toes and he sat with his fingers shoved under his armpits to keep them warm. And he was bored. He had seen nothing except a tawny owl gliding through the trees, sweeping over his head before disappearing in the branches. An hour ago, a small family of deer had come soundlessly along the path from behind him, before crossing the bridge and heading for the short brown grass in the fields opposite. This at least demonstrated to him that he could see enough by moonlight to identify innocent travellers from determined wrongdoers.

He guessed it was just before midnight that he again heard voices. This time he knew they were closer than the distant buildings and getting closer as the conversation continued. He also knew he had been asleep and that it was an alarm call from a vixen, somewhere over to his left, that had alerted him. He didn't want to turn to try and catch a glimpse of the men and so he sat stone-like against the tree trunk waiting for them to pass along the path.

It was two men, dressed in peasant clothes. Farmers, he guessed. They pushed a small handcart that seemed to contain large rocks, as well as a couple of sledgehammers, wooden planks and rope. He was, frankly, astonished that anyone was abroad, given the freezing temperature. He was prepared for a seemingly endless wait until Roger and the others arrived, and his heart immediately started hammering at his ribs at the thought that he might actually have to take action.

Although their intentions seemed pretty clear, he could not see any weapons on the two men – both of them large, but not particularly fearsome looking – and now his thought turned to what he was going to do. He couldn't just shoot two unarmed farmers for pushing a cart. He couldn't even shoot them if they started to smash at the ice. Could he just scare them off? Or maybe hold them as prisoners until the others arrived, God knows how many hours away? *Shit!* Perhaps he hadn't thought this through after all. He wondered what Roger would do, but even more he wondered what Hudde would do if they arrived to find a massive hole in the ice and Richard with nothing to show but a sympathetic shrug.

He would have to decide quickly as they were now approaching the bridge. They continued to chat, in low voices, but not whispering. They seemed unconcerned that anyone else might be around and started to unload the cart. Richard knew he could be quiet enough to get close before they spotted him and he suddenly got himself moving before his indecision totally paralysed him. As he got up into a crouch he nearly screamed, as his frozen feet and long-static leg muscles shouted their agony to him. Moving quietly and steadily, he pulled both pistols from his belt. He leaned slightly to make sure his scabbard swayed away from his body so it would not clank against his leg and crept closer, thankful that both men had their backs to him, one laying planks on the ice of the canal, the other tying the rope around his chest, under his armpits. He could now clearly see they must be father and son, so alike were they.

(AMSTERDAM, JANUARY 1639)

He paused on the path by the last tree, to gather his thoughts, then stepped quickly and decisively onto the tow path, raised both pistols and said in his best Dutch and his firmest and, he hoped, intimidating voice, "Stop!"

Both men jumped, the older one grabbing at his own chest, taken completely by surprise. "Hands up!" said Richard forcefully and, taking a step back, "Turn around!"

Both men turned their heads first, shooting a wide-eyed glance at each other as they slowly turned to face him. To Richard's relief it looked like his assessment of them was correct. He saw no anger, no craftiness, just good old-fashioned terror. He relaxed slightly but kept the pistols pointing at the centre of their chests. Without turning from them, he jerked his head back towards the path through the trees. "Go home." The father and son looked at each other, relief on their faces. Father jerked his head at the cart and the tools. "We take these?"

Richard was fast running out of Dutch. "Tomorrow. Now go. Now!" He let the volume of his voice rise.

Both father and son looked over his shoulder, towards the path, and then at each other, and then back to Richard. Both looked even more troubled. "Yes, yes. I am letting you go. Not kill you. Now go!"

And then the unmistakable sound of a pistol, or a musket, being cocked. Right behind his head. "No, friend." A new voice. "It is you who go." Badly spoken English. "Go into canal." The farmers relaxed, and the son started untying the rope from under his armpits. Richard felt a prod in his back – a musket then. He instinctively raised his hands, still holding the pistols. He knew that once he had cracked the ice, he would be going through the hole, straight to the bottom. He could almost sense already the deathly coldness of the black water closing over his head, and he felt himself struggling to contain bladder and bowels. Maybe they would let him go after he had swung the hammer, but somehow he doubted that. His mind started to jabber at him, losing control of any coherent thought.

Father farmer bent down and turned his back to pick up a sledgehammer from the ground behind him, and son was still trying to unpick his knot with cold, numb fingers. Both missed the slight grunt that came from the edge of the trees, but both heard the sound of a body impacting the hardened mud ridges of the towpath. The man behind Richard must have also heard, as there was a sharp inhalation before the *fizz-crack* of igniting powder and discharging firearm broke the stillness of the night. Instantaneously, Richard and the two farmers were struck by slivers of bone and splashed with blood and grey matter. A body catapulted past him, catching his shoulder and spinning him around. It took Richard a heartbeat to realise the gun which fired was not the one pointed at his own spine, and that the blood was not his own.

He dropped to one knee, eyes scanning the towpath, adrenaline now overriding fear as it dawned on him that he had somehow been spared. At least temporarily. He sucked in a deep breath, realising it must have been a long time since he had last dared to breathe. The body next to him, clothed in black wool and leather, was thankfully face down, missing the back of its head. It was only now that Richard realised to his surprise that he still held his two pistols, and these now swung round, one to cover the farmers, the other searching for a target in the edge of the trees.

But he didn't have to search long. Stepping out of the shadow of one of the trees framing the start of the path, was the shape of a man. Medium height, medium build and holding a smoking carbine in one hand and an undischarged pistol in the other. He stepped over a second body, lying at his feet, paused to lay the carbine on the ground and pick up a wicked-

(Amsterdam, January 1639)

looking knife, blackly slick with what Richard assumed to be blood, which he wiped carefully on the cloak of the fallen man.

Carrying the knife in his left hand, pistol in the right, he walked casually towards Richard. "Well met, Master Farrell. I thought it was you. Interesting company that you are keeping." English. Spoken by an Englishman.

Richard rose and peered at the man, his panting breath creating a cloud around him. He glanced sideways at the two farmers, who both wore expressions of shock and bewilderment, as well as a liberal helping of their former companion.

The man's face was shadowed even further by the brim of his hat, and Richard could not place the voice at all. "You do not know me?" The man sounded almost pleased. "But we have met before, Master Farrell." He pushed back his hat and the pale moonlight washed across his features. Nondescript. Average.

"Yes. Yes, I know you. Montague. We met in the office of Master Quarles."

Montague smiled. Even in the dimness Richard knew that the smile would not touch his eyes. "We did, sir. Well met again."

"Forgive me for asking," Richard was gradually recovering some composure, and wiped his sleeve across a wetness on his cheek, knowing it to be blood, "but what the fuck are you doing here?" He didn't smile. He kept both pistols up. One still pointing at a space between the two farmers and the other, surprisingly steady, at the centre of Montague's chest.

"A good question, master. I suspect we share the same objective here, although we work for different players in this… hmm… little exercise. I followed these men from Amsterdam. We have been watching them, and others, for some time. I wanted to see what they were intending with this shipment. You work for the supplier. I work for the customer."

"The King."

"Oh, well done, Farrell! I see you would have been wasted amongst Quarles's recruits. You have a razor-sharp mind." Again, the smile that wasn't. "It saddened me deeply when yourself and your… hmm… friend – Master DeLacey, wasn't it? – both felt you owed more loyalty to your purses than to your monarch, but there are many sadnesses in this world that will need setting to rights at some point in the future. But perhaps any fighting man that can be outmanoeuvred by such as these…" he nodded at the farmers, and the corpse lying behind him, "…is more of a liability than an asset."

Richard went from fury to embarrassment. He decided, for once in his life, that it was safer to say nothing. He stared back at Montague in the most intimidating manner he could summon. Montague didn't seem too impressed. "So what are you going to do with these two, boy?" No more 'Master Farrell' then.

"What? Nothing. Let them go. They are just peasants. They were just here to do the labouring." He looked at the two farmers who were, in turn, looking from Richard to Montague, desperately trying to follow the conversation. He swallowed in his throat as he saw what was coming. The father looked at him, pleading. He grabbed his son's hand.

"Nee. Alsjeblieft. Nee."

"They have seen you, boy. More importantly, they have seen me. They have raised their hands against His Majesty. They must die."

"They do not have the first clue who we are. They have no clue why they were doing this. You know this. You don't have to kill them."

"Well, one of us does. I was hoping you might show some shred of loyalty and do the deed yourself. But you are soft, boy. You have no cause but yourself. Don't pretend you do this for them. You refuse to shoot because you don't have the stomach for it. You think you protect your honour, but it is just selfish fear. Fear of doing the hard thing, even when it is the right thing."

"You are wrong. You cannot just kill in…" but before Richard could finish Montague's pistol arm came up and he shot the father through the heart. There was a moment of silence following the shot as realisation spread over the face of the son, and his father's body toppled backwards. The low wall of the bridge caught him behind the knees and he fell to the ice below, eyes staring upward, blankly, at his son. Blood spread slowly onto the ice around him, black under the moon.

"You bastard!"

"Move, boy!" The knife came up and forward, and Montague strode the few yards towards the son.

But now Richard's fury triumphed, fuelled by a wave of energy that swept across him as the father had fallen, dead before he hit the ice. He felt a now familiar surge of power. As Montague shouldered past him towards the young man, who still leaned over the parapet, unaware of his own approaching doom, Richard swung the barrel of one of the pistols down across the back of Montague's head with huge force. The King's agent hit the ground and lay in a heap. He made no sound. Carefully, with a pistol held to the man's temple, he checked if Montague was still breathing. He was, but blood was visible in his hair on the back of his head.

He looked up at the farmer's son, now slumped down with his back to the parapet, sobbing quietly as he stared at Richard. "Go! Run!"

The man shook his head. He seemed paralysed. In shock.

"Go!" This time Richard raised a pistol and pointed it. "Go!"

Now the man did move. He got up, eyes red and wide, and edged his way around Richard and towards the trees. When he got to the path he turned and ran, and Richard heard the sound gradually fade.

Now it was his turn to put his back to the parapet. *What have I done?* On one level, he knew Montague was right. There was so much riding on this shipment, politically, militarily and financially. You can't leave loose ends that will trip you later. But he couldn't slaughter people in cold blood. These farmers were like so many he knew back on his father's small estate. They were not faceless 'things'. They were people with their own lives, their own stories and challenges. Not just walk-on parts in more important events. Nothing was more important to them than their own lives, their families. No one had the right to take that away. Not when their ignorance of the underlying motivations was so apparent.

But he could also not get away from the fact that Montague had very probably saved his life. Without his ruthless intervention, it would be Richard at the bottom of the canal. He had no idea who the dead men were. Who they worked for. But their intention was very clear, and Montague had acted decisively and with great skill to thwart them. And now Montague was his enemy. An implacable, capable and highly motivated adversary, but still he could not bring himself to slit the man's throat. Instead, he took off the man's belt and tied his hands behind his back, but he couldn't just leave him, as Montague would surely die of the cold.

He went to the bodies of the two armed assailants and removed their coats and jackets. There was nothing on the corpses to give any clue about them, or their employers. One had a thick woollen scarf which he wound around Montague's head, to stem some minor bleeding and to keep his head warm. He dragged him to the edge of the bridge where he would be in clear sight of the first passenger trip along the frozen canal, and laid layers of coats and other clothes from the dead men over him. He threw all the weapons, except his own, deep into the trees. He went back to the towpath to see if he could recover the body of the farmer, but even though he knew the ice was thick enough to take the weight of thirty passengers in a *trekschuit*, he could not bring himself to risk his weight on it when there was no one there to aid him.

He collected one his primed muskets and settled himself with his back to one of the trees at the edge of the towpath where he had a clear and easy shot at Montague, should he need to take it. After about an hour he heard the sledges approaching with Hudde, Roger and the others. The ice was intact. There would be no ambush, but nevertheless, as he glanced at the still-unconscious Montague, he was not sure how happy his new employer would be with his night's work.

14

SIR WILLIAM BRERETON

(Handforth Hall, North-West England, January 1639)

The letter lay on his lap. Brereton had read it through twice and the contents disturbed him greatly. He had guessed that it was coming, but the physical presence of the paper was nevertheless a cold slap of reality.

The letter was signed by the lord lieutenants for Cheshire, Lord William Stanley, 6th Earl of Derby, and his son James Stanley, who held the role jointly. He knew the author would have been James, as his father had all but disappeared from public life, leading a reclusive existence.

Brereton had met both men and had to admit he was slightly in awe. William had managed to survive the political dangers of being a lawful heir to the English throne through Henry VIII's sister, Mary Tudor. But his loyalty to Queen Elizabeth had saved his life, and he had inherited, and been granted, estates-a-plenty, covering large parts of the north of England, Wales and the Isle of Man. Brereton had heard the stories of his wild younger life, travelling through France, before duelling and fornicating his way across Europe, Egypt, Russia

(Handforth Hall, North-West England, January 1639)

and even to Greenland. He was rumoured to have become a great poet, but perhaps sensing the risks of a high political profile, had then confined his attention to administering his estates, particularly across Cheshire and Lancashire. As a result, Brereton had had several dealings with him.

His son James was something of a chip off the old block. He too had travelled in his younger days and, at their first meeting, had exchanged tales and experiences with Brereton. James had also been a Member of Parliament, but ten years ago had been called to the House of Lords. Brereton had warmed to James, even though he was painfully aware of the gulf in their fortunes and antecedents, seeing a noble character and a great sportsman. He had heard that James had recently commissioned van Dyck to create a family portrait. His only misgivings were the rumours of the Stanleys' support for Catholicism, and he knew James to be utterly devoted to his monarch. Feelings he could not bring himself to share.

And now this letter.

For over a year he had been following events in Scotland with Charles's vain attempt to enforce Anglicanism on the Presbyterians in the form of the Book of Common Prayer, and his strengthening of the power of the bishops. Unsurprisingly, the stubborn Scots had reacted badly and had drawn up their so-called National Covenant. For all the protestations of loyalty to the Crown, and its careful drafting to show alignment with the law, it was clear to see that this was a threat to the authority of the King over church matters in Scotland. Drafted by the clever lawyer Wariston, the covenant had united the Presbyterians against the King's archbishop, William Laud. Laud was the driving force behind this attempt to subjugate the Scottish kirks, and Charles was standing firmly behind his man.

The Covenanters were now effectively ruling Scotland, and despite negotiations back and forward, and the holding of a general assembly to attempt to cool matters down, events had come to a war footing. The King was determined to assert his authority and the Covenanters equally determined to uphold their religious freedom. Brereton felt a lot of sympathy with the Scots, and he knew he was far from alone in this. He too resented the high-handedness of the bishops, particularly that crafty zealot Laud, but equally he felt affronted, as a proud Englishman, of this challenge to his sovereign.

But now this letter.

This philosophical, theocratic, theoretic debate was now knocking at his door in the shape of the King's demand for military support. Everyone knew the parlous state of the army – no more than a bunch of untrained, undisciplined, inexperienced militias – and everyone knew Charles had little or no money to raise, equip and train an army to take on the Scots.

So now the letter.

The lord lieutenants of Cheshire were writing to men such as him demanding they do their duty with financial support and the raising of troops to support the King's invasion of Scotland. Victory was certain – of course, it is the King who says so – and the English army would be supported by Scots loyal to the Crown (although many of these were openly Catholic in sympathy), by a landing of loyal forces from Ireland under Sir Thomas Wentworth (that fawning adviser to Charles) and an amphibious assault on Edinburgh under the command, as Brereton thought him, of the ineffectual Duke of Hamilton. He was 'encouraged' to respond as swiftly as possible, as the King was to muster his army at York within two months.

He knew he had to respond to the encouragement. But what to do? His duty to the King and his fear of repercussions dragged him one direction, but his increasing mistrust of those close to the King – and surely, he had been badly advised –

(Handforth Hall, North-West England, January 1639)

especially by Wentworth, Laud and his bishops, just as surely dragged him the other. He smiled wryly. *I am sentenced to be pulled apart by principles.* His only comfort was the knowledge that he was not alone and he sensed a tide was turning in the country.

He placed the letter on his desk and rang a bell to summon a servant to find pen, ink and paper. He had to find a middle way. Show his loyalty but take no action to support this rotten rule of the bishops. Show some solidarity with Covenanters, while keeping his head on his shoulders. He would employ classic political tactics: delay, flatter and possibly bribe. Perhaps he would invite James Stanley to hunt, which he knew Stanley could not resist, and while they were engaged in his favourite pastime, he would demonstrate just how difficult it would be to meet the King's request. He needed to buy some time to think this through.

Where to hold the hunt? And as he mentally ticked off Stanley's own nearby estates, his thoughts slid inexorably to the Forest of Macclesfield, and his recent frustration. It had been in the previous autumn when he had made his way back to Swythamley Hall. It had just been a pretext; his real purpose had been to try to find the woman again. She haunted his daydreams, and the obsession – he could think of no other word – was beginning to affect his marriage. He could not deny to himself the hold those chance meetings had over him, and he wondered at it. *Witch*, that horrible goodwife had called her. Was he bewitched? He had headed down the country lanes, back to the Dane Bridge, to find her and learn the truth about her. And perhaps about himself – where had those fine Puritan principles hidden themselves? But he had found her gone. The hovel she had occupied was now holding a family with a scarcely believable number of children. He had found none who could tell him where she had gone.

She had vanished. He learnt of Samuel Brassey's suicide and was told that 'Mistress Hume' had disappeared almost immediately after the midsummer fair. He wondered now if that was her real name. Some said darkly that the Brasseys had taken her and quietly done away with her. Others were now more inclined to believe the accusations that had been flung at her by Mary Brassey. But she had gone, and none had seen her for over a year.

Too many questions would have raised unwanted attention, and so his stay at Swythamley had been one of anger and frustration, much to the confusion of his bemused host, who was left not really understanding the purpose of the visit.

He had returned home praying to God to rid him of this succubus. But so far at least, there had been no answer.

There was a knock, and the servant had returned with writing materials.

15

WILL FLETCHER

(York, March 1639)

He pushed and elbowed his way through the press in the tight streets. The watery sunshine failed to penetrate between the overhanging garrets of the shops and dingy houses huddled around the great York Minster and lent a sense of dusk to the bright midday.

Will had marched in through Micklegate earlier that morning, his long stride eating up the well-worn cross-country trudge from the port at Hull. He had arrived back in England with a number of his companions from the continent as news of the impending conflict with the Scots had found its way along the mercenary grapevine. He had spent much of the preceding year trudging along the roads of Germany and the Low Countries, attached to this or that company, soldiering with other English, Swedes, Dutch or Scots, but seeing little action. As part of the body of foot in the Elector Palatine's ill-fated attempt to regain his lands, he had arrived too late to see any fighting at Vlotho, where Frederick's cavalry was destroyed or captured.

Word had reached him that King Charles was gathering an army in York to face the Covenanter Scots, and former comrades were leaving from continental ports to go either to

Leith or Hull, depending on how the financial offers, religious calling or patriotism stirred them. The city's population was already swelled by thousands of men and everywhere there was a crush of bodies.

Having only been in York a few hours he was already disappointed and concerned. The men being gathered to form the army fell well below the standards he had become used to across the North Sea. Poorly armed, poorly disciplined and with little or no experience. And the officers were little better it seemed. The usual crop of country gentlemen who saw the whole enterprise as a glorified hunt, but only a very few men used to leading, used to fighting, with any ideas of tactics or how to place or drill men. It would need a miracle to turn this rabble into a force able to take on the Covenanters, with their larger core of experienced mercenary fighters.

Even Will's limited experience marked him out as a veteran, which he found rather a bizarre thought at the age of eighteen. He knew he was an imposing figure, standing head and shoulders over the crowd, with his long fair hair and thin beard. His Swedish comrades had called him the English Viking, a term he had embraced for its martial overtones, and he had often found himself selected for the honour guard of his unit's colours, for his size, strength and skill with pike and mace.

He had added muscle to his already impressive frame, and the constant drilling of a professional army had brought finesse to the sheer brute strength he brought to a fight. When he reflected on his time traversing the roads of Europe, it was his thinking, and knowledge of the wider world, that he felt had developed the most. His ideas around privilege, wealth, fairness and God's plan for his people had matured. He had listened to Calvinists, Arminians, Lutherans, Presbyterians and Puritans. He had discussed the divine rights of kings, and the structure and role of a parliament. He had explored the perspectives of those born into property and those born into nothing. He had talked with ex-criminals, beggars and priests. But for all the listening to points of view and beliefs, after days and weeks and months spent in proximity with thousands of other men, he had found that observing what people actually did was a far better guide to the true worth and goodness of his fellow man, than what they said. The most ignorant, foul-mouthed peasant could put his life at risk for his fellows as readily as any lord or earl. A man sharing the last of his rations around a campfire was more valuable than any stirring speech. Being born into nothing didn't mean you were nothing. One man's life was as valuable as anyone else's.

Coming himself from a farming community, he saw with horror and pity the impact war had on commonfolk. Wherever he had marched across Europe he had seen the trail of destruction the armies left in their wake. Stealing food, burning crops, houses and whole villages, raping women, pressing the young men needed for the harvest into service.

And if a border moved by twenty miles, or if a king was replaced by an emperor, to be replaced by an elector, and then a king again, there was no help or benefit for the poor. They were not even pawns on the chessboard. They were invisible, or at best a grey, earth-coloured slow-moving backdrop to the glorious charge, the tragic defeat and the heroic stand that so galvanised the great and good that seemingly ran the world.

The commonfolk in the armies fared no better. They were required to risk their lives for one cause or another, often with little understanding of what they were fighting for other than a meal and a meagre wage. But at the end of it, when the dust settled, victory or defeat made no change to their lives. They were still poor. They still had no say in their own lives. Power and prosperity still rested with a privileged few, not the many who risked all.

He felt, strongly, that this was the voice of God speaking to him. Speaking to him directly, not through a written word, through a priest, through a psalm. He became more and more convinced he had the right of it. All men are born equal in God's eyes and anything else is a perversion of his design. Kings and queens claimed divine right. Their majesty handed down from God. But if this was the case, why would they fight so bitterly over a few acres of land, over a prayer book, over a marriage. They could not all be right in God's eyes. It made no sense.

He rounded a corner and came into the open space in front of the great doors of the Minster. His gaze was dragged up and up, and he felt his jaw dropping at the sheer scale of the building arising from the huddle of meaner buildings around it. He stood gawping until someone shoved him hard between the shoulder blades and sent him stumbling forward. "Get a move on, you great ox!" came the voice behind him. "Ain't got time to stand in your shadow all day."

Will swung round and glared at the man grinning up behind him. "Aye. Thought it was you, Fletcher. Well met!"

Will recognised the face immediately. "Captain Browne! Sir. This is good news. I am glad to see you here amongst this…" He struggled for the right word and gestured at the crowd of men milling around the streets and Minster.

"Rabble?" Browne frowned. "Yes. I have seen better. In fact, can't say I have seen much worse. Where have they dragged this collection of wastrels from? I have been 'ere a few days now and more keep comin' in from round the country, but the quality don't get better."

"Aye, Captain. And many have no weapons or equipment and them that 'as, don't know one end from the other. We're not goin' to scare them Covenanters into submission. That's for sure."

Browne nodded grimly, but then brightened. "Anyway, maybe we will find more of our former colleagues soon. I have

(York, March 1639)

command of a company which has a few good men in it and I would dearly love it if you would join us. Are you already attached elsewhere?"

"No, sir. I have just arrived and stored my arms in a billet not far from here. I were just exploring a little when you found me. 'Tis a marvellous thing." He nodded at the Minster looming over them both.

"Aye. It is that. A wonder. Something like that strengthens the faith when it is weak. A work like that can come only from God."

"Aye, Captain. But only with the sweat and labour of good men as well."

Browne smiled at him. "Indeed, Fletcher. And we both know about that. Where are you billeted? You must come and join our merry band. I need someone of your spread…" he stretched his arms out sideways from the shoulder, "…to scare the devil out of the useless sheep that I have to turn into soldiers. Let us go collect your gear."

Will's mood was considerably lighter having met Browne again. He was a good man. A godly man who would do all he could to preserve the lives of his men. And Will knew, there were precious few like Browne to be found in this army.

16

MARLEIGH HUME

(near Macclesfield, May 1639)

She glanced up from the streamside, peering through the trees to the bluff above her. She couldn't see the church tower but knew it was there. The sun, pleasantly warm, created small patches of wavering light on the grassy ground, always moving, as the breeze gently tugged at the leafy canopy. The Bollin gurgled behind her. Transformed from the pristine, crystal flow that rose in the Macclesfield Forest, it had become a befouled midden serving the town. Standing at its zenith, the sun illuminated numerous horrors floating slowly on their way to the good folk of Wilmslow, and then, with enhanced cargo, on to the Mersey and the Irish Sea.

Before long, her narrow path joined with the broader cart track that ran parallel to the river and, in another fifty paces, this in turn crossed a sturdy bridge, to become the long, exhausting, perilous road over the moors to Buxton. The cart track forked east to Buxton, north to the village of Tytherington and on to distant Manchester. To the west, her path reappeared, angling through thinning scrub to then wind back and forth up the side of the bluff towards the centre of

(near Macclesfield, May 1639)

the town. As she approached the first house, clinging to the steep ground, stone steps appeared, slippery with moss and algae, shielded from the desiccating power of the sun by the contours of the land and overhanging branches.

Stepping lightly, with hardly any quickness of breath from the climb, she rounded the final corner. The steps straightened, finding a passageway between tenements on the left, and a brick and stone building on her right. From the window above her head, becoming louder as the steps brought her ears level with its frame, she heard a rhythmic chanting. *"Pugno. Pugnas. Pugnat…"* Young male voices, perhaps between ten and twenty of them, led by an older, more mature voice.

"…Pugnamus. Pugnatis. Pugnant," she finished for them, smiling to herself. And then she was past the building, steps becoming a cobbled alley, and the rear of St Michael's loomed up in front of her. She hoisted her black shawl up around her shoulders, covering the back of her neck. Not because she was cold but for modesty, and to cover the brown, suntanned skin which would not be considered appropriate for a lady. Not that she was a lady; there was no escaping that. She might know more Latin, and Greek, than most ladies in the British Isles, but she knew better than to call any attention to it.

She came around the side of the old stone-built parish church. Stone from local quarries, dark and robust, coloured somewhere between brown and grey. It was market day, a triangle of commerce overlooked by the solid square tower of the church.

Macclesfield was a prosperous town, one of the largest in Cheshire. It lay on the eastern edge of the county, perched on the edge of the fertile plain that ran all the way to Chester in the west, to Wales, and the sea. The Chestergate ran arrow straight westwards from the marketplace, and was the site of shops, more tenements and an inn.

To the east of the town centre, the land fell steeply away,

down to the tree-filled valley of the Bollin, before rising quickly again to much greater heights, becoming the southern Pennines, the range of hills and high moors that cut the north country in half. She was in what was called the 'new town', being no more than 400 years old on this elevated site. The 'old town' lay slightly to the south, down the line of the Mill Street, past the old castle, now largely in ruins, to where the old manor house had stood and where the water mill still operated. This had also been a marketplace, situated where the Congleton Road met the road to Leek, but its popularity had waned as the new town developed.

The land fell away to the north as well, declining along the Jordangate, leaving the new town centre feeling like a last outpost of commerce, perched in the air, staring across at the wildness of the hills.

Stalls were set out in lines and ordered by produce. Livestock was at the northern end, rows of pens in front of the Guildhall and Royal Bakehouse, at the top of the Jordangate. It was mainly sheep from the common to the east, and fine fat cattle from the plain to the west and south. In the centre, vegetables and dairy products from the fertile western ploughland, and the southern end of the market, where the Mill Street left the marketplace for the descent down the long gradient to the water mill, objects in wood and metal, clothing, services such as shoe-mending, clothing repair and barbers.

The market was rammed with people. There were farmers, craftsmen and other trades. Well-to-do burgesses, with protective hands on their purses, children and wives – in that order of priority – pressed through the crowds of commonfolk. She wandered around the stalls, looking intently at the products on offer, but not catching any eye. She had been here before, but not with any purpose. Just passing through, or browsing for food items or materials for her seamstressing.

(near Macclesfield, May 1639)

From time to time, she glanced up at the sun, gauging the time, and keeping a careful watch on the church and the narrow streets which encompassed it. After a while she bought a cup of milk, warmed by the early afternoon temperature, and a slice of fresh bread, and sat in a small patch of shade at the southern end of the marketplace. None bothered here, being intent on their business and seeing that she had nothing to sell, or steal.

After a while she saw what she had been patiently waiting for. A line of boys, aged perhaps from seven or eight years old, up to around thirteen, made their way from behind the church, and the schoolhouse she had passed, into the marketplace. Some joined immediately with their families, all wealthy townsfolk, merchants, lawyers, local petty nobility. Others sat on the church steps, watching the crowd in front of them, pointing, laughing and occasionally throwing stones at some unfortunate passing too close.

This stopped abruptly when the tall figure of the priest appeared through the doors of the church, opening them wide and securing them with long metal hooks to rings set in the stone surround. In a long black cassock and broad-brimmed black hat, he was tall and imposing. She struggled to see his face, shaded as it was by the hat, but could tell from his movements and posture that he was no old man. He shooed the boys away, some going into the darkness of the church, others joining the crowd among the stalls. In their black gowns, she could see them here and there, chasing each other, laughing.

Sons of the rich and privileged, she thought. *Bestowed an education, by rote, in dead languages, based on a non-reality, featuring a non-existent deity, granted no knowledge of how things truly are. Superstitious, dry, dull, pointless.*

But not her concern. Not today. She needed to learn more about Master Priest because he was also their schoolmaster.

She needed supplies and what better place to obtain them than a school. The school was old, founded nearly 150 years ago – the Free Grammar School of Edward VI. *Good old King Edward!* And it had been on this site, School Bank, close to a hundred of those years. The great and the good of east Cheshire sent their boys here, and it was well endowed and would not miss a few scholarly items.

And she also needed money and a place to stay for a while. She was going to go travelling and needed to rest and stock up on essentials. So she watched Master Priest and Headmaster standing in the doorway of St Michael's and rehearsed her plan.

With school over for the day and the church doors opened, a number of people now made their way into the building. Many to pray, but also many to escape the warm sun and rest their legs sitting on the wooden benches. She followed them, keeping to the back corner. Always looking over her shoulder at the entrance. Always scanning the other people. Always alert.

The priest was kneeling at the front rail, a modest wooden barrier. He was scarcely visible in the dim light, made even darker by the strength of the late spring sunshine bouncing off the cobbles outside. She waited patiently. She watched him get up, busy himself with minor jobs around the interior of the church. Stacking prayer books. Adjusting benches. Replacing cushions in the choir.

He spoke to some of the parishioners, people he appeared to know well. She noticed he lingered longest with the more obviously affluent, adopting a humble attitude. Speaking quietly. His hat was gone and she could see him more clearly now. Unusually he wore his hair very short, but she could see that this was probably because he was losing it from a circular patch on top of his head. Although she put him at no more

(NEAR MACCLESFIELD, MAY 1639)

than thirty-five years old, he was already slightly grey of hair and his thin beard was speckled.

Inevitably he caught her eye once or twice – she had been kneeling now for nearly an hour – the second time with greater curiosity and a slightly raised eyebrow. But he didn't approach her. She thought he had an honest face, and could find no trace of malice, greed or zealotry which she found was so often present among the clergy. She thought he had a kindly face. She thought him not unattractive in an awkward, naïve way. This could make things very easy, or very difficult. Time would tell.

As the market wound down towards the end of the afternoon, the number of people in the church also reduced, until there were no more than ten including herself and the priest. Carefully, with minimum movement, she placed her hand into her leather bag at her knees and found the tied bunch of orange blossoms. She had liberated as many as she could carry from Fitton's pleasure garden of the Gawsworth Hall, and these were what remained. With a surprising strength, she crushed the delicate petals in her right hand, massaging the compressed mass into the palm with her thumb, extracting all the scented oil. Equally carefully, under the pretence of having dropped something to the floor, she bent behind the bench and rubbed her palm around her throat and carefully down the front of her waistcoat and petticoat, across her chest and under her armpits. She adjusted her coif, to make sure all her hair was modestly covered except for one tendril which artfully escaped confinement and curled down in front of her ear. Then she stood and made her way slowly down the aisle towards the altar rail.

The priest had just returned from a back room and was now alone, sitting on the front bench, apparently deep in thought. She stopped at the end of the aisle, just five paces from where he sat in reflection. Although her eyes were fixed to the front, she knew he would be detecting the aroma of the blossom. After the sweat of the boys, and the unwashed stink of the everyday commonfolk, she would be like a refreshing summer breeze to him. With long practice, she subtly bunched her long skirt between her thighs as she lowered herself to kneeling, knowing it would show the contours of her arse to best effect, but with no hint of an intent in the action. She bowed her head, and then affected annoyance at the tendril of hair, pushing it back under her cap. She closed her eyes and prayed quietly, but loud enough for him to hear her low voice.

When finished, she got up to go, but unaccountably her shoe slipped on the polished stone of the floor and she fell forward onto her hands with a small gasp. In a flurry of movement, he was on his feet. "Mistress! Are you alright?"

She looked back over her shoulder at him, at the outstretched hand to help her up, and deep into his grey eyes. She saw there what she was looking for. What she had hoped to see. "Oh, sir. My thanks! You are too kind." She looked up from under her lashes and she knew she had him.

*

Two days later, she returned to the marketplace.

She had been sleeping in a barn, little used now that the sheep had lambed and were out on the hills and common again. From the loft, she could see across the valley to the church, and with the prevailing wind coming from the southwest, could regularly hear the bells. She decided that two days was enough time for him to brood upon her, but not too long that she was consigned to memory as some aberration of faith.

She carried a small basket filled with late spring flowers as she retraced her path across the bridge over the Bollin and up

(near Macclesfield, May 1639)

to the steps below St Michael's. She timed her visit this time to catch him at the end of the afternoon. With no market, the area in front of the church was quiet. A few shoppers and tradesmen were wandering around as she slipped unobserved through the entrance into the dimness. Once her eyes adjusted to the gloom, she could see him to one side, lighting a series of candles.

She moved silently towards him and then coughed lightly when just a few paces away. He jumped in surprise, dropping the taper. "Oh! My pardon, sir! I didn't mean to startle you."

He knelt to pick up the taper and rose to face her. "Good afternoon, mistress." He bowed slightly, unusually, for she was clearly no more than commonfolk. "Ah! It is yourself. I hope that you are recovered from your fall?" He looked genuinely concerned.

"Aye, sir. I am well enough. My thanks to you. Here, I have brought you spring blooms for brightening the church. I am not so learned in church matters, but I hope flowers are an acceptable adornment?"

"They are God's creation. I am sure he is very pleased to have them in his house. You seem a little out of breath – will you sit?" He indicated the nearest bench.

"My thanks, sir. 'Tis all hills hereabouts. I just wanted to thank you for your kindness t'other day. I was tired, and my ankle just went from under me. Your kindness raised me up, it did."

"You are very welcome, Mistress…?" He paused, expecting a name in return.

Not yet. She looked down at her hands folded in her lap and then back up. She had conjured a small dampness in the corner of an eye. "Kindness is unexpected in these times, sir. A little goes a long way. I think you would have helped me whether you were a man of God, or not. God bless you, sir."

"Really, it was nothing. I am bound to help who I can, or what purpose am I serving here?"

"But, forgiving my boldness, sir, not all men of the Church would waste their time with commonfolk such as I. They are too enamoured of the glamour of the gentry. They do not have your goodness and fairness of heart." She had inched towards him so subtly he was suddenly surprised to see her thigh just a hands' width from his own on the bench. He smelled mint on her breath and suddenly felt a little lightheaded. And a little alarmed. Those eyes. He wondered how long he had been gazing into them. He knew he was aroused and quietly prayed this was not obvious under his clerical robes. She was silent and raising one eyebrow slightly in question. *Oh God, what has she just said?*

"Sorry! What were you saying? I... Er... Hmm."

"I was just asking about the school, sir. The school behind the church?"

He broke her gaze to look in the direction of the school. Thank God. A distraction. Getting things back under control. Breathe... "Ah yes. 'Tis my joy to educate these young men. We are so lucky to have such a school in the town. So many supporters. So many great families trust us with their sons."

Silence. She was just looking at him. "Erm. To be honest that is my main task here. I am headmaster, you see. On church matters I only assist. The priest of the parish, Master Ralph Stringer, is away in Chester at present. He returns shortly. I am sorry, mistress. What is your interest in the school?"

She looked up again. More dampness around the eyes. It was as much as he could do to not reach out and wipe away the moisture.

"Well, sir. I am not sure how best to approach this. I am in difficult circumstances. I am left on my own and need a fresh start. My husband has been gone these five years. At war on the continent. I fear he is dead, but there is no word. His

(near Macclesfield, May 1639)

family were never favoured towards me, and I now find myself without roof or bed."

She paused. *Not too much*, she thought. She heaved a deep breath and "But I am no beggar, sir. I want no charity. I prayed a long time here, not two days ago. As you saw. And I think God provided me with an answer." *Here is the crisis.* "I would ask about a position here, sir. I wonder if the school has a housekeeper? Someone to clean. To order the books and look after the materials? And you, sir? Do you have someone to mind your lodgings?"

He looked somewhere between horrified and eager. *This could go either way.* "And maybe, sir, I can help in other ways." She let him ponder that for a moment, letting him imagine exactly how she might help in other ways. "What I mean, sir, is that…" she dropped her voice to a whisper, "…I have some education myself and could perhaps assist you somehow."

Relief flooded across his face. He was so readable, like so many. So many. The thought of what she might have been proposing now made her actual admission seem banal, not the slightly shocking and highly curious statement it would have been in other circumstances.

"You, er… An education, you say? That's er… unusual in someone such as… er… What I mean is…"

"My father was a teacher, sir. He taught at a school not unlike this one. In Derbyshire, sir. I can read and write. I even have a little Latin. And I know a lot about the natural world, sir. Of plants and such."

He was fully recovered but now clearly uncertain about her story. "I am sorry, Mistress…?"

"Hume, sir. Mistress Marleigh Hume."

"An unusual name. 'Marleigh', that is."

"My mother's choice, sir. Been in the family for generations, she said." *Oh yes.* "You were saying?"

"I am not sure, Mistress Hume. It would be an unusual arrangement. I am not sure our patrons and the governors would approve."

"Yes, sir. I understand, but the teaching would just be an option. 'Tis not unusual to have a school cleaned? Any teaching work could be discussed later."

"Well. It is the case that our usual housekeeper is not currently available. She is elderly and has not been well the last week. The place needs some work." But he seemed unconvinced. "But what about your parents? I am sorry about your husband, but could they not take you in?"

"They are dead, sir. Both taken with sickness some years past. 'Tis hard for a woman alone. But, perhaps we could just try for a week or so, whilst your usual housekeeper recovers her strength?"

He stared at her for a while. A small vein throbbed at this temple. "Well, so be it, Mistress Hume. Let us start with a week and we can then discuss it with Master Stringer when he returns. Do you have lodgings?"

"Well, sir, I have been making do these last weeks, but I would be happy to sleep above the school if there is space? My needs are few."

"That is where I live, I'm afraid, and there is insufficient room for more. But I know of a place where you could lodge. 'Tis but a single room, but your pay would cover it. Not much to spare beyond that, mind you."

"Oh, sir! 'Tis more than I could have hoped for. I think 'tis God's will that brought my feet up that hill behind the church." She grabbed his hand in hers and kissed the back of it. "God bless you!"

"'Tis but temporary. Please do not forget that Mistress Hume. And let us hear no more about teaching. It is a cleaning and housekeeping post only. A woman teaching the

(NEAR MACCLESFIELD, MAY 1639)

sons of such eminent men would be unseemly. And 'tis my own task."

"I understand." She beamed at him, and he felt strangely warmed and uplifted, but just a slight nagging thought persisted at the back of his mind. A small shadow of misgiving in the blaze of her smile. "When shall I start?"

"Now?"

A shame that she had the job only at the expense of another, but people did get sick, especially the elderly. She would pray for the woman's recovery.

17

BRERETON

(Handforth Hall, North-West England, July 1639)

He sat in the garden in the early evening. The sun, tending to deepen its colour to ochre, was still warm, and cast long shadows from the oak and hornbeam trees that marked the boundary. It backlit the rose bed, turning flowerheads into miniature lamps and turning waving grass into golden flags, fluttering in the light breeze. William thought it a perfect temperature, soothing his bones, warming the skin of his face and the low-angled light compelling him to close his eyes from time to time, to give him relief him squinting.

It will not be long before I am asleep, he thought, and that notion did not seem such a bad one. The sun was slowly progressing on its downward arc and was now navigating the gap between two particularly large oaks. He had perhaps another fifteen minutes before it fell behind the heavy foliage and the bench where he rested would be in shadow. *What a metaphor for our times.*

He wondered how long the shaky truce the King had struck with the Covenanters would hold. A messy standoff at Berwick

(Handforth Hall, North-West England, July 1639)

had resulted in the 'pacification', a nothing agreement which covered the King's embarrassment at the inferior quality of his men and arms, and the Scots' reluctance to take the final military step against their monarch, for all their bluster and parading up and down. A few skirmishes between Scots loyal to the King and Covenanters, and a few lively rides through English border towns had been about it. No one wanted to take the fateful step to all-out war. But William thought it inevitable.

He knew now he had been naïve in thinking he could 'buy-off' Lord Strange, Lord Lieutenant of Cheshire with his hunting invitation, but bizarrely it had played out to his advantage in the end. The correspondence had wandered off into a dispute with Strange's agents regarding Brereton's duck decoy of all things, and by the time this had been rather acrimoniously resolved, what had become known as the 'Bishops' War' with the Covenanters had finished.

The more he heard about events in the capital, and the negotiations with the leaders of the Scots, the more he was convinced that further conflict was coming. The King was delaying, so he could boost his strength in arms and men, and continue their hasty training, and the Scots would soon realise the real power they had. The superiority of their generals, hardened in the continental wars, was evident, but more importantly, so was the superiority of their faith.

He admired their convictions and their commitment to their Presbyterianism. It mirrored so much his own views. He considered himself godly. It was his bedrock. His centre. The window through which he observed events.

It had not always been this way. Earlier, in his teenage years, he had of course believed, but it was a reactive faith. An instructed faith. It had not really impacted on what he actually did, other than the compulsory church attendance. But as the years had passed, he had found himself searching for his life.

He had looked to politics and had stood for Parliament as one of the two county members for Cheshire, but he had lost out to Peter Daniell of Over Tabley. He had felt the palpable excitement in the county at that vote, certainly more than the usual indifference, and so the disappointment had hit him hard and he had circled down into a melancholic state, almost an illness. He had then belatedly looked to God to help him in his endeavours, but God had not shone his light upon him. There was nothing to warm his soul in his feeling of emptiness. His wife had despaired for him. She thought him permanently broken.

But almost like the breaking of a fever, in the dark hour before his dawn, he had felt the unmistakable presence of Jesus Christ in his mind. He thought of it like a beam of white light suddenly entering a black room through a keyhole. A keyhole in a door that he had previously never even seen. He had let that light play across himself, crouched miserably in that dark mental cell, and then followed it until he beheld the door handle. Quietly. Calmly. Without fear, he had opened the door and finally stood in the blinding presence of God. A power had swept through him. A clarity of vision, and with it, a clarity of purpose. He recognised it now for what it was. He had read about this moment. He had heard powerful words from the pulpit to instruct him on its significance. He felt certain that he had been chosen for a specific task. A task that would be revealed in due course. He was now one of the Elect.

He looked back now on this rebirth, as he thought it, and smiled to himself. The wrestling with his conscience over his attitude to the King earlier in the year had been stilled. Now he knew the right of it. The direction he must take. Many of his peers around him in this county were feeling the same way. Prominent families such as that of his deceased first wife, Susannah, the Booths of Dunham Massey, but also the

Mainwarings, the Wilbrahams, the Delves and Ardernes. All perceiving the haze of popery that surrounded the King and his advisers, and particularly the Queen. All mistrusting of Archbishop Laud and his support for Arminianism. The campaign that the Bishop of Chester, and good friend of Laud, John Bridgeman, was waging against those of the true religion, who were now called Puritans. There was a rising tide behind him and he felt, for the first time in years, a cautious optimism that change was possible.

He had gone on to win election to Parliament in 1628, but this had hardly lasted any time before the King's high-handed dismissal of the House, and the start of his personal rule. And then the dark days of the persecution of those Divines who spoke the true word. Intimidation of preachers in parishes across the county – around Nantwich and Chester – and the harassment of the university clergy of the collegiate church of Manchester.

He had witnessed the journey of William Prynne through the county on his way to life imprisonment in Caernarvon Castle. The best men of Chester had ridden out to meet him and had invited him to their homes to sup and talk. Prynne was already a martyr to the religion, having had his ears cropped for speaking out against Laud's crusade. Bishop Bridgeman had had his revenge on some of his supporters, issuing fines and forcing recantations in the cathedral. *But at least Prynne had known he was loved and supported.*

He had also seen the charismatic Thomas Paget driven from England to seek refuge in Amsterdam. He had there taken over the running of the English Church in that fair city, almost at the moment that his brother John had laid down that burden and gone to God.

That was two years ago now. He had dined with John Paget during his own visit to the Low Countries a few years before that. He could still taste the fantastic strawberries Paget had served in that balmy June – the largest he had seen. And he had seen a freedom to worship as one pleased. He had seen different faiths co-existing peacefully. No man persecuted or scoffed at, no matter how zealous he appeared in his faith. Fierce debates to be sure, but no violence. No burning. No torture. No inquisition. Even Jews and Catholics were accommodated. In fact, he had encountered an English husband and wife who, desperate to make their fortune in the city, had converted to Judaism purely to access the incredibly rich trading circles that the Jews controlled. He shuddered at that memory – to compromise one's faith for riches. *Obnoxious couple!*

His memories of the conversation with John also brought to mind the highlight of his trip. One of Paget's supporters was none other than Elizabeth of Bohemia, the so-called 'Winter Queen' thus named on account of husband, Frederick V, the Elector of Palatine, only reigning for one season in Bohemia before being defeated by the Holy Roman Emperor. William had met Elizabeth in The Hague after a dinner with the war hero George Goring, who, at that time, was garrisoned nearby. *Boiled beef*, he remembered, *and some kind of suet pudding*.

A few days after the dinner, Lady Goring had taken him to a function where he was placed next to Elizabeth. She seemed very different to her younger brother, Charles Stuart. Approachable, down-to-earth, full of gossip and desperate for news from England, although this was not in short supply given the number of English travelling through the provinces.

On his bench, his eyes closed, his smile faded. The sun too now slid behind the oak, and the cool touch of shadow chilled him. He recalled the strange conversation he had shared with her. She had seemed obsessed with the supernatural world and had quizzed him about the Lancashire witch trial years before, around the village of Pendle. In turn, she had told him

(Handforth Hall, North-West England, July 1639)

of a village in Westphalia where *all* the inhabitants had been found to be witches and they had all been righteously burnt. She told him of an incident in Berlin where, at a dinner just such as this one, a woman had stabbed herself repeatedly in the leg, convinced that a demon was under her dress.

He had found himself discussing an equally uncomfortable event from his stay in Delft. He had been introduced to the daughter of a prince of Portugal who was living in a convent house. He had been told she was possessed of a demon. They talked for several hours, he curious to learn more of this condition. She became very distressed during the meeting and in the end he had to leave her. The following day her maid, English as it turned out, informed him that the possessed lady had told her of her dream that night. The Devil had appeared to her and told her that William was his witch. That William had come to take her to Satan, and the Devil would then take her to God. The Winter Queen had not laughed, as he had expected, but had looked at him in a thoughtful way, and that had unnerved him even more than the event itself.

He shivered slightly in the cooling evening air. The breeze had now picked up a little and he must guard against a chill. He had not thought about that conversation for a long time, and he was not sure if it was the temperature, or the warning he sensed, like a tolling bell, at the connection between this and his chance meeting with Mistress Hume. Was this some kind of test for him? Was he being nudged to go down a certain path? If so, the way was overgrown with doubts and uncertainty, and he knew not where to place his feet to start the journey. He admonished himself that her face came into his mind as often as Susannah's. His dear Susannah, dead now these three years. He knew not why God had decided it was time for her to go to Him, but he took comfort that she would be waiting for him.

His eyes were open now, and for a while he stared blankly at a sky slowly turning to gold above the trees, down to the colour of blood at the horizon.

He heard his valet announce the serving of his meal from the hallway and he shook himself back to life. His son Thomas, now eight years old, came running through the garden waving a wooden sword, also having heard the call. He stood, stretched the stiffness from his legs and back, and headed for the rear door, following his son. He passed the bed full of tulip bulbs, flowers now long finished. *Bought on his trip* from the Prince of Orange's own gardener! Reality reasserted itself. *William, he allowed himself a satisfied smile, you are worrying about nothing!* He looked proudly around his garden. *Witches are a fantasy to scare children and the commonfolk; you have enough in this life to consider without indulging in this foolishness.*

18

RICHARD FARRELL

(Amsterdam, August 1639)

All the doors and windows were open in an attempt to get a little relief from the stifling heat of summer. After several days of rain, the sun had come out hot, and the atmosphere was humid and oppressive. But Richard cared little. He was sitting in the small courtyard behind the tavern, mug of ale on the trestle table. Bright sunshine picked out small plants that had found some purchase in the gutters, on the windowsills and in cracks in the wood framing, but he and Neelie and Roger were cooling in the deep shade of the tavern eaves.

He felt good. He could quite easily have shut his eyes and drifted off to sleep, lulled by the ale, the task of digesting a particularly dense plate of Klaas's fare, and the rather half-hearted "uh, uh, ah, ah" coming from one of the upstairs open windows. It really was not the weather for that kind of activity, but there was never a shortage of enthusiasts at the Sailor. But the main reason he felt good was that he no longer resided in one of those upstairs rooms.

After their first job for the Marcelis brothers, they had found themselves extraordinarily busy. Hudde had been impressed by Richard's exploits, and while he had some initial concerns about the unconscious, trussed-up Montague, he had evidently been pleased at the humanity Richard had shown in trying to protect the two Dutch farmers. Though wary of the English agent, he did not like the idea of a foreigner assassinating two of his countrymen. If a helpless Dutchman needed murdering in cold blood, by God, he would do it himself! But Montague, it seemed, had been willing to forgive what he called Richard's 'youthful, if misguided impetuosity' and, as the precious shipment had not been disrupted, had gone on his way without a backward glance. He had accompanied the consolidated arms shipment back to London and, according to Hudde, had not been seen in Amsterdam again. So far at least.

The arms business was booming, and he and Roger had been in demand. They had carried out trip after trip, and more recently this had taken them out of the Low Countries, to Hamburg, Copenhagen and even to the foundries of the great trader De Geer in Sweden. Shipments of iron and brass cannon, powder and match, shot and ball, musket and blade were all pouring across the continent to the hub that was Amsterdam. Stored, tested, counted, consolidated and shipped. Amsterdam was frenetic, and it was not unusual to see hundreds of merchantmen, ships of war, river barges, barques and old holks pass through the harbour in a single day. A growing proportion of these carried the materiel of war, bound for Scotland, England, Ireland, France, Spain, Portugal and the New World, as well as the growing number of colonies founded or captured by the Dutch East India Company.

Richard was building a good relationship with Hudde and was picking up Dutch quickly, his young mind absorbing new words and phrases much faster than Roger, who seemed content to let Richard translate, and weigh in with a few choice profanities when needed. They were trusted and popular with their Dutch colleagues, working hard and reaping a good reward. The value at risk in the shipments was huge, and while their role seldom called for actual armed intervention, Hudde did not underestimate the deterrence factor, and paid them well. Richard had also come to terms, at least partially, with his hatred of sea travel, and his sickness was now restricted to the roughest of seas only.

Only once had they felt truly threatened and there had been the need for a skirmish. Coming through Germany, they had been menaced by a gang of men, almost starving farmers and labourers driven off their lands by war and unable to reclaim them. With hungry families to support, hiding in the dense forests they had seen the train of wagons winding through the trees on rutted tracks as a last desperate opportunity to survive. They had been obliged to fire on the mob, and Richard had ridden his mount into a knot of emaciated bodies to drive them from the cargo. Only when several had been killed or injured did the men draw off, some sobbing, some begging, all wretched at their wits' end. In the end, they had thrown them some of their own supplies of food in sympathy, and this, with the carcass of one of the cart horses that had been hit with a musket ball in the attack, would perhaps see them through a few more weeks of agony.

Most of all, Richard treasured the change in Neelie. With the good money he was earning, they had rented rooms right at the top of a nearby townhouse. She had said farewell to her previous occupation, and was healthy, happy and adding flesh over her skinny body. Her dark eyes sparkled with joy, and although she missed him terribly while he was away, fretting after his safety and imagining dalliances with ladies of loose morals in foreign parts, he could see that she was utterly content. It was a heavy weight from his shoulders to see her so blissful. He had dreaded coming back to find her the victim of a violent customer, a fate some of her colleagues had succumbed to, or sick with the pox, the most voracious killer of whores.

He leant back, looking at her through half-closed eyes. She had plucked a long feather from Roger's new hat and was using it to tickle the end of his nose and chin, experimenting to see how much she could torment him before he fully woke up. He thought her the most beautiful thing on earth, even though his travels had opened his eyes to the wider world, and the expensive uniform of the Marcelis brothers had made him and Roger a prime target for working girls. It only took a glance from those intense blue eyes, peering at him through her raven curls, for him to lose himself completely. She could ask him for anything and he would gladly give it. He loved her. Deeply. Achingly so. All thoughts of his family and return to England were locked away, and he had never felt so happy.

Roger, far from being disturbed by a feather being jammed up his nose, was now quietly snoring. He had consumed twice the ale that Richard had managed and would probably now sleep until sunset. Neelie had given up trying to tease him awake and looked over at Richard. She saw him studying her and smiled back bashfully.

She tucked her curls behind an ear and slid from her chair to come and sit on his knee. He turned to look into her eyes and she stroked his damaged left cheek. The compacted bone had healed well enough, but in combination with his broken nose, lent that side of his face a harder aspect than the still-boyish right side. Ironically, when he was away, she pictured his battered side when thinking about the mature, loving, kind, fairness-loving side of his personality, and his smooth, unblemished, teenage-fresh side with his frivolous nature and his quick, sometimes irrational, temper.

(Amsterdam, August 1639)

For her part, she felt she was living a dream. From less than a year ago, when she was a homeless orphan, surviving only by selling her fifteen-year-old body to fat, drunk merchants, or stinking sailors straight from six months at sea, to living with this handsome man-boy, with a good job and the money and skills to look after her. She loved him. She loved him. She loved him.

She put her arms around his neck and her head on his shoulder, and they fell asleep together in the shaded courtyard. No cloud trespassed across the deep blue of the sky. No black sail climbed menacingly over the horizon. No warning whispers slithered into their blissful thoughts.

19

MARLEIGH

(Macclesfield, September 1639)

There was just a straw-mattressed bed and a small oak table, with jug and bowl for washing, a chair and a chamber pot. But it would do very well. The room was a tiny garret, perched on the top of a tenement, just to the south of the church. Its single window looked east to the hills. A single irregular pane of glass distorted the view, but she liked the effect, particularly in the evening when the setting sun bathed the hillsides in gold. Heather, gorse and bracken quilted across the now-yellowing grass of late summer creating an image which shifted as the wind moved the glass in the frame, clouds created sweeping areas of light and shade, and the changing angle of the sun shifted hues from yellows, to oranges, to reds and through deepest purple to black.

But on glorious summer days it also felt a little like a prison. She wanted to be out walking in the hills and cloughs, to be on the rocks, to have her feet in the icy crystal streams tumbling over pebbles, in the verdant grass and late summer flowers by her pool. It was like a physical ache in her limbs.

(Macclesfield, September 1639)

A need to stretch her stride along the paths, exercise muscles which were starting to forget their purpose. The housekeeping could be a grind, but it was easy for her. Master Bolde – now she called him 'Master Thomas' – did not push her.

Old Ma Massey had not recovered from her sickness and had passed away. A surprisingly large number of people had turned up for the funeral, including some school old boys and two of the governors. She had stood with the group around the grave, looking serious and sad. Inside she felt very little. Why would she? She had no attachment to the woman. They had only met the once, about a week before she had first met Master Thomas. She laid a small posey by the wooden board they left as a headstone. She thought that a nice touch, and she made very sure Master Thomas and Father Stringer had seen her place it. Stringer was nice enough and seemed content to let Master Thomas take the lead. He focused on prayer, and study in the afternoons. She had been housekeeping now for over three months.

She needed the room, particularly thinking ahead to the winter. Needed the money. But more importantly she needed access to the resources of the school. By 'access', she meant 'opportunity to steal'. She sat now, table pulled up to the window, sketching out her thoughts on the sheaf of paper. Drawing circles and lines, arrows and boxes. Crossing out in frustration. Trying to connect her ideas. Trying to balance. Trying to understand how it all fitted.

The quill lay on the oak top. Her head down, balanced at the temples between two fingers of each hand. Squinting at her scribbles, forehead crumpled in concentration.

The sun. She knew this was near the heart of it all. She had read Galileo and Copernicus. She knew they were right, no matter what the Vatican decreed. Our world and the other planets revolve around the sun. The sun is the key to all life.

Light and warmth. Without warmth the plants could not grow. In winter, most lost their leaves, or certainly stopped growing. Only with the oncoming spring did life recommence. She knew. She had observed. She had measured. This was right. But then all farmers knew this.

Warmth was important, but light was essential. Without light, plants died. Put a plant in darkness and it would strain, and grow pale and sick, tortured, striving for light. For life. She wondered if they felt pain in the dark. If they felt tormented?

But not people, or animals. She had seen men emerge from mines after days in the dark. Released from prisons so deep the only light came from occasional candles. They survived. Children continued to grow. Somehow plants and animals were nourished differently.

Both needed water. Deprive a man of water he will not last long. Madness and sickness before a horrible death. She had seen it. Plants the same, but no words to express their agonies.

Plants 'fed' on sunshine, somehow taking light and using it in their tissues. Growing more of themselves. Her best visualisation was a water mill. The strength of the water in the mill race turned the wheel. The wheel drove cogs and wheels which turned the massive millstones, turning grain to flour to make the bread that fed the village. The power of the water was the key. Somehow, she felt sure, sunlight worked the same as the water driving a mill wheel. It drove some kind of process that turned rain, and the rich soil into which the plant stuck its roots, into more plant material. Light was the power that drove all of this. Light from the sun.

Man and animals ate plants, or ate other animals, which ate other animals, which ate plants. Plants were at the base of this pyramid. She had observed this. She had mapped it. She had studied it in forests, on moorlands, by the sea, in gardens.

(MACCLESFIELD, SEPTEMBER 1639)

Creatures with two legs, four legs, six, eight and more. The power that comes from the sun flows through these chains of creatures, the root of everything that lives.

But cut open a plant, an animal, a man, and there were no wheels, no cogs and certainly no trace of that light. She had watched people, animals, at the point of their death. Studied it closely, peering into glassy eyes, feeling flesh going cold. Somehow a light, a warmth, was leaving them. But how? Why? And to where does it go? A dying man released tremendous power, all that energy accumulated over a lifetime. She knew this. Had tasted it. *Used* it. But never understanding how.

But now the light in her room was fading and there was no candle left.

She needed more time. More observations. More measurements. But most of all she needed enlightenment. She needed to share her thoughts and ideas, her theories, but there was no one to share them with. The familiar problem…

*

She looked down from her window onto the sloping roof. A few yards below, trapped in the angle formed by a broken tile, a dead blackbird lay on its back. It looked at her mournfully with an eyeless socket. The flesh had receded from around the beak and there was a glimpse of grey bone. The flies and the ants had found it some time ago, and most of the body was a seething, crawling mass of small bodies.

Death to life to death to life.

Life was the organising force. Life brought structure and order. By living, not just existing, a tree could take air, water, soil – all things with little purpose or structure – and turn them into trunk, branches, twigs and leaves. To fruit, nuts and berries. To flowers.

A cow could take grass and water, and create muscle, bones, blood. It could provide milk to feed its young and a family of people. Unordered chaos, to structured form, sculpted by 'life'.

When life was over, the tree, the cow did not remain intact. Slowly, it disintegrated as time passed. It did not stay frozen in the state in which it died. Something was removed at death. Something that held all those pieces – the flesh, the wood, the blood, the sap – together had gone. Without it, the body slowly disappeared, merging back into the rest of nature. Eaten and defecated, dried and blown away, dissolved and washed away in the rain. Gone. Indistinguishable from the rest of nature.

She had seen human bodies at all stages after death. Eventually there was just dust, blowing away in the wind. Enriching the soil, creating more life in turn. A cycle. From dust to dust. The body given back to the earth at death, just bits and pieces to be reused. Sculpted form back to unordered chaos. But what happened to the life? The force that animated the flesh? Where did it go, and where did it come from? The Church had nothing to offer on this. She had investigated the idea of souls, or spirits, as the animator of life, but these were not answers. Nothing that convinced her.

Recently, Master Bolde had received a letter from his father, Thomas Bolde Senior, who lived in Lancaster. His brother William, young Thomas's uncle, was ill and may not survive his illness. Bolde Senior encouraged Bolde Junior to visit his uncle to ensure he could partake of God's word before the end, and to ease his passing. Uncle William lived in Knutsford, a short journey only. Young Master Bolde had asked her to accompany him on the journey as Uncle William had long lived alone and he feared what state his house might be in if his uncle had been in his bed for some time. She was to clean the place and cook for them all if his departure proved to be an extended time.

(Macclesfield, September 1639)

In all events, it had been a diverting trip. They had arrived by coach in Knutsford just in time to witness a hanging. As they arrived at one side of the town square, the hanging cart was moving away, leaving the condemned swinging on a rope. No swift death, as the fall from the cart did not break his neck, and there were none to pull on his legs. The sizeable crowd were hushed. No cheering or shouting, almost complete silence, so that she could hear the sounds of choking and the creaking of the rope from her vantage on the steps of the coach. The man was bagged and so she could not see his face, but she clearly *felt* the moment of his death, like a warm breeze spreading out like a ripple from the gibbet.

Uncle William was almost dead when they arrived, having had to push their way through the hanging crowd to reach his door. If he had been so inclined, Uncle William would have had the best seat in the house for the execution, but he was preoccupied with his own demise. Fighting for breath, he lay on his bed, eyes closed, the rasping in his throat gradually slowing, longer and longer pauses with each inhalation. Thomas Bolde knelt at the bedside, holding his uncle's grey mottled hand, praying quietly.

The room was well aired and tidy. In fact, the house was well kept throughout, and they had encountered a neighbour, a stout middle-aged woman, who had let them in, ushered them upstairs and made it clear that it was she who had been cleaning, and looking after Uncle William. The inference was that some reward was due, but she was too excited by the hanging to stand and claim it now. Far better it seemed to witness the violent death of a stranger than the peaceful passing of a neighbour and old friend.

So she sat and watched the old man die. His breaths came less and less frequently. The gaps between them longer and longer, and each effort more laboured. She resorted to counting the space between inhalations, with the low mumbling of Bolde's prayers as a background. Each time she passed a count of ten, she thought the last breath had been taken. But just as she thought his time was up, another rasping gasp signalled the struggle continued. She could feel, she could *see*, the remnants of his life leaking imperceptibly from his body. She wondered how long this had been so.

Uncle William's face was grey. His eyes closed. Finally, there was one more long exhalation. A sigh of termination. "He has gone." Father Bolde rose from his knees and stretched his back. He seemed to suddenly remember her presence. "I am sorry, my dear. I hope that was not distressing for you?"

"No, sir. I have beheld death many times. His end was peaceful, it seemed. Unlike the man dangling in the square."

He looked at her sharply. "There is no comparison. My uncle led a godly life." More gently, "We must see to the arrangements. The weather is warm and we do not want to delay proceedings unnecessarily. Please, mistress, would you step outside and ask for the local priest and enquire if Knutsford has an undertaker. I think we will need to remain here now for a few days, until after the funeral and the reading of the Will."

Two days later, they were back in the carriage, heading back to Macclesfield. The funeral had passed off smoothly and Thomas Bolde was quietly pleased at the outcome of the Will. Uncle William had died with no heirs, which was why Thomas Bolde Senior had been so keen to ensure his son attended the dying man.

They had stayed in the house, Bolde requiring her to take the room of the now-dismissed maid. She saw an opportunity for questions now that he was trapped in the carriage with her for the next few hours.

"Father?"

(MACCLESFIELD, SEPTEMBER 1639)

"Yes, mistress?" He looked up from his book.

"I don't often have a chance to ask about these things. You know, to have a priest all to myself. I... I have some questions. I want to learn more so I can strengthen my faith. May I ask you some things?"

"By all means. I hope I can help you." He shut his book and smiled encouragingly.

She beamed her thanks at him and he felt like a small sun had found its way into the carriage. He basked a while in its warmth. "When your uncle passed over, you said, 'He has gone.' What did you mean? He stopped 'is breathin', and 'is life were over. But his body were there."

He smiled back, slightly reprovingly. "Mistress. I know you are not educated, but you know about our immortal souls, I am sure. Uncle William's body is dead, but his immortal soul lives on. With our prayers, and his godly life, I sincerely hope and believe that his soul is now with God."

"Yes, Father. I know of the soul, but I confess I do not really understand what it is. What is it made of? Where is my soul now? In my heart? In my head?"

He pursed his lips. "Well. It is true that some of the things you ask are not known precisely. Your soul is the essence of you. It is what makes you, you, and not someone else. It is given by God and is your thoughts, your feelings, your emotions. It is your immortal soul that makes decisions on how you behave, not your earthly body. That is why it is your soul that stands waiting for judgement, not your flesh."

"Yes, I see." She nodded. "Is our soul made of light? Like what comes from the sun? Like what helps the crops to grow?"

"Well, I don't know if anyone knows what it is actually made of. People talk of God being the light of the world, and our souls come from God, so perhaps there is a connection. But that may just be words."

"Yes, I see." *That is quite interesting. I wonder why I have not heard that before. But let's press on...* "But words are important, aren't they, Father? You said, Father, that it is the soul that makes our decisions. If I choose to steal, or to do a murder, that is my soul that chooses?"

"That's right."

"What about if I just choose to visit my neighbour, you know, as a charitable act?"

"Yes, that is a choice that would please God and help your soul to gain heaven."

"And I s'pose if I choose to have a potato, rather than bread? Or if I have decide to walk to the school from the south or from the north of the church, it is my soul that makes the choice?"

"Er, yes. I suppose so. I am not sure where your questions are taking us?" He showed the slightest sign of irritation.

"Oh no! You are being so very helpful, Father. So, to take a decision, my soul must be able to see the world round me, to 'ear what people say to me." Bolde nodded, looking increasingly uncomfortable. "So, for a blinded person, or for them as can't hear at all, their souls must have been damaged too. What I don't understand is, if the soul is immortal, how can it be damaged in this world?"

He just looked at her.

She ploughed on. "I knew a man once. A friend of my father. 'E were a lovely man. Kind, looked after 'is family, doin' good turns for us and lots of others. Then one day, 'e's crossin' the street and gets run down by a runaway 'orse. Knocked 'im flat on his face. Cracked 'is skull open at the front, just 'ere." She indicated her forehead, above her left eye. "We all thought him dead, but no, he were stitched up and got better. Well, we all thought 'e were better. Wasn't ill or nothin', but it were like he were a different man – hitting 'is wife 'n' kids, and cursing.

(Macclesfield, September 1639)

One minute he were calm, the next he was coming after yer with a bottle!"

"Goodness!" exclaimed Bolde. "What happened to the poor wretch?"

"Well, they didn't know what to do with him, so they 'ung 'im."

"Goodness! They hanged him?"

"Seemed like the best thing for everyone in the end. He didn't seem to mind."

"Goodness!"

"I don't know about goodness, Father, but it were a lot quieter around the village. But the point of my story, Father…" and she looked intensely at him across the carriage, "…is that he were a different person after the accident. 'E made different, y'know… choices. I don't understand how a cracked skull could change an immortal soul, which is not of 'is flesh, but ethereal-like, as you said."

He stared at her, his mind a blank. He had matriculated from Brasenose College, Oxford, studied alongside some of the most learned men of his day. He had no answer. "Well," he said eventually, "we cannot hope to understand the mind of God and all his creation. I hope the poor man found peace and was reconciled finally with God."

He peered out of the window. *How far is it to Macclesfield now?!* His worry had been how he would be able to compose himself this close to her for a period of hours and days. Wanting her company, her closeness, but knowing it was a test from God. A tantalising temptation. He had thought her a very beautiful, but a very simple, creature. Now he was inwardly horrified and could not wait to escape.

"Don't worry, Father, we ain't even got to Chelford yet. There's plenty of time to continue our chatting. I wanted to ask you about some other things too. I heard that there is some great argument amongst some Christians. Some who believe that God has already decided, even before we are born, which souls are destined for 'eaven, and which are going to… the other place. But there are others who say that we 'ave a choice – like we was just discussin' – but God already knows which place we will end up, even though we don't. What do you think, Father?"

Ah. He thought. *Doctrine. I am on much firmer ground here.* "Well, mistress. I follow the instruction passed down from Archbishop Laud himself. We firmly believe that you have a choice, right up to the very end. God knows everything; it is what we call omnipotence, a big word, I know…" he smiled at her, confidence building again, "…and so He must know whether each of us, our souls, will ultimately decide to accept His grace or not. But He has not predetermined it."

"So, our soul is given to us by God?" Again, that intensity. Bolde nodded. *Every time she asks a question I get agitated. My heart is pounding like I have run up the bell tower! But is it fear of not knowing the answer, or is it what I hope to see in the depths of her eyes. God have mercy upon me…*

"So God gives an immortal soul to people he already knows will turn away from 'im and will burn in 'ell forever? Are you saying that some people are born just to burn? Not sure I see the reasonin.'"

He banged on the roof of the carriage. "Stop, driver! I need to relieve myself. Stop, man!" *I am just going to get out and keep on walking…*

20

MARLEIGH

(Staffordshire moors, October 1639)

She sat with her back to the gritstone, looking down on the purple heather glowing in the golden light of the late sun. She had not been back here for too long, but this sight, and the peace of the autumn evening, had revitalised her. A skylark exulted somewhere above and behind her, a sound she always associated with these moors. Her country. The stands of birch fluttered their yellow leaves against the sun, white trunks darkening in silhouette.

She had finally persuaded Father Thomas to return to the carriage and she had left him in peace the rest of the journey. He seemed wary of her now. She had known, of course, of his feelings for her. Had orchestrated it; it was a simple composition. She had seen the slightly desperate edge to his previous attention. Her questioning of the tenets of his faith had now made him think of her as more than a potentially available, simple, common woman. Now there was also an air of mystery, of uncertainty about her. There was a little more distance which she felt he was more comfortable with.

He had provided no new insights for her, although she

hadn't really expected anything. She had had this conversation with numerous men of religion – always men of course – and nothing rational ever survived beyond a few probing questions. These people were always... disappointing.

However, this idea of the soul as light was interesting, but she couldn't fit the idea of it being God-given into her patterns. This suggested it was a one-time 'gift' somehow 'inserted' into the body at the start of life. In fact, it *was* the start of life. But at what point? At the instant that the child was conceived? At the point of birth? This seemed unlikely. She had heard it said that souls pre-existed their physical body, and then, after the body died, returned to their ethereal state to be judged by God. This seemed a pointless exercise. Why judge a soul only after it had been in a body? If the soul was the thing that felt emotion – love, hate, sympathy, disdain – and made the moral judgements, what was the purpose of attaching it to flesh? Why create the whole physical world of flesh, rock, fire and water, to judge souls that were not of this world in any case? No. It made no sense.

A soul, in the religious sense, was not what she could *see*. What she saw was something more real, more... mechanical. It was something that could be replenished, because it was constantly expended in some way to power the body. Like a river refilling a mill pond, to replenish the water lost in driving the wheel. Life, or the 'stuff' that made life possible, was somehow of this world. And it seemed to be universal, used by all living things, not just people who looked to God for answers. She was close to understanding. So close. She closed her eyes against the red sun, echoes of its circle against her backlit eyelids.

Half an hour later she was making her way down from the Roaches to the path, navigating through smaller boulders and slabs in the gathering dusk. Suddenly there were noises behind her. Voices and the clink of bridles. *Two*, she thought, *maybe*

(STAFFORDSHIRE MOORS, OCTOBER 1639)

three? She was just reaching the flat bottom of the valley. No cover here, just heather, dry grass and peaty mud. She started to run as fast as her bulky long skirt and heavy boots would allow, back up the slope, back to the rocks and a multitude of hiding places.

But a shout told her she was already too late. The sound of hooves gathering speed on the peat track drove her on up the slope. Horses would be no use to them if she could gain the stone first. But the first rider was already cutting her off, long coat flapping behind him as he rose from his saddle to urge his horse on. The second was gaining on her from behind, although having to slow as he encountered more slabs of gritstone. They were shouting to each other. Not harsh and threatening but laughing and encouraging.

The first man was now between her and safety, and he reined in his horse, which circled on the spot. He grinned down at her, lank black hair sticking to his grimy, lined face and tangled in his beard. When he laughed at her, she saw he missed two front teeth. She stopped and gazed calmly up at him. She was only twenty yards from the rocky outcrops.

Now his companion came up behind her, talking to his mount. She turned and fixed her stare on him in turn. Younger. Much younger, maybe still in his teens? Straw-blond hair protruded from under a woollen cap. She saw that both carried cavalry swords; the older one also had a carbine in a saddle holster. *Local militia?*

The older one spoke. "Well met, mistress." Deep voice, still catching his breath from the brief chase. He was a big man, nearly six foot she estimated. The other one slimmer. Scrawny. Not yet filling out to a man's body. "Where are ye 'eadin'? And in such an 'urry... Did yer not fancy the company?"

"Be fair, who would fancy your company, Ralph?" the younger one laughed.

"Shut it, Tom. There's a lady present. Don't want to create the wrong impression, do we?" He hadn't taken his eyes off her and his smile now appeared a little more menacing than before. *A good-looking woman, by herself, in the middle of nowhere. There's a story here. And if not, perhaps we can start one...* "You ain't answered my question, lovely. What yer doin' out 'ere, all alone?"

As his horse started to circle again, he had to try to maintain eye contact over his shoulder, and she took that moment to throw the sharp-edged stone she had scooped up. It smacked against the bay skin of his horse's rump, and it snorted and reared in pain and surprise. Ralph fought to keep his balance and she set off towards the first shelf of rock, holding her skirts up around her knees, feet flying over the rough ground.

"Shit!" His horse back under control, Ralph spun it round and went to follow but soon realised the ground wasn't suitable for a further chase. He slid off expertly and set off after her. "Tie the horses and follow me!" he shouted back over his shoulder. She rounded a rock and lost sight of them both.

Tom watched the pursuit open-mouthed from his horse, before he jolted into action and he too slid down to the ground. He captured Ralph's horse and looped both sets of reins around a boulder. He then picked a different path up into the maze of angled stones. He could hear Ralph's boots on the rough gritstone somewhere over to his right, an increasingly angry voice cursing the woman who he had plainly lost in the jumble. Tom went for height and carefully scaled the steep face in front of him, finding plenty of secure hand and footholds. After a brief struggle, he pulled himself up onto the top of a flat-topped pinnacle and crawled over to the far edge.

Looking down he could see Ralph below him, standing

(Staffordshire moors, October 1639)

hands on hips, turning around on a flat area of earth surrounded by sheer rock faces. "C'mon, show yerself! Yer jus' bein' rude now. All we wants is a nice chat. It's been a long day in the saddle and we just needs some pretty company afore we set off 'ome. Don't mean you no harm. C'mon out afore we get really angry and it goes worse for yer." No reply, no movement, just the sounds of dusk in high places.

Tom, as quietly as he could, crawled over to the left-hand edge of his block. *Ah.* Just around the corner from Ralph, but hidden entirely from his sight, she stood, back to the stone. Tom could see the narrow cleft she must have crawled through to get there and there was a narrow path, probably a sheep or deer path, leading away down the opposite side of the rocks from their road, off into birch and rowan thickets. She could not move along, though, for fear of alerting Ralph. He could see her turning her head this way and that, searching for him, he knew. Once she looked up, but he dodged back just in time. She was very comely. Beautiful long, wavy hair of red-brown, loose around her shoulders, not stuffed under a cap. And her eyes! First thing he had noticed about her. *So, what's the word… intense?*

She had led them a dance and it was now getting pretty dark. He was happy just to get home. These stupid patrols they were now being sent on. Patrolling for what? But he knew Ralph would be even more of a bastard if he didn't get his way. He sighed and inched backwards, slithering back down the face of the rocks as quietly as he could. As his toes touched the ground, he turned, pulled his pistol and crept along the face. He leaned around the corner and *yes*, there she was. She had her back to him, listening to Ralph's venomous ranting, all pretence at friendly banter gone. He *was* a bastard, that one. Not a shred of decency in him, but no one wanted to cross him. Vicious bastard.

He crept around the corner and was within five paces of her when she turned. He brought his pistol up and she slumped back against the rock, defeat and resignation on her face. "C'mon, mistress," he said quietly. "Best come wi' me afore he gets even madder. Just give 'im what he wants, and we'll be gone."

"Just?" She arched an eyebrow. "Easy for you t'say, you fine gentleman."

"Let's go. Don't make it worse." He gestured with the pistol. "I got 'er, Ralph. We're coming through!"

They scrambled out through the hidden gap and into the small rocky amphitheatre where Ralph prowled. He stood, regarding them both. Tom stood a pace behind, pistol now back in his belt. "Well, mistress. That was a fine dance. Do you not like the look of us?"

"Please, sir, just let me go. I am expected home and they will be lookin' for me soon. They catch you with me, like this, and they'll hang you for it."

"Yeah? And where is 'ome, and who is they? Can't see no one. Did you see anyone up here, Tom?"

"No, Ralph. Not a soul. But let's just let 'er go and get 'ome ourselves, eh? I'm tired and hungry, and this is… wrong."

"Wrong? Don't give me that. It were you that first saw 'er. And now I've had to chase her, nearly fell off my horse, and scraped me knees and elbows climbing after 'er. D'yer think I'm just goin' to let it go at that? Fuck that! In fact…" he smiled, "…that's a much better plan, don't yer think, luv?"

He strode quickly towards her and grabbed her by the shoulders, leaning in for a kiss. His breath stank, and close up she could see the filth ingrained in his skin. She struggled back, but he took a firmer grip of her clothes and butted her sharply on the forehead. He let go and she went down in a heap. "Always had a way with women!" he laughed and winked at Tom.

(STAFFORDSHIRE MOORS, OCTOBER 1639)

"For the love of Christ, Ralph, be you an animal?! Leave it and let's go while we can." He looked around nervously but made no move towards them.

Ralph grabbed her ankles and pulled her, still apparently dazed, into the centre of the space. He pushed her skirt up her legs and dropped to his knees in between. She appeared to lose her dizziness and started to struggle, trying to wriggle out from under him, but he flopped his weight forward and pinned her, and slapped her hard to make his point. He was still fumbling awkwardly with his own breeches and the lumpy barrier her bulky skirt and underclothes made between them, cursing all the while.

Then, in the near dark, it looked to Tom as though she accepted her fate, and seeking to get things over with, he saw her bring up her knees on either side of Ralph's waist. Ralph saw this too, and relaxed his frantic struggles a little, again leaning towards her face. "Now that's better, luvly. Now yer behavin.'"

But the next moment, everything changed. Her hand on the far side came up from her boot and punched once, hard, at the side of Ralph's head. Ralph instantly stopped moving, all his weight slumped down, motionless on top of her. For a second, the briefest pause, there was stillness. Then, with seeming super-human strength, she rolled, tipping the inert body off her and coming to her feet in one fluid movement. Tom stared at the thin haft of the knife that sprouted like a strange flower from Ralph's ear. No blade visible. No blood. Just wide, staring, corpse eyes.

He looked up in shocked silence at the woman, hair wild about her head, feet planted apart, and at Ralph's pistol now in her hand, pointing at his face. She seemed to almost glow in the dark, like a paper lantern with a candle inside he had seen at a fair. She walked towards him.

"Stop! Wait! Please!" He took a step back, but she kept coming. "I didn't do nothing. You saw. It was him, not me. I did nothin'!" Pleading.

"That's right," she said. "I saw. You did nothin', Thomas. Is that something you feel proud of? You stood and watched him try to take me, and you want a reward? You think I should just let you go?"

He had no reply because he knew she had the right of it. *My God, what is she?* Now it made a strange kind of sense that she was out here all alone. *Is she some kind of demon, or witch?* "Please, mistress. Please let me go. I meant no harm. I was wrong. I should've helped you. That Ralph is a bastard. You did right in killing 'im. I won't tell no one. Please."

She pushed her hair back from her face and stared into his eyes. Her smooth unblemished skin and fluid movement made her seem as young as him, but the eyes which looked on him seemed from an ancient past. Her voice low, and slightly husky, came as a relief from that cold, relentless stare. "Turn around, Thomas."

He did as he was told. "On your knees." Down he went. He heard the pistol cock and lost control of his bladder. He started to mumble a prayer, eyes screwed shut. He got to the 'Amen' and started again. The second time he got to the end of the prayer the thought suddenly struck him that he was not, in fact, dead. It was nearly pitch black, with light clouds now masking stars and crescent moon, and there was no sound except a faint stirring of birch leaves. He held his breath and turned his head slightly but could see nothing. No voice came. More importantly, no ball or blade came. He turned around completely and stood, hardly aware of the warm wetness spreading across his lap. And then he heard the sound of two horses, moving slowly away down the hill.

21

BRERETON

(Chester, 3 January 1640)

"My word, sir, you have stirred my blood this day!" The preacher looked slightly shocked as his hand was pumped vigorously by the black-clad member of the congregation. "Never have I heard oratory such as this. Truly you speak the word of God, sir."

Having recovered his composure, the preacher clasped his left hand over their still-joined hands and smiled. "I merely say what must be said, sir. What we must all say. The truth. The truth that the Church in England is a sick patient. A patient that is expiring while the bishops enrich themselves and crush those who dissent. I will not be crushed, sir. I will not be silenced."

"Indeed, Master Eaton. You have elevated my soul and stiffened my resolve. The godly cannot take any lead from these popish lords. We must take the righteous fight to their doors."

"You have me at a disadvantage, sir. Clearly you know who I am but, forgive me, we have not been introduced. How should I address you, sir?"

"Duckinfield. Robert Duckinfield. I have followed your career, sir. From the disgraceful suspension of yourself by Bishop Bridgeman and your arrest and imprisonment by that… that popish hound, Laud! We had heard you had gone to Amsterdam, and then that you had gone to Massachusetts! But now you are here again in Chester. Oh, this is a great blessing for us!"

He turned and beckoned to another figure waiting in the shadows of the nave in St John's. "William. Sir William!" More frantic beckoning. "Come, sir, come. You cannot have failed to have been stirred by such a sermon. Master Eaton, please let me introduce my great friend, and a strong supporter of the godly, Sir William Brereton of Handforth."

Brereton, looking carefully around and then locking gaze with Eaton, nodded quietly and reached to shake his hand. "Robert is correct, sir. That was as stirring a sermon as I have heard for some time. I did not see you in Amsterdam when I was there, but I met with Thomas Paget, and he spoke very warmly of you and your brother Theophilus."

"Sir William. 'Tis an honour, sir. Of course, I have heard of your support for the divine. You do God's work, sir." Brereton nodded and smiled slightly.

Duckinfield looked slightly crestfallen that his own contributions to the cause had not rated any mention but pressed on. "Master Eaton, I would be honoured, sir. That is to say, I have an offer to make to you. A proposition if you like. At the Hall we have a private chapel and it would be illuminated to a burning star if you would consider making it your base. We would furnish accommodation and other support and can introduce you to the godly folk around the county. For beware, sir. Whilst we feel…" he nodded towards Brereton, "…that the tide is turning away from Laud and his popish dogs, there are many still who would not receive you as warmly as we."

(Chester, 3 January 1640)

Brereton nodded his agreement and, with his eyes only, indicated a pair of cloaked figures standing near to the doors of the church. "The bishop's men. I saw Sir Thomas Aston, one of the King and Laud's staunchest supporters, leave the church just before you finished. He will not like what he heard. You can expect some hostility. But, as Robert suggests, it is not how it was when you departed for the New World. There are many now who share our views on the corruption of God's word by the mouths of these popish puppets. Please consider Robert's offer. It is a good and sensible option for you, I think. We would keep you safe."

Samuel Eaton looked from one earnest man to the other. "My thanks to you, Master Duckinfield. I do see wisdom in what you suggest. My steps in this city are followed. This I know, for their tracking skills are not as keen or as subtle as the Pequot Indians with whom we have been warring in the New World." He smiled, but then his face hardened. "However, I must warn you that I did not return here to be 'safe'. The righteous way must be proclaimed. The unrighteous must be denounced. I will not sit safe in your chapel whilst others speak and bear the brunt of reprisal. I will be heard, and by as many as possible."

"That is understood, Master Eaton. We offer you only a place to base yourself and where you can return to friends and respite. Please. Take your time to decide, but in the meantime, take care."

"Thank you, Sir Robert. I will not keep you waiting. I will deliver my answer to you in a few days. Perhaps I can deliver it to your home in person when I can also view the chapel?"

"Of course. Fare you well, sir. We must be about our business, and there are others wishing to talk to you, I think." Duckinfield indicated several other men and women waiting for an audience and smiled. "You are much in demand already, sir."

"'Tis not me but God's word that they thirst for. God's words straight to their hearts, not from the mouth of a bishop." Eaton almost spat the final word out.

Brereton gently took Duckinfield's arm and steered him towards the doors. "That was well done, Robert, for he is already marked by our enemies. But now we are doubly so. We must take our own precautions too. I am already in conflict with the mayor and council over taxes and real-estate matters. This just makes me more and more unpopular with these gentlemen." He chuckled wryly. "How they would like to be rid of me."

They stepped together out into the cold of the January day and both pulled their cloaks about them as they looked for their carriages. They parted and Brereton strode quickly off down the street, recognising his waiting men and horses, and wishing them, or himself, to linger no longer than necessary in the biting air. But as he moved past the corner of the church, a cloaked and hatted figure emerged from the graveyard and stepped in front of him.

"Sir Thomas. Well met, sir. Enjoyed you the service?"

"Don't be a fool, Brereton." Aston's voice was low, menacing. Both hands were invisible under his thick, lined cloak, but William could see the contour caused by the hilt of a sword, and no doubt Aston's hand was resting on it. "How can anyone enjoy such fantasy? And dangerous fantasy too. It is all but sedition, sir. I had heard Eaton was back but did not believe that he would pick up again where he left off. After Bridgeman saw him and the Pagets off once before. Is he mad?"

"I think, Thomas, that he sees things more clearly than any of us. I believe he speaks truth, but that some find truth… inconvenient. But if you think him mad, then what harm can he do? Leave him be. Find others to persecute and let the godly worship as they will."

"And lose faith with the King? No, sir. That will not stand.

(CHESTER, 3 JANUARY 1640)

I said he is dangerous. I cannot deny the power of his oratory and charisma, and that is where the danger lies. He speaks against the policies and the divine right of his sovereign, who, as you well know, personally supports his archbishop. To rant against this is approaching treason, sir. Have a care, or you will be tainted by your association."

"No, Thomas. He is not speaking against the King, but against his odious, popish and misled advisers. They serve him poorly and set his people against him. You know, probably better than I, that what we see here in Cheshire from preachers and radical thinkers is nothing compared to what is happening on the streets of London, and the divine messages that appear ever-increasingly in the popular pamphlets. Change must come, Thomas. Think on it. Be our friend, not our enemy." Brereton took half a pace forward and placed a hand on Aston's shoulder. "We should be allies here, Thomas, for the good of the people of this county. For the good of the King. We should rid him of his ignorant and ungodly advisers. We should stand together."

With a sweeping motion of his arm, Aston knocked William's hand away and in so doing revealed the gleaming hilt and guards of his rapier. "Do not mock me, Brereton! There are many think as I do. You walk a fine line with your semantics, sir. You come close to treason yourself. It is you who should consider your next steps carefully."

"You come armed to church?"

"Church? That was no church I recognise. Just the rantings of some raving Massachusetts ne'er-do-well. I arm myself for protection against treasonous dogs who speak against their monarch." He took a deep breath. "But, Sir William, will you not relent from this madness? Yours is an old and respected family. Will you not renounce this and return to the King's church?"

"Sir Thomas. I cannot. I mean no disrespect to the King himself, but he is setting himself against his people by allowing Laud's vendettas. In conscience, I must stand with the divine on this. But the day is freezing and our men wait on us. Let us speak on this again."

"I pray that there is opportunity to do so in peace. My heart warns me that hope of a united people is sliding slowly towards an abyss. And it is men such as you, Sir William, who would tip it over the edge. Farewell." And Sir Thomas Aston stepped around him and hurried away without a backward glance.

William watched him go, thankful that he had not brought a weapon to the sermon, as this discussion might have ended differently. He knew that Sir Thomas's views were more representative of the Cheshire gentry than his own were. William had some powerful allies, but Aston could call on more. He had to think. He had to plan. He needed a clear goal rather than this posturing and sword rattling. When the time came, God would show him what to do.

He knew that Aston was right on one thing. He, Sir William Brereton of Handforth, would do all he could for the cause, would give everything that God asked of him, even if it meant his life. Even if it meant war.

22

ROGER DELACEY

(Amsterdam, February 1640)

Roger opened his eyes, slowly, carefully. Or tried to. This was harder than he had anticipated, as there seemed to be some type of sticky substance filming them closed. He gasped slightly as his eyelid muscles suddenly overcame the resistance and he got a jolting, painful burst of light straight to his brain.

It was only as his mind calibrated this harsh sensory stimulus that he realised the light was actually not that bright, but actually very dim. All things are relative. What he did have was an extreme close-up of wood grain, about an inch from his corneas, and it took him several seconds to get it in some kind of focus. His inner ear told him that he was, in fact, face down and, putting all of this evidence together, he came to the conclusion that he was either slumped on a table top, or sprawled on the floor. He appealed to his memory for help but received no reply. There seemed to be a temporary loss of contact.

Damnation! He would actually have to initiate movement to get a better view on his location and he knew from bitter experience that that would be a deeply painful exercise. *One.*

Two. Three! But on three nothing much happened. He knew he had instructed his neck muscles to raise his head, but there he was, still squinting at the oak. He tried again and confirmed to himself that his muscles had the message, but that his forehead was somehow glued to the wood. Pulling directly upward was not going to do it, not without having to exert so much force that his fragile grip on consciousness would be lost, and probably resulting in expansive vomiting.

Instead, he tried a gentle rocking motion, slowly rotating his head so that, little by little, his skin pulled itself free of the stickiness that was imprisoning him. As he became free of all but a residual tackiness, he steeled himself to raise his head again, knowing that this time he would have to confront whatever it was his head had been resting in for the last eight hours or so. He assumed it would be one of the usual three substances: wine, blood or vomit. He hoped for wine but expected one of the other two. At least if it was going to be vomit, he hoped it was his own.

Here we go. Ah. Wine. Thank you, Lord! He had smelt vomit and feared the worst. But no. His luck was in. He waited a moment for his senses to fully catch up with the movement of his head and, once everything was tentatively aligned, he made the brave decision to stand. *Here we go. Not so bad. Ah. I'm in the Sailor!*

He slowly turned, moving his entire body stiffly, so that he did not need to reorientate his head on his neck. This way the pain in his skull was just about manageable. He was just about getting a grip on things, and could see the way back to the bar, when disaster struck. The door to the outside world crashed open and this time the light piercing his retinas was a veritable bolt of lightning. He swayed, waving his arms uselessly to shield his eyes, and promptly fell over in a heap on the floor. *Bollocks! I think my head has come right off…*

(AMSTERDAM, FEBRUARY 1640)

The light dimmed slightly as a shape appeared in the doorway. A vaguely familiar voice bellowed at him, "Rog! Oh my God! Are you alright?" Why was the person shouting? He heard quick footsteps pound across the uneven wooden floor towards him. He decided his head was indeed still attached, but he now felt it spinning with increasing velocity. He closed his aching eyes to make it stop, but this made matters worse. His body took over, knowing there was only one way he could get release. He vomited long and voluminously, trying to do the decent thing and direct it away from where he had last heard the voice.

Now there was silence. So quiet he was sure he could hear the blood pounding through the arteries that surrounded his brain. He hoped things would stay this quiet forever but somehow felt this was unlikely.

And indeed, here came the voice came again. Talking more quietly, which was a blessing, but he felt sure the sympathy and concern he had previously heard had disappeared. He was right.

"For fuck's sake, Roger! What are you doing! Hudde's outside with the other boys. We are waiting for you! We are going to Rotterdam today. Remember?"

"Wha…?"

"Rotterdam! The big shipment has come in from Stockholm. We are escorting it back here. We talked about it only two days ago. How long have you been like… this? C'mon. This is a big deal, Roger. Can you walk? Can you do anything?" Richard's voice was a ferocious whisper. His blazing anger barely under control.

"Dunno. I'm… not well, Rich. Tell Hudde I'm sick. Sit this one out." Roger opened his eyes briefly, but the incandescence of Richard's face forced them shut again. "Sorry, friend. Tell 'im am sick." He could feel consciousness disappearing again and fought to stay in the conversation.

"Roger. This is the second time you have done this in the last month. He will start to realise what is going on. Unlike you, he's not stupid. He will stop using you. Worse, he might stop using me. You have to promise me, Roger. You've got to stop this!" He gripped him by the lapels of his filthy coat and shook him. Roger's head lolled and he groaned hugely.

"Promise. Promise, Rich. No more drink. Stupid Roger, no more drink." He half opened one eye, watching for Richard's reaction. Disgust. Anger. *Ah. Acceptance. That was better…*

"Don't screw this up for us, Roger. It's too good to lose. Please. Please, Roger."

"Promise." He paused as another thought crawled slowly and painfully across the aching floor of his skull. He frowned in concentration, trying to bring it into focus. *Ah. That was it.* "Rich. Friend. Money?"

"What?"

"Got no money." This was just above a mumble.

"What! How can you have no money? We just got paid a week ago. A good purse too! What the fuck have you done with it?"

In response, Roger slowly swept his arm around the scene of his triumph. "Been enjoying myself." He gave what he thought was a roguish, winning smile, but came across as more of a sickly leer.

"How could you drink and whore away that much in a few days?" Richard was genuinely shocked. In Roger's addled state, he took shock for admiration.

"'T'was a challenge but rose to the occasion, Rich." The leer appeared again but faded slowly when Roger saw Richard wasn't with him on this one. "Sorry, friend." He felt himself slowly sobering up. He put on his serious face. "Sorry. No more. Promise. Make it good for me with Hudde. Never again."

(AMSTERDAM, FEBRUARY 1640)

Richard's face remained stony, but he opened his purse and tossed a couple of coins onto Roger's belly. "We will be back in three days. The next shipment is to the Scots. I have told Hudde I can't do that one for conscience's sake. He understands, so we will have some relaxation time before we go again. Think on this, Roger. We have a chance for a good life. At least for a while. Don't ruin this for me. Friend."

Roger watched him stand and mutter some words to Klaas who had appeared behind the bar and was looking miserably at the mess around Roger. Another coin slapped onto the counter. Then the door opened wide again, and the blast of light and icy cold air was like a slap to his face. *No more than I deserve. Fucking worthless sack of shit that I am. He's a good boy. My boy. Never again, DeLacey. Is it so long since you lost Rose's respect that you've forgotten how this feels? And you never had the chance to make it better, did you, you shit?*

Tears streamed down his face as he tried to drag himself up the bar. He scrabbled for the coins as they fell from his shirt and stuffed them into his purse. *Fucking beggar now.* In a haze of fumes and melancholy he staggered for the stairs, heading for his mattress, and oblivion.

23

RICHARD AND ROGER

(April 1640)

"I cannot believe you have done this, Roger. I am lost for words. You know how I felt about this."

"Look, Rich, I know it's a bit of a shock, but really, it's for the best. And I can remember you weren't that bothered about whose side you were fighting for when we were looking to actually enlist. So what's the problem now?"

They both gripped the wooden rail, to steady themselves against the choppy water of the estuary. Richard was struggling with his usual nausea but just about had things under control. His temper was a different matter and he could feel the pressure rising in his chest. "Did you think I wouldn't notice? Did you think that just because I have never been to London, I wouldn't notice that we had actually landed in fucking Edinburgh! Did you really think that, Roger?"

"Well, no. There was a chance, I suppose. You can be a bit slow, but no. But look, Rich. It's money. It's a paying job. Good pay. And you told me you wanted to look good with Hudde. He was really pleased when I told him you were up for this job. Really."

(April 1640)

Richard rolled his eyes. "But that's not the point. You knew how I felt about working contracts to support England's enemies. You knew. And you lied to me. You lied to Hudde. And if you think you have done this for me, then you are lying to yourself. Why, Roger? Why?"

"Alright. Don't get so high and fucking mighty with me, son. You know why. I need the money, don't I. Can't pay my rent to Klaas. Nothing for food. Nothing for…" He tailed off, staring out at the coastline that slipped slowly past, trying to avoid Richard's eyes.

"Yes. That's it, isn't it? Nothing for gin. For wine. For ale. For sack. For whores. Christ, Roger, aren't you getting a bit old for all of that?"

"Oh, just fuck off then! So I lied to you. Grow up. Life's not fair, boy. Get over it and stop sulking."

Despite his anger, Richard's voice softened. Pleading. "I looked up to you. You got Will and me through Breda in one piece. I owe you everything, but you seem set on destroying yourself. Why? Just when we got a break. I don't understand."

There was a long pause as Roger stared across the grey-black water, waves cresting with white as they rolled up the muddy flats. His irritation had faded to black melancholy. "'Cos it's me, isn't it? It's what I do. I fuck things up. I'm like one o' them fairground tricksters doin' magic, except everything I touch turns to shit, not gold. All around me. I have seen countless men die in battle around me, but I don't get a scratch. I seen sickness wipe out whole regiments on campaign. Not me. My wife and kids fall to the plague, and I'm not even there to see them die. Never been sick, properly sick, in my life. It's like God thinks I'm so low I'm not even worth his attention for punishment. So I drink. It reminds me I'm alive. Then, when I remember, it helps me to fucking forget again. And now I am screwing up this…" He gestured to indicate the two of them. "You was like a second chance. And I pissed that away too."

"Stop being so self-pitying, you old bastard. You know Neelie would never let me leave you, even if I wanted to."

"She's a good girl, Rich. Don't ever let her go."

"Yes, she is, although I question her judgement when it comes to drunken old bastards."

"Fair point."

It was starting to get dark, adding to the gloom of the day. Grey sky, grey sea, green-grey land. The first signs of the city of Edinburgh started to appear along the shoreline. Roger had taken Richard aboard the merchantman after nightfall the previous day, persuading him that it was an unexpected contract that the Marcelis brothers had taken on when a rival arms dealer had failed to secure finance. He had said they were bound for London, with a shipment for the King's Ordnance Office, and had carefully kept him, Richard now saw with hindsight, away from the other crew members and Hudde's men. It was only when dawn had come, and the strong favourable breeze had driven them across the North Sea at an excellent speed, that he had guessed their destination was not what he had thought, and Roger could hide the truth no longer.

"Right. Seeing as we are sailing into the heart of a nation that currently hates the English, with a ship full of weapons, had we better have some kind of story?"

"No story. We just keep quiet. Pretend we are Dutch and no speak no Eeengleeesh. Hudde's men know the risk for us. They won't give it away. We just lurk around at the back, keep our mouths shut and play like dumb guards. Easy money."

"We'll be entirely in character then. What's the arrangement?"

"We dock. We unload onto the waiting wagons. They inspect and test some of the merchandise immediately and

(April 1640)

hand over the finance papers for half. They test the rest later, and Hudde sends someone, not us, to collect the balance later."

"Right. So once we finish overseeing the unloading you and I get back on the ship. The others can handle the testing. Agreed?"

"Agreed. See, no fuss required."

"Except that these guns, matchlocks and blades could be cutting down our fellow Englishmen in a few weeks' time. That's quite a fuss, don't you think?"

"Oh, don't get so moral 'n' righteous about it. You're happy to take the money when it's other nations' sons getting killed. What difference is it what flavour they are? You been a soldier. At least for a while. You seen dead men of all countries – they look that different to you? They all got mothers, brothers, kids. Probably most of 'em didn't want to be there. Do you feel a duty to Charlie-boy? Are you like that bastard Montague? If you don't like it, quit. Go home to your folks in the fens and take Neelie with you. You got the balls to do that?"

Richard was silent, he too staring into the grey gloom. "You're right," he said, finally. "And I'm not sure that I do have the balls to take her with me, if I'm honest. And I hate myself for thinking it."

"Welcome to the world of Roger DeLacey, King of Bastards. You can be my Prince of Bastards. How do you like that?"

*

Two hours later and they were finishing tying up the ship in Leith. From their vantage point on the rail, they could look down onto the quayside and see the activity there as men rushed to make ready the wagons that had been sent for once the ship had come into view. The strong wind that pushed them so quickly across the North Sea from Amsterdam now ushered in rain, coming alternately down and then sideways in the swirling gusts. The dock workers were in the lee of the ship and a little sheltered from the worst of it, but up on deck they were soaked through in minutes.

The captain and Hudde's senior representative, Jan Kuyter, were engaged in animated conversation with several Covenanters at the foot of the gangplank. Richard and Roger watched from above, sheltering under canvas sheet as much as possible. They were both armed – a pistol each, and swords – largely concealed under their heavy leather coats, collars upturned. Both had broad-brimmed hats pulled low over their eyes.

The Covenanters had posted guards all around the quayside, presumably alert to Royalist sympathisers and spies, and the wagons, also with protective canvas covers, had been drawn up in front of a large warehouse area. Seemed that the Scots wanted to come aboard, but the captain was having none of it, and there was something of an impasse. Roger seemed very relaxed, humming quietly to himself and cleaning under his fingernails with the point of his dagger, normally kept hidden in his boot. "Well, I guess we get paid either way. Quite happy to turn around now if needs be."

"Something's not right," said Richard, peering through the drizzle and the murk. "Why don't we just unload and get on with it?"

"Probably payment issues," Roger replied. "It's always about money. And the Scots are tighter than a virgin's…"

"…Yes, alright. What would you know about virgins anyway? I just wish they'd get on with it."

After several more minutes, Kuyter came back up onto the deck. He beckoned his men together; there were five including Richard and Roger. "Look," he said, "they want a demonstration before they pay, and we won't unload until we see their finance paperwork. So go to the hold and bring out two cases of matchlocks; they want to be able to pick some out at random. And bring match, powder and ball as well. They want the whole performance! I need you all to lend a hand," he said, looking at Richard and Roger. "I know you want to stay on the ship, but we need to hurry now. Just carry the cases and stand in the shadows somewhere. The others can do the shooting. Right. Let's get moving."

In fifteen minutes, they were tromping down the gangplank, heaving the weight of a wooden case of matchlocks between them. Richard backed down, Roger peering over his shoulder and giving a quiet commentary. "Right. Slow down. We're coming to the quayside. Go left. No. Your left. That's it. Keep going, keep up with Jan. Head down. Good. Nearly at the warehouse. Some torches set so keep your bloody head down."

They passed out of the driving rain and into the relative quiet of the warehouse. "Keep going straight towards the wall. Jan is telling us to stack it next to the other one. And… Jesus Christ!"

Richard looked up at Roger quickly, but there seemed to be no immediate danger. Roger walked off to the side, towards the open doors and away from the nearest torch into shadow. He leaned his back against the wall and folded his arms across his chest. When Richard did likewise, he whispered under his breath, "Over there. At the back of the group of Scots. Recognise anyone?"

Richard looked. While their colleagues stood around the now-opened crates with the Covenanter representatives, another group stood slightly to one side. In this group of four was a mid-sized, plainly dressed man, with mid-brown hair and unremarkable features. He carried a notebook and seemed to be recording events, watching procedures closely. Now he strolled over to the crates and peered in, checking the makers' names and noting these down. He glanced briefly across to Richard and Roger in the deep shadow near the door but gave no sign of registering them.

"It's bloody Montague!" hissed Richard.

"Yes. It is."

"What the bloody hell is he doing here? He's the King's man through and through!"

"Yes. Interesting. Isn't it?" Roger was ensuring he looked down so as not to catch Montague's eye, but squinted sideways to keep him vaguely in view. "Seems to me there's two possibilities. Either he is a turncoat and has defected to the Scots, or he is posing as one to get intelligence for Charlie-boy. Which do you think?"

"Well, I am guessing the second," Richard whispered. "I just can't see him turning his coat so quickly when the war has not even started! You didn't spend the time with him on that canal bridge. He is a fanatic."

"So if that is so, and I think you are probably right, he really wouldn't want us to point that out to his new employers, no matter how he has presented himself to them. So *he* won't want to give *us* up as being English dogs, for the risk we expose him."

"If he even sees and recognises us."

"Oh, he has seen us, don't you worry. The crafty fox doesn't miss anything. Look, he is talking to… who is that? I do believe it's Sir Robert fuckin' Moray! He commanded the Scots Guard of Le Roi." He saw Richard's vacant expression. "Louis. King of France? Good man. Good soldier. What the fuck is 'e doin' 'ere. It's that crafty fucker Richelieu, I'll bet. Plant his man among the Scots to create maximum pain for Charlie.

(April 1640)

Montague has his ear, that's for sure. He'll want to stay close to him one way or another. But why would they allow a simple turncoat such access? It still doesn't really ring true."

Suddenly there were three loud cracks as their fellow guards fired off a volley from the three muskets that had been selected for testing. Three good hits were registered on the wicker target that had been set up at the far end of the workshop. Kuyter wandered casually over to them while the Covenanters selected three more weapons at random.

"So, Master Kuyter, they are happy with everything?" Richard asked in his best Dutch. Kuyter gave him an encouraging smile.

"Yes. So it seems. We must play this game, though, before they part with their money."

"And who is the gentleman with the notebook? It seems I have seen him somewhere before."

"Him? I doubt it. But he is the reason we are doing all this extra work. He is the money man. Well, he represents the money men. He is an agent of the City of Edinburgh, which is funding this shipment."

"Really? I am sure I have seen him before, but that was not his role."

"Hmm. Tell me, Richard. Who do you think he is? I do not want anything to go wrong given the amount of money that is at stake here."

But at that moment, Moray called over that he wanted to see samples of cuirasses, blades and match. Kuyter nodded at them. "OK, you two. It has to be you, the others are busy. Bring a case of each."

With a mixture of relief and reluctance – it was still raining hard outside – they jogged off towards the ship. Fifteen minutes later the additional crates were open on the floor of the warehouse. The Covenanters and Montague crowded around the goods. Cuirasses were tried on, buckles tested, blades examined, match lit and closely observed. Moray turned to Kuyter with a tight smile. "We are happy, sir. Have your men unload the full cargo. We can loan you extra hands from the wagonmen outside to speed things along. I guess you will want to be on your way under the cover of this weather. Easier to avoid the King's ships, eh?"

Kuyter waved his men back towards the ship. "My thanks, sir. And yes, it was only last week that two Swedish vessels were stopped and the goods impounded." Richard shot Roger a look. Kuyter continued in his broken English, "We would not want that fate. Alliances are fragile things at this time, and we want to keep trading with all we can."

"Ah, the call of the coin. I cannot blame you, sir. Your country has suffered greatly at the hands of the damnable papists." Roger could not help but smile at this, coming from the servant of the cardinal, but Kuyter clearly did not know who he was dealing with. "I did not expect to be raising armies in my own country, against my own king. And yes, I know you also supply the English. The King's attention is on us, but he is sitting on a powder keg in his own backyard. The longer he delays calling Parliament, the more grievances he is storing up. A spark, and the lot will go up." He smiled again. "Perhaps they see us as that spark, but I can say, with my hand on my heart, that we wish the King no ill. He is badly advised and must rid himself of his popish bishops and advisers. If he will but relent on the matters of faith, he will see he has no more loyal folk than we."

Richard caught an ironic smile on Montague's face, carefully hidden as he pretended to poke around, but then he felt Roger grab his arm and pull him away towards the ship. They had a long night ahead unloading the shipment.

"Did you hear him, Roger? The English are stopping

(APRIL 1640)

and seizing ships. We should thank God that we weren't intercepted on the way in."

"Stop worrying, lad. Here we are. Job is nearly done. Pay is as good as given. What can they arrest us for, a pleasure trip to the great city of Edinburgh? Save your energy for lugging these bloody crates!"

Near dawn, they were finished, and exhausted. The last of the crates were being carefully strapped to the wagons, and the draught horses had been fed and watered and were being led to the harnesses. The Covenanters gathered around, Moray to the fore. "Master Gray, bring me the promissory note, if you would. I am sure Master Kuyter would wish to check all is in order."

From ten yards away, Richard watched Montague step forward, swinging a large, stiff, leather satchel from under his coat where he had sheltered it from the rain, which had now just about stopped. Moray gestured to Kuyter. "Here, sir, as agreed. The payment is guaranteed by the City of Edinburgh. Our fundraising has been better than we hoped for. You have no need for concern on payment. Please, study it carefully and if you are happy, I will sign, and you can witness my signature. Gray, give him the note, please."

Montague extracted a single page from his satchel and handed it to Kuyter. He then crouched down and extracted pen and ink from the bag, which he now deployed as a makeshift table. Satisfied, Kuyter nodded to Moray and returned the note to the crouching Gray/Montague. But in trying to offer up the quill to Moray he fumbled the satchel which fell to the quayside. Cursing he bent down again and rummaged around to reorder the necessary items. "Sorry, Sir Robert," he mumbled in, Richard thought, a very passable, soft Scots accent. He offered the satchel up with the note laid on it, inked quill in his other hand. They all watched as, leaning on the stiff, flat casing of the satchel, Moray briskly signed away a sizeable portion of the Covenanters' funds.

"My thanks, sir," Moray nodded at Gray/Montague, "and now Master Kuyter should countersign in witness." This was played out and the atmosphere among the men immediately seemed to relax. Smiles broke out and backs were slapped. Richard began to feel that perhaps he had been overly hard on Roger. This was not so bad, and even though it was clear Montague had recognised them, he did not seem inclined to make anything of it, his own safety probably hanging in the balance. It was clear now that he had not turned his coat, but it wasn't clear what game he was playing here. Richard didn't care as long as it did not impact on him. He just wanted to be safely home with Neelie.

The carts and wagons had already started winding their way off the quay and onto the roads from Leith back to Edinburgh. Moray and his group of Covenanters recovered their own horses and swung into the saddle, escorting their shipment. Kuyter and the others were already heading for the ship; he and Roger started to follow. Roger swung an arm around his shoulder. "See? I told you it would be fine. Job done. They are already getting ready to sail. Let's get aboard and let's get a drink. We could both do with one. I know I could!"

But as they approached the gangplank, a voice called from behind them. "Gentlemen! It is such a pleasure to see you both again."

They whirled round. Montague emerged from the shadows by the warehouse where all the torches and lamps were now extinguished. His face was grim. Richard doubted that he ever really found anything truly a pleasure, except perhaps strangling kittens.

"Yes," said Roger, rain again dripping from the brim of his

(April 1640)

hat, "a strange twist of fate that brings us all here. Tonight." His tone was questioning.

Montague stared back. "I see you persist in your treasonous activities. You are just a little more brazen about it now. Now you do not just deny the King your service, but you openly conspire with his enemies."

"And perhaps you also have some explaining to do, *Master Gray*. What brings you to be supporting the Covenanters in arming themselves against your King?"

He turned his cold gaze on Richard. "Duty, sir. As always. My notebook is full. Names. Dates. Connections. Even quotations from the key persons present, sir. There is much that I have..." he tapped the left-hand side of his coat, indicating the location of his notebook, "...that will be of great value to the King and his officers."

"And what happened to the real Gray? Had an accident, did he?" Roger enquired.

"Unfortunately for him. Cut himself shaving, I believe, although why he would be doing that stood on the very edge of the quayside I really couldn't say. Fortunately for me, no one remembers the clerk. The accountant. The notary. Just a dull, ordinary man."

"Perhaps his family will remember him. Did you ever think about that?"

"No. And I couldn't care less. There are more important things for me to consider. Did you know these Covenanter bastards have appealed to the French for help? We intercepted their letter! Louis is too canny to provide money or troops, but Moray is here. I am sure *you* noticed him, DeLacey. If I were you, I would take care of your own safety. The world is a dangerous place and accidents happen all the time. Think of your family, friends and, hmm, companions." He looked steadily at Richard. "I can forgive your actions when we met before, sir, but this? You mark yourself, and those connected with you, for death." He smiled. "Your dangerously outspoken brother in the clergy, who rants against the archbishop? Yes, we know him. Even your skinny Dutch whore."

Richard's hand shot immediately to his sword hilt, his rage suddenly boiling over, but Roger's grip clamped his wrist. "No, Richard. 'Tis what he wants. He is in our hands. He can do nothing while we have the power to expose him as an English spy."

"But who will you expose me to, sir? My Scottish friends have all departed. It is just you and me here."

Richard nevertheless took a pace forward and thrust his face down into Montague's. Nose to nose he hissed his hatred. "If you ever harm any of my family or friends, you are a dead man, Montague. And not a quick, honourable death. You will regret ever having been born."

Montague, taking no step back, smiled slightly as Richard stepped back. "I doubt you have the stomach for it, boy. For that's what you are, for all your bravado and your fury. You may think yourself the man in your smart uniform..." he backhanded Richard's chest, "...and with your flashing blade, but you are just a silly young boy who is playing with things he doesn't understand. Well, understand this. You have gone too far. You conspire against your King. You arm his enemies. You are a traitor, boy, and you will be punished. Not here. Not today. But the day will come when you will understand that justice has a long arm, and then you will be the one full of regret." And he spun on his heel and walked away across the quay, splashing through the black puddles towards his tethered horse.

Soaked, and chilled by the wind off the sea, Richard shivered. He felt his eyes moist with rage. Trembling with cold, anger and frustration he whirled on Roger. "You see what you have done! Here are the consequences of getting me involved in this job! You lied to me. You lied. And now they are all in danger. Because of you, Roger. Because of you, and your pathetic drinking!" He shoved him with both hands to the chest and Roger staggered to avoid sitting down on the puddled stone.

Roger stared at him, a theatre of different emotions playing in his normally inscrutable face. Then he nodded to himself. "Then we kill him now, Richard. Then there is nothing for you to fear." He pulled his pistol from his waistband, took aim at the retreating figure and pulled the trigger. Nothing. The rain and damp had got to the powder.

"Damn you, Roger!" Richard took off in pursuit, struggling to draw his rapier from under his heavy coat as he ran, splashing the rainwater. By now, Montague had turned, his own blade out, and was reaching behind for his poignard. He looked calm, balanced, focused, everything that Richard was not. At the last minute, Richard gathered his wits and skidded to a stop, a few yards in front of him, breathing heavily.

"This is rash, boy. I should just administer a beating and be on my way, but I am heartily sick of you and happy enough to rid the world of such a sorry excuse for a man. I hope you know how to use that," nodding at the wavering tip of Richard's rapier. "It is a while since I had any exercise worth talking of."

"Talking seems to be what you do best, Montague." He was gaining his composure now. Gathering his wits together and dropping into a fighting stance, sword arm extended forward, knees flexed. He knew time was on his side, Roger was here to help. He could hear him coming. His confidence grew. He even smiled as he feinted forward.

In a flash, Montague flipped the poignard in his left hand, grasping the blade between thumb and first two fingers, and threw it just to the right of Richard's head. There was a gasp, a curse, the crash of a body hitting the ground. Richard risked a glance over his shoulder. Roger was down, the hilt of the blade sticking out of his shoulder. *Stupid!* Because Montague was on him now, and only a rapid step backwards and a sway of his head avoided the loss of his right eye.

The attack was relentless, and Richard was forced back dodging and parrying and feinting to buy himself some time. "Roger! You OK?" he shouted in a brief lull as Montague caught his breath.

"Got a fucking knife through m'shoulder! What do you think!"

Montague smiled and winked at Richard.

"But I'm reloading. I'll shoot the fucker this time."

The smile dropped from Montague's face to be replaced by grim determination. Richard manoeuvred himself to stand between him and Roger. If he could shield Roger long enough, and stay alive himself, then maybe this would turn out OK. *Concentrate!*

He gave up any hope of attack and focused on keeping the man at bay. But Montague pressed his attack, looking to dive through Richard's defence. High, then low. A vicious backhanded slash nearly opened his throat and as Richard took a long backward step to evade the stroke, he caught his heel on Roger's leg. He fought to maintain his balance, but as Montague moved in he knew it was better to let himself fall. He held out his blade as he fell to keep Montague at bay, but a dodge to the left and a swift lunge in return took Montague's blade just past his face as he fell. Montague's momentum carried him forward and with amazing dexterity he aimed a sharp kick that took the pistol out of Roger's hand. He stood over them. Roger unarmed and clutching his shoulder, Richard crabbing backward to get some distance so he could stand again.

(April 1640)

Montague appeared to calculate, opted for Roger and drew his arm back to push the blade through his chest, thinking to take the easier kill before he pursued the other. But as he thrust forward, his rapier was deflected by his own dagger, Roger having dragged it out of the meat of his shoulder with a howl of pain and anger. It bought him a few seconds, and as Montague readjusted for the inevitable killing blow, the crack of a musket came from the ship and the lead ball ripped the air apart as it flew over Montague's head. He froze, looking up, and saw two other muskets leaning on the rail and levelled in his direction. Kuyter's voice roared at them. "Stop! This! Madness!"

Montague reached up and touched the brim of his hat. "I so enjoyed our little dance, gentlemen. Another time!" He turned and strode away before pausing and looking back over his shoulder at Roger. "Oh. Keep the knife, DeLacey. 'Tis a good one!"

He broke into a trot, reached his horse and galloped off into the drizzle.

Half an hour later, as the ship made its way back down the Firth of Forth, Richard sensed he had also started on a new journey. The image of Roger DeLacey's invincibility had dissipated. He was no longer a surrogate father. He could not trust him as he thought he could. He could not rely on him and he must look after himself. There was a bigger picture than feeding his own self-worth. He must look after Neelie. He worried for his family. Montague knew of Lionel? If he was being watched, he must find an opportunity to warn them. *He* must grow up, damnit! A grimmer, colder Richard watched a pale sun emerge from the clearing grey smudges of cloud to the east.

An hour later he heard two cries of anguish from below the deck. The first was Roger; his shoulder wound was being cleaned and stitched. The second was Kuyter, who had just realised that Montague had switched the promissory note during his staged fumble, and that the paper in his hand was worthless.

Montague, for his part, was jogging along on his horse, drawing in the sharp, freshened air that follows rain, shadowing the arms shipment back towards Edinburgh. Already his mind was planning the unfortunate, devastating fire that would sweep through the building where the arms were to be temporarily stored. A temporary setback for the Covenanter cause, but they would not be replenishing with more arms from the Marcelis brothers. Not after last night. Really, when he reflected on it, things could not have gone much better.

And then he thought of home. A home he had not seen in months. A home that at times he never expected to see again. His daughter Mary would be waiting. And little Thomas. *Not so little now*, he thought with a mixture of pride and a sadness that these precious moments were passing him by. And Grace. Her calm brown eyes, her seemingly inexhaustible patience and love, and a fierce passion which none of their family and acquaintances would ever guess at. His pleasure at his cleverness and success was washed away in an instant as a flood of guilt and melancholy coursed through. He shook himself. He had to regain his focus. He had to concentrate on his duty. To his King and to his country. Grace would understand. He had to believe that.

24

MARLEIGH

(June 1640)

Life went on. Throughout the winter and early spring, she had maintained a low profile. Staying indoors, restricting her forays to the market, local shops and immediate countryside. She was in no doubt that the missing militiaman, Ralph, might raise no end of questions, particularly if the amazing fact that he had been overcome by a mysterious woman became known. But she also wondered whether the conscience, or the common sense, of his companion, Thomas, would have found another explanation to give to the militia commander, and to Ralph's family.

Nevertheless, she was careful. But no one came to find her. No proclamations in the marketplace. No announcements by local magistrates. Everything was quiet except for the worrying news from the north and the anticipated invasion by the Scots. She began to roam more widely again and, as the solstice approached, promised herself a journey back to her place. A performance of her rites of summer. It had been a while.

She made her excuses to Bolde. A sick cousin in Leek. She would be gone at least the week and hoped that would be acceptable. Bolde nodded his stern approval but in truth was delighted and disappointed both. He walked the knife's edge of desire and denial, an exquisite torture which made him feel more alive than at any time in his life, but one that exhausted him. He had begun to resent the hours he spent teaching at the King's School, as it kept him from thinking of her, from watching her when he thought she didn't know she was being observed, and talking to her when he dared. There had been no further discussion of philosophical matters for which he was eternally thankful, but she intrigued him, alarmed him, aroused him in equal measure. He was bewitched and utterly lost.

Just after dawn she had set out for the hills, which were masked by a faint but persistent drizzle. She hoped that the sun would be visible for the solstice, but it wasn't essential. It would be present even if the clouds obscured it.

Towards midday she halted, breathing hard after the climb up from Wildboarclough, and looked down on the hamlet of Gradbach. For the last hour she had moved warily. She was known in these parts and her leaving had been controversial. She had no desire to meet either friend or foe, particularly anyone connected with the Brassey family, who would see her dead if they could. But all looked peaceful down in the valley, the sound of the Dane River carrying to her above the breeze and the plaintive noise of the ewes.

She unwrapped a cloth parcel containing bread, cheese and one of last year's preserved apples. She put her back to the rough bark of a Hawthorn tree and her mood brightened with the clearing sky, now showing blue through thin, high clouds, filtered by the branches. The soft bubbling and chirping of greenfinches sounded above her head, and she caught a glimpse of the male, the darker line above his eyes making him appear severe and disapproving, despite his colourful clothes.

(JUNE 1640)

She smiled and nodded a greeting at him, but he disappeared with his mate in a blur of khaki and yellow.

Lunch completed, she angled down across the grassy bank towards the water, rushing fast under shielding beeches. She entered the dim, green-tinged, slightly close atmosphere of the wood, the humming and buzzing of insects magnified by the thick canopy. Here and there oases of sunlight dotted the floor where the cover was incomplete, flowers proliferated, and saplings took their chances to surge upwards and claim their share of the world.

She navigated through the trees, following game tracks, following her memory of the place through the seasons and across the years. After careful observation, she slipped back into the gritstone chasm, located her cave and changed from her usual clothing into the lighter, more comfortable, more natural garments she wore for her time up on the moors. For her rites. Her shoes were discarded, and all her clothing carefully wrapped in an oilskin and placed against the damp of the cave.

As the afternoon drew on, she emerged back into the daylight, and found the path up the side of the brook and up onto the moor. The familiar rocks reared up on the horizon like a stony wave about to break onto a beach she couldn't quite see. She stood for some time, hidden, scanning across the dry grass, reeds and heather for any sign of travellers, or shepherds out looking for wandering stragglers from their flocks. But there was nothing. No one.

She moved cautiously across the open ground and up the slope to the slabs, boulders, towers and high corridors of gritstone. She found her place, surrounded on three sides by towering stone, but open to the east. Facing the point where the sun would rise on midsummer's day. She laid down her packroll, dug out a few morsels to eat, and the wire and anchors for her rabbit trap. She anticipated a good meal, as she had seen a newly dug warren on her way up the slope, and the grass and heather were full of fat, happy rabbits, nibbling contentedly in the evening light. Traps set, she had a little time to kill and wandered along the rocky ridge, keeping below the horizon, to the place where she had encountered Ralph and Tom, around one hundred yards from her camp.

Uncertain what she might encounter she crept up the rounded back of the rock tower from which Ralph had spotted her hiding place to see what, if anything, remained to mark the events of that autumn dusk. At first, she saw nothing. The flat slabs were marked with lichens, a scattering of sheep pellets and edged with ferns, but the body had gone from where she had left it. She climbed down, carefully placing her feet. If she fell here and broke a leg or ankle, likely she would die there, for none visited by chance.

Down on the slab, memories of that evening washed through her mind. His angry face and fetid breath. The pain in her forehead from his headbutt and his weight and frantic fumbling as he pushed himself between her thighs. She had been unnerved but had remained calm, waiting for the time that he lowered his guard, when his alertness receded, for when he was vulnerable. And then, with all her thoughts concentrated on the muscle flow, she had brought boot up to hand in a natural signal of acquiescence and then plunged the needle-pointed knife into his ear and straight through to his brain.

And then. Oh, how she had longed to feel it again. As his life force fled his corpse, she had welcomed it in, absorbed the power, the energy, whatever it was that she searched so hard to name. To define. She grasped it before it dissipated into the environment, *seeing* the flow behind her eyes, in her mind. Somehow. Somewhere. Knowing it and controlling it, without truly understanding how, or what, she was doing.

(JUNE 1640)

And then. Channelling that energy to *her* limbs, into *her* brain. She pictured it like molten steel flowing into a mould. Like spring meltwater coursing over a millrace, driving the wheel at speeds where it could barely hold together. With the strength of two, and the heightened alertness and speed that always came with the borrowed power, she had easily levered Ralph's corpse off her, her hand grabbing the pistol from his belt as he rolled and her body flowing with the momentum to roll up and to her feet. The look on poor Tom's face as the cocked pistol finished a foot from the end of his nose.

But she couldn't hold on to it for long. Within hours of Ralph's death, the additional energy was nearly all gone. Like water in a canvas bag, the greater the pressure of the water within, the more leaked out through seams, or through the material itself. It was only intended to hold so much, and adding more and more eventually led to the excess seeping away. But while she could hold it, control it, direct it, the things she could achieve! She had unlocked an ability beyond her imagining.

It had been her life's work. Acquiring this gift appeared to be random chance. For a long time, she had not understood where it had come from, and it had taken years to actually realise what was happening to her. But the realisation had come like a lightning bolt to her brain. She had connected the proximity of an ending life with the wash of power, and she had become able to actually perceive it. Like the flow of molten gold, yet transparent, light, airy. As the body died, the energy that animated it sought a route back into *nature*. It was the only way she could describe it. This process was entirely unknown to those affected, although she knew, through her own experiences, and time talking to others, that many people observed the moment of death in others, not as an *end*, but as a *departure*. The difference was, she could actually sense it and, increasingly, see it. She had sought out death and the dying, human and animal, and found that by extending herself, in some way she couldn't explain in words, she could touch this flow of life and, eventually, divert it to herself. She could feel it flow through her, coursing through her body seeking to reconnect itself to the earth. She had the strong feeling that, in some way, it was *returning*.

In time, she had found she could visualise this golden flow going to parts of her own body and she was able to claim its power, the departing life of another, for a time. The sudden flood running through the millstream, generating power incredible enough to grind the millstones, before the flood subsided. Always she sought to learn more. This gift had opened her eyes to the world and she had so many questions that needed answers.

She cast about, looking for traces of Ralph's body, and found it. What was left of him was lying face down, under an overhang of rock, almost smothered by vegetation. The cold winter had preserved much of the flesh, partly by temperature and partly by limiting the number of scavengers, but with the coming of the late spring, and now summer, nature was taking him back to herself. Insects and their larvae had invaded his tissue, and grass, flowers and ferns pushed up through the emerging ribcage. His physical being was being dispersed to create more life, the nutrients of his flesh, blood and bones being absorbed by the world around him. Having been delivered to a life of thirty years, dragged into the world, made of earth and water, fed and fuelled by the sun, he was now going home, merging slowly again into the life all around him. Despite the horror of his decaying substance, there was a beauty to it, she thought. That inevitable cycle. We are pulled together from different substances and materials, and crawl around on the face of

(June 1640)

the earth for a brief time, but then we must give it all back. Everything. In a world where most people still lived the hard, relentless grind of rough labour, she thought it ironic that those whose lives were consumed by digging the soil were themselves then consumed by the soil.

She recognised the difference between the fate of flesh and the fate of that which animated it, but knew there was a connection. She grasped at the idea that there was no infinity of both. As humans, as other animals, as plants, they were formed from a pool of life, materials and energy, but then returned to it at the end. She had explored, endlessly, the view that this energy was a soul, but had rejected it. It didn't make sense to her. She looked at what remained of Ralph, his skeletal grin pressed to the rock as if sharing a joke with the gritstone. Was he, was she, even a separate being? Or were they a finger, a hair, a fleck of existence on something altogether larger? Was the living world itself some kind of being in its own right that could think, act, create, suffer and… die? Where did that end and she, as a human, begin?

She thought of the changing balance she had witnessed in her life. More and more people, needing more houses, more villages. Houses went up, hamlets grew to become villages which expanded to become towns. Trees were felled, wells dried up, rivers diverted, the animals of the countryside hunted. Is that how it was? There was just so much material and energy, and when it was used in one place, it meant less in another? Where would that end?

She had heard stories brought back from the New World, brought back to Europe by the Spanish conquistadors. Years before, after persistent and often dangerous enquiry among some of the adventurers still to be found around the taverns of Bristol, she had heard of a grandson of Hernán Cortés, a son of his firstborn Martin Cortés, who had been exiled from

Mexico to Spain. He was still living and had accounts and stories of human sacrifice on an unbelievable scale. He had a house in Léon, in northern Spain, and was old but still full of tales from 'New Spain'.

She had sensed in her gut the importance of this and had been driven to find the truth of it. She had managed to attach herself to a party of pilgrims intent on completing the journey to Santiago de Compostela. They were initially suspicious of her, and because of their deeply held Catholic faith, wary of everyone at that time in England, but she had convinced them of her sincerity, and they had taken her passion and commitment to finding Fernando Cortés to be a burning passion for the pilgrimage itself.

She had kept herself to herself on the stormy journey from Bristol to Bilbao, and had followed the Camino de Santiago along the coast and then through the mountains, suffering from hunger and oppressive heat, to the ancient city of Léon. Here she had parted from the pilgrims and spent a week, using her knowledge of Latin to talk with the local priests, to try to find Fernando Cortés. In the end, she had discovered the information she had from England was out of date. Fernando Cortés had been dead for a year. She had been distraught, despairing of the time wasted and the risks she had undergone for nothing.

On the point of starting back on the long and tortuous road to Bilbao, she had wandered past the house in Léon where she had been told he had lived. As she approached it, lying in the streets between the awe-inspiring cathedral and the monastery of San Marcos, she encountered an old woman leaving the property through a rusted iron gate, nearly twice her height. She had approached her and asked in a mixture of some recently acquired Castilian and classical Latin about Fernando. The lady was a maid and had been with the family for decades.

(JUNE 1640)

She had confirmed Fernando was dead. *Was the house now to be sold?*

No! Of course not!

Why?

Because where would his sister, Doña Ana, live?

She enveloped the poor maid in a hug of such amazement, joy and relief that it took her several minutes to recover. It occurred to her that after weeks of travel and rough living she looked and smelled terrible and had nearly asphyxiated the old woman. But she regained her composure and responded to frantic questions that she would speak to Doña Ana on her behalf, and that she should return later in the evening to learn the response to her request. She went immediately to the banks of the river, and after wandering for an hour, eventually came to a place where she could wash her herself and her clothes completely undisturbed.

Returning in the cool of the early evening, she had been admitted and spent several hours with Doña Ana Cortés. She had lived an extraordinary life, the daughter of a Spanish conquistador, one of the first mestizos and granddaughter of the infamous Hernán. She welcomed her as one more exotic visitor, keen for conversation now that Fernando was gone, and as a willing ear for her reminiscences.

Always she tried to steer Ana towards her grandfather and her memories of Mexico. *Were there any documents, diaries, journals? Could she remember anything he had said about the Aztecs and their practices?* They went round and round, with stories of palaces, gold, silver and handsome suitors drawn to her exotic beauty. As the sky grew darker and the stars shone out, they moved in from the rear terrace, and the maid, Maria, lit candles and closed the shutters. Strong local red wine had been drunk and Ana relaxed even further, sometimes even seeming to slip into a light sleep. She concluded that she would not achieve anything more than an entertaining evening and a slight hangover. *She is too old, or too stubborn.*

But as the time approached midnight, Ana seemed to reach a decision and nodded quietly to herself. She leant forward and asked for her forgiveness, her eyes more focused and intent. *Why should I forgive you, Doña Ana?* And Ana had smiled and admitted that she knew what was wanted. What was hoped for. *There is a chest in the library. It has everything you want,* she had said. *But you cannot take anything away. You must read it here. When I wake in the morning, we will have breakfast together, you can bathe and you can leave with nothing more than you came with except, perhaps, a few coins to see you safely to Bilbao. Do we have a bargain?*

She had spent a feverish night, regretting the wine and fighting to stay awake. Maria, who apparently did not sleep anymore, fed her chocolate and sausage and olives, and kept the candles alive. She waded through old journals and maps, copies of Aztec codices and other papers collected, Doña Ana had said, by her father and brother, searching for references to the human sacrifice practices. She found notes from Hernán Cortés himself, and others such as Sahagún and Durán.

It had taken her hours, but she found what she was hoping for, and it meshed so closely with her own experiences and thoughts that she saw a truth underlying their observations.

She departed León exhausted but clean and well fed and, most importantly, closer to an understanding. She had passed the coins received from Doña Ana to Maria with her thanks, and had rejoined the Camino de Santiago, walking against the flow of pilgrims.

Now, sitting with her back to the stone escarpment in Staffordshire, the pictures conjured up by the accounts from the exotic lands were vivid in her mind. Hundreds, sometimes thousands of people – men, women and children – sacrificed to the gods. Sometimes willing, and honoured, volunteers. More often captives or forced offerings from subjugated tribes. Still-beating hearts cut from the bodies at the top of giant pyramids, the remaining flesh eaten by people or animals. Some of the accounts thought this was to intimidate and divide their vassals, others that it was repayment to the gods who the Indians believed had themselves sacrificed their divine lives for the land and the people. She thought differently.

That amount of released life force, of energy, could carry an adept individual – a priest, she guessed – to great heights of power. Perhaps they did this to perform astounding feats, to cement their positions and even intimidate their kings. She had always thought this was the case with the druids. An annual sacrifice at the spring equinox or summer solstice, reaping the released energy to create some kind of magic spectacle and keep the tribe believing. She knew there was not enough power from an individual death to influence the vastness of nature, to guarantee a good harvest, or the onset of the spring growing season, but had the Aztecs in the New World found a way to channel mass sacrifices to influence the land around? Using released life force like a fertiliser to enhance the harvest? To redirect energy from a few thousand consumers of food to the crops needed for the population as a whole. It was an intriguing prospect.

Abruptly, her thoughts swirling like a mass of starlings, she reached a sudden insight, as if the flock had formed into some kind of sacred symbol. She knew what she must do. Too long she had focused on death, and the release of this strange fire, magic, energy... whatever it was! She had nowhere else to go with her thinking, she needed to make a change in her approach. And she wondered why she had been blind to this idea for so long. She would not wonder at the departure of life anymore. She would study its creation. She stood and walked back over the rocks, through the stiff heather, to check her traps and prepare her meal. She would finish her rites of midsummer. She would return to her room. She would turn her thoughts forward.

She would have a child.

25

WILL

(Newburn, near Newcastle, 28 August 1640)

Like the fallen branch of a tree wedged between rocks in a river, he held his pike horizontally out in front of him, fists gripping the centre, knuckles white as he tried to interrupt the flow all around him. He stood at the rear of the hastily erected earthworks above the Tyne, a twin of one a few hundred yards away, as men flooded past him. They avoided his eye as they dodged around the ends the wooden shaft, fear-driven, ashamed, but determined. More determined to escape the terrible bombardment than to defend the crossing from the Scots.

Will shouted, threatened, pleaded, but soon there were but a handful left sheltering behind the mud and wooden walls. The others, the handful of trained soldiers still trying to do their duty, looked at each other helplessly. Some cursed the fleeing troops; others were clearly of a mind to join them now that the cause was clearly lost.

Three iron balls from the Scots artillery landed almost

simultaneously, ploughing into the earth and mud that had been hastily piled into a defensive wall. Two of the three buried themselves feet deep in the ground, but the third skipped off the bank and ploughed a bloody furrow through the press of retreating men, compounding the panic. Shrieks and moans of agony and shock added to the symphony of hell all around them.

Will looked past them, down the slight slope of the Stella Haugh, to see massed Scots cavalry, supported by musketeers, advancing in disciplined fashion to the ford, now passable after the tide had retreated back towards the city of Newcastle. Viscount Conway, the English commander, had known the odds were stacked against him after the Scots had merely bypassed his defences at Berwick and, caught out, had raced his small force of 3,000 foot and horse to defend Newcastle and its rich coal fields. When the Scots had avoided the strong northern defences of the city and headed west to find a place to cross the river, Conway had hoped to hold them at the Newburn ford. But his 3,000 were faced by five times that number of Scots. And the Covenanters were led by experienced officers who had fought on the continent. Their troops were well armed and well provisioned. Not like the English. *A rabble*, thought Will, *with too few officers who carry any respect.*

After the rather pathetic stand-off with the Covenanters the previous year, what had become known as the Bishops' War, Will had left York when the northern militia was disbanded and headed home. Back to the fens and his family. But with the renewed desire of the King to subdue the upstarts north of the border, this time an army was raised in the south. If the previous one had been green, this year's crop was rotten. Poor behaviour, looting, desertion, even the murder of two officers suspected of Catholicism, or so he had heard. And in trying to hold back the tide of the Covenanter army, Charles had split

(Newburn, near Newcastle, 28 August 1640)

his force between Northumberland and Yorkshire allowing the Scots untroubled passage through the north.

The Scots were crossing now, the dark waters churning white around their horses' legs, and with the musketeers holding their matchlocks high to keep the matches dry and smouldering. Blue bonnets, sashes and flags made a moving wall. There was nothing to hinder their advance. But then came shouts and cheers from behind them and the slow building sound and tremor of a mass of horses on the move. Their own horse! He had assumed all were on the retreat, but here was a charge building pace towards the river. Lord Wilmot's troop gathered speed, fired their pistols as the distance closed, swords flashing out. The Scots horse responded, and were backed by their steady, well-trained musketeers. On both sides men collapsed from their saddles or were dragged among the pounding hooves. But by far the most were on the English side.

From the raised vantage of the earthen fort, they could see Wilmot's troopers fighting hard and bravely, but it was soon apparent that they were hopelessly outnumbered. The weight of Covenanter men and horse was telling, and the English were giving ground. Those at the rear of the press, who had not even been engaged, started to turn and spur away from the inevitable. Feeling a void opening behind them, more turned and followed, while those at the front had no knowledge that their colleagues were deserting them and fought on grimly until the final collapse came, when they could see they were flanked and in danger of being completely enveloped. They broke and followed their mates back up the slope and away from the harsh steel, blood and death. The Scots pursued, but before long they stopped and let the English fly unmolested.

Will had had to admire the strategy. Leslie, commanding the Scots, while the tide still blocked a crossing, had paraded a small troop of his cavalry to the shore and drew out the pathetic response from the four light pieces of artillery that the English possessed, split between the two forts and badly positioned. Pinpointing the position of the English guns had then unleashed the response from the Scots, who enjoyed a hugely superior artillery train, including eleven nine-pounders and a host of lighter pieces. They were marshalled by the experienced Alexander Hamilton, another who had learned his trade fighting for the Swedes. The forts were targeted and the effect was devastating. Will, attached to the soldiers placed in the forts to guard the guns, had experienced exposure to the terrifying power of big guns before. A few ranging shots built the tension for the occupants of the earthworks, but as the range was found, and some pieces that had been hauled to the top of a nearby church tower also opened up, he knew the bloody carnage would begin in earnest.

Despite the foreknowledge, it was a physical, visceral, bowel-opening fear that rolled over him and the other men. Huge detonations, earth-shaking impacts of the solid shot and the horror of the effect a nine-pound ball of iron, travelling at high velocity, had on the human bodies around him. The earthworks turned into an abattoir, with gore-spattered men desperately, but hopelessly, trying to return fire. Men exploded in fountains of blood and body parts, leaving unidentifiable mounds of flesh in heaps. As officers fell, all authority to hold the men in place evaporated, particularly as many had strong sympathy with the Scots' cause in the first place. Will and a few others had not been able to stop the rout, and with Wilmot's brave charge all in vain, there was nothing to keep them there. At least the cavalry action had silenced the guns. No point in wasting ordnance now.

As Will and the few others looked at each other for a decision, a horseman skidded to a halt at the rear of the

(NEWBURN, NEAR NEWCASTLE, 28 AUGUST 1640)

earthen fort. Red-faced with exertion, he bellowed down at them to wait. To hold their position and secure the guns. Colonel Monck was sending horses, and a detachment from his regiment that was still holding its ground, to bring the guns to safety as they retreated towards Newcastle.

Monck! Will had known his regiment was on the field, but he had not seen him. It surprised him little that Monck's men were still holding. The iron will and discipline of their commander would have allowed nothing else. The horseman pleaded with them to hold and then, seeing them willing to do so now that the cannonade had ceased, wheeled away back towards his regiment. In minutes, as Will and his mates crouched in the lee of the earthen walls and tried to comfort the dying heaped around them, two harnessed trains of horses arrived, with outriders and a jogging company of musketeers about twenty strong.

They dragged the two guns out of the earthwork and secured them to teams. Together they wound their way up and away from the river. Will thanked God that the Scots seemed content to depart with no further bloodshed. The meagre English artillery train was enveloped by Monck's men, who marched away in good order. Will watched them go and then set about trying to find his own battered and bloody men.

Later in the evening, around campfires to the south of Newcastle, what remained of Will's unit sat silently in circles. Somehow around thirty men had been rounded up, or had found their own way to the camp, and were now sullenly contemplating the gathering darkness and the lack of any food beyond what they themselves were carrying. Will's anger at their flight had dissipated, and although he was probably the youngest there, he had also seen the most actual fighting, and his huge size made men look up to him. They had little choice in that.

He looked around their faces, seeing exhaustion, shock and a dead flatness of expression. These were not soldiers. They had been pressed, pushed, threatened or bribed to be there. Forced into fighting by lords who cared nothing for their lives. For the harsh poverty from which they were dragged and the even harsher fate that stalked the widows and orphans left behind with no hope. If a lord won a victory, he could expect honours and riches, respect and reward. If he was captured, he would be treated with all due respect and honour, and ransomed back to his family. If he was unfortunate enough to be killed, his family would have pension, estates and wealthy relatives to fall back on.

For these men? They were just part of the landscape. Like livestock. Like hedgerows. Like the mud and earth. But without them, what then? It was only through the labour of men like these that fortunes were made and spent. Long days of endless, patient toil in the fields and workshops that produced the wealth for others to spend.

He had to speak. He needed to.

When he stood, he had no clear idea of what he would say, but somehow the words came to him. He had little education, but he had a natural authority, and now, as he peered through the gloom at the gathered men, messages started to flow from him.

At first, he spoke of the battle and the rout. He questioned the justice of their cause and why God had not been with them. "No shame," he had said, "for we knew not what we fought for, and we were outnumbered in men, equipment and the power of heaven."

He started to talk about what he *did* believe in. "I know not the intricacies of the politics that brought us all to this battle, but there are some things I do know." He spoke of how all men are created equal in the eyes of God, and that the accident of your birth should not count for you, or against you. How it is the quality of your heart, and your deeds, that should count. That all men should be level, not with some uplifted above the mass.

(NEWBURN, NEAR NEWCASTLE, 28 AUGUST 1640)

He could see that his words washed over many, too far gone in pain, hunger and fatigue to listen. But he also saw men nodding, silently connecting with his quiet passion. When he had finished, and he could only maintain his speech for a few minutes, he felt uplifted himself, like after a powerful sermon. He felt refreshed, and that something had been released within him. He had been encouraged that none had shouted him down and that his words were received positively by at least some of the men.

Later when they woke in the chill of the pre-dawn and started to move out to find the rest of the English force, two of the men sought him out. They had been moved by his words, they said, and asked him where he had heard these ideas. Surprised, he had replied that they were his own, that it was the first time he had shared them with anyone. It was their turn now to be surprised. Earnest men, they were of Puritan faith, from London, and they talked in subdued voices of others who spoke the same way. In St Stephen's ward in the City, around Coleman Street, were many who were of the same mind. Powder, just awaiting the match. London, they said, was growing tired and suspicious of the King's advisers, particularly Archbishop Laud and Strafford. The people wanted freedom to pursue their faith, without interventions that smacked of popery. Will should return with them. The London Trained Bands were in need of real soldiers to train them. To lead them. They had the numbers to make a difference but not yet the quality. When the day came, and they were needed, the Trained Bands would be the power in the City. And there were many in the Bands who thought as Will did.

Will thanked them, listening intently. He was excited. He had no concept that any thought as he did. For the first time he saw that he was not alone in his ideas. In truth, he was less concerned about religious freedom, and more concerned about the basic freedom of men to live and work fairly, but religious oppression was oppression just the same. He saw the sense in allying himself with the Trained Bands. An income perhaps. A cause and a mission. Something practical that he could do while he could engage in discussion and debate, and grow his ideas. He would be useful, perhaps even valued for his skills and experience. He would go to London as soon as his current duty allowed.

26

MARLEIGH

(Macclesfield, September 1640)

The days passed, and summer slid into autumn. The weather was wet, and it was unseasonably cold, although this seemed to be the new pattern, she thought. Her garret room started to reflect the coming chill and damp of winter, and she fretted at the confines of the walls with their rotting plaster and exposed wooden frame.

Now she had a new direction, a new plan, she wanted to be pursuing it. A child. Something she had considered and rejected so many times. But it was no maternal pull. No aching to fill a void in her life. It had never been the right time. She had seen it as a distraction, an anchor that would drag behind her when she needed to move quickly. To escape, or to follow an idea. Now she had turned all of that onto its head. Perhaps the answers were in the child. New information. New observations to make. New ideas to add to the pile. She was excited.

She knew how she was different and she knew there would be no problem in conceiving. Her *talent* would ensure success, but she also knew she must consider the other half of the equation. The father needed to be the right one. Not love. Not even desire. But a man who also had *talent*, even if he didn't know it.

And all her searching had so far been in vain. No hint, no sign, no indication that she had even come close. But what she did have was patience. She had waited so long for her answers, a little longer to find the right match was nothing to her. She swallowed down her eagerness, adjusted her coif and set off down the narrow stair to cross the market to the school.

The rain slanted in from the south-west, black-edged, grey clouds sweeping unhindered across the plain like ships, until they encountered the rise of the Pennines and deposited their cargo on the hapless citizens of the town. She pulled a hood over her head and trotted over the cobbles towards the school door. No children today, but Bolde had asked her to come in to do a thorough day's cleaning before they arrived back for the new term. She cursed him quietly for dragging her out in this weather, but he had been strangely insistent, and she didn't want to sour the relationship and put her job and accommodation at risk.

She shouldered the door open; it was always sticking in its frame. She half fell into the hallway and just stopped herself from skidding her wet boot on the slick wooden boards. She was soaked. She made her way to the large hallway cupboard where she kept the brooms, buckets and cloths. She removed her woollen jacket and gave it a snap to shed the surface water. Her cotton top clung to her where the rain had seeped through to her shoulders. She took off the coif and used one of the cleaning cloths to loosely towel her hair.

As she emerged from under the cloth, she developed the unmistakable feeling that she was not alone. As she started to turn to look down the corridor, Bolde stepped from the shadowed doorway of his office, further down the corridor. He coughed into his hand to make sure she knew he was

(MACCLESFIELD, SEPTEMBER 1640)

there. He seemed agitated, and as he took in her uncovered, dishevelled hair, and the suggestion of her form through her damp clothing, his state of nervousness increased. She saw him flush, look away, look back, and then away again.

"I'm sorry, sir." She took the initiative in the awkward silence. "Didn't know you was in yet. I was just tryin' to dry off from this rain. 'Tis a day for Noah to be buildin.'"

"Er, what? Ah. Yes. Yes, indeed."

She smiled back at him, trying to put him at his ease, but he just shifted from foot to foot. He was building up to something, but she wasn't sure what. She scraped her hair up and back into her coif, not entirely successfully as the dampness and her towelling had caused it to become wild and unruly. She replaced her jacket and buttoned it and saw his expression pass from relief to disappointment and then to… what? Fear? Determination? She really didn't like the look of this.

"Please, Miss Hume. Would you mind stepping into my office for a while. I just wanted a word." He disappeared back through the doorway leaving her alone in the corridor with a sense of foreboding. She stood for a moment, without moving, wondering whether it might be best just to retreat back into the rain.

But his voice came from the doorway. "Miss Hume? Just a moment of your time?"

She sighed, and walked to his office, feeling like a condemned prisoner, even though she was not aware of any offence. As she entered, she felt a pleasant warmth from a fire he had set in the grate. Two chairs were drawn up either side of the flames. He was standing behind the furthest chair but gestured that she should sit.

"Thank you, sir. This is very welcome on a day such as this." She sat on the edge of her chair, trying to make the most of the heat while remaining entirely alert and ready to move quickly. He remained standing, looking down at her.

"You really are wet, aren't you? Please, if you wish to dry out your jacket, we can hang it from the mantel. Let me help you."

She allowed him to take the jacket from her and weigh it down by the collar with a pile of books, so that it swung gently in the eddies of warm air. She thanked him and again caught him staring at her chest. It was now very clear the way his mind was moving, and she wished she had opted for the cold rain rather than the warm fire. This was disastrous, not because she felt threatened, but she could see no way forward that didn't end badly for her.

She hunched her shoulders forward, trying to disguise her contours under the cotton. She clamped her knees together and linked her hands together on her lap. She avoided his gaze and looked into the fire. And waited.

"Mrs Hume. How long have you been with us now?" Still he stood behind his chair.

"I'm not sure, sir. Would it be about a year now?"

"Yes. About a year. And still no word of your husband?" She shook her head, trying to appear sorrowful at the reminder. "Such a tragedy. War is so..." he floundered to describe something of which he had not the first idea, "...dangerous," was the best he came up with.

"So it is. You see things so clearly, sir."

"Do you think there comes a moment when..." he paused and gathered his determination, "...when you must accept he is lost and start your life anew?"

She looked down to conceal her dismay and also her growing anger. *Why can't he just leave well alone? Aren't men of God supposed to practise denial?*

"I don't know, sir. 'Tisn't anything I have thought about. I

(MACCLESFIELD, SEPTEMBER 1640)

thought once I was married, I was married forever. 'Til death do us part. I don't know that death 'as parted us yet."

"Quite so. But what I mean is, although you are married in name, you may wish to reorientate your affections elsewhere."

"I'm sorry, sir. Such big words. I'm not sure what you mean."

He looked even more awkward, but his course was set now. "I mean that perhaps you could learn to love another, even if in name you were still wed."

She did her best to look surprised and shocked, staring at him open-mouthed. He blustered on. "Of course, as a man of the church this is a topic on which I am well versed. There is much evidence among the scriptures that the Lord looks kindly on widows and wants happiness for them."

"Truly, sir?" *You lying bastard.*

"Oh yes! I have studied this very carefully. You can trust my clerical knowledge in this matter."

"Goodness me. I had no idea, but I suppose that makes sense." She watched him trying to position himself close to her without seeming to actually move. He was really bad at this and she had had enough. She knew what was coming next and it wouldn't be pretty. She sensed this might be her last chance to escape without a confrontation.

"Well, thank you, sir. That gives me something to think about and no mistake." She stood up quickly. "I'd best get on."

He placed his hands on her shoulders and tried to force her, gently but firmly, back into her chair. She could sense the desire in him, burning hotter than the fire. His eyes were wild, unrecognisable, and his passion was evident in an obvious and undeniable way. But although he pushed down increasingly firmly, she stood her ground. Her strength and suppleness, borne of hard manual work and endless walking across the hard landscape, made her like a rock to his thin arms. She saw his anger and frustration at her resistance.

He stepped back and glared angrily. "Mrs Hume, you know you are here only as a result of my goodwill. Without me you would be out in that rain, not in here by the fire. Not in employment. Not in accommodation. You owe all of this to me!"

She looked at him from under her brows. "Aye, Master Bolde," she said, her voice just above a whisper. "I know that. But that don't give you the right. Do it?"

He hissed back, "Well, yes it does. Actually. And if you don't like it then you will be back on the street like a whore. Just how you came to me. I am not a fool, Mrs Hume. You knew exactly what you were doing."

"Maybe. But more fool you are, if that is what swayed you. You are supposed to be a man of God, sir. Don't give me that rubbish about heaven countenancing adultery. What about your so-called immortal soul!"

He stared. His features writhed as he considered his next move. He had thought to browbeat her if his original gambit had failed, but he was clearly out of ideas. His normally peaceable, rather meek, expression was totally transformed. He was on the verge of tears, and on the verge of murder. He drew back his hand and went to slap her, but she caught his wrist easily and slapped him herself with her other hand, staggering him back.

His hands went up to his face, and he peered at her through his fingers. She strode to the door, jerking her jacket from its perch and scattering his books on the hearth. He scrabbled to rescue them from the flames but shouted after her as he did so. "Get you gone! I want you gone from here. And don't think about working in this town again, your reputation will be in the gutter from this day on."

(Macclesfield, September 1640)

"So be it, Master Bolde. But look to your own name, for you, I and God all know the truth of what has happened here. You are weak and evil. How suited you are to the Cloth!"

She was through the door and out into the weather. The rain had stopped, but the sky remained leaden. She was torn between frustration and elation. The difficulty presented by having to move on again, offset by the joy of being free of the monotonous existence at the school. Men like Bolde were just boring. Nothing new. No original thought. Just utterly predictable. She paused at the door to straighten her clothing and catch her breath.

She had two weeks of her rent paid up. She could plan her next move. She really didn't want to move again, but Bolde could poison her name, and with the incident with the Brasseys still a nagging threat in her mind, another scandal might be the end of her; she would become 'noticed'. She needed anonymity. She needed time to find the man for her child. She curled her lip when she thought again about Bolde. She felt her anger return. She would not let him win.

*

A week later and the townsfolk of Macclesfield were mourning the loss of their priest and schoolmaster. His body had been found at the foot of the long, steep path of stone steps that led down from the school to the valley below. A tragic slip on the rain-slick surface and a sharp contact between a granite edge and the back of his head. His eyes stared up, unblinking, seeking out God in heaven, but giving no sign if his search had met with success. His cleaner suspected not, but did not offer this opinion to anyone, particularly not the new priest when he arrived and confirmed her continuing position at the school.

He was a kindly man, and suggested she take a week to recover from the shock, and to grieve, and she gratefully accepted. The new priest was in his fifties and a genuine scholar of Latin. The boys' education benefited from the change, as Bolde had unaccountably become distracted and the quality of his teaching had deteriorated. The boys had noticed and told their parents. Perhaps it had all worked out for the best.

27

RICHARD

(Amsterdam, October 1640)

Richard sat with his head in his hands. The candle, which was the only light in their small sitting room, threw his shadow onto the faded plaster wall, a silhouette of some Greek philosopher, lost in thought.

"Fuck him!" he suddenly bellowed and that image had gone for good. "Fuck him everyway there is!" He banged his fists down on the table top making the candle leap and topple. He fumbled to put it back in the squat holder, burning his finger on the hot wax. He turned his face to her, red-eyed with tears of frustration.

"Can't you see it, Neelie? It is just lies! He is like a child, striking out because he hasn't got his way. You do see that?"

She too was crying. Sitting in her nightdress on the trunk by the window. A blanket wrapped around her shoulders, which quivered with sobs. "But he's my friend too. Why would he lie to me? And where have you been, Risch? It is late. Where have you been until this time? I'm scared…"

"Was he drunk? Had he been drinking when he came round?"

"Well, he smelt of it, but he often does now. Why would he lie? He said he just wanted to warn me, and that he had been drinking to get the courage to come."

"I'll bet he did. And why do you think I would lie to you, Neelie? Have I ever lied? You know how I feel about you."

She sobbed again but made her way over to the table. She sat next to him and took his hands in hers. She stroked her fingers along his ruined cheekbone and looked up at him through her long lashes, her black eyes huge and blurred with tears. He stared back, faces six inches apart. He could smell her warm body and the hint of mint on her breath.

He caught her fingers and kissed them and leaned forward to kiss her on the forehead. He closed his eyes. "He lied to you to get back at me. I went to see Hudde today. He had asked to see me. He said he wanted me to take on more work for him. More responsibility. He is expecting to do more trade with London, but there have been setbacks. Some shipments have been rejected by the Royal Ordnance, and he wants me to go and meet them and see what is behind this. I guess it is a promotion. 'More thinking, less fighting,' he said. He seems to think I have a future with the company."

She brushed some hair from her face and smiled. Her tears were drying up and she wiped her nose on her nightdress sleeve. Richard cupped her face in his hands and wiped the tracks of her tears with his thumbs. "That's good news. I mean, I don't want to see you travelling away from me again, but I understand this is important. For you and me."

He nodded. "Yes, I think this is a turning point for us."

"But I don't understand what this has to do with Roger?"

"As I left Hudde's office, Roger was waiting outside. It was early afternoon, Neelie, and he already reeked of wine and gin. He could barely stand. He asked me why I was there and I told him. He was happy and asked when we would be leaving for England. I told him I didn't know, but Hudde had not mentioned Roger, Neelie. He was only talking about me."

"What happened? What did Hudde want with Roger? Did he have different work for him? You always work together."

"I waited for him. He was only in there five minutes. When he came out, he came straight over to me and took a swing."

"No!"

"Well, he was drunk, he couldn't have hit his grandmother in the state he was in. He ranted and raved at me. Caused a real scene right outside the office. I had to drag him away. Hudde has fired him. He said he couldn't tolerate his drinking and no matter how good a sword he was, it wasn't worth it to him. He said he was a liability."

Neelie put both hands to her mouth in shock. "What will he do?"

"Well, I hope the first thing he does is sober up."

"Yes, but after that. Is there nothing you can do to help?"

"You asked where I have been until this late hour? I have been with Hudde. I tried to convince him to give Roger another chance. I took him out to dine. We discussed it for hours, but he would not back down. In the end I had only one option left. I told him I wouldn't take the job in London, the promotion, unless he reconsidered about Roger."

"Risch! No! You didn't!"

"He agreed. He hated doing it, but he agreed. But I am his bondsman now. Next time Roger fucks up, we are both out."

"That's great. Isn't it?" She looked at him, her broad smile fading as she weighed up the chances of Roger not fucking up. "But where have you been since then?"

"Looking for the ungrateful bastard. I went round every bar in the area trying to find him, but nothing. And then I come home and find he has been here all along, poisoning you against me. What was it? Whoring his way along the dockside? He still doesn't know I saved his arse."

"I will find him tomorrow, Risch. I will tell him what you have done for him, and I will make sure he understands."

"I hope that's the end of it, but I just can't see him changing now. He has sunk so far. He hates himself so much. I am not sure he can pull himself back together, to be the man he was when I first met him."

"Enough talking about him now. I want to talk about us." And she gave him the smile that always preceded… something. "Unless you are worn out from all your whoring, perhaps we can go and celebrate your promotion." Her hand slipped under the table, and all his tiredness and frustration was forgotten. "You seem to be very excited about it."

28

WILL

(London, November 1640)

He leaned on his pike, sixteen feet of polished wood, a padded leather bag where the steel point would normally be. He was panting and blowing, his breath creating clouds around his head in the chill air. He was exhausted. He had spent the last two hours drilling, or at least trying to drill, the designated pikemen of the 5th Regiment of London's Trained Bands, the so-called Green Regiment, on St George's Fields.

He had been impressed by their willingness to learn, their enthusiasm and their dedication. He had been less impressed by their skill, their discipline, their fitness and the quality of their equipment. But he felt it had been a good start and he had something to build on. He had shown them stance, how best to grip the pike when marching, when on the defensive against horsemen and when acting offensively against other units of foot.

He had pushed and bellowed, shoved and cajoled. He had been patient. He had knocked any number of them on their backs as they practised 'push of pike'. None could compete with his size and strength, and his skill and experience. But he loved how they kept coming back for more. Good men.

He was trusted by his captain who, in truth, was rather in awe of Will. The captain was a good and godly man, but lacked the strength of character and experience to lead his men effectively. He leaned on Will, and Will knew it but didn't resent it, because his reward was that he had found his home. He felt he was at a pivotal time in his life. He had found the anchor for his drifting thoughts, because a few weeks ago he had met a man who had become a walking, breathing incarnation of his vision for a fairer world.

He had been returning to his room in the parish of St Stephen's, making his way along Old Jewry, when he had heard the sound of a crowd approaching along the road, the sound building as it funnelled between the leaning houses. Some thirty or so men and women were cheering, shouting, some even dancing, as they made a slow procession along the dirty cobbles. At their centre was a man, heavily bearded, looking thin, drawn, exhausted, but laughing and smiling and returning shouted comments with wit and enthusiasm.

He pressed himself against a shop front to allow them to pass and grabbed the arm of a man at the back of the crowd. "Sir! Please! Tell me, who is this? What is happening here?"

The man looked like he had spent the afternoon in the alehouse and slurred his words as he shouted into Will's face from just a few inches, spraying him with spittle. "Don't you recognise John? John Lilburne has been in the Fleet these months and years and now is released! Three cheers for the Parliament men, for this is their doing!" The man lurched on, stopping now and again to steady himself against the wall of a house, or shop.

Lilburne. He knew the man by reputation. A fierce opponent of injustice, of bishops and, some said, of the King

(London, November 1640)

himself. But he had never met him or seen him, as Lilburne had been imprisoned in the Fleet gaol for most of the time Will had been in London. The press of people moved off down the street and Will, tired as he was, attached himself to the back of the group straining to see the great man up ahead. After a few hundred yards, the crowd slowed and halted as the throng squeezed itself into the alley that ran north through to Windmill Court and the Windmill tavern that stood there. Will followed on, finding himself closer to the front of the crowd as some more abstemious supporters peeled away when the destination became clear. But a hard core remained, and Will stepped over his previous informant who had succumbed to the effects of ale and excitement and was now just waving happily at the passing people from the cobbles.

In the dim light of the Windmill, a seat was found for Lilburne near the fire, as the weather was raw outside. He slumped gratefully into it and, rather like an enthroned monarch, accepted the praise of his subjects. The crowd, now swelled by its tavern-warmed counterparts, formed an impromptu queue, shaking his hand, thumping him on the shoulder, some of the women even kissing him. Will shuffled along with them until he found himself at the head of the line. He leaned down to shake Lilburne's offered hand, ready to move quickly on, but he felt the grip tighten rather than loosen, and he looked up from the floor and met Lilburne's intense gaze.

"I don't know you, sir. For I should recognise and remember a giant such as yourself. Indeed, I am amazed you made it in through the door!" His crowd roared with laughter. They would probably have laughed at anything he said that day. Despite the humour, Lilburne studied Will coolly. "What is your name, friend?"

"Fletcher. Will Fletcher, Master Lilburne. Congratulations on your release."

"I thank you, Will Fletcher, but I am no man's master. Call me John, friend. And what do you do, Will? Are you 'prenticed in this parish?"

"No, master… I mean, no, John. A soldier." He paused. "Was a soldier, I suppose. I am with the Green Regiment. The Trained Bands. I train the men."

"Well, Will Fletcher. That is an honourable profession. You have seen action yourself then? I am surprised in one so young."

"Aye, sir. At Breda, and various scrips and scraps on the continent. And at Newburn. I fought the Covenanters at Newburn. Not that it was really a battle. A rout more like. Many good men died 'cos they weren't trained. Didn't even know how to hold their weapons. I didn't want to see that again, so now I am here."

Lilburne nodded. The line behind Will was getting restive, and so he leaned forward and said, "I would speak to you again, Will. Now is not the right time, though," as he saw an elderly woman vainly shoving at Will's bulk. Will seemed not to even notice she was there. "I will be here often. Find me here, and we can talk again."

And Will nodded and moved off, smiling as the woman planted a toothless, wet mouth on Lilburne's cheek in triumph.

He did return to the Windmill. And he followed Lilburne to the Whalebone as well. And the Saracen's Head. And in all these taverns were men and women who talked together quietly, earnestly, with passion and conviction. He learned from John, and from his new friends, as he now thought of them, much of what had been happening in London. He learned more about John himself, and he came to marvel at his courage, endurance and purpose.

(London, November 1640)

John had come down to London from the North-East of England, some eleven years ago. He was the second son of a land-owning family and like many, destined not to inherit and been drawn into apprenticeship. At the age of fourteen he had been apprenticed to Thomas Hewson, a draper at Londonstone in the City, one of many thousands learning a trade, working long hours for little pay but receiving reliable board and lodging. He had served with Hewson for six years before being given his liberty.

While many apprentices spent their free time drinking and discovering the pleasures of the flesh, many others were of a more Puritan outlook, and were drawn to oppose the imposition of the Common Prayer book. They were sober, but passionate in their outlook, and many had come to follow the words of those like John who stood up against the bishops. John was from a Puritan family, and Hewson was a Puritan. John had spent his money on words. Words that had shaped his mind and fired his soul. John had got drunk on the Bible and the Book of Martyrs. He had not whored but had absorbed the views and thoughts of the radicals who had attended on evenings at Hewson's house. Men like Winthrop, Kiffin and Jessy, Rosier and John Bastwick. Men passionate about separatist churches and also passionate about the need for freedom from the established order, because a separation from the King's church meant a separation from the King. Whispered words that came easily from Lilburne's mouth but which chilled Will to his core, for they went far further than he had dreamed. Denying the role of the King felt like denying God himself.

He learned of Lilburne's own imprisonments and how his association with these martyrs brought him under the cold gaze of the Crown's agents, forcing his flight to Holland. On his return to London, John had been arrested by Archbishop Laud's agents. After a defiant stand in front of the Star Chamber, seeking to exercise his rights as a freeborn Englishman, he had been imprisoned, fined and then flogged, tied to the back of a cart, all the way from the Fleet gaol to Westminster. Will had heard this story before. Of John's defiance before the Star Chamber and how he had fought off paid assassins sent to get rid of this awkward man in the gaol. Food had to be smuggled in to him, when he had been left to starve. But even with his hands fettered, John Lilburne had managed to write his own protest pamphlets, smuggle them out and later learn they had been printed in Holland.

Will would have doubted much of this had he heard it about another, but looking into the cool, calm eyes of Lilburne he believed every word. More so when he saw the mass of scars across John's back and had read his pamphlets, particularly 'Cry for Justice', which had sparked the first apprentice riot against the archbishop.

About one year later, the archbishop had called out the Trained Bands to keep the peace when the authorities learned of an apprentice plot to attack his palace at Lambeth. Over the ensuing days there had been a stand-off, a riot, a break-in at the gaol to release prisoners, before calm had been restored, although John Archer, one of the leaders of the riots, was tortured and executed for his defiance. Some of his new friends in the militia had been present at the unrest and had been sympathetic, doubting if they would have actually fired on the mob if ordered to do so.

Will wondered at Lilburne's apparently charmed life, as all knew it was really he who was at the root of this violence and revolt. He was in awe of the man. He thought to himself that this was how the Disciples must have felt to be near Jesus, and immediately berated himself for his sacrilege. But later, in the dark of his room, he admitted to himself that he did see John as his saviour and accepted the thought as truth.

Now, with the Parliament restored, the tide had turned with a vengeance and a storm was gathering on the horizon. Visible to all. Visible to the King. Within days, freeborn John was free again, propelled from his cell by the fiery oration of a Member of Parliament, one Oliver Cromwell.

But perhaps even more than his disbelief at the bravery of Lilburne, he was amazed beyond belief at the role played by the women in the movement. He met John's most loyal supporter through his dark days in the Fleet, Katherine Hadley. Katherine, who had not only braved the horrors of the prison to visit John but had also smuggled out 'Cry for Justice' and been caught and sentenced herself. She too was only newly released, and bore the hardships stoically, unfailing in her allegiance to Lilburne and the cause. Will had never met anyone else with the same intelligence, courage and sheer bloody-mindedness as he saw in Katherine.

He followed the advice of his new associates and joined the Honourable Artillery Company, meeting more like-minded men. Men such as Owen Rowe, an officer in the Green Regiment of the Trained Bands, who had great knowledge of the colony in Massachusetts, firing Will's ideas of a new and fairer land. His thoughts spun in his head like the merry-go-round at the village fair, and every time he met a new friend of Lilburne, their words gave his whirling mind another hard spin.

Slowly, he had begun to form his own viewpoint. He cared about the Puritan faith. He railed at the bishops and championed religious freedom, but he had come to realise that what really interested him was a more universal freedom. A freedom from tyranny of every kind, not just religious freedom. The freedom of a human being to make his own place in the world and to have his say. To be as valued as the next man, no matter who his father was, or what land he owned. And his eyes had been opened to the scandalous disregard for the thoughts and voices of women. These matters were not the real focus of his new friends, but he was patient.

He lamented his poor command of letters, for so much of the cause was driven through pamphlets, and he could not get to grips with the texts. He knew that one day, he would want to write his own words and see them read, digested and acted upon. For some time, it had seemed a forlorn hope, but through his new association with yet more prominent radicals in Lilburne's circle, Daniel and Katherine Chidley, he had met their daughter, Sarah. She was just a little younger than him but had become his teacher. Showing the determination so characteristic of her family, she drove him tirelessly until he could grasp the meaning of the pamphlets churned out by the secret printing presses in the district. He loved her, and she him, although both were too shy to say it out loud.

He spent his days training his body, honing his skills and feeding his mind. Looking across the tavern board at Sarah Chidley, he knew he had never been happier.

29

BRERETON

(London, 18 December 1640)

It was dark in the room, lit only by a few candles placed on the tables. It was dark outside, the weak sun never piercing the layers of grey clouds of the frigid December day. No light penetrated the tiny, dirty windows that looked out onto Fleet Street. William nursed a tankard of ale, alternately holding it in his lap and then replacing it on the sticky table top. They were late. Very late. He could understand it, though. What a day it had been!

The Cheshire Cheese was busy, the evening customers starting to arrive in numbers, stumbling through the doors wrapped against the winter cold, seeking the fireplaces. And, in fairness, he had been early. He had wanted to secure a good table for the discussion, close enough to the window to observe the street, but not too far from the warmth of the roaring flames. And he had wanted to explore the inn; it had seemed wholly appropriate to have arranged this as the meeting place, given his origin and the topic for discussion.

The place was old. The bartender had told him it had already stood for nigh on a hundred years, and the cellars, he said, used to belong to the Carmelite monastery that stood on the site. He had stood in contemplation under the vaulted ceiling and tried to imagine how it had all appeared in those times.

The ale was good, but he resisted the temptation to finish this one and secure another before the crowd built further. He had to keep his head clear, excited as he was, and heavy drinking was a great sin. He wondered again where they were. Making their way through the grimy streets from Westminster, he guessed. Another fruitless glance through the translucent glass gained him nothing but another ratcheting of his tension.

As he waited, he reflected on the tumultuous events of the last year. It had started with the continuing breakdown of the truce with the Scots, and the King bowing to the inevitability of calling back Parliament. He needed their support. More importantly he needed the money that only they could grant. He had travelled down to London in anticipation in the spring and saw, for the first time, some of the great men of the day in action. John Pym in particular had caught his attention. He was known as a relentless campaigner against Catholicism and had been placed under house arrest some twenty years earlier. He had led the fight against the traitorous Duke of Buckingham, and was a passionate advocate against an absolute monarchy, treading a very delicate tightrope across the pit of treason.

It was Pym who had stood firm at the spring Parliament, leading the argument that the King must listen to the many fiscal, political, legal and religious grievances of the members of the House, before any funds would be granted to strengthen the army against the Scottish Covenanters. He had printed and distributed copies of his great speech, and William's copy was one of his treasured possessions.

The King had made half-hearted gestures to secure the House's support, but these had been rejected. And so, with the

(LONDON, 18 DECEMBER 1640)

words of his most loyal adviser, Sir Thomas Wentworth, Earl of Strafford, in his ear, King Charles has dissolved Parliament and sent them home, determined to find funds from elsewhere. Determined not to be beholden to the ordinary men of the country.

But it had availed him nothing. The Scots lost patience and in August their cavalry had crossed the Tweed with the objective of taking Newcastle and its coalfields – to hold the south to ransom. Behind them had followed the foot, and artillery train, and they had shown impressive discipline under the leadership of Alexander Leslie, a veteran of the Swedish army and the conflicts in Germany. It was like Caesar crossing the Rubicon, as the pamphleteers coined it.

They had pounded the meagre English defence of the Tyne crossing at Newburn, and had soon pushed on to take a largely undefended Newcastle, Tynemouth, Sunderland and Durham. The King was in York, but even with Strafford urging him to fight on, he saw that he had no option but to recall Parliament yet again and explore a peaceful resolution with Leslie. But any peace deal would have to be negotiated and agreed through Parliament, and the Scots remained in Northumberland, and were paid to remain there by Charles. It was humiliation.

As much as he hated the thought of his country under threat from an invader, William could not but help admire the fervour, and the restraint, of the Scots. There had been no real looting and the English prisoners of war were treated well. The Scots made clear their loyalty to the King, but that this was conditional on their gaining true religious freedom from the Crown, and an end to episcopacy. And William knew he was not alone in his admiration.

The King recalled Parliament, and Pym, John Hampden and their supporters had lost little time in pursuing their advantage. First, they had pushed successfully for the impeachment of Strafford, and he had been arrested and imprisoned the previous month. And today! What dramatic events. What excitement and hope for the true religion. Denzil Hollies, another fine gentleman, had moved the impeachment of Archbishop Laud in the House of Lords, and the damnable man was now in the custody of Black Rod. A huge step forward, and surely the start of better times.

He beamed, and allowed himself to swell a little with pride at the thought that it was today, of all days, that he had received word that the great John Pym wanted to meet him. *But where was he?* He looked again through the thick glass.

As he turned back from the window he saw them pushing through the clientele to his table. Pym, a small man approaching his sixties, was to the fore, waving his hat at him. "Well met, sir. Well met!" An icy handshake, then dropping down into his chair, leaving proximity to the fire to those who followed him.

"Master Pym. It is a pleasure to finally meet you, sir! I am honoured."

"The honour is mine, Sir William. And please let me introduce you to my companions. Perhaps you already know John Hampden?"

"By reputation, sir, of course." William pumped Hampden's hand. "A real pleasure, sir. The country owes you a great debt."

"Thank you, Sir William. You are most kind, but t'was nothing. A man must take a stand where he perceives wrong. Wouldn't you agree?"

"Of course, sir. But not all take the step."

Pym indicated the third member of the party. "Have you met Master Cromwell, Honourable Member for Cambridge? You and he should get to know each other."

William had seen him around Westminster, an active committee man a few years older than himself, longish nose

(LONDON, 18 DECEMBER 1640)

and blue-grey eyes framed by brown hair, strongly built and of serious countenance. Not a man who would be pushed around, William thought, and also another leader of the true religion. An ally. Cromwell nodded, holding William's eye as he reached to shake hands across the table. *There is a passion there*, William thought, *the slow burning fire of conviction.*

"Well met, Master Cromwell. My congratulations to you on the release of John Lilburne. He is an admirable man, and beloved of the people. T'was a good deed to obtain his freedom." Cromwell merely nodded his thanks, but William had been in awe of the man's oratory that day in the House.

A tavern waitress arrived with a tray of four ales. Pym thanked her and distributed them around the table. "Not something I would normally countenance, but I think a celebration is in order. How are the mighty fallen! A toast to Master Hollies on a job well done. Laud is done, I think, finally. We need the trial, of course, but his days are over."

"Well, John," laughed Hampden, "only a fool would drink water this close to the Fleet!"

"True enough!"

They all raised their mugs together. He watched Cromwell over the rim as he drank deeply. He had heard rumours of Cromwell's rather less than abstemious past and noted his slight hesitation before joining the others in the excellent ale.

Pym wiped his upper lip with the back of his hand and addressed William, fixing him with a piercing stare. The switch from jovial companion to hard-bitten inquisitor was instant, and stark. "Well, Sir William. We have heard encouraging things about you."

William returned his stare, desperately trying to convey a gravitas that matched Pym's. He said nothing.

Pym's gaze softened slightly. "Tell us. How is it in Cheshire? How does the land lie?"

William spoke for around ten minutes, laying out the antagonism of Bishop Bridgeman, trying to stifle the Divines in the county from his seat in Chester. He outlined his views of his fellow MPs. Sir Thomas Smith and Sir Francis Gamull for the city, Peter Venables, his fellow MP for the county. Gamull and former MP Sir Thomas Aston were passionate supporters of the King; the others were more sitting astride the fence.

He named the families who supported the true religion and his conviction that the commonfolk were sympathetic to the views that he held. Above all, he tried to give the impression that he was their man, one that could be trusted to work for the cause in the North-West.

The others nodded along, Cromwell quietly observing, Hampden making sympathetic noises, Pym scrutinising, questioning, probing. As William finished, Pym glanced at the other two and received barely perceptible nods in return. He turned back to William.

"As I am sure you realise, Sir William, we did not ask for this meeting just from a yearning to know more of your fair county. Today has been a great day, but there is much work still to do." He glanced around him, assessing the likelihood they could be overheard. Satisfied, he continued, "Firstly, we must deal with the Scots. I am sure, like us, you feel some sympathy with their cause?" William nodded slowly. "You know that is a treasonous viewpoint, sir?" William did not respond, so Pym pressed on.

"They will push the King, and Parliament, for all manner of concessions, and there will be little choice but to acquiesce. But perhaps not such a bad thing in the circumstances, eh? The King is under great pressure. He has been humiliated at all turns and is seen as weak and indecisive. Now his greatest counsellors are disgraced. He is in a corner."

(LONDON, 18 DECEMBER 1640)

He paused to take a swig. William did the same. *Where was this going?*

"We must take advantage of this weakness to push forward the agenda. This is our opportunity to kick popery back into the pit where it belongs! You have heard, perhaps, of the work that George Digby has started?"

William shook his head. He knew of Digby, but they had never spoken.

"He is preparing a paper. A list of grievances that could be said to have root in the conduct and decisions of the King. A remonstrance, if you like. He is a good man, and we will support him."

Pause, drink.

"But we know not how the King may react. Push him too far and we may face his wrath. Wrath backed by the Tower and steel. I am getting old, and my health is not good. I care little for myself but could not bear to see our righteous cause come to naught. The people rely on us. We must not fail. But to secure the future, we must lay plans. We must be organised and anticipate any event, and be able to react in the right way."

Personally, William felt that the commonfolk were probably oblivious to anything beyond their next meal, and perhaps the next harvest, but he was gripped by Pym's intensity.

"What do you need me to do? I know very well we walk a fine line here, but I put my trust in you, gentlemen."

"That's good, Sir William. As we trust you, in sharing this conversation." Brereton nodded his head in response.

"Strafford is gone. Thanks be to God! But his departure weakens the King's hold over Ireland. Whatever you think of Strafford, he ruled that land with an iron grip. With him gone, all is uncertainty, but two possible outcomes can be seen. Firstly, if the King needs troops to prop him up, he has the army in Ireland to call on, as long as that country remains peaceful. Whilst he couldn't land them at Dumbarton to assist him against the Scots, it is not to say it couldn't happen through a different port. Secondly, if the papists revolt, the Irish army will need support, which means recreating an English army to help crush them. We need to ensure that any such army raised is under Parliament's control, not the King's."

"Yes. I see that. There are very many powerful Cheshire families with ties in Ireland. Ties to estates and offices that go back generations. Why, on my own travels through Ireland a few years ago I met one of my own tenants running a tavern in Dublin!"

"Precisely." John Hampden now spoke. "And through which port would any army come and go between England and Ireland, Sir William?"

Ah. Now all became clear. He was being given his task. "Through Chester, sir. Through Chester."

Pym again. "We assessed your colleagues from Cheshire as you yourself did. Our conclusion was that there is only you we could rely on to deliver that city to our cause. Will you help us, sir?"

"I will do whatever I can. But 'tis no easy prospect. Bishop Bridgeman is entrenched, and it is not easy to say which way the key men will lean. Still, you have my word. You can rely on my best endeavours." He looked up from his study of the wine-stained table top and looked each in the eye in turn.

Finally, Cromwell spoke, and William suddenly realised these were his first words. "We may need more than your best endeavours, sir. We need your success. We need Chester for the cause. God leaves us with no alternative if we are to serve His will. When God is on our side, we cannot fail."

"Of course, Master Cromwell. As you say."

(LONDON, 18 DECEMBER 1640)

Rather more gently, Pym continued, "First task, Sir William, is to observe. We need you to maintain alert to any developments that might impact our plans and keep up a regular, but secret, correspondence so we may stay abreast of events. You may need to think about recruiting agents who you deem sympathetic to our cause, who can help you to stay informed. You will need to be highly discreet, and trust as few people as possible. Chester is the backdoor to England. You must be prepared to lock it."

"Yes, gentlemen. I will do as you say." William paused, thoughtful. "My main concern in this relates mainly to the border with Wales. I have some influence in Cheshire, but the northern Welsh are a different matter. I would anticipate them being fervent in their backing of the King. I think that is where our greatest danger lies."

"These are now matters for you, Sir William. Just keep us informed. We want no nasty surprises."

The conversation now turned to more general matters. Voices lowered and were easily drowned out by the growing clamour in the Cheshire Cheese. The cold drove more and more people inside to its fires, and there was scarcely room to move.

Hampden led a discussion on the parlous state of the army and the lack of decent arms in any quantity. "The King has been importing from the Danes, and through the Low Countries, but often the quality is very poor. His agents are either incompetent or are defrauding him. The Scots have a much more efficient network, although the navy is intercepting some of their shipments. I think the King is at the end of his tether with men like Quarles."

Cromwell was a more active participant in this discussion. "I have heard that it is not always that the foreign arms are inferior. Remember, some of these are coming from places like Solingen, or have already been proved in action. No. I have heard that fortunes are being made by our own manufacturers and they collude with the Ordnance Office. Men like Browne and Stone. You know of them, I am sure. They have secured virtual monopolies in iron cannon and blades, and it is not in their interests to see a flood of foreign weapons."

"What are you saying, Oliver?" Pym responded, and William was shocked; this was all new information for him.

Hampden butted in, "Last year, when the army was desperate for weaponry, a very large consignment of blades and other arms arrived from Hamburg. They were rejected – perhaps you remember?"

"T'was a scandal," remarked Pym, nodding. "There was great criticism of Sir Thomas Roe. He defended himself stoutly, I recall, but there were many who said he had been tricked by King Christian IV himself. Kept all the best weaponry and sold Roe the dross."

"But who rejected them, John? T'was not the ordnance officers themselves. They were appraised by three senior men from the Gunmakers' Company! No wonder they rejected them, more competition is bad for business. The weapons never even made it as far as the Tower. There's the scandal."

"The problem," Cromwell continued, "is that the Ordnance Office is starved of money. They pay their officers so little that some are always on the lookout for ways to make a little extra. And the English producers make so much profit they can easily afford to buy a few clerks. They are not all crooks by any means. Many of the Ordnance men work hard, and honestly. But it only takes a few."

"Look at the situation with blades, swords and pike heads." Hampden picked up the tale again. "It is difficult to know if things are getting better or worse. The Cutlers' Company had their monopoly broken by Ben Stone, but now he has just supplanted them with his own. He kept rubbishing their work

(London, 18 December 1640)

– yes, he did invest in bringing over all those Germans from Solingen, but they made him the official cutler for goodness' sake! Now he can pass his own work through in priority and reject the Cutlers' Company blades as he pleases."

Pym and Brereton looked at each other and shook their heads. "If you wrote it as a story, people would call it fanciful," said Pym.

Hampden continued, "And we hear that these wealthy, wealthy men are engaged in sabotage on the continent. They are trying to disrupt the supply at source while they scale up their own production. The investment needed is large and they can't afford the imports to suppress prices when they are borrowing such large amounts. Even though we have a degree of peace in the Low Countries and Germany, they are certainly gambling heavily on a larger conflict."

Pym summed up. "If we ever come to a time of war in England, and God forbid that we do, this is an issue we must resolve once and for all. Gentlemen, thank you for opening my eyes to this. I must think on it further. But now I am away. We are going to be busier than ever following today's glorious outcome!"

Brereton followed the others out into the cold. He reflected again on his naivety as he trudged towards the Ludgate, where his lodgings were. So many layers. So many plans. On the one hand, he felt a little lost, despite his excitement at mixing with some of the great men of his age. On the other hand, finally he had clarity of purpose. He had his task sent down from God. He must master his county for Parliament. For the true religion. For God.

Thoughts of balmy summer evenings sitting in his garden were hazy pastel in the long distance against the bright, stark, burning urgency of the new reality of his assignment. He had a lot to think about, but right now top of his list was finding better rooms, closer to Parliament!

30

RICHARD

(Amsterdam, April 1641)

For the third time, he stopped. This time pretending to look in the shop window of some fashionable shoe and boot shop. He used the reflection in the glass to look over his shoulder, to the left and the right, waiting for a figure to appear from the alley on the far side of the street. The alley he had just left. Watery, late afternoon sunlight struck the glass making it difficult to peer into the shadows, but he was convinced he saw a head peer around the corner and quickly pull back.

For a week now he had had the sense of being followed. Ever since his return from Copenhagen he had half seen, or half heard, a presence over his shoulder. But he had never quite caught a clear sight of his ghost. The man was clearly skilled and, after two days of this nagging feeling, Richard had taken to daily strolls around the district, purposefully trying to get a better sight, or maybe even challenge him. But no success, only half-imagined glimpses. The tension had built in Richard as his attempts to resolve his situation failed time and again. He had started snapping at Neelie when she expressed her

(Amsterdam, April 1641)

own concerns, his patience quickly exhausted and his temper explosive as ever.

At her suggestion, he had made two trips back to the Sailor, swallowing his pride and trying to cajole Roger into helping him corner the shadow. But Roger had not been interested, only willing to watch from an upstairs window to try to observe if Richard was indeed being followed. He reported that he had seen a man, hatted and cloaked, emerge from a doorway when Richard had left the Sailor and follow him carefully up the street, but he was not willing to help further. Roger was continuing his slide into what seemed a terminal melancholia and had become almost unrecognisable as the seemingly indestructible fighter who had adopted Richard and Will.

So, Richard had come out of his rooms again, resolving to stay on the street until he addressed the situation. And now he at least had what he felt was definite proof and, what's more, the man was just ten yards away on the other side of the street. He pulled the brim of his hat down an inch, slipped a hand under his cloak to find the grip of his poignard and walked purposefully down the cobbles, swinging right into another of the tight alleyways of the district. As soon as he rounded the corner and was out of sight of the man's hiding place, he sprinted halfway along, took a sharp left, ten yards, took another left and crept back towards the street he had just left, peering carefully around the corner, his own hat removed.

Back up the main street, he saw a figure emerge from the alley on the far side and walk slowly down the cobbled pavement to a point where he could see down the passageway that Richard had initially entered. The man stopped and peered across the street, trying to penetrate the gloom with his stare. He then picked up his pace heading over the road, dodging two men on horses trotting westward, and disappeared in pursuit of Richard. Immediately, Richard left his hiding place and jogged quickly up the pavement to the same alleyway the man had just entered, and for a second time, he walked into its gloom. Ahead, silhouetted against the light at the far end, he saw the cloaked figure walking slowly along one wall, staring ahead and trailing his right hand behind him along the stone. He paused at the left turn which Richard had previously taken, peering into the shadows and, seeing nothing to interest him, pressed on along the alley. Richard followed, moving quietly, but quickly, fully intent on catching up with and surprising his quarry, a week of anger speeding his steps.

He gained quickly and as the distance closed to less than ten paces, drew his poignard, just as the man finally sensed the presence behind him and looked back over his shoulder. He fumbled under his own cloak, eyes widening as the point of Richard's needle-like blade narrowed the distance in seconds. The tip hovered an inch in front of the man's blue left eye and Richard gestured for him to slowly bring his right hand out from the folds of his cloak.

When it emerged it was empty, the man now fully turned to face Richard, two empty hands held out from his sides in a stance intended to calm his assailant. Richard now swapped his knife to his left hand, and with his right drew out his rapier, resting the point in the hollow of the man's throat. With a quick flick, he tipped the hat off the man's head, revealing a young face, with blond shoulder-length hair and moustaches, and a neat goatee beard. If the man was afraid, his face didn't show it, but his eyes were watchful and alert, fixed on Richard's.

"My friend. In my city, this is not considered a polite way to introduce yourself." The voice was steady and, Richard thought, slightly mocking. In any case, the man had made the possibly fatal mistake of calling him 'friend'. He hated this device, and his rage ratcheted up another notch.

(AMSTERDAM, APRIL 1641)

"In anyone's city, it is not considered polite to follow a man around for days. Although some would consider it dangerous." He tried for ice-cold menace but was not convinced he was achieving it given the lava-flow of emotion he was trying to control. *This fucker is intruding on my life, threatening my peace of mind and posing who knows what kind of threat to me and Neelie.*

The man smiled broadly at him. Confidently. "I am sorry, my friend, but I do not know what you are talking about. This is my way home. I go about my lawful business. I follow no one. Perhaps you have an inflated idea of your own importance? If you care to put away your various weapons, I am sure we can forget all about this."

"The only place I am going to put this," Richard raised his rapier so the point centred over the man's face, "is through one of your lying, fucking eyes. Friend." Richard was rather disappointed with the effect this had on the man, whose gaze did not falter. "Perhaps you can start the process of your redemption by telling me who you are, who you are working for and why I might be of interest to you. Perhaps then you will get to walk away from this without leaving any pieces behind." Richard had heard DeLacey use that line and had always liked it.

But blond moustache man just stared back, smile on his lips. "As I said, my friend, I do not know what you are talking about and my patience is wearing thin. I do not know you and I do not want to know you. Put away your arms and perhaps we can yet resolve this peacefully."

The anxiety and frustration of the last few days threatened to undermine Richard's cool as, for the first time, he realised he could not just kill the man in cold blood, and he clearly wasn't for scaring into talking. *Why does nothing ever seem to go to plan? Why did I not tell Hudde about this rather than go* to Roger? Useless arsehole! Me, or Roger? "No. That's not going to happen. This is going to happen." And he swept the blade down and drove the point through the outside of the man's left thigh, piercing the large muscle, but avoiding the bone and major blood vessels.

The man's leg collapsed under him and he crumpled against the wall of the alleyway. His standing leg then slipped on the greasy surface and he slid to the ground. Richard had learnt many curses in Dutch, but here were some new ones.

But Richard became aware of activity behind him and he glanced over his shoulder, taking a step back as he did so to put himself out of range of any tricks the wounded man might try. He saw a small group of people at the end of the alley, peering through the dimness to try to ascertain if it was safe for them to venture down. He had no desire to draw further attention to himself or face the law, so it would have to be intimidation rather than interrogation. He squatted down onto his heels and pushed the man's chin up with the point of his dagger, looking him in the eye. "Luck is with you. No death today. But if I see you again, I tell you straight, *friend*, it will be your last day on this earth." He stood and then abruptly swung his boot into the man's face, cracking his head back against the stonework. As he slumped unconscious, Richard reached under his cloak, removed his knife, purse and searched for any type of paper, any clue to the man's identity and purpose. But nothing.

Infuriated that the mystery continued, he gave the prone body another hearty kick, stepped over him and strode to the far end of the alley. He walked quickly away, taking random turns to throw off anyone who had tried to follow him. As the sun lowered, he headed to Hudde's house. Time to tell his employer of his concerns. And his actions.

(AMSTERDAM, APRIL 1641)

*

Slumped in a leather armchair close to the fire, he studied Hudde's back as the man gazed out of the tall window, a forest of masts waving gently beyond him against the cold grey sky. It would be fully dark soon. The firelight and a few candles were the only sources of illumination and shadows wavered on the walls, now and then shooting out shoals of darkness as the flames twisted.

He was concerned. Hudde hadn't spoken or turned from the window in minutes. Minutes that felt like hours in the silence of the room. He admired Hudde. He liked Hudde. He was grateful to Hudde for employing him, and then trusting him with more and more responsibility. Pieter Hudde was his mentor, and he held Richard's future and growing prosperity in his hands. From a simple guard, he had become one of Hudde's trusted traders, responsible for carrying the company's terms of business to foreign capitals. Conducting preliminary negotiations with buyers and reporting back. Outlining catalogues of materials and discussing methods of payment. He was good at this and he knew it. But more importantly, Hudde recognised it too, and the recent trip to Copenhagen had been the next stage in his education. Closing a deal to purchase Swedish-made cannon and to allow their passage through Danish waters to Amsterdam.

The last thing he wanted was to bring bad news, or plant the seed in Hudde's mind that he was trouble. Not to be trusted. A liability.

Finally, Hudde grabbed the wooden shutters and drew them together, bolting them shut. "Well. I don't think anyone followed you here at least, although it is no secret who you work for." He gestured to the golden initials woven into Richard's dark blue waistcoat. "I know this must be troubling for you. It is troubling to me as well. And it would trouble my employers." He held up a hand as Richard started to speak. "No. I don't blame you, son. What I mean is that it is just another brushstroke in a picture that is already confused, and worrying, and cannot be easily interpreted. It is not a masterpiece from Master Rembrandt. It is more like something my dog would throw up onto the kitchen floor. Too many things are happening that are unclear, and this is just one more."

"I thought we thrived on confusion and conflict?"

"Normally, yes. Uncertainty means powerful people want to safeguard what they have, or take something that belongs to someone else while attention is distracted. That means business for us. Quietly, carefully, in the shadows." He emphasised his point with a sweep of his arm to the unlit corners of the comfortable lounge that served as an office at his house. "But this is different. Events seem to be centring on us, and that is not a comfortable thing in our line of work."

"I don't understand. What things?"

"Most of it is things that don't concern you. We are in a very competitive and secretive business. There are often disputes, bad debtors, untimely deaths. But I am wondering if this recent event – you being followed, for I do not doubt your tale – is tied up with the failures we have been having with your mother country? It is perhaps stretching reason to link the two, just because you are English, but I wonder if there is connection with our troubles with the Royal Ordnance Office in London."

"How so, sir?"

"Our last few shipments, small consignments only as your King is broke again, keep getting refused on the grounds of quality. Not all the goods, but always the blades. And the musket barrels. Problems with quality, they say. Inferior steel,

(AMSTERDAM, APRIL 1641)

they say. We know the steel is good. It is Spanish steel, or from Solingen. OK, we might slip a few rejects in from other shipments. Everyone does this. But it is whole consignments. It is bad business and bad for our reputation. But I can't see a connection with you apart from your Englishness."

"No, sir. And I have no connections with the Ordnance men. Nor has my family, nor any of my acquaintances. I do not think this can be the reason. I think it has connection with the unfortunate events in Edinburgh. And with my help to Monsieur de Sête those months ago at the warehouse. I think perhaps I made a bigger enemy than I thought with Montague, the King's agent."

Hudde leant against the edge of the massive oak desk and raised an eyebrow. "You think you are so important to him that he has you followed? You have risen well, Richard, in our business, but you are not yet such a player that you would attract the attention of an agent of King Charles. It seems unlikely."

"I agree. But it seems personal, somehow, with Montague. A hatred of myself and DeLacey."

"Well, a hatred of DeLacey is easily understood," Hudde said, "but this seems an extreme reaction. You say your shadow had no papers on him?"

"No. Just his dagger, which was locally made. And his purse. I haven't counted it, but it seems not out of keeping with the man's clothing and grooming. He was surprisingly cultured for a common footpad."

Hudde extended a meaty hand, gesturing with his fingers to receive it. Richard tossed it underhand and it smacked heavily into Hudde's palm. He emptied it onto the desktop and pushed the coins around, dragging a candlestick across the green leather surface to let him examine them. "Well," he said, "either the man is well travelled, or he has been transacting with a countryman of yours recently. Half of these coins are from your London mint. That is an interesting piece of information."

Richard rose from his chair and joined Hudde in looking at the gold and silver discs.

"It seems that the answers to at least some of our questions may lie in London. Perhaps you should go there and dig around a little." He paused. "And perhaps I should come with you. I will seek a meeting with our friends at the Ordnance Office, and meet up with our own agents and listen to what they know."

"England! I… I have not been back there since Breda. I am not sure I will be welcome given we have been supplying the Scots so recently!" Richard was genuinely unnerved.

"Oh, don't worry on that. We also supply the English against the Scots. And the French against the Spanish. And only whisper it, but also the Spanish against ourselves. We are a necessity. No one said we had to be popular. Just profitable and reliable. And, at the moment, King Charles needs us more than we need him."

"Then I worry for Neelie. If this man is connected with Montague, I am wary of leaving her here without my protection. And DeLacey is no good for that anymore, it seems."

"No indeed. Very well. Bring her too. I doubt she has ever travelled much outside the city. When our business is done, take some time. Visit your family. Your family is near London? You can introduce Cornelia. I am sure they will be delighted to see you both!"

Yes, thought Richard. *Delighted.*

31

RICHARD

(London, June 1641)

He walked along Moorgate, arm linked with Neelie's. Her head was constantly turning; he was surprised she didn't injure her neck. Everything was new. Everything was different. He thought her interest in the London fashions was shallow. He thought her people-watching and her gawping at some of the London landmarks made them look like country mice, lost in the big city. He felt half amused and half embarrassed. Maybe this had been a mistake. But then he realised he was doing much the same, for despite this being his country, he had never set foot in London before.

He fretted about how much they stood out in the press of people. Their different clothes, their behaviour, the fact he had to keep asking directions. He was used to this feeling when he was on business for the Marcelis brothers. When he was alone. But now, yes he was on business, but somehow Neelie complicated his feelings. She interfered with his usual confidence and sense of purpose. Now he worried about Hudde's business, the potential danger he was in, but also about Neelie. Her safety. And, he couldn't deny it to himself, that he felt slightly resentful of her presence.

They had arrived after dark, mooring against one of the quieter quays, down river of the Tower. A short row up, with the tide, had taken them close to their lodgings at the ambassador's grand house. Hudde was on good terms with all of the most important of his country's ambassadors, as the arms dealers in many ways were just extensions of the government – given all of the subsidies, tax and trading concessions they received. Richard felt safe within those walls, but that first night when they were received, had cringed and sweated when questions and pleasantries were directed at Neelie. With his upbringing as minor gentry, and with a few years of polish in the employ of the Marcelis brothers, Richard had built up a passable knowledge of etiquette for dealing with his betters – which was most of the people he dealt with in business. But Neelie's experience was limited to a whorehouse. However, she had played a part well, he had to admit, and guessed that every successful whore had to be resourceful, and a good actress, to keep her customers and keep the bruises from her face.

Now they were out in the streets, dressed as plainly as he could contrive, and he was torn between feelings of exasperation at her tourist behaviour, and feelings of pride and anger in equal parts at the admiring glances her youthful beauty attracted from passing men. But above all, she was a distraction, and he could not focus properly on his job.

Hudde had told them to go and enjoy themselves while he met with the ambassador and sent runners to set up meetings for them at the Royal Ordnance Office, and with importers with whom they did business. He had indicated that it might be some days before they could get down to serious business, even with the letters of introduction they had sent in advance. So here they were, wandering the busy streets on a muggy,

(London, June 1641)

overcast summer day, thinking about lunch after taking in the Palace and Abbey in Westminster and strolling towards the Guildhall. Despite Hudde's confidence that their movements would be unobserved and seem unremarkable, Richard's experience in Amsterdam kept him alert for anyone who might seem to be watching them, or actively following them. He had left his rapier in his room, but his hand sometimes rested on the pommel of his poignard, concealed under his jacket. But he saw nothing and gradually relaxed as the day wore on, responding more to Neelie's questions and forcing himself to take in more of the city and his surroundings. He had to admit that while it was a great city, it did not have the wealth, the bustle, the feeling of being the centre of the world, in the same way as Amsterdam.

But it did feel tense. Twice they had pamphlets thrust into their hands by fierce-eyed men and women. Small crowds gathered here and there to listen to orators at street corners and in small parks and courtyards. Always the words called the change. For freedom. "Down with the bishops!" "Down with Laud and the Pope!" "Freedom to worship as God intended!" To his surprise, he heard support for the Scottish Covenanters who had only recently been fighting the King. Richard smiled to himself. *Hudde would be delighted with this*, he thought.

The Guildhall loomed ahead of them as they walked along. As they crossed the opening to a narrow street, a figure emerged from the shadows and paused, studying the pair closely. As they strolled across the courtyard, Richard tried to appear knowledgeable by pointing out aspects of the architecture, but Neelie got the giggles at his pomposity, mimicking his tone and gestures. He bristled, but her laugh was infectious and he joined her, having to concede she was right. He was an arse sometimes.

As they struggled to regain their composure, the figure closed the distance between them and a heavy hand fell on his shoulder, just as his shadow fell across Richard's peripheral vision. Although he had relaxed, Richard had learnt to react in an instant. As the hand pulled back, starting to wheel him around, the poignard was out from under his jacket in an instant. Neelie was still largely unaware of anything happening until she saw the bright steel flash past her face.

As he saw the blade coming for the centre of his chest the big man managed a sharp step back, almost tripping on the cobbles. But instead of going for a weapon of his own, he just held both arms straight up, palms showing to them both, empty. With space for a breath, Richard now focused on his adversary.

"Woah! Calm yourself, sir. And I was right! It *is* you! Richard Farrell, as I live and breathe." His arms came down and spread out, giving him a huge wingspan.

"Wha... No! It cannot be. Will? Will Fletcher? My God, but you have become a giant!"

"Not quite, Rich." Will smiled warmly. "And I think you can put that away now." He nodded at the knife, whose tip was still circling in front of him. "I don't think you will need it."

"Quite so. Sorry. I am a bit on edge today and I didn't see you coming." He seemed to be chastising himself for his lapse in concentration, but a second later he was drawn into a massive bearhug and could scarcely breathe.

"It is good to see you, Rich! In these times nothing is certain and I thought you probably dead on some adventure on the continent."

"Not yet. But I bet we both have stories to tell. Have you eaten yet? Can I buy you lunch? Is there somewhere near here you can recommend?"

"Aye. There are stories a-plenty. And I see one is standing right in front of me." He turned and gave Neelie a huge smile

(London, June 1641)

and offered his hand. "Hello, my lady." Neelie let him gently shake her hand as she blushed and giggled. "This is one of the reasons why I was not sure it was actually you. Never I have seen you with one so beautiful."

She whispered to Richard in Dutch, "You see. I *am* a lady. And your friend is so big! This must be the one you have talked to me about so often?"

Richard was pleased and embarrassed in equal measure. "William Fletcher, I have the honour to introduce Cornelia Coeymans, my..." He paused, suddenly feeling horrified that he did not know how to describe her. He looked wildly to Neelie for help.

"His companion..." Neelie finished for him in the halting English she had picked up from Richard, Roger and some of her former clients. "But call me Neelie. Please. Everyone does. And I am pleased to meet you, sir." And she curtsied, blushing prettily again.

Will stood back and looked at them standing together. "You make a lovely couple," he said. "I am so pleased to see you again. Truly. And yes, you may buy me lunch for I am both hungry and poor today. And you look like you can afford it – which is another story, I am sure. And Rich?"

"Yes?"

"You should not take the Lord's name in vain."

"Did I?"

"You did. But now to lunch... and many stories!" He stepped between the two of them, grabbed their arms and strode off in the direction of the Windmill.

*

They stayed in the Windmill all afternoon, enjoying the dim coolness of a corner booth, while the heat and mugginess increased outside, the threat of a thunderstorm building. Will had a small amount of Dutch, but Neelie's English was better, so with Richard doing some translating they were able to converse reasonably freely.

Richard relayed most of what had happened to him since they had parted after Breda. Will was fascinated about his stories of how he started work with Hudde and the Marcelis brothers, and laughed 'til he cried over the story of Richard's infamous fight with the pavement, which Neelie had eventually learnt the truth of and never missed an opportunity to tell the story as her means of revenge.

Will was saddened to hear of Roger's decline but suddenly interrupted the narrative. "But here is a strange thing! DeLacey is not such a common name and so when I heard it used, just last week I think it was, I took note. Now where was this?" He paused, then snapped his fingers. "It was one of the shops on Cheapside. A baker? Or butcher? Anyway, I was just passing, and through the open doorway I heard a customer refer to one of the ladies serving as Mistress DeLacey. I immediately stopped in my tracks and looked in, but the shop was busy and there were several women working in there. I have meant to return but never found the opportunity and now my memory of which shop it was has rather faded. Do you think there could be a family connection? I know his wife and children were lost to plague, but maybe an unmarried sister or cousin?"

"I don't know. As you say, not a common name. We will be here for a few days, maybe weeks. Perhaps we can go in search of this mysterious DeLacey. Roger could do with some good news and this might give him some hope."

Richard did not give Will all the details of the reason for his visit but relayed his run-ins with Montague. Knowing Will had connection with the London militias he thought the name might mean something to him.

(LONDON, JUNE 1641)

"I am sorry. It is not someone I have heard of." He dropped his voice to a lower volume. "But the King and his loyalists have agents everywhere. There is much unrest, and much righteous protest at the oppression of independent religion and belief. Many call for the end of episcopacy, and some dare to say, even openly, that if the King supports the bishops, the King should be made to change his views. People are arrested. The Star Chamber issues what the King calls justice. But his popularity wanes, Rich, especially here in London."

Richard had had a sense of this from what he had observed on the streets but had little idea how deep the resentment ran. He was little concerned about the religious conflict but could see why Hudde was keen to make positive relations with the Ordnance Office. Will then told his own story and became increasingly animated as he spoke of his new friends, and Lilburne in particular. He was surprised and pleased, but also a little concerned, to hear his old friend talk. Will had clearly found himself a role in life. He looked strong and fit, and his conversation showed an intellect that Richard had never previously seen. He guessed that the hours of listening to and reading – he was amazed that Will had learnt to read – the words of his new circle of radical activist friends had awakened an eloquence that neither he nor Will had known was there.

He felt a pride in his friend. Here was an example he could follow perhaps. A man with a purpose beyond money and just living from day to day. Richard had ambitions. He wanted to succeed in the business, but to what end? For success itself?

He noticed Neelie was nodding; the effort of keeping up with the language, and all the new names and places, had finally meant she had just shut out the discussion and had resorted to watching the locals come and go from the tavern. And now she was quietly snoring on his shoulder.

Will called a halt. "You must come here again, Rich. I cannot go for years again and not see you until we have exhausted our stories. And there are people perhaps you should meet. I know you are not excited by the rhetoric. I understand that. But perhaps there may be a more professional interest for you. I will enquire and get a message to you at the ambassador's residence."

Richard looked intrigued and nodded. "Of course. Should I bring Hudde with me?"

"Perhaps not the first time. I would then leave it to your own judgement. But let's see what can be arranged." He paused and looked Richard in the eye. "But I have one more question for you before you go."

"And what is that?"

Will looked at Neelie, her head resting on Richard's shoulder. "You have not wed her, Rich? She is beautiful, and kind, and good. You cannot disguise her past from me, I know enough of war to understand how young girls can get lost. But she has been *found*. Her love for you is so clearly sent from God himself. She has a good heart. Marry her. Make her an honest and respectable woman. Will you not consider it?"

Richard sighed. "Do you not think I have, Will? But life is complicated. Perhaps we can talk on this another time?" and his eyes slid down to the sleeping Neelie and back to Will.

"Of course. What I say is only in your best interest, and because of my own love for you."

"I know." He put a hand on Neelie's shoulder and gently shook her awake. "Come. We have to get ready for dinner at the ambassador's house. You cannot snore through that too!"

She looked horrified. "I snore? Oh no. I am sorry, Will. I am so embarrassed."

"He is just teasing you." And Will playfully punched Richard on the shoulder, Richard feeling the weight of it and wondering what being properly punched by an angry Will, who really meant it, might feel like. He didn't want to find out.

They parted, with Will giving them directions on the shortest and safest way back through the London streets. They could smell rain in the air and some distant rumblings in the darkening sky lent speed to their feet as they made their way back. And all the way back, and all through dinner, and all night as she struggled to sleep, Neelie pondered on the reasons why Richard had not married her. And she weighed up Will's words, because she had not been fully asleep on Richard's shoulder. She could see no answer, but one. Despite his words, perhaps she was just not good enough for him. An awkward embarrassment. And the tears dried on her cheeks as she lay awake in the dark.

*

"We are called to the Tower."

"What? Today?" Richard dropped the bread he was holding and looked up at Hudde, who had finished his breakfast and was holding up a note.

"Aye. Finally. Our ambassador has secured us a meeting with Sir John Heydon this afternoon. We must prepare." Hudde had a grim smile in foreknowledge of the difficult discussions to come.

It had taken days of lobbying to gain the meeting. It was not that the name of the Marcelis brothers was unknown, or not respected, more that the Royal Ordnance Office was in a state of barely organised chaos. Trying to arm the country for possible further war with the Scots and in anticipation of possible conflict in Ireland, with minimal budget and resources, left little time for entertaining foreign guests.

"Come, Richard, bring that with you," he said as Richard

crammed the loaf and jam into his mouth. "We must go over the plan again to make sure we know what to say and when."

"I will be with you in just a few minutes, sir. I will let Cornelia know I will be occupied today and come straight to the library."

"Of course. Is she feeling any better today? She has been so pale and so unlike her usual self. Perhaps it is the dampness of the air in this backward place," and he gestured towards the grey murk outside the window. "This closeness and the warmth are not good for the lungs. She needs the cool wind from the North Sea to clear her passages!"

Richard scurried off, taking a plate of bread, butter and jam with him to try to tempt her. Hudde was right. She was not well. Ever since the meeting with Will, she had seemed downcast and inward-looking. She could not summon up enthusiasm to go out again and had taken to her bed the previous day complaining of tiredness and headache. She had slept on while he had gone down to enjoy the rich breakfast that the ambassador's staff prepared.

When he got to their room, the shutters were open and Neelie was sat up in bed, her face deathly pale framed by the ringlets of her raven hair. But even her hair, normally having a life of its own, seemed lifeless. She stared out of the window, the greyness of the day reflecting flatly on her skin. She didn't turn her head when he came in.

Richard was becoming increasingly worried about her. She didn't seem ill. There was no obvious fever. Just a melancholy, a malaise from which he did not seem able to rouse her. "I've brought you some food. Please try to eat something. It will help you to feel better." No response. "How is your head? Do you still have pain?" A slight shake of her head.

He felt desperate. This was so unlike her. This was more like him.

(London, June 1641)

"Please, Neelie. Tell me what is wrong. What can I do?"

She heaved a sigh. "Nothing, Risch. I am OK. I am just tired. I will get up now. Perhaps I will read."

"I am very sorry, but I can't spend much time with you until later. We finally have our meeting at the Royal Ordnance Office. We must go to the Tower this afternoon. I must go and plan with Hudde now, but I will be back this evening."

"That's fine. I will rest. I hope it goes well."

"Neelie..." He didn't know what to say. "We'll talk again later."

"That will be nice. Now go. I don't want to hold you back when you have important things to do." And she turned and looked at him, and he thought he had never seen anyone look as sad as she did.

He felt a lump form in his throat, and his eyes moistened. "Neelie..." he tried again, but just then a soft knock came at the door and the voice of one of the ambassador's staff came from the corridor, with a request from Master Hudde to join him in the library. "I am sorry. I have to go." He turned quickly and strode out of the room.

*

The carriage journey to the Tower was short, and they did not talk. Hudde stared intently out of the window, but Richard just sat looking at his hands and trying to make sense of the situation. *Don't want to hold you back.* That was the key to it. She knew. She knew he was wrestling with the dilemma of their relationship, and she had concluded that he had made up his mind. That they could never marry if he wanted to secure a place in society that would live up to expectations. *Whose expectations?* he thought. *Hudde doesn't care. My family probably think me dead anyway, but would they care? Of course they would… If I go and visit them, can I take her? Can I take her if we are not wed? But can I marry her?* And around and around…

The carriage left them at the Coldharbour Gate, which loomed over them, adding to Richard's gloom and general sense of unease. He sweated in the close humidity of the day and ran his finger around his collar, already damp with sweat. He nodded to the guards at the gate and followed Hudde through and towards the White Tower.

An aide of Sir John Heydon guided them to the meeting, and he stood making conversation with them while Heydon finished a preceding meeting, deep in the Tower. He introduced himself as Nicholas Cox, the Royal Ordnance Office's messenger. "Anything that Sir John asks me to do," was his response to a question about his duties, "but mainly I liaise with the other armouries and ordnance offices, and the artisans and merchants. We are very stretched in these difficult times. I do the job that two men used to do. Sir John drives us hard, but we make progress, day by day." Cox then showed them in to Heydon's room where he awaited them at a table.

Heydon proved to be a shrewd man. It was he, as lieutenant, who ran the operation and clearly seemed to have little time for his superior, the Earl of Newport. "I go straight to the King, whenever I can," he had told them and it seemed no idle boast. Hudde's mission was clear: to find out what lay behind the rejection of so many shipments they had made, and to try to establish who was behind some of the dirty tricks and surveillance they had experienced in Amsterdam and elsewhere on the continent.

Heydon could shed little light on this. He stressed the difficulty they had carrying out proper proving of powder weapons, and inspections of blades and other equipment. "We are at the mercy of the guilds who demand monopolies.

(London, June 1641)

They fight us every step and our importing of arms from those such as yourselves is a key weapon to keep their prices honest. But they whisper, and they bribe, and they manoeuvre, these fine upstanding, God-fearing men of commerce. I suspect it is from amongst them that your challenges arise, sir."

He described the ongoing dispute between a certain Benjamin Stone, who had broken from the Cutlers' Company and set up a blademill on Hounslow Heath, and some dominant members of the company: William Cave, Robert Moore, Robert South and John Cobb. Stone had invested heavily in the mill and brought over German craftsmen from Solingen. His blades were of good quality, but the company tried to thwart his supply at every turn. In the end, he had advised the King to award Stone with the title of official cutler to the King, and he had known Stone had then used his new power to block delivery of competing blades.

"If it is your blades that are being rejected, then it could be any one of these who are paying for that disruption. I would welcome your supply, it is healthy to have options and competition. But my officers are so poorly paid that we know they look to supplement their income. As long as we make progress, I turn a blind eye, unless it gets out of hand. I cannot help you directly, gentlemen, but on my honour, it is not I who have a hand in this."

Heydon did promise to send a harsh message to the businessmen he had named, warning them off any dirty tricks, but he could not promise it would have any effect. "...But I am sure you are able to look after yourselves, gentlemen. Your own company did not get where it is by running scared of competition, I'll warrant."

The meeting finished and realistically they had accomplished all they could have. Hudde was inclined to believe Heydon and his protestations of innocence, seeing what he felt was a man of honour. Richard was relieved that the lack of Crown involvement seemed to suggest that Montague was not involved in his recent skirmish in Amsterdam, and that it was simple commercial rivalry. Not that that might be just as dangerous.

Nicholas Cox met them in the hallway and led them out into the sunlight. The air had cleared and a cooling breeze was coming in off the river. Richard felt a weight lifted from him. "There is perhaps someone you should meet," Cox said to them over his shoulder as they walked between the heavy wooden gates. "I know something of why you are here and you might be interested to speak to Master Benjamin Stone? The King has granted him premises within the confines of the Tower for blade sharpening, dressing and the mounting of hilts and such. Although he is often in Hounslow, he comes here now and again to oversee his men. He is here today. Would you like an introduction?"

Hudde was keen to meet this man and weigh his character, and Cox diverted them towards a long wooden lean-to construction, built against the inside of the massive outer walls of the Tower. Sounds of industry escaped through the open door, and Cox leaned through and peered into the gloom. He gestured for them to follow him in and they ducked under the low doorway, particularly cramping for the tall Hudde.

They waited near the door, their feet illuminated in bright sunshine, their upper bodies in near darkness. But the shed was alive with activity. Sparks flew from numerous grinding and polishing stones as steel was honed. Artisans glued, pinned and wound to set blades to hilts. Scabbards were hanging all around the walls awaiting their razor-edged lodgers. In the midst of it, Cox was speaking straight into the ear of an intense-looking man, who Richard guessed was in his fifties. Cox nodded over in Richard's direction, and the man, presumably Stone, shrugged and wandered over. With his head, he gestured that the party step out of the harsh noise of the workshop and into the comparative peace of the sunlight.

Outside, Stone glanced at the embroidered 'MB' on the waistcoats of Hudde and Richard, and took in Hudde's height and the impressive hilt of Richard's rapier. He seemed unimpressed.

"Well met, sirs." He reached out and shook both their hands. A warm, strong grip, contrasting the ice in his eyes. "Master Cox has said you have come to add to my burdens. What can I do for you?"

Hudde took the lead in his halting English. He was direct, hoping this approach would flush out any lie if he gave Stone no time to construct a story. "It has been suggested that the sabotage to our business has its roots in the blade suppliers to the King. We have had shipments rejected, our people harassed and followed, our quality and reputation impugned. I am very keen to know, sir, if you might know anything about this?"

Stone held his gaze and did not immediately respond. "I make allowances for your unfamiliarity with our language, sir. From an Englishman..." and here he looked briefly at Richard and Cox, "...I would take that as a grave insult and an assault on my honour. Is that your intent? Please speak plainly for I have no time for this."

Hudde peered down at him, and his shoulders relaxed slightly. "My apologies, sir. In my country, we do speak plainly and simply and like to get to the point. I think I have the right words and I mean what I say. But I do not accuse. I would like to know if you have any knowledge of what is happening to our lawful commercial activities. That is all."

Again, Stone just held Hudde's gaze for an awkwardly long period until he appeared to reach some kind of decision and again shrugged. "Yes, I believe I know something of it. But this is not the place to discuss things. I will be dining at the Seven Stars tonight. Any driver will know it. Meet me there at seven. Perhaps we will both find something of value." He looked at Richard and then meaningfully at his sword hilt, the red gem catching the June sunshine. "And you won't need that, sir. Don't come armed, gentlemen. I shall not be."

*

They arrived just before seven. Neither man wore swords, but both had knives concealed in their boots. While Hudde said he had a positive feeling about Stone, Richard had advised some degree of caution. But he felt distracted, his mind drifting back to the awkward, unsatisfactory few hours he had spent with Neelie. Every look had seemed to stab at his conscience, although she would not acknowledge her melancholy. She was fatigued. The London air did not agree with her. He now realised that she was painfully aware of his dilemma. Of course she was. She was the cleverest uneducated person he had met. The fact that he had not made a commitment to her was a knife in her loving heart, even if she glimpsed the reason behind it.

He wrenched his concentration back to the present. He had Hudde wait outside the tavern in a courtyard just off Minories, close to the Tower, while he scouted the surrounding streets. He paid particular attention to the rear entrance of the Seven Stars, waiting in the alleyway for several minutes and observing the trickle of people braving its dank and fetid atmosphere.

Satisfied, he returned to Hudde and gave the all-clear. They found Stone already seated with a pint of ale in front of him. He stood as they approached the table and, again, they all shook hands. He was alone and had his back to the tavern wall so he could observe the room. Hudde sat opposite and Richard took one end of the table so he too could observe the other clientele. Stone recommended the mutton chops and ale. They ordered and they ate.

To start with, the conversation rambled innocuously as they discussed the situation on the continent and the relative position of the Spanish and German steel and blade industries. This inevitably led Hudde to discuss the difficulties they had been experiencing and Richard was initially amazed at how brazen Stone was about his role in these. "Yes, I abused my position with the Ordnance to block some of your shipments. But would you not have done the same? I invested heavily, borrowed heavily and have spent all my energy to build the mill on Hounslow Heath. It is a wonder, sir. Water-driven. We can produce a thousand excellent quality blades every month. I produce more, and better quality, blades than any of the others in the Cutlers' Company. I started to pick up bigger contracts. And they resented it mightily. 'Resent' is perhaps too light a word. They hated me because it highlighted how poor and inefficient were their own efforts. They were shown to be complacent and intent on reaping reward for inferior goods. My own efforts merely illuminated their incompetence with a bright torch." He warmed to his narrative, leaning across the table.

"My colleagues started to try to undermine me, but none could argue that my blades were not superior. But through their influence, their contacts and their money, and by intimidating those I did business with, they gradually wore me down. Some years ago, as a direct result of their actions I was facing bankruptcy – as I said, I have borrowed heavily to finance the mill. I faced arrest for non-payment. But in the end, it was the King who came to my rescue. Realising that he was about to lose the best blade-maker in the country, he awarded me the monopoly of supplying the Ordnance. Or at least I thought this was the case. In truth, these villains still supply the Ordnance, but I am given preference in trade.

"And now Heydon and the King play us off, driving prices lower to the extent that I am only just keeping my head above water, even with the mill at full capacity.

"And yes, you probably got caught up in this. At the time, I was trying to establish my goods as the premium quality offer. The last thing I needed was the water muddied with more German imports. And why do I tell you this? Why not more circumspect?"

He paused to finish the last gristly piece of chop, swilling it down with the last two inches of his ale.

"Because now, gentlemen, I need you. And I reason that I can only regain your trust through honesty. I surmise that this is something you value?"

Hudde nodded thoughtfully, his face giving nothing away. "And so?"

Stone smiled. "So. Now they are trying other methods to ruin me. Oh, I know that most of them do not have the brains or the balls for this. Cave, South and Moore are being led in all of this. They are greedy, but not wicked. But Cobb, he has a black heart. Him and his son. I wager he is the one behind your other troubles."

Hudde exchanged a glance with Richard.

"Now they have stopped their supply to the Ordnance. They do this for two reasons. Firstly, to create a shortfall, just as the King's nervousness about the state of the country is increasing his demand for weaponry. They look to drive up prices, and plead this disaster, or that supply problem, or the weather, to justify their lack of production. But mostly they do it to highlight that, despite my innovations, I cannot meet the

(London, June 1641)

market. As the King's main supplier, I am unable to deliver to the quantity required and I let down my sovereign in his hour of need."

Stone looked at them, the depth of his hatred and his despair written in the dark rings around his bloodshot eyes. "That is not a good position to be in, sirs. The King's agents sniff around and I know that several of them are also drawing coin from Cobb. He is a clever bastard. I have no doubt that it is he who is trying to sabotage your imports. The last thing he would want is to see the shortfall made up by some enterprising foreign company."

Richard and Hudde looked at each other. To Richard it rang true enough, but he was not sure if Hudde was buying it.

Hudde looked back at Stone. "And so?"

"So. I am proposing an alliance, sir. A commercial agreement whereby I acquire blades from you directly. This is risk-free for you, as you no longer have to submit to Ordnance inspection – that is my risk alone, but I am confident in your quality. I am able to meet the Ordnance's demand, and I salvage my reputation with the King and protect my business. I pay you for your blades and add a minor mark-up only when I sell them on the Ordnance. We both profit from this and we both get the satisfaction of screwing Cobb."

Hudde blew out his cheeks, finally allowing an expression of some description to gain a foothold on his face. "I am interested, Master Stone. Of course I am interested. But I need to see your offer, and to see it in writing. You say there is no risk, but I am concerned that this man, Cobb, will step up his activities and cause some real damage. I do not want to get into a real war, sir. I do not want to see blood spilled or embarrassment to my government. But show me your offer and we can talk again." He paused. "But your war with Cobb is not mine. I do not know him and I do not want to." He leaned forward across the table to shake the hand that Stone offered and at precisely that moment, Richard saw the tavern door swing open to crash against the plaster, and several men bustled in from the gathering dusk.

Stone looked up. "Well, sir. It looks like you are about to get to know him. Word of our meeting has obviously reached Master Cobb." Richard noticed, without really registering the fact, that Stone did not seem particularly surprised.

The group of men marched across the dimly lit room in a phalanx, halting right by the table. Stone, Hudde and Richard were all standing. Richard's left hand had already found the handle of his dagger as he stood, and he palmed it from his boot so that the blade projected up his sleeve and the hilt was hidden by his hand.

John Cobb was a bear of a man with thick black hair and beard, and would easily have been Hudde's height if he was not beginning to bend with age. He stood at the apex of a wedge of five other men. Richard had little doubt all were used to violence, although the young man behind Cobb's left shoulder, and nearest to Richard, was dressed in a more refined way. In fact, as Richard studied him, it was clear that this must be Cobb's son, although he didn't yet have the bulk of his father. He did, however, have his father's sneer, and Richard was treated to a close-up view as both men stared across the table at Stone with genuine hatred. They made a show of ignoring Hudde and himself, focusing purely on Stone, but the other men were watchful, hands concealed in pockets and under cloaks.

Cobb Senior gripped the edge of the table, almost standing on Hudde's feet, and leant right over the oak. "Did you think, sir, that this little meeting, this petty treason, would go unnoticed? I thank God that there are still those who would uphold the honour of their country, of their company, of their craft! You, sir, would sell out your own to these…" he spat onto

(London, June 1641)

the table in front of Hudde, "...foreigners!" He didn't even look at Hudde, who regarded him impassively.

Stone said nothing but merely returned his gaze. Cobb was not done. "You fail your King. After all your boasting, your promises. Yes, sir! You have failed him. All your attempts to ruin the honest men of the Cutlers' Company, and now you cannot keep your word and cannot match the need of the King at this crucial hour for the country. You are a disgrace, sir."

"Have a care, sir, that you do not say a little too much." Stone even managed to smile. "I suggest you sit and join us in a drink. Cool your passion in some fine ale. These are heated words, even for you."

Cobb's fist slammed down on the table making all the plates and jugs bounce and roll around. "Do not mock me, sir. This..." he waved at Hudde and Richard, still not looking in their direction, "...will not go unreported. The Ordnance will hear of this. The King's men will hear of this and their loyalty will not allow this to go unpunished, even if Heydon is of a forgiving nature."

Richard immediately thought of Montague. *Now there is a man who is not of a forgiving nature. I wonder if he is in Cobb's pay? I doubt it – Montague is too much of a zealot to have divided loyalties.*

Stone stirred. "You are verging on bravery, sir. Unfamiliar territory for you. I know you prefer to work in the shadows and let others take the risk for you. Do not threaten me. I am sure you know that the King himself has been purchasing from the continent – these are idle words. All is known to the authorities. But have a care you do not overreach yourself, for I cannot let all such words pass unanswered. Do not think yourself safe because you come with four men at your back."

Cobb betrayed his confusion with a half-glance over his shoulder. "You are mistaken, sir. There are five with me."

"I think not. I only count four *men* behind you. Oh, and of course James." He nodded at Cobb's son. "Good evening, James. Have you been setting your fires again and trying to intimidate my workers. Have you been skulking around my friends and family again? As I said, I only see four men."

James Cobb's face screwed up with rage, an arrogant sneer smearing into a mask of hatred. His hand came out from under his jacket with a flash of steel and he lunged forward across the table, the blade's tip halting just in front of Stone's face.

"I wouldn't do that if I were you." Richard was impressed that he managed to keep his voice cold and level as he tried to manage his excitement. His own blade was held against James Cobb's throat, the flat of the blade making a depression in the skin, the point drawing a speck of blood from under his chin. "I really wouldn't."

Cobb's eyes rotated down, trying to see the dagger without shifting his head a fraction of an inch. Everything had happened so quickly that Cobb's men had not shifted, hidden hands frozen, gripping weapons. Cobb Senior went pale beneath the black frame of his hair and beard and stepped back from the table edge. No one else moved or spoke for what to Richard seemed like an hour but was only a minute.

Cobb cleared his throat. "Put your blade down, sir. There is no need for this." He tried to keep his voice steady, but it cracked at the edges with tension. "James, lower your arm and place the knife on the table. We did not come to fight."

"I will move when he does," Richard replied, and kept the pressure on James Cobb's throat as the young man's steel rolled over once as it clattered among the plates on the wood. He lowered his own arm and stepped back, keeping a careful

(LONDON, JUNE 1641)

eye on Cobb's thugs. "Master Hudde, I think it best we leave now. Come and join me here." He was concerned that six men stood between them and was not expecting any help from Stone, who just stood with his arms folded, a faint smile on his lips.

Hudde nodded and edged his way round the group to stand with Richard. Sensing the immediate danger had passed, James Cobb's sneer had found its way back to his face. He straightened his waistcoat, adjusted the lace of his shirt cuffs and looked Richard in the eye. Richard saw shamed arrogance competing with fear. Arrogance won out.

"You attack from behind like a craven? You cannot deal with a man face to face? I put it down to your youth, your low station and your lack of honour." His voice trembled slightly as he strove to control his emotions. For a big man, his tone was slightly shrill.

"Be quiet, son. We have made our point. We will talk to the King and…"

"What did you say? I'm sorry but you must speak louder so we can all share your wit." Richard was also struggling to control his anger as he felt the familiar red tide rising.

James Cobb hesitated and shot a look at his father, but even in that moment, seemed to reach his own conclusion. "I called you a craven, with no honour and no decency. A man who supplies the King's enemies. You dishonour your employer, your family, such as they are, and God with your behaviour. You…"

The slap rocked him back before he could evade it, Richard backhanding him and leaving red stripes from his fingers across Cobb's white cheek. "Apologise!" he shouted into Cobb's face. His knife was out again, held towards the body of men who now openly displayed clubs and hammers in their hands as they edged towards him.

"Not to you, scum." Cobb spat out the words along with a gobbet of blood and mucus.

"Then I demand satisfaction, sir. In front of these men..." he gestured at the group around the table, "...and all of these," his arm encompassing the fascinated clientele of the Seven Stars who watched open-mouthed as the drama unfolded. "I demand it," he repeated more quietly. "Tomorrow morning. Or apologise now and walk away with your life."

"For God's sake, James, just apologise and let's begone from here." Cobb's father looked imploringly at his son.

"Tomorrow morning, sir. And it will be I who walk away. Perhaps to pay a visit to your whore." He managed to smile, but Richard could see his heart was not in it.

"Do not shame me, Father. How can God smile on the likes of him? He will be with me tomorrow as I slit him from belly to neck, like a pig." He looked back at Richard. "We will send note of where to be. An hour past dawn." He turned and strode to the door without a backward look. Cobb Senior looked across at Richard with hate in his black eyes.

"If you harm my son in any way, you will pay for it. And those who hold you dear." He looked across at Stone. "And you, sir, your part in all of this will be told. I will see you ruined, or I will see you dead."

He gestured to his men, and they followed him out into the night.

*

The heated passion of the previous evening had cooled in the dark of a sleepless night and now, with the dawn, the events of the tavern seemed long ago, and like they had involved someone else.

(LONDON, JUNE 1641)

He stared out of the bedroom window, his back to the crumpled bed where he had spent the night talking and talking to Neelie. She had finally slept, but they had lived every emotion from anger and bewilderment, to fear, to sadness and melancholy, before a cautious joy. Joy, because he had come to a realisation and a decision. A decision that he wondered at. Not because it was the wrong decision, but because it had taken so long to arrive.

She had fought him and shouted at him for his heartlessness and stupidity. How could he put himself in such danger? How could he risk leaving her alone? Alone again, after all that had happened to her. Richard was confident that he had the beating of Cobb, but she had warned him that these things didn't end so easily. The father's revenge. The actions of someone in the crowd. Or just that James Cobb could get lucky.

And then Richard had started to doubt and, not for the first time, rued his inability to control his temper. Neelie had slumped into an even deeper despair. He could not gain any spark of emotion from her, but neither could he persuade her to rest. He replayed the events in his mind, trying to analyse how he had got himself into this situation and, at around four o'clock in the morning as the dark had begun to lift into a flat steel grey, he had his epiphany.

He thought about the insults and antagonism he had heard from James Cobb, and he knew that this had not really roused him. He had been called worse things, by better men, in his time since leaving home. He now knew precisely what it was. The attack on Neelie. The focus on her past, the label people had attached to her. Whore. Like there was nothing worse on this earth. But they didn't know her strength. What she had had to do to survive by herself, at such a young age. They did not know of her beauty, or the unselfish kindness of her heart. She was just an object of scorn because of the tragic circumstances that had forced her to live in the only way she could.

He knew then that if he was willing to die for her honour, not his, then what possible reason was there for him not to marry her. It was so far beyond pity, or duty, or a need to protect. He realised truly for the first time how he loved her and how his stupid, misplaced sense of decorum made him little better than Cobb. He understood that he could give her what she desperately wanted and, he realised, what he wanted and needed too.

He took her by her hand and drew her up until she was sitting on the edge of the bed, kneeling in front of her. There was no understanding in her eyes of what he was about to ask of her, just a melancholy so profound that he feared she might die from it if he made the wrong move or said the wrong word. He knew he was no poet, so he didn't try. "Neelie. Forgive me. Forgive my stupidity, my pride, my blindness. It has taken this ridiculous duel to truly open my eyes. If you can forgive me, if I survive this fight, I ask you to do me the honour of being my wife. If you can do this, I am yours forever." He held his breath as he saw waves of emotion pass across her face. She couldn't speak but rested her hand on his head. And then she fainted, falling backwards onto the bed.

When she had come around, and he had contented himself that she was not ill, they had sobbed uncontrollably in each other's arms, a release of tension, passion, hope and dread that had been bottled for what felt like an eternity. And then such joy. Such happiness, until they remembered what awaited them in just a few hours, and the sensible, pragmatic Neelie re-emerged from the chaos of battered emotion.

They talked calmly now of possible outcomes and how they would react. If Richard were to prevail, he would have to quit London quickly. There was no saying how Cobb's father would react, and duelling was frowned on. He could be arrested, particularly if Cobb's bought agents were present.

(LONDON, JUNE 1641)

Richard would leave immediately for his family home. It was years since he had seen his father and siblings, and here was a perfect opportunity. Neelie would return to Amsterdam with Hudde, and Richard would sail home from the East Anglian coast later. Then they would wed. With this settled, Neelie slept with her face lined by the streaks of her earlier tears. But for the first time in what seemed like months, she slept with a smile on her lips.

As he looked on the slate dawn sky, Richard now thought about Hudde. The man was calmness personified, which Richard knew hid a steely determination to see business done. But for all that, he could be a passionate man. After the incident, as they walked back to the embassy, Hudde had sympathised with Richard and his actions, but at the same time he knew they were on the verge of a significant new contract. "We underestimated Stone. We were played, Richard. Whether he engineered Cobb breaking into our meeting, or if he just knew it was a good bet, he gambled on how things might play out. Of course, he could not know the precise outcome, but he clearly guessed Cobb's attitude might drive us into his arms. It couldn't have worked out much better for him, no wonder he was smiling fit to split his face."

Richard had been focused on Cobb, but his peripheral memory had an image of a smug-looking Stone. "I am sorry, master. I acted rashly, again, and I put you and your business in danger. You would be justified if you never wanted to see me again."

"Don't be stupid for a second time tonight, boy. You are a good man. An honourable man and I think you can go far in our business. If you had not stepped in, then I may well have done so. But listen to me carefully. I know not how tomorrow will go, although I think you have his measure. Regardless, you should retire from business for a while. Go into the country.

Leave London. I don't want to see you again for a few months. I must stay and conclude business here, and Neelie will be safe with the ambassador, whom she has completely charmed, and she can return with me."

"My thanks, sir. Sincerely. I owe you so much already."

"So, repay me by doing as I instruct. Go to your family. And if you can avoid killing Cobb's son without getting yourself killed, then try to do so for all our sakes. I think we have seen he is not a man to cross lightly and putting holes in his son's belly will not endear him to us further."

*

Half an hour later, there was a knock at his door and Hudde greeted him with the details of the location for the duel. "There were two messages delivered late last night. This one comes from James Cobb. We are to meet him and his entourage – he stipulates no more than two companions so as not to draw unnecessary attention to the contest – back at the tavern. There is a small courtyard to the rear where, at this time of the morning, we should not be disturbed."

"And the second note?" Richard frowned.

"His father. Clearly, he believes that his son is not a match for you and asks you to stay your hand. He accepts that swords must be crossed but believes you can demonstrate your superior skill without taking his life. He believes his son will apologise once he sees he cannot win. What do you think, Richard? Can you accept this?"

Richard smiled and felt a weight lifting from him. "Yes. I can certainly do this. My rashness from yesterday evening has given way to joy and relief." And he told Hudde of his betrothal to Neelie and their discussion of just this possible outcome. "I have no wish to kill him. If I can draw first blood we can call it over and done, with everyone's honour intact."

"I am proud of you, boy. This is the best news in weeks. It is about time too!" He paused and looked worried. "But take care. If all your thoughts are on your wedding, and on trying not to kill your opponent, be careful he does not catch you with your mind wandering! Do not be too relaxed."

Richard slapped him on the back. "Don't worry. I have too much to live for now. I will do my best to keep him alive, but there is no way he is sending me to the grave. Not when I have a wedding to go to. And we are agreed. After the duel, I will away home, but I ask you to ensure Neelie returns safely with you to Amsterdam."

"Of course. She will be safe. Have no fear on that." The words were solid and reassuring, and Richard allowed himself a sigh of relief.

*

They arrived after Cobb. Richard, Hudde and a footman from the embassy stood in the small courtyard opposite father and son and one of the henchmen from the previous evening. James Cobb was in black breeches and waistcoat and long-sleeved white shirt. His long black hair was tied back and his beard was freshly trimmed. He seemed nervous, slashing at the air with his rapier and trying to warm up his muscles. He was already sweating, although the day was only just starting to warm up.

Richard unhooked his cloak and passed it to the footman. He undid his swordbelt and made a show of passing it, with the poignard still sheathed, to Hudde, drawing his own rapier as Hudde took it. He wore the dark blue waistcoat with the embroidered 'M' of the Marcelis brothers on the left breast. He was not only younger but also a couple of inches shorter than Cobb, and when they met in the centre of the courtyard with Cobb Senior and Hudde attending, Richard had to tilt his head back slightly to meet James's gaze. He saw determination there, but also fear and apprehension.

"Sir. Please. Will you now apologise for your remarks last night? I care not about your thoughts of me, but I cannot stand by to hear my family, and my lady's name dragged down. Please consider, sir. Will you not apologise so that we can end this now?"

John Cobb put his hand on his son's shoulder. "Come, son. Much is said in anger and the heat of the moment that we later regret. Let us not waste our time on these trivial matters. We have other, more important things to attend to."

But James shrugged the hand off and glared at Richard. "I cannot apologise. I will not apologise. I have been challenged and I will not lower myself to walk away. You wanted satisfaction, sir. I intend to give it to you. Let us get on with it." He turned his back and took five long strides away. As he turned on his heel Richard saw him slide slightly on the greasy surface of the cobbles. Not a big movement, but he filed it away as important. He smiled to himself. DeLacey would have been proud that he had remembered this from his hours of instruction.

He too retreated some paces and relaxed into his stance. He saw Cobb remove his poignard from its sheath and pass it to his father's man. He brought the hilt of his rapier up to the bridge of his nose and then swept it down in salute. Richard just nodded slightly in return. He felt good. No nervousness, no distraction. Just a clear focus. He imagined himself back at the barn outside Breda with Roger and de Sête. He took a deep breath and blew it out, rolling his shoulders before settling back and waiting for Cobb's move. He moved slightly forward and back, testing the surface and the quality of grip, and confirming his earlier impression that the surface was slick and treacherous. *That's a leveller*, he thought. *Let him make all the big moves and risk the slip. Stay relaxed and compact and move as little as possible.* He saw Hudde catch Cobb Senior's eye and give a slight nod. The father visibly relaxed.

James Cobb suddenly stepped forward rapidly, closing the ground between them to fencer's distance, blade tips overlapping by around six inches. Richard held his guard slightly open, giving his opponent a clear path to his chest. Having seen Cobb move and warm up, he now had little doubt he was quicker, more experienced and more skilful than his opponent, but he wanted a little time to make sure this was not just a clever bluff.

Cobb slapped Richard's blade aside and lunged forward. *Reckless*, thought Richard, as he stepped half a pace back and parried. Again, he saw Cobb's front foot slide half an inch as he sought to regain his balance. Two, three more times attacks came in and Richard evaded comfortably. Careful, watchful but with increasing certainty that there was no bluff. Cobb was barely competent, and seemingly entirely inexperienced. Richard risked a sideways glance at Hudde, who shrugged slightly and gave him a grim half-smile.

The next time Cobb launched an attack, Richard could see that Cobb knew that he was not going to win this fight unless something untoward happened. This time Richard did not retreat and parry but kept his position and actually leaned forward. Cobb attempted to cut under the parry, but Richard saw this coming from a hundred miles away and had already started the counter that saw him circle the other man's blade before a snap of his wrist sent the rapier flying end over end to the cobbles. He slammed on the brakes as his momentum continued to carry him forward and his leading foot slipped on the cobbles. He ended up on one knee, looking up at Richard.

Richard stepped back to allow Cobb to rise. He made no attempt to attack, wanting Cobb to understand the gulf between them so that when he took his chance to nick his skin somewhere harmless there would be no desire to continue. He noted the discordant sound the blade made as it struck the stone; a weapon of real quality would ring like a bell. *Must be one of Cobb's own blades.* The lack of quality was apparent, but he admired the man's loyalty to his own product.

Cobb slowly got to his feet, blowing slightly with the effort he had already expended. Richard waited for him, stance relaxed, guard slightly open as usual. He could see Cobb gather himself for the next attack, and he resolved to finish it while his opponent still had control of his mind and was not so fatigued that he might take a foolish decision or make a wrong move. While he had no desire now to kill the man, he wanted to leave his mark on him, so he would remember his defeat. *The cheek slit*, he thought, *or perhaps an ear trimmed.*

The lunging attack came, feinting high but cutting down to stab at Richard's extended front leg, but again the extravagance of the move caused him to skate on the slick stones, and his blade instead angled towards Richard's heart. Richard was momentarily surprised by this unintentional thrust and had to react rapidly, slapping Cobb's blade down with the flat of his gloved hand, and as the momentum carried his opponent past him, he flicked the tip of the Toledo rapier across the back of Cobb's neck, leaving a thin slash of crimson on his white skin.

He heard Hudde bellow excitedly, "First blood! Farrell has first blood!"

Cobb's father shouted across to his son, who was trying to reach the cut and then inspecting his dripping fingers, "Stop this madness. James! You have your honour intact,

(LONDON, JUNE 1641)

and Farrell has his satisfaction. Come, boy. Enough! Let us depart this place!"

Richard wiped his blade on a cloth from his breeches and looked across to Cobb Senior. "That suits me, sir. Let that be an end to this. I am prepared to shake your son's hand, if he is also willing." He started to half turn when he saw the blur of movement coming towards him. James Cobb was clearly not about to shake anyone's hand. Richard's trained eye located the sword point heading for his back. With no time to bring his own blade around he waited for the thrust and arched his back to avoid the steel. Cobb struggled to keep his feet as his momentum took him past and behind, and Richard thrust his boot backward, clipping Cobb's heel and tripping him. James Cobb cursed as he fell. There was a sharp metallic crack and then the dull thump of him hitting the cobbles.

Richard span around to face him, recovering his stance, but as he did so, he felt a thing he had not encountered for over a year. A wash of heat coursed through him, electrifying his body, shocking his mind like a bolt of lightning. He felt a sudden rage building and fought to control it. As he stood looking towards the prone figure, almost bouncing up and down with barely suppressed energy, he already knew that James Cobb was not going to get up from the cold stone.

"Get up, James! There's no shame here if we finish this now. Come, lad. Get up and let us leave." There was no movement and Cobb Senior was getting exasperated. "Get up, I tell you."

Still James Cobb did not move, but now a slow trickle of blood became visible and started to run and pool in the gaps between the cobble stones. Cobb's father barged frantically past Richard. He laid a hand on his son's shoulder and gently rolled him over. The tip of James Cobb's rapier had caught between two cobbles as he fell forward, and the blade had snapped as it reached the point beyond which it could bend no more. The ragged steel end had gone straight through his heart and his surprised eyes stared through his father, seeing nothing at all in the grey London sky.

There was a moment of absolute silence that seemed to last forever before a wail escaped John Cobb. It grew louder in its intensity, climbing into the dawn above the courtyard, summoning more faces to the upper windows where there was already an audience. Richard felt a hand on his shoulder. Hudde. "We should go," he whispered. "Now." He started to drag at Richard's shoulder, but it was useless. Richard was rooted like an oak to the spot. "An accident! We were finished. You saw what happened. If he hadn't…"

"No!" James's father span around and onto his feet. "No, sir! Your cowardly tricks have robbed me of my son. We had an agreement! An agreement, damn you! You lied! You have cheated me and now he is dead!"

"No! You saw what happened. Everyone saw! How can you…" He could have easily avoided Cobb's punch, but he chose not to and it caught him on the ear. Felling him to the ground. In his state of heightened strength and emotion he felt nothing and quickly regained his feet, but now he let Hudde drag him away.

"I will not forget this, Farrell. I will pursue you, boy, until the ends of the earth! May God be my eternal witness!" His shouts continued to echo around the courtyard as they ran towards their waiting cab.

*

Two days later he walked his horse quietly through a copse of oak and elm. He had left London at dawn and made good progress along the Cambridge road. He had met few people, and the fields had been quiet as the people rested from the

(London, June 1641)

warmth of the day and built the strength for the slog of harvest. He had removed his long black jacket and rolled it behind him across the saddle. Now he was wiping his brow with his kerchief and rolling up the sleeves of his linen shirt. His waistcoat was already unbuttoned.

He halted at the edge of trees, reluctant to leave the comparative cool of the shade. In the distance he could see a church tower which he knew was home, Godmanchester. And beyond, the larger town of Huntingdon, across the Great Ouse. For the last hour he had been recognising features of the countryside. Places he had ridden and walked. Hamlets where he had run errands for his father in a childhood that now seemed like ancient history.

He wondered to himself why he wasn't nudging his horse on, but still he sat on the fringe of the copse. His horse became bored and lowered its head to find food, and Richard loosened the rein to let it. In fact, he would take a right turn along a narrow path not much wider than a deer trail. His family's manor lay a couple of miles to the east and he could be there in a half-hour of leisurely travel.

The anticipation of seeing his father, brothers and sister again was a strange kind of excitement. He had not left home on bad terms. He had sent and received half a dozen letters with John and Angelica, and a couple with Lionel. He knew his father had uncertain health after the initial scare, but it was now six months since he had had any news. Yet he felt strangely tense about the reunion.

He knew he had changed, physically and emotionally. He had seen more of the world in the years away than his family had witnessed in a lifetime. He was the only one who had travelled abroad. The only one to fight in war. And, he assumed, the only one to have spent a significant amount of his time in the company of whores and arms dealers.

But he was also eager to see them and live for a while that quiet uncomplicated life of the country. He looked forward to walking the lanes with Angelica, swapping gossip about the tenants and talking of their dreams. He knew in his heart that Angelica would love Neelie. They shared an air of innocent mischief and he also knew they would tear him to shreds if they ever got together. He smiled to himself, half in dread, half in anticipation.

He was not sure what to expect with his father. His father's attitude to him had always been a shrug. Not annoyance. Not hatred. Not love. Just a kind of 'what to do with you' indifference. He had been concerned about his health, but he was not sure how much he would mourn his death when it came.

And it was this thought that spurred him to regain control of his horse and kick it forward into the late afternoon sun. *Hello, again. I am a killer accused of murder and am about to marry a harlot. Please pass the parsnips…*

While he had his horse moving again, it was not taking the right turn, but angling along the main road towards the town. *Perhaps one quick ale in the tavern before I go. Just something to loosen me up.* Then definitely home and a long summer evening of reacquaintance.

Opposite the church, across a hard-packed earthen square, was the Blue Boar. All seemed quiet and only low tones of conversation drifted through the tavern's open door. He tied up his horse in the shade cast by the church tower and wandered into the cool dark. He did not expect to recognise anyone in the bar and at first he struggled to even see anyone after the bright sunlight.

He put his elbows on the bar and removed his broad-brimmed hat, placing it on the polished oak. The tavernkeeper nodded in greeting and soon placed the mug of ale in front of

(London, June 1641)

him. "Passing through?" Richard assumed it was a question, but it could have been an instruction given the stare he got from the man. He wondered at that. His memories were all of warmth and friendliness and good humour. But then he remembered his sword belt, his pistol and the damage to his nose and cheekbone, and could understand the reaction from an innkeeper in a sleepy country tavern.

"Actually, I'm coming home, sir. My family are south and east of here. I have been in the war, in the Low Countries. I have not been back for years."

"Then welcome home, sir. We have a seen a few such as yourself over the last few months. Gentlemen coming home or passing through from the coast. I hope it is one war finishing, not the scent of another one about to start."

"And why would you say that my good man?" The voice came from behind Richard, somewhere in the dark depths of the room, far away from the blazing void of the doorway. "Are you aware of talk of war in England?"

The tavernkeeper blanched and looked back over Richard's shoulder. "No, sir. I meant nothin' by it. Just thinking about them Scots camped in the north. And we hear tales from Ireland too now and then. 'Tis all I meant." Now he looked sullen, like a schoolboy angered at a rebuke, but scared of the consequence.

Richard turned and put his back to the bar counter, resting an elbow and trying to look casual. He thought he knew that voice, but surely it couldn't be. Not here.

"Oh my word. I did wonder if I should see you here, Master Farrell, but did not really expect to be so lucky to make your acquaintance again." Montague emerged into the light and Richard could now see he had left a table where two others were also seated in the corner.

"Master Farrell!" The tavernkeeper's voice came from behind him. "You are here for the funeral? You are only just in time, sir. 'Tis in the morning. Half the county will be going."

Richard was momentarily dumbfounded. Montague here! Funeral? What was happening? What had happened to his quiet drink?

His open mouth provoked a smile from Montague. "Your face is an open book, sir. I see that this is news to you. I am sorry to tell you, genuinely sorry, Farrell, that your father is dead. Two days ago. As our host here says, the funeral is tomorrow and the fact that half the county is going to be there is reason for me to be there too."

The tavernkeeper looked distressed. "I am sorry you heard the news this way, sir. I assumed that was why you were here. Your drink is on the house. Your father was a good man and will be missed."

Richard found his wits and his voice. "Thank you. Both. This has come as something of a shock to me." He paused to swallow, take a deep breath and buy some time to think. "I was but coming here by chance. It seems I was almost too late." Although his voice was level and calm, inside he was flailing to make sense of things. *Dead! Why now? Is it fate brought me here today? And why is Montague here? He did not know my father.*

"Almost, Farrell. But tell me. Why were you returning now if not for the funeral? What brings you back to this backwater after your adventures on the highways and by-ways of the continent?"

"What? Oh. I was in London on business, which has now concluded. I was taking a chance to visit my family. I knew my father had been ill, but he had seemed to be recovering these months."

"A summer sickness took 'im, sir." The tavernkeeper wiped his own brow. "It can be cruel on the older folk."

"Yes. Of course. Thank you." He was slowly herding his

(London, June 1641)

thoughts together and was aware that Montague was studying him closely. This, more than anything, snapped him back into shape. "But why are you here, sir? I assume this is not a social call?" He, in turn, now studied the King's agent and glanced meaningfully over his shoulder at Montague's companions, sitting quietly in the corner. "Who do you pursue?"

The tavernkeeper shot them both a worried look and moved himself away and busied himself wiping tables as far away as possible. Montague smiled again and nodded at Richard's hand, now resting casually on the pommel of his rapier. "You won't need that, Master Farrell. I am watching bigger fish, meaning no offence to you. It seems there are many in this county who may have questionable loyalties in this difficult time. Men of importance and profile. Your father's funeral will draw some of these men together and I would hate to, ah, miss that." Again, the slight smile. "How is your brother? Not the oldest, he seems quiet enough. I'm thinking of your brother the priest. Lionel, isn't it? He seems much more interesting."

Richard's eyes hardened. "Lionel is a good man, Montague. He does not warrant your scrutiny. His thoughts are only concerned with God. He has no argument with the King." But even as he said this, he knew it wasn't true. The letter he had had from Lionel had perturbed him. So much passion directed against the bishops. Such passion could make him of interest to such as Montague and that was dangerous. If Lionel was writing to his absent brother in such extravagant language, what was he saying, and perhaps actually preaching, to his friends and congregation? And who was listening? Montague, or more likely one of his creatures.

"As you say, Farrell. I am sure you are right." He took a step forward and actually slapped Richard on his shoulder. Another smile, but colder this time. "Nevertheless, Richard, as you will be seeing him, perhaps a quiet word in his ear would be a kindness to him. And now we will leave you to your grief and your drink. I sense we are making you uncomfortable. Perhaps we will see you on the morrow. I hope so. I do so enjoy our meetings." And he walked out into the softening light, waving his companions to follow.

Richard watched them go. The first an older man with close-cropped steel-grey hair and a hard face. *Ex-soldier*, Richard thought. The man didn't glance at him. The other was much younger. Probably younger than Richard himself. The lad gazed at him curiously as he sauntered past, trying to appear as dangerous as his companion, but failing. Something about him made Richard look twice as he swallowed down the last of his ale. He could have sworn he knew him from somewhere. He looked very familiar. A childhood friend? He couldn't quite place the connection and it worried him.

But now he definitely had to get home. The long-awaited reunion had taken on an extra edge. He slapped a coin down onto the oak and thanked the tavernkeeper.

"Give my regards to your family, sir," he called after Richard. "Your father was a gentleman. And, sir?" Richard turned in the doorway. "Careful of the likes o' him." He nodded at the table where Montague had been sitting. "For all 'is manners, and 'is smiles, he's the Angel o' Death, that one."

As he urged his horse across the fields, Richard had to agree.

*

He lay in his old, now rather cramped, bed. Now he was home, he could even remember the view from his window so clearly that he could tell that the oak outside had grown in the years he had been gone. He had found his childhood wooden sword and hobby horse in a cupboard and could picture summer days riding the wooden stick with horse head carved by his older brother John through the fields, hacking at nettles with the flat blade of ash. He had been the Black Prince, Richard Lionheart and all manner of other martial heroes. And he always vanquished his legion foes. There were none like Richard Farrell, feared and admired by all. Things never quite worked out how you think they might.

He studied the cracked plaster of the ceiling. The room had seen better days. He guessed the uncertainty of his return had meant his family were reluctant to spend time and money keeping it well maintained, but couldn't quite let themselves repurpose it.

His surprise return had made quite the impact. As he had made his way along farm tracks and fields high with barley, he had passed a few tenants, some that he recognised. He had enjoyed the slightly puzzled stares he received when he called out to them by name and watched their faces as they tried to match his appearance with someone who might know them well enough to greet them personally. Occasionally, the penny had dropped and a shout followed him down path – "Welcome home, young Master Farrell!" He liked that. In fact, he was surprised how much he liked that.

Although his family were only on the first rung of minor gentry, it had been a long time since he had felt respected for who he was, rather than what he had done. He wondered what Will would think of that.

His encounter with Montague had receded quickly and he felt a warmth that was not all to do with the late summer sun. He had turned off the narrow hawthorn-hedged lane, occasional beech trees shading the path, and into the open space in front of the two-storey manor.

Ochre-coloured plaster covered local bricks. He could see

it had been repainted recently and the building looked fresh, glowing in the warm light. Huge oak timbers of the frame were newly pitched. The manor had a long frontage with a central massive iron-studded oak door with the symmetry of two windows to each side. At each end of the house, wings marched backwards to create a small semi-courtyard at the rear which collected the afternoon sun. At the back, to the right, were stables and farm buildings. Five windows occupied the upper floor at the front.

The shade was deepening at the front of the house by the time he had tied his horse to the rowan tree that stood opposite the front door. There were several other animals similarly tied, and he could hear many voices coming from inside the building and carrying from the rear. Preparations for the funeral, he assumed, and again this stirred a conflict of emotion within him. Joy that he would be reunited with his siblings and sadness at his father's passing. Guilt too, as he acknowledged that the joy outweighed the sadness by some margin. And behind it all, a lingering dread from the memory of Montague's words that seemed to wax as the light waned.

In something of a turmoil, and after several deep breaths, he had thumped the iron lion's-head knocker down and listened to the boom reverberate through the interior. Then a voice, his oldest brother John's, he thought, calling out to someone, "T'will be the ham, I expect. We have been waiting these hours for it." Boots crossing the stone-flagged hallway, a bolt thrown back and the heavy door pulled open, allowing slanting sunlight to stream out, flowing through the house from the rear ground floor windows, and lighting the cool blues of the early evening where he stood.

John stood silhouetted against that light. Close-cropped hair and sparse beard, in white shirt with rolled sleeves and black breeches. Richard immediately thought something must be wrong with his brother. *What has happened to him? He has shrunk!*

For his part, John stared. And stared, through a silence that appeared to go on forever. Tears started in his eyes. "God be praised," he whispered. "God be praised." He took a step forward, boots crunching on the gravel, and threw his arms around Richard, burying his head in his shoulder, and sobbed. Richard had never even seen his brother cry when they were children. Always the quiet, dependable, steady John. He felt his own eyes burning, and taking his brother by the shoulders eased him back so he could look at him, realising stupidly that it was he who had grown, not his brother having shrunk and he was now half a head taller.

"John. Please. Stop. Please. You will have us both flooding the garden. It is so good to see you. I don't think I had really understood until now how long it has been."

John was wiping his face on his sleeve and regaining his composure. "But how did you know about Father? We wrote to you in Amsterdam but yesterday. How are you here now?"

"I was in London. On business. My employer gave me leave to visit before I go back there. I stopped briefly at the Blue Boar and heard about Father. I am so sorry, John. So sorry not to have seen him before the end."

"'Tis almost like a miracle. You were meant to come now. Ah..." he ran his fingertips back and forth through his stubbly hair, "...Lionel could talk to you about God's plans. I am better with sheep and barley and horses. It is good to see you, you... giant! You are so changed." And almost for the first time he really studied Richard's face. "And you have seen some things, I reckon, in the time we have been apart. You have many stories for us, I think." He also caught sight of the hilt of Richard's sword, and his eyes widened. He looked up at Richard. "Yes, many stories, I have no doubt."

"John. May I see to the horse?" He nodded back over his shoulder.

"Of course. What a host I am! Take it round the back. Tom is still with us, and he can see to it."

It had been an extraordinary evening. His reunion with Angelica was more floods of tears. No longer the little girl, she was now a young woman and, Richard thought, much changed from his memory of the vivacious, pretty and wickedly humorous. She was handsome, no doubt of that, but she had seemed a little worn down. Much of the burden of caring for their father had fallen on her shoulders and it seemed some of her spark had gone. Her blonde hair was drawn tightly back, and to Richard she seemed so small and a little fragile. But as the evening wore on and Richard, John and Angelica were left alone by the well-wishers and tradespeople, her mood lifted and she begged Richard to tell them more of his adventures.

She made a rewarding audience, and while John had to keep leaving them to organise some arrangement for the funeral, Angelica was on the edge of her seat as Richard played out the siege at Breda, his adventures across the continent and the encounter at the bridge over the canal. She traced the line of his crushed cheekbone and the numerous small scars on his hands and arms.

She was by turns in hysterics and disbelieving horror at his stories of Roger DeLacey, but he kept a few things back. Montague, his recent duel and, to his own surprise, he could not bring himself to talk of Neelie and his intention to marry. *There will be time for that*, he thought. *I must pick my moment. After the funeral.*

When he asked after Lionel, there was a moment of silence as John and Angelica exchanged glances. "Well, you will meet him tomorrow. He will come with Anne, his wife.

(LONDON, JUNE 1641)

We are worried about him. He has a running feud with the bishop. Lionel attacks episcopacy in print and from his pulpit. He is a marked man, I think, and Anne is shaped from the same stuff. They egg each other on with a passion I have seldom seen."

Angelica added, "And he is surrounded by more and more people who are of a similar mind, and they become bolder in their defiance. You will meet some of them tomorrow too. And not just any local firebrands, Richard. Important men. Members of Parliament and landowners. They will not conform, and speak loudly of tyranny and a need for change. With the invasion of the Scots as well, all seems uncertain."

As if they all suddenly wanted to move off this topic, they spoke of more prosaic things. The weather, the soil, the coming harvest. John hunted and spoke to Richard of the beauty of his horse and dogs. He coveted a hawk but had not yet taken the steps to ownership. And eventually, as they all felt the urgent need to sleep before the trying day to come, Richard asked to see his father. They led him to the cellar, the coldest place in the house, gave him a candle and left him alone.

Now, as he lay on his bed with the early morning sun slanting across his sheets, he acknowledged that the opportunity to say goodbye to his father had been necessary. Finally, the emotion had come, and as he looked on his father's face by the wavering light of the candle flame, he could see how the years and illness had carved away his flesh and left him gaunt and stretched. He looked what he was, a man who despite the good fortune of a prosperous farm and lands, and the love of his children, had never found joy again after the loss of his wife. He thought he understood the indifference he had always felt from his father. *We were no consolation. He had one great love, and he lost it too soon.* He prayed that he would never be in the same position. He would never let that happen. He kissed the ice-cold forehead and lowered the oak lid on the casket.

He could hear the sounds of people moving around the house. Preparations for receiving villagers and local dignitaries after the funeral were all-consuming, but he wanted to lie just a little longer in the sunny peace of the morning and remember. Golden days. Playing with his siblings in the fields and woods, and around the house. He remembered endless games of hide-and-seek on rainy days when they were very young. Richard laughed out loud as he remembered how every time it was Angelica's time to hide, she would run to the same big wardrobe in their father's room and hide among her mother's old dresses, the dresses that his father could not bear to get rid of. In fact, she often forgot the game, so lost was she in exploring the clothes and trying to capture some scent or presence of her mother, and always looked so surprised when she was first to be found.

John had been the one he looked up to; in many ways he acted as a father. Dependable, reliable, there to get him out of scrapes but also to scold him when he went too far in his exuberance. And it was usually Angelica that would get him into those scrapes. A cheeky, daring, endlessly laughing Angelica who would be forgiven everything. That Angelica now seemed from a very different time, but Richard had seen, the previous evening as they talked, glimpses of her former character, as though dark blinds were slowly being opened to allow the light to shine through.

He had forgotten the joy of a simple life. The rhythm of farm life following the rhythm of the seasons. After the tense and frantic recent past, death and disaster swirling around him, this felt like falling asleep. In fact, why not? And as he felt himself drifting off again, he imagined life here with Neelie. Would she love it? Hate it for the quietness and lack of bustle

(London, June 1641)

and excitement that Amsterdam brought? Would she get on with Angelica?

And as he contemplated these 'ifs' with eyelids drooping, there was a sharp bang on the door and Angelica's voice: "Are you ever going to get up and help us get ready?"

"Sorry! I am on my way, dear sister! My, but you have become a brusque old maid!"

From the other side of the door she laughed. "Wait 'til you get downstairs! I'll 'old maid' you with the back of my hand. You don't scare me with your sword and your scars, brother! Come and learn what working for a living is really like."

*

It wasn't until the service at the church that he met Lionel again. And then only as the sizeable congregation slowly filtered out into the sunshine after the ritual was complete.

Lionel had always been a bit of a mystery to him. He shared Richard's quick temper, but always seemed to be thinking on a different level to the rest of them. Now the shortest of the three sons, he was also the darkest. His hair, beard and eyes were almost black, but his eyes carried a fire. He was the one more interested in news from beyond the village. More prone to argue with their father, and other adults, and always wanting to get to an understanding of what lay at the heart of something. Richard knew all children go through the phase of asking 'but why?' over and over again, but Lionel had never stopped. Right up until the point Richard left home, Lionel was still infuriated when he could not get to an answer, to a truth he knew was there but couldn't quite grasp. And as a result, he had always seemed on the edge of rage and it burned within him. When he had announced that he wanted to become a curate, no one was surprised.

Now, with their father's body in the earth he had farmed all his life, he found himself walking back from the village to their house with Lionel. They were near the head of a long line of mourners winding along the lane under shading oak and beech, like a black snake whispering through the countryside. Richard had decided Lionel's wife, Anne, was even more frightening than Lionel, and she had fixed him with a steely stare from her grey eyes and interrogated him about his work in the arms trade, where he was evasive, and about the different Protestant groups in Amsterdam, where he was ignorant. Having seemingly labelled him as a warmongering heathen, he was thankful that she fell in step with Angelica and did not deem him worthy of further discourse.

Lionel had seemed little fazed by seeing him again, as if it were the most natural thing in the world for him to have turned up just in time for his father's funeral. "I pray for you every day, Richard. And I prayed for your return as I knew no letter could reach you in time. And here you are. I am glad to see you again. You are much changed, though."

"Really? Do you truly think so? I feel little different inside, despite the things I have seen…" and he continued more quietly, "…and the things I have done. I am trying to control my temper. You more than most know how I can be, but I have had some success. Perhaps you sense I am worldly? A bit more informed?"

Lionel smiled. "Yes, but that's not really what I mean. That is experience, not any progression of your character." *Oh*, thought Richard. *Right.* "You are… harder? I am not sure that is the right word. Not just because of your face…" Richard kept forgetting his damaged cheek and nose, "…but inside. Perhaps it is difficult to truly perceive oneself accurately. But you seem deeper, more thoughtful, more analytical. Perhaps there is a little coldness to you. I am sorry, brother!" He

(LONDON, JUNE 1641)

suddenly laughed, something unusual for Lionel. "Now I am merely being rude. I analyse too much and speak what I am thinking. It will do me damage someday. At least that is what our brother and sister tell me constantly. Perhaps they are right. You left us at such a young age and I admit we were never sure we would see you again. It is good to see you!"

Richard winced slightly at this. *I must speak to him on this when we can be alone. I must tell him of Montague and his eyes and ears.* As they passed along the leafy mile to their house, Lionel updated him on their story. He had aimed for the clergy but had found the Anglican rituals and trappings too lavish for what he considered a purer approach to God's grace. He had rejected this and was engaged in dialogue with like-minded people in the area, and further afield in London and other towns and cities. He aspired to writing his own pamphlets and that triggered a memory of his meeting with Will in London.

"You remember my friend? Will Fletcher from the village?"

"I think so. Yes."

And Richard proceeded to tell Lionel as much as he could remember of their conversation. Of Will's acquaintance with pamphlet writers, some of whom Lionel had heard of, and his particular devotion to John Lilburne. At that name, Lionel started, and swung round to face him. "You know Lilburne? Really?"

"Not I, I'm afraid, brother. But Will knows him well. They talk religion and politics, but it goes over my head."

"You must meet some of my own acquaintances, Rich. I am even hoping Master Cromwell will come to our house. He knew Father and wants to pay his respects. He is very much the coming man. He will be interested, I think, in your knowledge of war and the way of the arms trade, although he is himself a godly man. I admire him for his courage to speak out. I wish there were more like him in their devotion to the truth."

"I would be honoured, Lionel. But afterwards, you and I must talk. There are some things I must tell you. Will you be staying at the house tonight?"

"I fear not. That sounds very mysterious! But we will find time, brother. Don't worry. Now, Anne, I know you had some more questions for my little brother. She is very curious to learn more of how our brethren care for fallen women in Amsterdam. It is a cause close to her heart! Come and walk with us…"

Richard gave her his best smile.

*

Some hours later and most of the villagers had paid their respects and wound their way home through fields and along the lanes, stomachs full and some heads spinning from the local cider. Immediate family remained, and many of their tenants had stayed to talk with John about the harvest, and market prices for their barley and oats. Richard sat on a bench in the sun with Angelica, her head on his shoulder. They had talked of their father and their pride that so many had come to pay their respects. They had always seen him as a quiet, unassuming man, a little cold, a little distant. And in his final years, Angelica had sometimes found it hard to love him as the coldness grew and the distance extended, as he seemingly became more and more detached from his life, adrift on an ebbing tide of melancholy.

His death was a release for all of them in the house, and they lifted the heavy shrouds from the windows and let the warmth of summer finally penetrate and banish the shadows. It had felt like a final gift, the only one he had been able to give his children in the end. His absence.

(LONDON, JUNE 1641)

And it was while Angelica was quietly telling him of the final days of his life that Richard, before he had intended to, told Angelica of his own love. He faltered over the words. Feelings and thoughts about Neelie, which had seemed to whirl so beautifully around in his head, stumbled out of his mouth like drunks leaving a tavern, and he felt ashamed at his lack of eloquence, like he was in some way belittling the strength of his love, and Neelie herself, through his inability to express himself.

He had expected Angelica to whoop and shout and start shouting instructions for the wedding, but in fact she hardly shifted on the bench. She just cocked her head slightly and looked up at him from under black mourning lace, face framed by her golden curls. "I would love to meet her, brother. This fine woman who has you so under her spell. I can feel the happiness and the... hmm... now I can't find the right word. Yes, I don't think *adoration* is too strong a word. I can feel how you feel about her — you don't have to speak any more. Bring her here to us when you can, so we can love her too. You will come back to us now, Richard? Are the days of your adventures over? Do you think you and she would be happy here?"

"That is the question I have been turning over ever since I came back here," he replied, watching a beetle skirting the toe of his boot in the gravel. He watched it gain the safety of the grass of the small lawn in front of them. "I honestly don't know, sister. I have to admit, I thought this just a passing visit, an opportunity which came up by chance, but I had forgotten... all of this. I realise I have missed you all. I have missed this place. I left because I saw no prospect for me here, but now, after what I have seen in the world, this peacefulness is attractive. And I know that Neelie would love you. I just don't know if she could face leaving her own home."

"Well of course, you must discuss this with her. You cannot

just drag her away from her family and her friends. It is not so easy to uproot yourself when you are settled in a place."

"Angelica." He paused but had to go on. "She has no family. Her father was killed in the wars with the Spanish. She was separated from her mother and younger brother, and she believes they must be dead. She is very likely right. She came to Amsterdam a penniless orphan."

"But that is terrible. War is so terrible that it does this to families. How did you come to meet her, Richard? How did the poor thing cope in such dire circumstances?"

He sighed, and turned to look at her, easing her head off his shoulder. "And that is the other thing I must tell you about her, but I would ask you not to tell anyone else this. Not at the moment."

And Richard told her, sparing no detail of how they came to be together, and Angelica cried a little and laughed a little, and at the end flung her arms around him and promised to tell no one of Neelie's history but that she was even more determined that Richard should bring her home. But as she excitedly started to plan how all these things could come to pass, a shadow fell across them as Lionel approached.

"Richard, Anne and I must soon be on our way, but I want you to meet a few people, and wasn't there something you wished to tell me? Come, let us walk a loop around the house so you can tell me this dread secret before we rejoin the group."

And for the second time he found himself divulging his secrets to a sibling. This time not so joyous, or so liberating. He shared his conversations with Montague. He shared his concerns about what the man was capable of and he warned Lionel urgently to take care of what he said, to whom he said it and about the company he kept. "Please, brother, these men are dangerous and would do you harm if they could. Any slight against the King, directly or through your words on bishops — I confess I do not fully understand the subtleties of all this — could see you hang, or worse."

"Worse?"

"Worse. His kind would see hanging as a soft option for traitors."

Lionel paled in the warmth of the late afternoon sun as they came around from the shaded side into the courtyard area. "I hear you. I will think on what you say. But I find it amazing that a King's agent from London could be interested in my modest preaching here in Huntingdonshire! I cannot change my beliefs, Richard, but I would bring no harm to Anne. Anyway, at least meet my acquaintances while they are here and see for yourself if they are not fine men, with the finest of intentions."

He gestured to a small group of men, dressed predominantly in mourning colours, standing in the middle of the modest lawn, between the house and the first of the barley fields that lapped like a green-gold sea at the end of their garden, the light breeze raising waves and ripples through the heads of grain. And, as if in a waking dream, Richard saw a mirror-like reflection unfurling in front of him. Equidistant from the group on the far side, emerging on a narrow path through the field, were two men, walking purposefully towards them. He recognised Montague and his young companion, and as he looked beyond them to the copse on the far edge of the field, he saw the other man, the old soldier, holding the three horses.

He grabbed Lionel's arm and thrust him behind him as he picked up the pace. "Montague," he hissed over his shoulder, "the one I was telling you about." They arrived at the group of four men, who were dividing their attention between the approaching parties, seconds before Montague. Richard strode through the middle of them, ignoring an outstretched hand, and planted himself in Montague's path. His glance strayed to his left hip involuntarily, but he remembered he had left his blade in his bedroom. He had not, however, neglected to bring his small dagger in his boot, which was a little comfort at least. He folded his arms across his chest, as the men behind him muttered and stirred uneasily.

"Well met, Master Montague, although most of our visitors tend to arrive at our front door."

A faint smile on Montague's lips as he swept off his hat and bowed slightly to the assembled group. "Well met indeed, Master Farrell. I did say I would pay my respects, and here I am."

Richard glanced at the other man, but he made no move and Montague showed no signs of introducing him. "You could have come to the chapel, sir. Why do you impose on our private gathering?" Richard knew this was provocative, but he was sick of the man and the tension and fear that he always brought with him. "You paid your respects, and you have our thanks. I am sure you are busy and need to be on your way."

Richard sensed a figure next to him and glanced to his right. A tallish man from the group of guests. Brown hair cropped conservatively, Puritan dress and a stern face. "Master Farrell. I do not think you understand Master Montague's true purpose here. He does not come to harass you. He is here to observe us. That is his job for the King. He is here to see who is meeting with whom. Who is saying what, and where and why. Who went to the non-conforming service at the chapel. It is my misfortune to see Master Montague on many occasions. He seems to have a particular interest in me and my affairs."

Montague bowed again. His smile still fixed in place. "Master Cromwell and I are old acquaintances, Farrell. He is such an interesting man. So many interesting friends. So many strong opinions on this and that, particularly his

(London, June 1641)

opposition to our sovereign's will in relation to prayer and worship. That is why I could not come to the chapel, Farrell. The stink of Puritanism makes me nauseous. I need to breathe cleaner air. Careful, sir, that you do not catch this disease from your brother." He nodded towards Lionel who stood behind Richard's left shoulder. "It seems to be a plague in these parts."

Richard felt a little lost. He could understand threat and intimidation, but the subtleties of religious differences were not in his vocabulary. Cromwell motioned Lionel to silence. "We will not debate with the likes of you, Montague. Our direction comes from God, not from fat, greedy bishops that seek to influence our King. Begone, sir, and leave us in peace!"

Montague's eyes hardened above the smile. "I am not someone you can just dismiss, Master Cromwell. And in any case, Master Farrell and I are firm friends. I cannot just leave so abruptly. It would be rude."

"Believe me, Montague, when I say that you are no friend of mine. Your departure would be a blessing. We are here to mourn my father, not fence with words. I understand you have a duty to perform. You have performed it. Now please leave."

"I am hurt, Richard. To my very core." He shrugged. "I expect I will get over it. But it was nice to see you again, and in such illustrious company. And nice for me to meet your family. Lionel I am aware of by his reputation as a bit of a firebrand. Take care, sir, that you do not light fires you cannot put out. And your brother John, who hosts these interesting men on his estate." Richard noticed his brother had come to stand next to Lionel. "And, of course, the lovely Angelica Farrell. Mistress…" He again swept off his hat and bowed low. "I never forget a face or a name. And they say you can tell a man's character and loyalties by the company he keeps." He looked hard at Richard. "Farewell, Richard. And take good care of your family in these uncertain times." He spun on his heel. "Come, sir. We must be a long way towards Westminster before dark." His companion followed him back along the path they created by wading through the barley.

Cromwell turned to Richard. "Come, sir. I would talk with you."

*

He had stayed with his family longer than he had intended and it had been a wrench to leave them again. He had helped with the harvest. He had ridden and hunted with John. He had spent long hours talking and plotting with Angelica, and had time with Lionel and Anne, trying to understand more about the tensions that existed around their Puritanism, and trying to educate them in what men like Montague were capable of.

Richard had been impressed by Cromwell. He had been grim, and serious, but a man of strong passions and determination. He showed no fear of Montague's threats and was resigned to being spied upon and intimidated. Richard felt he was a man who could be relied upon to keep his word and stand his ground in a tight situation. They had talked for some time, and Cromwell had been keen to learn more of Richard's military experiences, his connections with other mercenaries and soldiers from the wars on the continent. They had discussed the practicalities of the procurement and manufacture of weaponry and how this was managed discreetly. Richard had wondered at his motivation, but Cromwell had revealed little. "We are beset by enemies, Master Farrell. We are loyal to the Crown but fret at the poor and selfish advice he receives. Papist bishops desperate to retain their authority and self-seeking tyrants like Strafford. We only wish to protect the

(London, June 1641)

true faith and the people. We serve His Majesty, of course, but we must not be caught unprepared."

He had written to Neelie, guilty at the delay in his return, but had received a response full of understanding, joy at his reunion with his family and love for him. She counted the minutes until his arrival but did not begrudge his time at his home, she who knew the empty feeling of loss in relation to her own family.

But now it was October, and he was nearly there, his ship rounding the point on its approach to the Amsterdam dock. The crossing had been rough but swift, the trader hurried along by the strong southwesterly, crashing over the swells and reacquainting Richard with his difficult relationship with sea travel. Feeling the relief of one who had imagined salty death at every moment but now stepping shakily on to solid stone, he hoisted his pack and set off south through the teeming streets around the harbour. People and carts and animals in never-ending rivers of commerce. He had forgotten the almost tangible feeling of money being made all round him. The fear of not being involved. Of missing out on a fortune. Not like London. Everything there was tension and fear. Here, nothing could stand in the way of business. It was like the wars had never happened.

He pushed his way through the crowd towards the rooms he shared with Neelie, minutes from Hudde's grand home and office. No more than ten minutes' walk through the wind that now blew his hat and hair around like the traders' sails.

He rounded the corner. He stopped. He had not expected to see her out. The picture in his mind all the way across the North Sea had been of him striding into their home and surprising her. Carrying her to the rug in front of a roaring fire and, well, becoming reacquainted. But she was returning to the front door from some errand, wrapped up against the autumn wind. Her arm was linked with that of a tall man, and she stared up into his face, his hair blowing and masking his features, and hers. His other hand clamped his broad-brimmed hat on his head, but he gave up the battle and swept it off. As she smiled up at him, he bent and kissed her tenderly on the forehead and she flung her arms around him. Her face appeared over his shoulder as he half crouched to bridge their difference in height. She did not see Richard, but he saw her expression. He could think of no other word to describe it than 'bliss'.

He found that he could not move. His brain numbly registered Neelie leading the man up the stairs to the front door, and then disappearing. He slumped back against the wall, trying desperately to erase the moment from his mind, but the image of her smiling, contented face was seared into him. He couldn't process it. Couldn't make sense of it, but there was no mistake in what he had seen. He stared blankly at the doors and windows of the house opposite him. What to do? He felt no emotion, which surprised him given his usual hot-tempered response. No anger, no sadness. Just a coldness and a sense of disbelief.

He found himself turning away. Swivelling on the heel of his boot and walking slowly back towards the dock. He took a right turn. A left. He bumped heavily into a couple of city scouts who were patrolling the dockside taverns, but he didn't hear their angry shouts. He stepped in front of a laden cart pulled by a team of two enormous draught horses which had to stop so quickly they danced with an agility belying their heft. With no conscious intent, after an hour of aimless wandering, he found himself outside the Sailor, his feet having more awareness than his fogged mind. Hans was delighted to see him, largely because it had been a slow morning in the tavern. Unbidden, he brought him ale and a sausage and

(London, June 1641)

helped himself generously out of the purse Richard pushed in his direction.

The warmth of the room seemed to melt his frozen brain and with the thaw came a quickening flow of questions with no answers. And the quicker they came the more it stoked the fire of his emotion. Who was the bastard? How could she have done this to him, so soon after his proposal? After all her melancholy act in London? Because he saw now it must have been an act! Is this why she had encouraged him to stay on with his family? How long had this been going on? Why was he always such a fool? Why had no one told him of this?

And now the icy trickles of the thaw had become the boiling rivers of fury. He slapped the mug of ale across the table, startling the tavern cat and drawing a shout from Hans. He kicked back his chair and, not realising payment had already been taken, slammed more coins on the counter and pushed his way out into the early evening light.

Ten minutes later he was hammering on DeLacey's door, demanding to know why his former friend had not found a way to stop Neelie's betrayal, or to have warned him. But Roger, surprisingly sober, clear-eyed and rational, had not seen or heard anything of Neelie. He was shocked and saddened too, but challenged Richard's version of events. Was he sure? This was so unlike Neelie. He let Richard's anger slowly blow itself out becoming, in the end, a mess of sobs and snot.

Eventually he suggested Richard go to Hudde to see what he knew, seeing as he had brought Neelie home from London, to which Richard silently agreed. But before Richard left, he also told him of his recent encounter with Captain Browne in Amsterdam, of strong rumours of conflict to come in England, Ireland and Scotland. They were trying to re-form the company and Richard should consider joining them. The acrid scent of war had cleared Roger's head and given him a new focus. This was the Roger DeLacey he had first met outside Breda years before. The man he had admired. That man was back and through the haze of his misery, Richard marvelled at the transformation. Here was a man who had regained his purpose, just as Richard seemed to have lost his own.

Hudde was pleased to see Richard back in the city but had no good news for him. Yes, he had also seen Neelie with the tall young man. He had not approached them as they seemed so engrossed in each other, strolling the streets arm in arm, laughing and talking. No, he had no idea who the man was or where he had come from. He had no tasks for Richard for a month or so, so his time was his own for now. Why didn't Richard just go around and talk to Neelie? Maybe there was a simple explanation?

But Richard couldn't. He just couldn't. The shock of betrayal was too great. The damascene realisation of his love for her, of his total commitment to her happiness, had been flung back at him, slapped him across the face and fallen like a wet cloth at his feet. He couldn't step over it and confront her. He just couldn't.

A week later he was back in London, looking for Will.

32

MARLEIGH

(near Macclesfield, October 1641)

The woman was trying to walk along the path without making a noise. It was something she tried to do at every opportunity. To be like one of the creatures of the woods. To be part of the silence that hung between the branches. She avoided twigs and stones, trying to step only in the sandy dirt of the thin trail. She ducked low branches and side-stepped projecting foliage, placing her feet carefully as she made slow progress towards the Edge. She knew she was good at this. She had had nearly sixty years of practice, and her age and crookedness had not restricted her abilities. Perhaps had even heightened them. A few small birds twittered off to her right. Firecrests, she thought. And now, with a shift in the light breeze, the noise of the distant rookery, harsh voices of the birds carrying as they circled, argued and communed.

She was here for herbs and other plants for her store. And she was here for mushrooms for her pot. A rabbit hung in her shoulder bag, and she was already picturing the fragrant stew that she would prepare back in her small hut on the fringes of the trees. She swallowed saliva and tried to focus on her task. She had promised to visit the Harpers in the morning to see to their milk cow, and to talk to Meg about her 'problem'. She knew the answer to that one already and it would need none of her herblore. Just stopping fucking every farmboy in the neighbourhood. A simple poultice to cure her immediate need and a stern talking to for the longer term. She chuckled to herself as she approached the cliff through oak and hornbeam. She liked Meg for her wit and kindness, but one day her God-fearing husband would find out and probably kill her, or worse.

She knew where the plants she needed grew. They liked the airiness of the Edge and occupied crevices in the sandstone. She would gather a good bundle which would do for Meg and could be dried for other needy customers. She stopped as she reached the first viewpoint. The Edge at Alderley was a thing to see and she never tired of gazing from the cliff path out over the plain of Cheshire below her. A strange and sacred place where the red sandstone cascaded down to the green lands below. A view framed in trees, many with their autumn painted leaves clinging on. Others, with their naked limbs, revealed the intricate lace of their branches and twigs, contorted and black against the flat grey of the October evening.

She pulled her shawl around her as she started to feel the coolness of the day taking hold. She would not linger here today. She knew the legends about the place. That King Arthur and his knights slept below the stone, waiting for the last day. For Ragnorak. For the horn that would summon them forth for the final battle. She set no store by that. But she also knew the other stories. That this was a place of reverence for the old ones. The faeries of the forest and the spirits of the earth. Those who were here before the Romans, before the Christians, before there were many people here at all. Not many knew these stories, but she did, and she had seen too much and learned too much to discount the tales.

(NEAR MACCLESFIELD, OCTOBER 1641)

Yet she had no terror of the place, just a healthy respect, and she limited the time she spent on these rocks for fear of giving offence. Even now she felt the closeness of the air. The gentle breeze of earlier had faltered, and she felt the hairs on her neck and forearms rise and knew this wasn't entirely down to the chill of the air.

She knew others would be oblivious to this, but she felt it. A vaguely ominous feeling of dread. Not malevolent, but like a pressure, pushing her away. Resisting her. She felt uneasy, but no more than usual. She had not been to this part of the common for some weeks and today felt... odd. Tense. Waiting. She hurried to gather the plants she needed, to be on the path home. She tried to make light of her nervousness and started to hum a song of Pan. She hoped they would like that.

After a few minutes, as she bent to gather leaves and stems, her knees protesting, she felt eyes upon her. Slowly, she straightened, and turned, looking along the face of the escarpment to the trees that started again on the far side of the expanse of bare red rock. Nothing.

There! A shadow moving among the tightly packed birch trunks, along the path she would normally take home. Moving towards her. Curious. She so seldom encountered any folk along these paths. She couldn't have run if she wanted to, so she sat on a stone ledge, and waited. The figure emerged from the trees onto the other end of the broad ledge. The ground fell away sharply to the newcomer's right, and rose twenty feet or so to her left, to the summit of the Edge.

She could see the other was a woman. Dressed in the usual black skirts, white coif on her head, with a few strands of red-brown hair dropping down the sides of her face. But she was carrying her boots in one hand and had a leather satchel over the other shoulder. The woman looked up across the red, dusty space between them, and smiled. She walked slowly, carefully, in her bare feet. As she got closer, the older woman could see that she was quite beautiful. High cheekbones and full features. She had the colour of those used to being outdoors, but her skin was clearer, and less lined with hardship. The smile was warm, genuine and welcoming, but as she came within a few feet of the old woman, it faded and was replaced with a look of concern. She halted in front of the ledge and looked down, worry in her eyes.

"Good mistress, are you unwell? You are pale and you shiver. Do you have a fever?"

The old woman was shivering but only partially because of the cold. She didn't know who it was stood in front of her, but now she was close she somehow sensed that something wasn't right. The young woman in front of her appeared far older than her face suggested. She felt unsettled as she looked up into brown eyes, flecked with green, and saw a depth of… of what? She couldn't think of the right word, but her long years of herblore and exploring the secrets of the cunning folk had tuned her senses and now, somehow, she felt herself in the presence of something… ancient. How could this be?

"Can you hear me, mistress? Are you unwell?"

She mastered her speech. "I am well, my lady. Thank you. I was just catching my breath and taking in the view before I follow the path home."

The younger woman's smile returned. "Aye. 'Tis wondrous on the eye. I have not been here for some time, but I came, I think, for the same reason as you." She glanced at the older woman's bag. "I mean no insult, mistress, but I do not imagine those herbs are for you?"

Now the old woman smiled in return, regaining some confidence. "Indeed not, m'lady. Those days are long gone. So you too have those who rely on your herblore then?"

The younger woman stepped forward and sat alongside. She looked at the old woman cautiously. "Some, aye. But I

(near Macclesfield, October 1641)

must be careful how many know of this as, in the past, I have been accused of more unwelcomed practices. And it seems to be getting more and more dangerous for folk such as you and me. You know what I mean, I'm sure?"

The older woman nodded. It was a constant risk and threat, particularly with the spread of this new Puritanism. She had heard distant rumours of accusations, trials and hangings. Burnings even. She shivered again. "Aye, m'lady. I know of what you speak. I heard of them two Rainow girls dragged to Chester for trial. Them n'ere came back to their 'omes."

The proximity of this other confused her. She felt a powerful presence, which awed and frightened her equally, but also an excitement. A thought came to her mind and she spoke before she had time to think on it. "I live but fifteen minutes' walk from here, my lady. Would you visit with me? I seldom have any visitors and none who have knowledge that I might learn from, even in my shadow years. And I have everything we need for a good supper." She held up her bag.

"I thank you, mistress, but you do not even know my name. Perhaps you should be more cautious. And please, do not call me 'lady'. You see I am dressed no better than what I am. I have escaped Macclesfield today for air, and to replenish my stock. As I mentioned, I have not visited here for some time and it is a special place."

"Aye, 'tis special. But why do you think so if you don't mind me asking?" *Perhaps she is a faery herself or something like, for she ain't no normal woman, no matter what she says.*

"Well, so many of the plants and herbs I need grow in this one place, I s'pose. Maybe 'tis the red rock and the soil it makes. And I am plain Marleigh. Marleigh Hume. I work as housekeeper at the rich boys' school in the town. Nothing more grand than that."

That does not sound so fay, but I am not mistaken, she

thought. *There is more to her than that.* "And I am Alice Mellor. Although as you can imagine, 'cos folk 'ere abouts know of my cunning, they have to give me another name. I am also known as 'Old Mother Edge', although only God knows why."

They both laughed, and Alice felt herself growing warmer as if the chill in the air had receded.

Feeling emboldened Alice turned to face Marleigh. "Mistress Hume. May I ask you a straight question?" She got no reaction beyond a slight smile, so she plunged on. "I know 'tis rude to be so blunt but forgive me, there is something about you that riddles me. I have a good eye, you know, for certain things. I see you in front o' me, but I don't see you clear. You must know the stories o' this place. I have to ask you…"

Marleigh interrupted her. "Am I one o' the faery folk? Is that what you ask?" She frowned hard at Alice.

Alice swallowed, panic again rising in her. Her tongue cleaved to the roof of her mouth. With an effort, beaten down by the combination of those eyes and the now-angry expression, she managed, "Or maybe a tree spirit, m'lady? I mean no offence."

Marleigh rose, towering over old Alice, her face contorted with fury. But after a few seconds she took pity on Alice and her features reassembled around a torrent of sudden laughter. She collapsed back onto the ledge, helpless. Alice was bewildered and was more and more convinced she had walked into some kind of dream, or nightmare. Finally, Marleigh regained control of herself and shifted again to kneel in front of Alice, taking her veined old hands in her own – smooth, brown, unblemished. "Alice, I ask your forgiveness for my prank. But truly I have not laughed so in a long time. It has done me more good than any infusion of herbs you could give me. But no, dear Alice, I am none o' them things. In fact, nothing could be further from the truth."

(NEAR MACCLESFIELD, OCTOBER 1641)

Marleigh could see Alice harboured no anger at her joke, but rather her eyes reflected a certain disappointment, mingled with a little relief.

In a soft voice she asked, "But what is it that you think you really want to know?" Marleigh looked deep into Alice's eyes and saw fear there, but also a desperate curiosity. She recognised a yearning to 'know'. To understand more deeply. A feeling that gnawed at her own soul every day of her life. She saw in Old Mother Edge one who had scratched at the edges of real awareness without ever being able to get to the heart of things. Again, she took pity.

Alice swallowed hard, her old eyes rimmed with tears. "All," she whispered. "I would know all there is."

"Then let us go to your home and prepare that coney."

*

The musty darkness of Alice's old cottage was illuminated by a blazing fire. She had been accumulating firewood all year and she was prepared to build a good flame for such a visitor. Her excitement confused her fingers and it took her longer to light the kindling than it normally would have done. Between them they skinned, cleaned and jointed the fat coney and set it to stew slowly with rosemary and the mushrooms that Alice had gathered.

They sat either side of the ancient oak table, probably the most valuable thing in Alice's possession, with elbows propped and hands cupped around cups of a steaming herb infusion. In truth, Marleigh did not really know why she was here or what it was she intended to say. She just knew she had a yearning to share her thoughts with one who might have a glimmer of understanding. It had been so long since she could speak openly of her passion, her beliefs. She knew she was taking a risk, but here was one who would not want to be anywhere near a mob chanting "Witch". And she liked Alice. She was not one who would use her knowledge for revenge, or petty dispute. She had a good heart and, in many ways, she felt that if she had allowed herself, she might have been something like Alice was. She felt a sudden warmth for the woman who seemed intent on treating her like royalty, although she felt King Charlie might turn his nose up at the earthiness of her hospitality.

As the evening deepened, they talked of their lore. They swapped recipes for broths and infusions. They freely gave away their secret places where certain plants and herbs could be found, although Marleigh's knowledge of local geography was far more extensive than Alice's who had seldom travelled from Alderley. Nevertheless, Marleigh was delighted to find she was learning from the old woman and their friendship grew.

And Alice told her of the spirits that she believed haunted the woods around the Edge. To her regret, she had never met them, but she felt them everywhere. In the trees, in the rocks, in the air around her. Like a thrill or a shiver. Like a sudden shaft of sunlight that lights you, that warms you, but then is gone. They come from the earth but are not solid, not something she could see and touch, but real enough to her. "Do you know of this?" she asked. "Do you see them? What is it that I feel?"

Marleigh decided to move things on. "Alice. Are you a Christian woman?"

Alice peered back at her over the rim of her cup, marvelling at the perfection of the woman's skin in the bronze light of the fire, and the way it reflected back from her brown-green eyes. "Aye. I suppose I am a Christian, mistress, but I am never sure what that means. I have seen so many flavours of Christian in my life, that I no longer remember what it is I am told is truth.

(near Macclesfield, October 1641)

All I know is that 'tis a crime to stay away from church. So I go. Does that make me Christian?"

"To many, aye, it does. For many, that is all that matters. Stand in that cold stone house. Say the words you don't understand. Kneel. Stand. Kneel. Turn around. Do all the man in black tells you from his big book and say 'Amen'. All will be well. Yes, Alice. Do all that and eternal life is yours."

"Then I am a Christian, 'cos I do all that. But I hope life eternal don't mean livin' in this 'ut forever." She smiled at Marleigh.

Marleigh laughed out loud. "So, Alice, tell me. What happens when you die?"

"Well, my dear, I shall be vexed for sure... But 'ow d'yer mean?"

And for the next hour, until the rich smell of the stew could no longer be ignored, she laid out her thoughts, her studies, her experiments and her observations. While they ate, savouring the savoury, melting meat, Alice was quiet. Marleigh had tried to answer her questions and forgiven her many interruptions, but now she could see Alice was trying to digest all she had heard and to make sense of it.

And as Marleigh waited, she knew that it had been in vain. It had felt empowering to be able to talk openly through it all, and a relief that it still sounded like truth to her ears when spoken out loud, rather than only turned and churned in the quietness of her own mind. But she could see Alice's resistance. Her reluctance. Her disappointment and her fear. She could read it all and she could feel her shoulders slump involuntarily.

Finally, Alice had looked up from her bowl, every scrap of food consumed. She had looked on the edge of tears. "I don't understand."

Marleigh had smiled. "I know," she said. "I know. I would have been 'mazed if you had, but I wanted to keep my side of the bargain. I have told you all I can and I can see you do not know what to believe."

"I see no place for... for..." She grasped for the word.

"Magic? You see no spirits, no faery folk, no great god Pan? Do you not think it magic – what I have told you I can do?"

Alice frowned. "I ain't a child. I know what I know. No. There's no wonder. T'ain't magic if you can explain it." She shook her head. "Not that I really understood a word you were sayin'. Millponds and wheels turnin' and such..."

"I know. And I once thought the same. But to me, now, there is more wonder in the knowing, than in the hoping. I have told you of my skill. Of my cunning, if you like. But now I understand, at least a little, of where it comes from and how it... works. And for me, that is almost more wonder, more magic, than I can contain."

"Well, mistress, you are a wonder yourself and that's the truth. If you can do 'alf them things you say you can, then I am a'feared of you. But thou should take care. Tell this to no one, as there are many will not like the power you hold and will have less understanding than even I have. You know what they will call you. And what they will do."

"Aye. I know well enough. I have not lived as long as I have without care. But I tell you, Alice, I grow weary of the burden. I cannot carry this weight in me forever. I can only lessen it by sharing and you have helped me here tonight to reduce my load. I thank you for more than just the coney."

"Watch out for her as they call the 'Oly Maid. It were she that fingered them two poor lasses from Rainow and they got their necks stretched... They say she gets her words direct from God. I seen 'er once. Some say she is blessed."

"What do you say, Alice?"

"I say she's fuckin' mad. I'll take the faery folk over fire and

(NEAR MACCLESFIELD, OCTOBER 1641)

damnation every day thank'ye." And she tapped the side of her head with a gnarled finger.

Marleigh laughed again but also wondered why she had not heard of this 'maid' before. "Do not worry for me, Alice, I will take your warning to heart. But now I will be on my way. I can move quickly in the dark and there will be none out there to harm me at this time."

She gathered her possessions and stooped to kiss Alice on the forehead. "Fare you well, sister. I am sure we will meet again in this world."

As she slipped quietly out into the dark Alice strained to hear her on the path, but in vain. She did not know whether to pity her, to fear her, or to fall down and worship her.

33

BRERETON

(London, October 1641)

William pressed himself further back into the heavily shadowed north-eastern corner of Westminster Hall and silently prayed to Almighty God that this idiot would keep his voice down. Sound echoed freely down the great space, with nothing to absorb anything more than a whisper, from the stone flags to the vaulting wooden beams. The jackdaws that loved to hop around in the artificial forest canopy above their heads were providing an intermittent shower of droppings, and he was at least thankful for his wide-brimmed hat that he kept pulled forward to hide his face.

He felt nervous, edgy, stressed by the constant need for vigilance which seemed to be the payment required for his increased profile and engagement in the great cause. And still this idiot lawyer prattled on. *And I hardly know the man! Does he not understand the sensitivity?*

"So you see, Sir William, all of Cheshire stands with you. You are seen as the great man of our times there. A staunch defender of the faith, sir!" John Bradshaw beamed at him. "I am proud to be associated with you. We Cheshire gentlemen must stand together at this critical time."

I am not so sure about your claim to being a gentleman, Brereton thought acidly. *More jumped-up country busy-body*. He assembled a grim smile and leaned in closer as he lowered his voice. "Now, Master Bradshaw, let us be a little more circumspect. Indeed, we must stand together, and I thank you for your kind words, but we both know that Cheshire does not stand with us. Far from it, as the events of this year have shown."

Bradshaw seemed finally to get the message and he now tried out the type of whisper that actors could project to the back of a noisy theatre. "Ah, your tussle with Aston over that blasted petition. You came out of that rather well, I thought, Sir William. Honour intact. There were many that applauded your righteous stand." He put a friendly hand on William's shoulder until the ice in the look he received in return persuaded him to move it off again with haste. It flapped around awkwardly for a few moments as he tried to find a way to land it without a loss of face. He placed it against the cold stone of the Hall and tried to appear nonchalant.

William's recollection of the affair was rather different and he still squirmed with the memory of it. While he had been meeting with Pym, Cromwell and Hampden, back in Chester and the surrounding county, Calvin Bruen, son of the godly John Bruen, had been creating a stir with his Root and Branch petition for the reform of the Church. Bruen's name and involvement would strike fear and uncertainty in the hearts of Archbishop Laud and Bishop Bridgeman, as they saw the fiery torch of Puritanism passed from father to son.

William, buoyed by his new acceptance into the godly circle in Parliament, had been swept away by Bruen's passion, and the rising tide of sentiment that the Puritan ministers were preaching across the county, from Chester and Tarvin to Little Budworth,

Barrow and Thornton. He had himself presented the petition to Parliament and forever sealed the enmity of Sir Thomas Aston. He now reflected that his action in supporting the petition may have been overhasty. Perhaps this was exactly the type of activism that lent Laud his power. Perversely, paranoia over Puritan plots might actually strengthen his arm. *Patience, William, patience.*

Regardless of this, Aston had responded furiously. Clearly, he saw in men like Bruen, Holford and Eaton, and their belief that nothing and nobody should interpret the word of God to members of a congregation, nothing short of a plot to exterminate nobility, gentry and all order in the country. He had organised a counter-petition in defence of episcopacy and, a little over a week later, presented his document, supposedly signed by four noblemen, eighty knights and esquires, seventy divines, 300 gentlemen and 6,000 freeholders, to the Lords.

William might have left it there, but others, incensed with a belief that the Aston petition was a fake, had taken extraordinary steps for revenge. In just a month, a response was printed and circulated by printers and booksellers, already under scrutiny from the King's agents. Men like Henry Walker, Hoode, Bankes and Bates had created thousands of printed copies, with signatures purporting to come from Cheshire. Brereton's name was immediately attached to the pamphlet, but he had, in truth, had little to do with it, and was dismayed when he saw the obvious signs of fraud. The authors had merely doubled the numbers of signatures that had appeared on Aston's petition and no one believed the truth of it.

Those behind it had been arrested and bailed, and would be forever under suspicion, and William had felt he had to support them, even with the misgivings he had over the exercise. He had only avoided greater censure by Aston's arrogance and heavy-handedness in his response. He had produced a further pamphlet, calling out Walker's document as a fraud and calling for heavy punishment of those involved. His mistake was his claim to be speaking on behalf of Cheshire gentry, and while they may have had strong sympathies with his views on Puritanism, nearly fifty of his supposed supporters had disowned him for taking their names in vain without their direct permission. The whole episode had gradually faded, as neither Aston nor William had the energy to pursue things further.

The whole saga had been playing out against a backdrop of increasing violence across the churches in the county to the extent that the Lords received a report from concerned citizens. William had felt a mixture of pride and worry as he learnt that his new wife, Cicely, had been to Neston church with some of his staff and smashed stained-glass windows. He saw the story of the rising passions that these events told of, but he also saw how greater political powers were shifting events at the national level. He was torn between rolling his sleeves up and getting more involved in the fight in Cheshire, and a belief that he had a role to play on the national stage. *Pride is a sin*, he told himself, *but surely I am called to great things. I must play my role as befits my station.*

It had been a momentous year. The triumphs of Strafford's trial and execution and Laud's imprisonment. But also, the rise and rise of tension and intrigue. The army plot that Pym had uncovered and the fleeing of its leaders to France, that den of Catholicism. He was sure it was this that had helped persuade the King of the need to execute his beloved adviser, Strafford. The papal envoy had been banished from court, and the loathed Star Chamber had been abolished. Bit by bit, piece by piece, the King's authority was being whittled away by clever men like Pym and Hampden. William felt his contribution had been minimal and that the farcical events of the petitions and counter-petitions may have been an irritation and a distraction to his godly colleagues.

August had passed more promisingly for the King as he finally laid the Scottish problem to rest. Or so he thought. The army of the Covenant had been largely disbanded and he had peace with the Scottish parliament, but back in England the tide had turned against Laud as Parliament legislated against many of his ideas. But every day new reports of plots, conspiracies and agitation reached the capital and tensions ratcheted up.

William focused again on Bradshaw who seemed to be waiting for a reply. He had been lost in his thoughts and now had not heard Bradshaw's question. "I am sorry, Bradshaw, what did you say?"

"I said, these men are approaching with some purpose, don't you think?" He nodded over William's shoulder. He seemed to shrink in on himself a little. William turned slowly.

Striding along the Hall towards him were two men he recognised immediately. Pym and Hampden. Parliament had only reassembled a few days ago, after a recess of a few weeks. He had not seen either man for some time, but it was clear they were headed for him. *Obviously they are not here for Bradshaw*, he thought.

He felt a thrill of excitement. He knew that this was his destiny arriving, and he straightened his back and stepped to meet it, Bradshaw completely forgotten.

"Sir William, well met." Pym looked up at him. "We were told you were here." *Who told you?*

Pym looked hard at Bradshaw who just smiled back at him. "Would you please give us a moment, sir? We have matters of Parliament to discuss."

Bradshaw blushed, swept off his hat and bowed, before walking backwards towards the doors. Brereton did not even turn to gesture a farewell; his eyes were locked on Pym. "Is it the Remonstrance? Is it complete?"

"It is not about that, although we are so nearly there.

(London, October 1641)

No, Sir William, it has begun. Sir Phelim O'Neill has seized Dungannon. The uprising in Ireland that was long predicted is on us. You remember our conversation from before, sir?"

William swallowed, feeling the sweat break out on his forehead even in the frigid air of the Hall. "I do remember it well."

"Then you will need to be gone to Chester today, sir. There is no time to lose. You must make that great city ours. We must control movement to and from Ireland. I will write to you, sir. Make haste and remember that whilst you are a loyal servant of the King, we all serve a higher cause." He turned on his heel. Hampden leaned in and shook Brereton's hand, laying his other hand on Brereton's shoulder. Brereton wished strongly that Bradshaw's hand had not already lain there to taint this moment in his memory.

"We are confident in you, Sir William. We know you will not let anyone down. But be careful." His voice dropped to scarcely a whisper. "The King has eyes and ears everywhere. Be careful who you trust." And then he too was gone, catching up with Pym and moving out of sight among the knots of people at the far end of the great vaulted Hall.

William stood for a moment, transfixed. Here was his role. Here was his challenge. As he turned to go, he locked eyes with a smartly dressed but rather nondescript man. Medium height and build, very forgettable but apparently very interested in William, or so it seemed. The man smiled slightly and touched the brim of his hat, before disappearing into the crowds. William felt the warmth of his excitement and passion suddenly chill. *I have entered another world now,* he thought. *Hampden is right. I must be more careful.*

He left the Hall and emerged into the bright light of an October afternoon, heading for his rooms. Bradshaw was waiting in the doorway and opened his mouth to speak, but William was past him without a word or a backward glance.

34

RICHARD

(London, December 1641)

He sat near the fire, nursing his ale and wondering, again, if Will was going to show up. Not that he blamed him. The city was a-fire with violence and protest, or rumour of it, and the Trained Bands were heavily involved. Richard knew little of what was happening, or what was at stake. Nor, in truth, did he care. He was focused on his own turmoil and had little time for revolution and anarchy – to foment it, or stamp on it.

He knew Will was feeling horribly conflicted. He wanted to be rioting with the apprentices and his God on earth, Lilburne, but he knew he had a duty and a chain of command to respect. He was being torn apart, and while Richard was convinced it was he, himself, who possessed all of the pain in all of England, he felt for his friend and allowed that he too was tormented.

He had news of his own he wanted to pass on. He had no contacts, no friends in London. Only Will. Selfishly, and he knew that, he wanted him here to give him some attention. Here he was, almost at the end of a year which had seen him go

(London, December 1641)

from being a well-respected, well-paid, ambitious businessman on the rise, with a beautiful fiancée, to a spurned, betrayed, unemployed no one, accused of murder and constantly looking over his shoulder for assassins. He struggled to remain patient as he waited for his only true friend. Surely he would not let him down, the day before New Year's Eve.

He was just on the verge of taking the decision to head to the door, or the tavern bar, when there was a sudden building of noise in the street outside and the door banged inward; a small crowd of armed and armoured men spilled in, blowing plumes of breath in the cold air, shouting and banging each other on the back. Their phalanx headed for the bar, gently easing chairs, stools, tables and people out of their way. At the rear was a giant of a man, bowl-cut blond hair and trim beard emerging from beneath his helmet which he tucked under his arm.

He shouted to the men at the bar, "Lads! We have an hour. No more! Drink. Eat. Get warm, but don't get too comfortable. We have God's work to do. And poor Jonah is freezing his balls off guarding the pikes while we rest here."

Richard looked on in amazement at the man his friend had become. Calling hard men twice his age 'lads'. But it was not just his size, he had an authority about him. A confidence that Richard knew he himself had never felt. He could scarcely command himself, let alone a squad, and he wondered where Will had found this strength and certainty. As Will scanned the room, Richard waved, almost shyly, to gesture him over to the fire. He pointed to the second cup of ale on the table to prevent Will from having to wait at the bar, and Will's tired face split into a broad smile.

He crashed down onto the chair and started to shrug off bits of armour, Richard helping him off with his breastplate. He rubbed his hands together by the fire and turned to look at Richard over his left shoulder. Smile gone, now looking earnest and years older than his true age. "My apologies, Rich. We have been in the middle of things for a few days now and this is our first break for some time. I am sorry that all of this," and he swept his hand around him to indicate 'London,' "has got in the way of our meeting." He smiled. "But tell me, how did you fare?"

Richard was about to launch into it, but he felt a twinge of guilt and he reined in his excitement with an effort. "No, Will. I think you are the one with the tales to tell. As you say, you have been in the heart of things, how do *you* fare? I am a little distant from it all, but I should learn more of the political situation now I am employed." He immediately groaned to himself, disappointed. He just couldn't resist dropping that in.

"Employed! Rich, that is great news. Tell me!" And he buried his face into the ale, drinking in huge gulps.

Resisting the strong temptation to do just that, Richard held up a hand. "No. That will keep. You come from the heat of the fight, my friend. I would hear your story first."

Froth was wiped away with the back of a huge hand. "Very good, but where to start? It is an important story, do you know what I mean? I mean, it will be important in history. Does that make sense? Oh, I am not sure I have the wit to tell it well, but I want you to hear it so that someone other than me will remember it."

"Don't get distressed, Will. Just remember who it is you are talking to. It's just Rich, not some hellfire preacher, or great politician. Tell me like we were back digging latrines outside Breda."

Will spluttered into his ale, snorting globs of it out of his nose. He slapped the table with a meaty hand, beaming back at Richard. "Those were the days, eh? Life was simpler then."

"You speak like we are approaching dotage, Will. These

(LONDON, DECEMBER 1641)

are still those days. I think it is us who were simple, not the times. I think we have both seen something of the world since then." He looked down, overtaken by an incoming wave of depression as his memories lapped around his feet. "A lot has happened. Not much of it good in recent times."

Will placed a hand on his shoulder. "Come, Rich. I know you are hurting over Neelie. I am sure you have the wrong of it. She did not strike me as the type to betray you. She seemed, well, you both seemed, so…"

"In love? Aye. I thought so. But I have the clear evidence of my own eyes, Will. I cannot deny to myself what I saw. In daylight. With no shame." He stared into the fire but with a shrug. "I have done things I am not proud of. This must be God's punishment for me. I must bear it."

"Rich. None of us can know God's plan. I think there is more to your life than this." He paused, uncomfortable. "Come, let me take your mind off this with my tale and please don't laugh if I stumble. Remember, I have heard much of this from others. I am in no place to know much of this, so I must keep my voice lowered. Please. Tell no one of this."

Richard nodded, already intrigued, and his black mood temporarily forgotten.

"You have heard of Colonel Lunsford? Yes? The lieutenant of the Tower? Well, former lieutenant now, I suppose. Well, much to many people's anger, that swaggering reformado was the King's idea of a man who could command respect with his military background and keep safe the Tower, the Mint and all the wealth of London's merchants that is deposited in that place. The King is nervous. Since publication of the Remonstrance, the Irish revolt and all the trouble these reformado scoundrels are causing in the streets, he feels the need for a strong arm to protect his back and chose Lunsford. He is indeed badly advised, if he thought that a good move!"

"A hothead, I have heard. You are right. What the King needs now is cool heads around him."

"Just so. I fought Covenanters with him at Newburn, although I have never met the man. But he is fiercely loyal to the King and, in these times, that trait seems to trump wisdom and restraint.

"Anyway, only shortly after his appointment, just before Christmas Day, the City men asked the Parliament men to have him removed and they tried. But the Lords blocked it. So then the 'prentices came to Parliament, and many good citizens with 'em. Good and godly men protesting at the appointment of this dangerous fool. A man they say fled his debts to hide in the Dutch wars and is a hardened drinker and debaucher. No wonder the godly object."

Richard thought of DeLacey and tried to hide his smile. Will ploughed on.

"So the Commons told Henry Marten to seize the weapons of Lunsford and his men and good folk, and some others started to find their own arms. No one wanted to be caught with no defence should it come to blows. Someone was even printing pamphlets telling good citizens to arm themselves. I tell you, Rich, I didn't know if it was God's judgement day a'comin' with a rebellion of the godly and the downtrodden poor, or if we..." and he waved his hand towards the crowded bar, "...were goin' to have fire on our own.

"Anyway, things just kept getting hotter, and the merchants, they started to take all of their gold out of the Tower in protest. Nothing moves the King faster than that, I can tell you. After the mayor had been to the King for the second time to warn him the mob was turning ugly, he finally kicks Lunsford out, against his better judgement, I expect."

"But that obviously didn't quieten things down. I have seen the mob and heard the fighting."

(LONDON, DECEMBER 1641)

"No. Once the mob gets going it is difficult to stop them. Some are just there to cause trouble and take the chance to loot and burn, but there was also a core of good men and diligent 'prentices.

"Two days after Christmas Day, the mob forces its way into Westminster Yard, and are shouting and protesting against the bishops. I would have been with them, Rich, but my duty is to my commander. Anyway, to add fuel to that fire, who marches in but Lunsford and some tens of his friends, and they incite the mob with their own shouts."

"That took balls. To stand against the mob."

"Maybe. Soldiers with swords, against 'prentices with a few clubs? And then, one of Lunsford's fellows draws his sword and threatens some citizens with a cut-throat.

"Then Lilburne came with some sailors and armed men at his back. He drew his own sword and disarmed the fellow. Hide, his name is. Seems he was just a blustering coward, and probably drunk. They took him away, but he was soon let go. What does the fool do but head back to Lunsford when the whole lot of 'em just started cutting at the crowd with their weapons. That was when I arrived. I had been sent by the officers to scout the situation and report back. Oh, Rich, it was a sight to see. Brave and godly men arrayed against these bullying, ruffian cavaliers! It was push and shove and slash and block. Many fell injured and worse, and it looked like Lunsford would carry the day, but Sir Richard Wiseman... do you know him?"

Richard shook his head, gripped by the story and captivated by the passion with which his friend stoked the vision of the mayhem at Westminster, his voice low but intense, eyes reflecting the flames from the fireplace, and arms re-enacting each cut and punch.

"Parliament man. A true man of the people, Rich. He rallied the 'prentices and the good citizens and pushed

Lunsford back. More 'prentices came flooding in then and it was Lunsford's mob who fled. We chased them down to the Thames. I have to say, Rich, that by this time I was not scouting, I was running with the good citizens and kicking arses with the rest of 'em."

Richard laughed out loud, picturing the effect of being kicked up the arse by one of Will's tree-trunk legs. "You must have kicked one clear over the river!"

Will laughed in return. "Aye. Just about. But I was sober by the time we got to the water. His followers had slunk away and Lunsford was left knee-deep in the shitty mud, wavin' his sword to keep the mob at bay…" Will mimed the flailing arms, "…just long enough for someone to come and rescue him with a boat. Oh, it were glorious to see. I ran back to report and found that the King had ordered us all out onto the streets to keep order.

"I thought that might be it, but we were back out the next day, with hardly any sleep. The mob were back in Westminster and were besieging the Abbey. Nearly got hold of the Archbishop o' York, which would have gone bad for 'im, I reckon, but he escaped by the skin of his teeth. Probably had to drop all his golden rings and chains so he could run faster." Will mimed the hitching up of clerical robes and he ran on the spot, shooting terrified looks over his shoulder. His acting had drawn a small group of his men over to their table and their laughter joined Richard's, who was seeing a side to his friend he had never dreamed existed.

"The mob had heard there were 'prentices taken prisoner in the Abbey and they weren't goin' anywhere until they were freed. Anyway, there were men on the roof of the Abbey throwing slates and bricks down onto the crowd, and later a bunch of men burst out with sword and pistol and fired into the press. They say Lilburne was hit, and Sir Richard Wiseman too." The comic pantomime became tragedy. "Lilburne will live,

(LONDON, DECEMBER 1641)

they say, but it looks bad for Sir Richard. There will be murder if he should die. The 'prentices would follow 'im anywhere.

"We were called to restore the peace and at least for the time being, we were able to pacify the mob. Many were known to us, and they listened to reason and dispersed. But I have never seen so much anger, Rich. And anger allied to hope. They had seen that they were strong, and they knew that many of us would have gladly joined them if duty did not forbid."

Many of the soldiers were nodding agreement and a few quietly banged fists on tables. It was at that point that Richard noticed a figure in the shadow towards the back of room. Some way from the fire. He had seen him before when waiting for Will but not thought anything of it. A man like himself, having a quiet drink and waiting for an acquaintance. But now he stood out for his inaction. All in the tavern were in some way now listening to Will's story and had edged closer to get a better view. But not this man. Richard stared over at him and for a moment even thought it might be Montague, spying on them, but no. No one he recognised. Just another anonymous figure. Sensing that he had been noticed, the man quickly leant back and busied himself studying the floor and sipping his ale.

Will had now moved on to the events of the previous day, not noticing Richard's attention had faltered, now he had a larger crowd.

"And then yesterday, well. There must have been 10,000 out on the streets around Whitehall. The King had gone and made Lunsford a knight. Him! A knight! There were some of the King's soldiers out on the streets too, as well as the Trained Bands, but those men have no sympathies with the mob and it quickly fell to fighting. And of course, swords against clubs ain't a fair contest.

"Word came down that the bishops had complained to

the King that the Commons were obstructing the work of the Lords, but then Parliament had 'em impeached! The King is losing control, Rich. These are wondrous times. The ordinary people are on the rise. 'Tis a thing to see..." His tone had dropped, and they fell to discussing detail of the momentous events. People drifted away and they were alone again.

"I tell you, Will, you will be a Parliament man yourself one day soon. You really have your finger on the goings-on and you can tell a good tale. I see great things ahead for you."

He waited for Will to come back with his usual self-deprecation, but he was in for another surprise. "You said that to me just six months ago, I would've called you a fool, Rich. But now. I really think I have found myself. I can't describe it, but it's like a new Will has hatched out of the shell o' the old one. And it's Lilburne, and listening to others like 'im. Such ideas, Rich. Such passion. 'Tis no wonder it is rubbing off on me too. We are at the start of something grand. A change is comin', the tide is on the turn and I am part of it.

"I don't know if I will see it as a soldier, or in some other way, but I am determined to play a part. It is too important to miss. I would see the world turned upside down, Rich. Where goodness is valued, not wealth and birth."

"Well, I am happy for you, Will. My world has already been turned upside down. No..." he held up his hand as Will started to speak, "...not because of any of this. Some misfortune cannot be explained. I don't want pity. I need to find something in myself, as you have. Something to drive me forward. Something so I can forget what I have lost."

"I was going to say the same thing, Rich. If you don't mind my honest opinion, you have been letting yourself wallow in your sorrow like a sow in shit. You have allowed yourself to give up when there is so much you could turn your hand to. And anyway, you told me you had found a job. Tell me about

(London, December 1641)

it. That surely sounds like your luck has changed. I just hope you have signed on to go to fight the Irish!"

Richard smiled thinly. "No, Will. No fighting for me. I do welcome your honesty. And these days it seems you always have the right of it."

Will clapped him on the shoulder, making him wince with the weight of it. "Now, tell me your news. I do not have long and I must be on the move again. More trouble is expected tonight."

"You mentioned that the merchants had removed their bullion from the Tower? Well, there have been many calls on their money recently. The King must finance his army in Ireland. They need weapons to fight the papist uprising, not just strong words and high intention.

"He managed to get 50,000 pounds a few weeks ago, but now he has gone back again, turning the screw harder and harder until a further 100,000 has popped out of their fat purses. And all that gold is going to buy and ship arms. But how to get it to Ireland with all speed? And who has experience of managing such shipments?"

He smiled triumphantly at Will.

"Who? Someone at the armouries in the Tower perhaps?"

Richard looked aghast. "No!"

"Ah! There is someone in the Trained Bands they will look to then?"

"I see that when you hatched out as a new Will, you emerged with a very poor sense of humour!"

Will had collapsed in silent giggles, pointing helplessly at Richard. "Oh, your face. What a picture!"

When he had recovered his composure and straightened his face, he motioned Richard to continue, not daring to speak. Richard looked at him, unimpressed. This was not how he had hoped to pass on his news.

"So in fact, William, it is *I* who have been entrusted by Master Nicholas Cox of the Ordnance Office to manage the delivery of the first train of wagons heading from the Tower to the port of Chester. 'Tis an office of some great responsibility."

"You are right, Rich. Forgive me, but when we were younger, it was always I who was the butt of your jokes. I never thought the shoe might be on the other foot."

Neither did I, thought Richard. *How our fortunes have shifted.*

"It is indeed an important job. The King is at least right in this. The papists must be stopped. They massacre innocent Protestants. We have heard stories of terrible cruelties. To whom do you report in Chester?"

"I am working with a man called Thomas Gibson to coordinate shipments, and I will accompany the first one to agree the best route and offer some protection. I have the name of my contact written down somewhere." He scrabbled about in his jacket for the note from Cox. "Brereton. A Sir William Brereton. It is not a name I know. Have you heard of him?"

"Indeed I have. An upcoming gentleman apparently. Beloved of Pym and Cromwell. A good man, and a great friend of the godly, they say."

After a little more discussion of the task Richard had been given, Will gave his apologies and led his men out of the tavern and into the cold dark of the last days of the year.

*

Within two weeks, Richard was starting out for Chester at the head of a line of wagons, all heavily laden with arms. 1642 had started cold, but the temperature had done nothing to cool the heat of events.

(London, December 1641)

Richard had met with Will a final time, and he had relayed that the Trained Bands had been admonished by the King himself for their laxness in controlling the mob, and more power was given to the City Watch. Whether out of a newly born sense of power, or frustration at being constantly hemmed in by Parliament, the King had gone with force to Parliament to arrest five of his tormentors, including Pym and Hampden. The Trained Bands had been told to stay away and not to answer any pleas from the Commons, and Will and his men had sat frustrated in their barracks. But the five had escaped and when the Commons knew the Trained Bands could not protect them, they moved en masse to the Guildhall.

Again, the King tried to arrest the men, but he was defied and he was in danger of running foul of the mob that had gathered to protect the Parliament men.

And the unthinkable had happened. The King tried to shore up his control of the military, but it finally became clear to him what was known by all. He had lost London. The Trained Bands were with Parliament and a few thousand militia were summoned from Buckinghamshire, together with another thousand armed sailors, massed to add their support. More than 10,000 'prentices and good citizens were there, all armed, and to Will's obvious delight Philip Skippon, veteran of Breda, was put in charge of London's forces.

The King had fled from Whitehall to Hampton Court, and the five Parliament men returned to Westminster, with all of the Trained Bands, mounted troops and cannon as escort. Will was in tears as he told of this return of his heroes and could hardly contain his joy in the telling. The people now held London and the King had fled again, this time to Windsor.

Richard had had word from Cox at the Ordnance Office that all was to proceed as arranged. Move with all haste to Chester. Hand over the arms to none but Brereton. And to keep the movement of the arms convoy as quiet as possible, using back lanes wherever possible and where the winter weather allowed.

It was against this background of excitement, dread and confusion that Richard led the wagons onto the road to the North-West. The rain fell, cold and portentous, on a land that would not see peace again for many years to come.

35

BRERETON

(Chester, April 1642)

Although the watery sun was doing its best, a deep chill still hung around the courtyard. Winter was overstaying its welcome, and William wondered why they were plagued with such unremitting cold and grey weather. He had needed the air, though, and had ordered a table be carried outside so he could work at his papers without the closeness and the smoky atmosphere of his study.

And so much paperwork! He felt the weight of his task crushing his spirit, and only the frequent prayers, psalms and reading of the Holy Word kept him moving forward. He had yearned to be more involved in the great work of his age, as he saw it – protection of the godly and the support of the great men of Parliament. But now, all his days were filled with complication, confrontation and, above all, frustration. He was succeeding in moving men, materiel, horses and supplies to Ireland, but he faced problems of payment and credit, poor communication on the snow- and rain-bogged roads and the ire of the good people of the city of Chester, who resented the billeting of common soldiers in and around the town, with the inevitable disruption that comes with idle soldiery.

He knew he was reliant on the goodwill of the leading townsfolk, but he was also painfully aware, as he was reminded almost daily, that he had few friends and little reserves of goodwill to support his cause. His family had owned this house, 'the Nunnes', in Chester, for almost exactly one hundred years, and the Breretons of Handforth had often resided here. The site of the old Benedictine nunnery, it had escaped the dissolution relatively intact and after it had been granted to the family, they had repaired and extended the property and buildings. Situated north-west of the castle, just within the old Roman wall and shadowed by the church, it was an arrow flight from the River Dee where it broadened to the sea. But despite this solid connection with the history of the great city, the Breretons had always seemed outsiders. His religious views and support for the likes of Bruen put him at odds with the bishop and many of the local gentry and merchants. With this, his arguments with mayor and corporation over payment of the murage tax – *damned money-grabbing pedants* – and the endless land disputes that seemed to come with his personal business ventures, his supporters in the city were thinly spread.

More instructions and demands came up the road from London on a weekly basis. Some were business-like instructions to deal with this or that logistical challenge, and he prided himself that his education and lawyer's brain had made him an admirable planner and administrator, beyond even his own hope and expectation. But others were more political, more frantic and extremely secretive. It was clear his sponsors in Parliament felt the country slipping helplessly towards a civil war with the King and that they were reluctantly, so they said, laying plans and building alliances to ensure a proper and godly outcome would ensue if the King did raise his banner in the coming months.

(Chester, April 1642)

Parliament continued to wrestle with the King in some kind of preamble to actual conflict. Even now they petitioned the King to move the northern armoury down to the Tower and even now the King rode to Hull to secure its contents, amassed for the second fight with the Covenanters. Sir William predicted disappointment for his monarch, as Sir John Hotham who held Hull as military governor did so at the specific request of Parliament. He would not admit the King and his entourage without permission from London.

The Covenanters, against whom the Hull stockpile had been arrayed, had now also sent troops to Ireland to fight the insurgency and now he had no instructions on whether he should also try to support their supply line. Complexity, confusion, indecision.

The letter in front of him now was another burden laid on his sagging shoulders – a short note only, but bringing a cartful of worry and additional responsibility. He became aware of a shadow across the table and looked up from the paper to the man who had brought it to him. He had completely forgotten him in his anxiety to open the letter. "Do you wait for a response, sir?"

"No, sir. I do not believe a response is required. But if you read to the end, you will see that I am at your service. It was mentioned to me that you may require my services to fulfil the letter's request. Not that I have read it…" he added quickly, "… but it was what I was requested to say to you once you had digested the message."

William looked back to the letter and, turning the page, now saw to his embarrassment and annoyance that he had missed the postscript. He looked up again at the young man in front of him and frowned. Something about him.

"Have we met before, sir? You seem familiar. My apologies, but I have so many men of a military type passing through my doors these days." He squinted up at the silhouetted figure and noted the quality of his clothing, albeit battered from the early spring weather along the quagmire roads.

"We have met before, Sir William. In fact, we have met on at least two previous occasions. No! Please do not feel awkward. I know you for a very busy man. The cares and responsibilities upon your shoulders are heavy. I would not expect you to hold all your acquaintances in your mind. Let me reintroduce myself. I am Richard Farrell and we have met in connection of the delivery of materiel from the Ordnance Office. I am Master Nicholas Cox's representative and have been accompanying the cart trains delivering in support of the cause in Ireland. I have had the pleasure of obtaining your signature on the bills of delivery."

William now felt thoroughly out of sorts. Of course! Farrell. An honest, and if he admitted it to himself, rather intimidating man for someone of such slender years. With the pale sun temporarily cloud-obscured, he now more clearly saw the slightly unnerving contrast in the young man's face. A handsome fellow from one side, but a distorted cheekbone and evidently poorly set broken nose presenting a much more world-used aspect to the other. His travel cloak revealed the hilt of an expensive-looking sword, not that Sir William was an expert in these matters, and Farrell stood with an air of detached competence.

"Of course! Master Farrell. Of course. I am not myself, I am afraid. Sometimes I am so deep in the task that I think the niceties of society have all but deserted me. My apologies, sir, you must be weary from the road. I assume you have not come all this way with just this letter? You have escorted more supplies to us?"

Farrell's expression had not changed. He seemed to take snub and apology with equal disinterest. And this, William remembered, was what he found at once fascinating but also unnerving. Despite an obvious intellect, the man displayed no engagement or passion for the cause he was so ably serving, and apparently had no desire to further please his social betters.

"I have, Sir William. It is being checked and warehoused on the dock. I will return later today with your auditor, or more likely tomorrow, and bring the bill of receipt for your signature."

"Thank you, Farrell. I am confident all will be in order."

"And the letter, sir? As I said, I have not read it, but wondered if you would require any additional service from me? As I mentioned, it was made clear to me that I should ask."

"Asked by whom, may I ask? Not Sir Nicholas, I am sure…"

"No, Sir William, indeed not. I received this letter from a friend of mine, who I will not name. He, in turn, had been asked to deliver it to me by a group of Parliament men. Who *he* did not name. He said you would know from whom the message came."

"Aye, sir. I am pretty sure. But I am learning to be more careful. Perhaps too late. You trust your friend? He is a good man?"

"I do. With my life. And likely he is a better man than me. He is certainly more motivated by your cause than I. Aye, sir. You can trust him."

William thought on this. "You are not a believer in our cause, sir? You are not a supporter of the godly men who would see an end to papists and the persecution of those who would speak the word of God without interpretation by the bishops? What then, sir, motivates you to this task? And perhaps I asked the wrong question. Why would your friend entrust you with this message?"

Farrell smiled. "'Tis a better question indeed. I have known my friend since we were children together. We joined His Majesty's armies in the Low Countries together, we fought together at Breda. I suppose I saved his life there. He knows me better than almost anyone and he knows that I have but a simple motivation. To be paid, sir. To be paid."

William was not entirely reassured by this. Surely a man motivated solely by money was easily bought, but he had to believe that any letter from his godly colleagues would not have been entrusted lightly, and he was convinced the signature on the note was genuine – certainly it was the correct, agreed seal.

"Well, perhaps God has a plan for you yet, Master Farrell. Certainly, I did not see my own path through many dark years. I have now stumbled, undeservingly, into His Grace and now he shines a light for me, guiding my way. I have a certainty and a purpose that I cannot now doubt. Perhaps he will reveal his will to you, sir. Perhaps when you least expect it."

"Perhaps he will, Sir William. I mean no disrespect, but so far I have seen precious little of His love. Neither on the field of battle, nor in the ways of commercial men." Farrell paused, his eyes unfocused on his surroundings. "Or indeed in the ways of women. He speaks nothing to me. He... No. I have said enough on the subject, I think. My apologies, Sir William."

"Indeed, you have. Have a care, sir. There are those who might misinterpret your words to your disadvantage. Let us hear no more of it. Let me instead consider this note more fully. Perhaps we will speak again of possible additional tasks when you return with the papers. And now, I will return to the fireside. This chill is too much. On your way, please ask my man to come and return my table to the study."

He watched Farrell leave. He didn't really need time to consider the note. The message was clear enough. *"The crunch*

(CHESTER, APRIL 1642)

is coming. Shore up your allies and identify your enemies. The time will soon be upon us when we have to take action on both." It was true that he did have many friends and supporters in the county, but much of his powerbase, and that of the other godly men, was to the east and north. *Precious little in Chester*. Now was the time to cement those friendships. Test the loyalties. Assess the capabilities, of friends and enemies both. And he could not be everywhere at once. He needed a series of trusted lieutenants to carry his word and to be his eyes. Shrewd men. Hard men. Reliable men.

Men like Farrell? On the one hand he admired the leanness, the coldness, the obvious competence. Clearly Farrell's military experiences had honed him into a formidable person, and he had an intelligence to go with it. The shipments that he had managed were reliably delivered, with little loss on the long road from the capital. Not something that could be said for many of the shipments he had been sent. On the other hand, his lack of belief, his lack of any *investment* in the cause, left him uncertain if he should place his trust.

He resolved to find out more about Master Farrell. When his man had replaced the table and his papers in the warmth, he asked him to make his way down to the dockside. To find some of the men who had accompanied Farrell and find out more of the kind of man he was dealing with.

That done, he started to compile two lists of names.

36

MARLEIGH

(Macclesfield, late May 1642)

It was her day for cleaning the tenement where she still boarded, or at least the common area of hallway and stairs. She was on the landing outside her own top floor garret, cleaning the thick, cheap, distorted glass of the windows. There was a fine drizzle from a grey sky and her arm was getting damp as she leant out to try to reach the outside surface of the panes.

She had a head for heights but had hooked her toes under the rim of the top stair so she could stretch out to clean the whole width. As she strained for a few more inches, sound and movement below caught her attention. The window looked down onto the Jordangate, and if she looked to her left, the town square in front of the church.

No market today and the town was quiet. Now as she peered down, retracting her body back in through the window, she saw two horsemen trotting their animals briskly into the square. They pulled up as they reached the junction with the Chestergate. One of the horses, a handsome animal, black with three white stockings and blaze, danced around in a full

(MACCLESFIELD, LATE MAY 1642)

circle, the rider skilfully maintaining poise as he took in the surrounding buildings and streets.

Not the usual farmers or merchants comin' to town. There was a different bearing to the one on the black mare. Straight back, comfortable on good horses, no sack of potatoes in the saddle. *A lord, then? Or a soldier?* He was well dressed for the road, but she couldn't quite see his face under his hat. Water dripped from the brim as the steady light rain dreared on, and flicked right and left as he turned his head to peer down the different streets trying to find their destination. The other man was older, she thought, fatter. Certainly, he was no stranger to hearty meals. More richly dressed and handling his horse competently but with none of the natural flair of what she perceived as the younger man. She thought she saw a beard. A gentleman perhaps?

She was intrigued, and that in itself was just a little exciting. She had not felt curious about a person for a long time. She would really like to see the younger man's face. After a brief discussion, they both swung down from their horses and started to lead them away from her, up the Chestergate. *Going to the Bate Hall tavern?* Only place with stables and rooms in that direction.

She really wanted to see his face and didn't understand why she felt this so strongly. A decision gripped her and her hand moved before she could stop it. Her small tin bucket hurtled down from the window, turning over and over, to crash noisily down the stone steps below the door of her building.

Both horses spooked at the sudden noise and both riders hauled on their reins to gain control. Fat-man, as he was now named in her mind, struggled to stop his bay rearing. He pulled hard and beat its shoulder with his crop, while its eyes showed white with panic. It dragged him several yards up the Chestergate, away from her building.

The younger man's mount was soon calmed, and even now he was leading her back towards the bucket rolling slowly back and forth in the thin mud at the edge of the square. His riding cape was parted and she saw his right hand moving away from the elaborate pommel of a long rapier as he saw he was in no way threatened. As he approached it, he looked up, scanning the windows in the adjacent tenements, looking for where it had fallen. Although her landing window was the only one open, she had stepped back into the shadow so that she could see him, but she remained hidden. Nevertheless, she felt his eyes, an interesting sea-grey, she thought, piercing the gloom to meet her own stare.

My, he is interesting, she thought. He was young. Much younger than she had first thought, but he had a face worn by experience and, she thought, not a little sorrow. He held up the bucket, head back and face to the drizzle.

"I pray you, please come and claim your property. I will do you no harm even though you startled my mare and my companion both." He smiled broadly, and she saw how this transformed his face from the melancholy she had seen. And as he continued to search up and down the row of windows for a response, she saw the cruel wounds that blighted his face on one side, giving him a far rougher and somewhat intimidating aspect.

"Please. The least you owe me is an opportunity to ask you for directions, for we are strangers to your town. Please, I pray. Come down and assist us. I think you owe us that."

By this time, his companion had returned to his side, having finally calmed his large bay. Red-faced and flustered, he seemed less inclined to linger.

She could not let this opportunity escape her. She had no certainty that this man was what she sought, but this seemed to be the most promise she had encountered since she had made her resolution. She leant out of the window and called

(MACCLESFIELD, LATE MAY 1642)

down, "Oh, sir! I cannot apologise enough! The pail slipped from my hands and I did not mean to cause you both such inconvenience. Please forgive my clumsiness. I will be down in but a moment."

She did not wait for a response but walked swiftly down the stairs. At the front door she paused, straightened her pinafore and teased a strand of chestnut hair from under her coif, for all the world an agitated and embarrassed maid. She took a deep breath and hauled the heavy oak open.

They were standing three steps below her, looking up. The rain had finally stopped and both men now swept off their hats, spray flying. "Good day to you, mistress." *Fat was perhaps a little unkind, she now thought. He is brawny and strong-looking, but perhaps I was too hasty with fat.* She bobbed a slight curtsey and put on her best humble but uncertain smile.

"My thanks, sir. And good day to you both, gentlemen. I must apologise again. Never have I dropped the pail in all of the times I have swabbed them windows. Perhaps 'twas the surprise of seeing two such fine gentlemen in our streets. And two such fine animals."

The younger man now spoke. *From Norfolk,* she thought. *Certainly from that part of the country.* "You have an eye for horses, mistress? For truly you would find few better than these in these parts."

He is very young, she thought. *Scarcely in his twenties I would judge. But with a look of one who has seen more than one o' his years should have seen. Been to the wars, I reckon.*

"No, sir. Not really. But I see 'em come and go when the market is on. And none are so pretty as these. I thank you again, sir!" as he climbed two steps and passed her the bucket. He looked into her eyes. She had been correct, a restless grey, like the North Sea whipped by strong winds. And carrying some sorrow.

"You said you were after directions. Can I help you, gentlemen?"

"Aye," said no-longer fat-man. "We are looking for lodgings and were recommended..." he looked down at what seemed a list of names on a curled sheet of paper, "...a Bate Hall? It is an inn here in town, I think? We were recommended to stay there. Do you know it?"

"Aye, sir. I know it. And you set me an easy task as I can see it from here, almost." She descended the steps, hitching her skirt to show her ankles as she picked her way down. She gestured for them to follow her and after no more than ten or so paces pointed back up Chestergate. "'Tis but a short way along, sirs. On your right side. There is an arch to the stables at the back. They are good people, I have heard. They will treat you fair, even though it is clear you are not from these parts." She looked at the younger man and raised an eyebrow.

He laughed. "It seems you have an eye for horses and an ear for men. But you are quite correct, mistress. I am from the country between Cambridge and Huntingdon. I am here on business. My country is flat, a lot like the land between here and Chester, for that is where we have ridden from. But I see that to the east, all is up and down here." He gestured past the church where the hills were starting to emerge from the clearing rain.

"You are come from Chester." She looked in mock wonder from one to the other. "They say it is such a grand city! With cathedral and walls and castle and the river. Our little town must seem like a backward hamlet!"

"Well, mistress, I am from these parts," said the other, wringing some of the rain from his beard. "I hale from Chester myself. And I thank you for your directions, but now we must be off. You say 'tis a small town? So it may be, but it is an

(MACCLESFIELD, LATE MAY 1642)

important one and we have need of settling in for a day or two, as there are many we need to meet."

The younger man looked at him hard and she got the strong impression that his companion had said more than necessary. "Aye. We had best be on our way. Thank you, mistress, for your kind words and assistance. Perhaps we will see you again before we depart."

"Oh, I do so hope, sirs," she said looking at the young man. "I do so hope. Let me know if I can be of any further assistance with directions. I have duties cleaning yon church, as well as the school, so I know many of the important men by name and by sight. I would be happy to help you. As a repayment, you know, for your not seeing my clumsiness in too harsh a light."

She summoned all her power and channelled it into the smile she bestowed upon him, and she could see the touch-paper spark and catch behind the cool detached grey of his eyes. She half turned, curtsied slightly to the other and was on her way. As she turned to open the door, she saw him standing, rooted to the spot, watching her, mouth slightly open. The other smirked, grabbed him by the arm and led him away like an injured soldier up the muddy street to the inn.

She shut the door behind her and leant against it, looking up to the flaking ceiling of the hallway. She breathed her thanks to the universe, for this was the one. Or at least the best option she had encountered since her decision to have a child.

As soon as she got close to him, the younger man, she had felt the raw talent within him. She could also see that he was no adept, but the marks were there to be read. He had encountered this force, the energy of life, presumably as a soldier, but had no control or awareness as far as she could see.

He seemed strong and had some intelligence. And, she

smiled to herself, she liked his eyes. She felt something stirring inside her that she had not felt for an age. Desire? Passion? Perhaps it was no more than the excitement of something new to explore. A way to advance her plans. But time was against her. It seemed clear that he would not be here in the town for long. She would have to be bold, and bold meant risk. She had no choice. Something told her that she would have to wait a long time to improve on this youngster. She had enjoyed a few years of quiet contemplation and low profile. She had become attached to the country, and even to the town. But now she had to risk that, to risk exposure and the dread that brought, if she wanted to finish her work.

As she reclimbed the stairs, she started to plan, and realised she didn't know his name.

*

No more than a few hundred yards away, Richard stood brushing the road from his horse's coat and mane. He felt a hand on his shoulder. Matthew, his companion and Sir William's trusted right hand, had come back into the small stable in the courtyard of the inn.

"Are you still here? Do you want me to show you how to do it?"

Richard looked at him quizzically.

"Only you've been doing this for an hour. The lad finished my horse and has been inside and had his supper, and you're still here. What's the problem? Ah. But we know the problem, don't we, young fellow?" He winked at Richard and fluttered his greying eyelashes inexpertly.

Richard had to laugh. "Matthew! Your master would be horrified that you would think such ungodly thoughts. Not that I know what you are getting at, of course," he added. He

(MACCLESFIELD, LATE MAY 1642)

continued to brush the mane stubbornly, trying not to catch Matthew's eye.

"I am a sight more godly than thou, Master Farrell, but that wouldn't be too hard. The mouth on you – Sir William would have you whipped, scourged and purified in vinegar if he heard some of the words you had been using the past few weeks!"

"Vinegar? That's for picklin' not purifyin', you old fool." They both laughed.

"Well," said Matthew, snorting, "something unpleasant. Brimstone or sulphur or the like. He'd have something handy, I'm sure."

"He would not be happy to hear you speak of him so," cautioned Richard. "Remember he may have ears in some of these towns and word may get back to him."

"Ah. The only ears in here are yours and the horses' and whilst I reckon they got more sense than you, I don't think they will tell Sir William anything. Unless of course it's about yon lass from the street. I have a strong feeling that that is what is occupying your mind."

"And yours too?"

"Now now. I may not be as godly as my master, but I am a married man and takes my vows seriously. I will not blaspheme and I attend church. I have more godliness in my little finger than you have in your whole body."

Richard looked at him with a raised eyebrow but got no more reaction. He had been wary of Matthew when they first set out from Chester, fearing a stern and devout character would drag on the task they had been set. But he had soon shown that much of his austere behaviour was reserved for the presence of Sir William and his friends and supporters, and while it was true that he would not tolerate blasphemy or drinking, he had a ready sense of humour and Richard saw him as a more gentile version of his erstwhile companion Roger DeLacey. Certainly, he was more stable, coherent and predictable, if less riotous, dangerous and competent with a blade – not that they had encountered anything other than harsh words so far.

"Well, Matthew, you are right. I have been at this long enough, and if I can't fill my body with the grace of the Lord then let us see if the landlord's best ale and stew can fill the void. Or…" and he poked Matthew's generous belly, "…have you already partaken of your supper? Looks like you ate the stableboy!"

Richard packed up the brushes and flung a blanket over his mare, kissing her on the white blaze and wishing her goodnight. They passed through the rear door and along a short corridor and past the stairs up to the few rooms, to the bar. They found a table close to the fire. Business was slow and they had the landlord's full attention as two well-dressed men on important business.

With ale in front of Richard and a cup of milk for Matthew, they waited with some enthusiasm for the arrival of a roast chicken – as it was a special occasion, according to their host.

"So, what did you make of her?" Richard asked, watching Matthew over the rim of his titled mug.

"What, the landlord's wife? Not my cup of milk, boy. 'Tis the beard that spoils it for me, but maybe that's what you youngsters go for." He smiled, the milk collected in his moustache giving him the look of a wise old professor.

"You know exactly who I meant. What a strange meeting that was. Do you think she dropped that bucket a'purpose? To get our attention?"

"She certainly got Baron's attention. He reared and set off up the street like Satan had prodded his arse with a pitchfork. I nearly shat myself!"

(MACCLESFIELD, LATE MAY 1642)

"Now who has a foul mouth?"

"Well, I have spent three weeks with you, boy. That's where I have picked up these wicked habits. And maybe you're right." He became serious for a moment. "She didn't look the clumsy type to me. Something about her. Can't rightly say what, but… well, something a bit out of the ordinary. Still, why would she want to speak to us? She doesn't know us, and she can't have heard of our coming, or be a spy for the King." This last bit was whispered.

"No. I agree. She cuts an unlikely cavalier." *How quickly these terms have come into common use. Roundhead! Cavalier! Insults thrown across the rioting streets of London now adopted across the land.*

"Perhaps she just liked my arse?" Matthew said, smiling smugly.

"More likely to prefer Baron's arse to yours! But it was terrible strange. I have to say that I have seldom strayed since… well, you know, my misfortune. But I have never been looked at by a woman in such a way, and seldom seen one as striking."

"Aye. I am with you there. She had a fey look to her. Made me uneasy without really knowing why. Likely we won't see her again, though."

"No. I suppose not." He felt a little relieved at that thought but also, somehow, incredibly disappointed. Her face still occupied his unconscious and, disturbingly, he suddenly had difficulty remembering Neelie's face – a ghost that had haunted him up and down the roads of England.

"Let's put such idle imaginings to one side. At least until we are both alone in our rooms. We need to concentrate on the reason we are really here. Do you have the list of names for Macclesfield? My copy is with my bag in my room."

Richard dug the list out from inside his jacket. Now much crumpled and ragged at the edges, it was a faithful copy, in his own hand, of the pages Brereton had given them both. Both had taken copies so that if they fell into the wrong hands, the King's agents could not trace the handwriting back to Sir William. The rack, thumbscrews and hot irons, even just the thought of them, would probably have done the trick just as well as a comparison of penmanship, but he had insisted.

He flattened the page out on the oaken table with his hand, avoiding debris of food and small puddles of ale. "Let me see. Which of the local well-to-do, self-important burgesses do we need to speak to?"

There were nine names under the heading of Macclesfield that they were to try to meet. Organised as ever, Brereton had listed them alphabetically. Matthew read them out.

"Samuel Atkinson
Arthur Birtles
John Brocklehurst
Peter Davenport
Harold Legh
Henry Oldfield
Stephen Ridgeway
Josiah Rowe
Samuel Walker.

"So, how do you want to play it this time? Do we write our letters and get them delivered? I guess this place is a suitable place to meet unless we get invited to their residences."

Richard was about to respond when he saw the innkeeper heading their way with a huge tray, steam rising from the large golden chicken, surrounded by potatoes and carrots. "Oh my!" he exclaimed and gestured to Matthew to look over his shoulder. "Sir, you have done us proud. It has been a long and wet road to get here, but this makes up for all. Your inn shall be made famous wherever I travel from here."

Matthew gasped his thanks also as they both suddenly

(MACCLESFIELD, LATE MAY 1642)

realised how famished they were. The innkeeper beamed at them as he set down bowls, knives and forks and set about to carve the bird.

"Don't worry 'bout that, sir, we can fend for ourselves from here," Matthew said, and he actually rose and hugged the man in his joy.

"You are both welcome, sirs. We get many a traveller through here; the town is prospering, and people come from across the county and over the wild hills from Buxton, and up from Stafford-way. Come to buy 'n' sell. We treats 'em well and they come back again and again. Good business for me. Is that what you gentlemen are here for? For the button trade?"

"Buttons?" They looked at each other blankly.

"No, my friend," said Matthew. "We are here surveying the land. Our master has a thought to invest in some property, and maybe some acres for hunting. We are here to make contact with a few of your well-to-do folk, well-positioned burgesses and owners of property. Perhaps we can meet some of them here? Do you have suitable rooms for such a purpose?"

"Ah. Why of course. We have a quiet room towards the back of the inn. No one will disturb you there. Oh, except o' course unless the Grey Lady pays you a visit!"

He clapped Richard on the shoulder and gave him a grin. "And who is the Grey Lady?" Richard asked, not really sure he wanted to know.

"The Grey Lady o' Macc. Our famous ghost. She do haunt this inn and other buildings along the Chestergate. I seen 'er just recent myself. We have a few such extra guests here. But Her Ladyship and our little kitchen helper we see most often. A little lad, no more than ten year old, he's about all the time. But friendly, that one is."

He laughed again, this time clapping Matthew on the shoulder. "But don't worry, gents. No one has died o' seein' 'em.

At least, not yet. And most folks never do… see 'em, that is. Anyway, enjoy your supper and I'll be back to clear up later."

They both sat and looked at each other in silence for a while. "Well, he's a character," Richard said. Matthew snorted. "Don't pay attention to rubbish like that. That's just for the tourists. There are Grey Ladies haunting every building more than a hundred years old between here and Chester. Whoever she is, her fame has made her popular. It hasn't numbed my appetite so let's get going on this!"

For quite a while, neither of them spoke, the excellence of the supper, and perhaps the thought of spirits wandering through their rooms, occupying minds and mouths.

When all that was left was grease and bones, chins were wiped and bellies patted.

Richard, with something of an effort, returned to Matthew's earlier question. "Inviting them all here is going to take too much time. We have to be back on the road in no more than five days. We are to cover Nantwich on the way back to Sir William. There is no time to linger. And having a line of local dignitaries trooping in 'ere one after another is not goin' to go unnoticed, even if they choose to respond to a letter. People, important people, are gettin' nervous and careful."

"So what's your cunning plan, Farrell? We knock on every door 'til we find 'em? If we don't send the letters, we can just get directions from our friendly innkeeper, can't we? He'll know 'em all."

"And of course he won't talk, will he? Even if he bought your story of land surveyin' – nicely done, by the way – he might still pass on what he thought were harmless details to some who might be more suspicious. I tell you, everyone is expecting war between King and Parliament, and believe me, Matthew, I have seen the King's agents at work and they are ruthless bastards. People are right to be a'feared of them!"

(MACCLESFIELD, LATE MAY 1642)

"Well, I can tell you have a plan, you smug so-and-so, so why not just bless me with your wisdom?"

"What day is it tomorrow?"

"Sunday."

"Where do the good and godly go on Sunday?"

"Church. Well, at least most of us." Matthew looked disapprovingly at Richard. "Because it's the law."

"Exactly." Richard ignored the reprimand. "All we need is someone who might be able to recognise our men and point them out to us. But who? Hmm."

"Oh! That is a cunning plan. On many levels. Congratulations."

"Thank you. I am a cunning bastard."

*

He had lain awake for hours, sleep eluding his tired mind. He tried to focus on his work, this task he had been given by Brereton, but it was like trying to peer through a fog. Eventually he had slipped into a dream occupied by three women wandering through this fog, appearing in turn out of the mist and vanishing again, as if on some infernal carousel.

Neelie, smiling and laughing with her new consort in Amsterdam, stoking the rage that always simmered at the edge of his thoughts. Try as he might he could not rid his mind of her. But then, as she slowly turned away, with strands of mist clinging to her, the woman from the marketplace took her place.

This stirred a very different emotion. He liked the way the rain had plastered a strand of her chestnut hair to her high cheekbone and could still picture the droplet clinging to the end. He saw himself reaching out to collect that precious water. She gave off an air of health and strength and… what?

But it was her eyes that captivated him. Large and slightly upward-sloping, patterned like some rare gem of the orient, she seemed to have a slightly Moorish cast, reminding him of travellers from the Barbary Coast who occasionally traded in Amsterdam. She had seemed older than he was, but it was difficult to say how old. On that grey afternoon, with the dampness of the rain weighing his clothing and his spirits, and the weight of the task bearing down on him, her smile had been like the sun ignited, blazing just for him. It had hit him like a physical impact, leaving him stunned but strangely energised. The intensity of the light seared thought of Neelie from his brain.

But then another image emerged, as she turned away and back into the mist. A smaller figure, hooded, in a long grey cloak. The face was shrouded in the dark of the hood, but he was sure it was a young woman. The cowl turned away from him, but the figure held out a pale, slim hand towards him, and he slowly took it, feeling the coldness of its touch.

She led him slowly into the mist and all sound was lost. He turned to look at her, but the hood denied him a glimpse of her face. All he could think of was the innkeeper's words and he felt a helpless terror. After a short time, the mist thinned and he found himself standing on a low cliff, looking down onto a beach. He realised the figure was gone from his side. He felt he recognised the view but could not place it in his memory. It was night-time, and it was cold. The pebbles of the beach glistened black under the pale silver of a full moon, as if they were wet from a recent wave.

Small, sluggish waves disturbed the stones. He felt it but could hear nothing. He watched the scene for what seemed to be a long time until he finally made out a slight figure, cloaked and hooded in grey, staring out across the sea. She held out her hand, backwards, towards him. An invitation. He found

(MACCLESFIELD, LATE MAY 1642)

he could make no movement toward her – for he was sure it was the same figure that had led him to this strange shore.

And now he recognised where he was and recollection turned to sick horror. Sudden lightning from the now-pitch-black sky illuminated the tidal wave of blood slowly mounting over the shingle. He found he was on his knees and nothing could move him from the spot.

The receding liquid revealed the black, faceless figures looking like black statues smoothed by the endless action of the viscous sea. Hundreds crawling relentlessly over the pebbles. Silent and grim.

He shouted as he always did. *Run! Run! For God's sake, run!* But she never moved, other than to sink onto her knees, but still he shouted. Useless, impotent. As one, the creatures reached down and picked up large black stones, raising them above their heads. Then, as they reached, she turned her face to him in silence, as the darkness of the creatures and the crashing, silent wave of blood enveloped her.

He woke with tears streaming down his face. Sweating like in a fever. No fear, but the horror of helplessness in the face of inevitable heart-wrenching loss.

Why had he been revisited by this dream now? It always felt like a warning – that is how he had interpreted the dream before – but no event had followed. Was Neelie in danger? Was she trying to reach out to him in some way? Or was it some kind of message about the woman in the marketplace? He stared blankly at the decaying plaster of the ceiling, waiting for his heaving chest to quieten.

He knew he could not return to sleep, so he rose and dressed. He welcomed the cold rain as he stepped quietly out into the pre-dawn dimness of the deserted street.

*

At first light he was standing by the doors of St Michael's, pushing himself flat to the old oak to gain shelter from the drizzle. He had pushed a note under Matthew's door to inform him of his intentions and now he wished he had stopped to at least have breakfast. There was a chill to the melancholy dawn and he hoped his encounter with this strange woman would chase away the flat depression that he had awoken with.

The streets and marketplace were deserted. All good folk still abed. All quiet and all well. He felt cheered by the thoughts of home, and almost like an accompaniment to the lightening of his mood, he suddenly heard the faint sound of singing through the massive doors. A woman's voice, low but clear. He must have missed her arriving, must have come in through a side door. That would make sense.

With his back still to the door, he thumped the wood with his fist and kicked hard with the heel of his boot. The singing stopped and there was silence. He couldn't hear footsteps, but the door was thick oak. He thumped again. Nothing.

He half turned and put his ear to the oak, straining to hear. He cursed quietly and raised his hand again, but his wrist was caught in a remarkably firm, warm grip. "No need to rouse them in the crypt, sir. I heard you." He whirled around, embarrassed that he had not heard her approach. She didn't release his wrist but pulled him gently but firmly after her, as she headed for the northern corner of the building. Suddenly his dream was back in his head and a chill swept over him. He had little choice but to follow. He felt like he was on a string, being led like a puppy on gritstone slabs along the side of the church. Abruptly she pulled him in through a narrow doorway and into the dim light of the vestry. She threw back the hood of the cloak she was wearing, scattering rain drops, and fixed him with a gaze. *Oh, those eyes.* "Sorry, sir, but there's no cause

(Macclesfield, late May 1642)

to open the main doors at this time. The noise would waken the goodly folk and people are comfortable with routine. Don't want to mess with that. Now we be out o' the weather. Was it the priest you were to see? It's early for him to be rising." She continued to fix him with an intense look. "Are you alright, sir? Looks like you may have a fever or something like?"

He realised he must have been staring and hoped his mouth wasn't actually hanging open. He pulled himself together and saw a tick of a smile at the corner of her mouth. "Er, no. Actually, I had hoped to speak to you before you started your duties." He saw the besom broom leaning against the doorway.

"Me, sir? Oh dear." Now she looked distressed. "Did my clumsy hands cause a hurt after all? Please say what I can do to make it right. I could not afford to lose this job." There was definitely something other than worry in her expression now. He was sure of it. And it made him feel decidedly nervous and uncomfortable.

"No, mistress! No. Of course not." She looked relieved but expectant. "My colleague and I had thought on what you said yesterday, and about how you knew all the godly folk in the town. That might be of great use to us. We are in need of identifying certain men of property, as our master is looking to invest in the town. We hoped you might be able to point some of them out to us this morning. We are happy to pay."

She seemed to relax. "Oh, sir, I am that relieved. But that is but a small service and I am happy to do this to make up for your shock yesterday. Please tell me how I can help."

"Thank you, Mistress…?"

"Hume, sir. Marleigh Hume."

"A pleasure to meet you, Miss Hume. My name is Richard Farrell, and my companion – who is still asleep, I deem – is Matthew Briggs. Master Briggs is the appointed representative of Sir William Brereton. I understand that is a name well known in the town?"

She suddenly seemed wrong-footed by this. "Actually, it is Mrs Hume, sir. My husband is fighting in the Low Countries, although it is now some years since we last met. I have heard nothing of him, and I fear the worst." She lowered her head to hide her face and Richard assumed she was overcome with emotion. He reached and placed a hand on her arm.

"I am sorry, mistress. I did not mean to upset you. I too have fought in those wars. It is a cruel business, but there are many fates which he may have encountered. He could be prisoner or be recovering from a wound. He may just be struggling to afford passage back to England. There is no saying he is… dead." *Stupid! That will have cheered her up.*

However, she did seem recovered and looked up at him again, although she was almost as tall as he. Clearly, she was not the woman from his dreams.

"Do you have a paper with the names of them as you want to meet?"

He was again caught studying her. "What? Oh yes. But. You can read? That is… unusual."

"My father was a schoolteacher, sir. I can read and have some letters, although I have little reason or opportunity to use them."

"Well, that certainly makes things a lot easier. Yes, I have a list. Here." He unwrapped the page and handed it to her. She scanned it, moving her finger down and along the names, and she silently formed the words with her lips. He looked hard at those lips. *For God's sake, pull yourself together. This is business!*

"I know all of these names, Master Farrell, but I don't think all will attend this church. These, I am sure these will be here." She pointed to five of the names on the paper.

(MACCLESFIELD, LATE MAY 1642)

Richard was a little disappointed, but this was a good start. After all, he thought to himself, this plan was designed to bring a number of benefits.

"That is excellent," he said. "How will you identify these five to us?"

She thought for a moment. "If you gentlemen arrive early and position yourselves at the back," she pointed to the rear pew on the right, "I will sign you when they enter the church. I will hold up one finger for number one on your list, three fingers for the third and so on. Will that do?"

"Yes, Mistress Hume. That will certainly do. You will need to be careful so that you are not seen. We need to keep our business quiet so as not to alert Sir William's, erm… competitors."

"Do not worry, sir. I have had a lifetime of careful. I will not let you down. May I ask a question, sir?"

He nodded, smiling.

"Sir William, sir. Will he be coming this way soon himself? I hear he is an impressive and godly man."

He wondered at that question, for no matter how innocently put, there seemed more than purely idle curiosity behind it. "Not that I am aware of. He is fully engaged with the Irish situation. That is primarily why he has despatched Master Briggs and me on his behalf."

"I see. And if Master Briggs is Sir William's man, what is your role, sir, if you don't mind me asking?"

He smiled. "I think you would describe my role as helping to ensure Master Briggs's safety on the road. And helping him in negotiations, should he need to show these gentlemen Sir William's determination to achieve a successful outcome."

"That would be your experience as a military man, I expect. You look as though you might have seen some fighting in your time." To his astonishment, she reached out slowly and gently brushed the line of his broken cheekbone with the warm tips of her fingers. He jumped back as though a bolt of electricity had passed through him. She started, bit her lip and looked down. "I am sorry, master. You have got me thinking of my own husband. I forgot myself, and where I was. Please forgive me." She looked miserable, and his surprise at this unexpected behaviour was quickly submerged by a tide of other emotions that ran through him.

He cleared his throat, straightened his jacket, now almost dry from the drizzle, and shook his head. "Think nothing of it, Mistress Hume. We all have people whom we miss. It is forgotten." *Not for a second.* "We will see you later, and thank you again for your help."

He strode out into the clearing day, his own fingers touching the skin where hers had lingered moments earlier. Now he had an appetite for breakfast. The horrors of his dream entirely forgotten.

Around noon, Richard and Matthew sought out Marleigh Hume in the dim depths of the church. It could not have gone any better. They had spoken to Atkinson, Birtles, Legh and Oldfield as a group. In a corner of the church, in plain sight, but quietly, with no excitement or high emotion. A gathering of men discussing possible business cooperation, or perhaps, if asked, discussing the finer points of the sermon just delivered. Matthew had completed his job in exemplary fashion, all four committing their support to Brereton, Parliament and the fight against episcopacy. All were well informed and fully understanding of the potential conflict to come. Matthew was delighted and thanked them all vigorously for their promises.

Only one, Samuel Walker, had evaded them. Richard had intercepted him, but he had pleaded a prior appointment. Unwilling to lose the opportunity completely, he had extracted a commitment to meet with them early the following day.

(MACCLESFIELD, LATE MAY 1642)

But for now, Matthew and he were in good spirits, and Matthew pressed some small coins into Marleigh's hand to show gratitude. As they were parting, she put her hand shyly on to Richard's arm. "Sir. I do not want to impose further, but I wonder if I can ask a favour? Although, as I said, I have letters, I am not experienced at composition. My husband has been gone these years and I know nothing of his being live or dead. I thought I might write a letter to someone who might have news. I wondered if you could spare me a moment of your time to help write it?"

Richard looked at her and felt a wave of pity pass over him. Other, contrasting, emotions quickly followed, and he felt little choice but to smile, nod and agree. He would meet her towards the end of the afternoon at the side door to the church that they had used earlier.

*

Her back was propped against the cool plaster, strands of hair across one eye, more lying on the thin sheet that covered her breast. The line of the cloth followed the left side of her torso, down to her waist. His head lay on her left hip, the remainder of the sheet falling at an angle across his shoulders. She stroked and played with strands of his hair, knowing that soon she would need to move, partly because he had an important appointment to keep, and partly because the weight of his head was getting uncomfortable. She shifted slightly, trying not to wake him. Not just yet. With a light finger, she traced a long pale scar across his shoulder blade. Not a deep wound, but the mark ran for several inches. A sword wound, he had said, a keepsake of some skirmish. He had quite the collection, including a nick on his inner thigh, where a pike thrust had skewered his mount and only just missed his femoral artery and his privates. A narrow escape all round.

She had enjoyed the evening and the night-time more than she had expected. Not such a dull soldier after all. He had had an interesting life for one so young and he told a story well. She had warmed to his willingness to laugh at himself and she had laughed along with him as he recounted how he had received the wound to his face. And she could see how his relationship with his Dutch girl had given him skills that had surprised and delighted her. In fact, she had fed him from her power several times to keep him going, and he had responded with enthusiasm, entirely ignorant of the source of his stamina.

But more than the unexpected pleasure, she had taken what he had offered of himself and, knowing her own body intimately, was confident she would conceive. In the pre-dawn hours, she had strained her consciousness inwards, searching for signs in the flow of energy through her body that the seed had taken. This was just excitement and anticipation; she knew it would be some time before she could be certain.

But by God, he was the right choice! Under the pretence of wanting to understand a soldier's life, on account of her dear fictional husband, she had led his story towards his experiences of battle and death, and he had given accounts of the impact it always had on him. The strange rush of heat, the strength that seemed to flow into him as his combatants passed over. He was clearly unnerved by it but had no explanation – rather trying to hide it and push it from his mind.

In return, she had told him of things she claimed to have learnt from her father, about the fearsome Viking warriors from the North, who went beserk in battle, fighting with the strength of several men. She had said how that terrifying image of these unstoppable killers had frightened her as a little girl. Could Richard somehow be possessed of this same

(MACCLESFIELD, LATE MAY 1642)

beserker ability? She saw him thinking on it but remaining unconvinced. She had no doubt there truly was a link, although these pagan warriors had never been able to tame or control the talent, or to bring it on at will. Only in the presence of violent death and heightened raw emotion – fear, hate, fury – had it manifested. She had got beyond that and her child would help her to understand everything.

He was stirring as the dawn light started to illuminate them on the narrow bed. His hand, which currently lay under the sheet, was slowly moving over her skin between her right hip and her knee and she could sense his breathing change. His warm palm now crested the firm muscle of her thigh and headed slowly but determinedly upward. While she was sorely tempted, there was no time for that now. She rolled quickly away and out from under the sheet, his head thumping on the mattress. He looked up at her through the tangle of his hair.

"You are right. I must go. But I must see you again before I leave. After all…" he smiled mischievously, "…we have not finished your letter."

*

He had met Matthew at breakfast at the Bate Hall. Matthew gave him a look as he joined Richard's table and tore into a loaf. Richard had expected a wink and a joke but got a frown and a lecture.

"You are your own man, Richard. God knows you have seen more of this world in your lifetime than I have. But what were you thinking?"

Richard looked back dumbly. Taken off guard.

"She is a lovely woman, but did you for a moment consider *her* reputation, and yours, afore you bedded her? Because I assume that letter did not take all night to write?"

Still he found no words.

"What you may not know is that our Mistress Hume already has something of a reputation. Our friendly innkeeper saw us talking to her in the church and whilst he does not suspect your rendezvous with her, he passed on a little of the local gossip. You can't look like that and not attract attention, particularly as she tries so hard not to. Folk are nervous of her. They whisper things about her past. The whereabouts of this mysterious husband and if he even exists. A suicide laid at her door – she leading him on and then turning him down with no mercy. Hanged himself. There have been accusations of witchcraft in the past, although those were known to be malicious and few pay 'em any attention. But the point is, your nocturnal games could push opinion against her should you have been seen comin' or goin' from her door."

"My friend, you are right. And you are also right that this could have damaged our own affairs. I apologise. It was wrong. I was wrong to take advantage of her... kindness. I had no idea there was a risk to it for her." He looked thoroughly miserable, and his appetite had vanished.

"Apology accepted. Just think on. Anyway..." he brightened, "...I hope it was worth it because you look exhausted."

"Matthew. I don't know what to say." And he really didn't. "I have never, ever had a night like it. She is an amazing creature. I have never been capable of, well..." Lost for words, and lost in his memory. "It was almost like whenever I was wilting..." he blushed hard, "...you know what I mean! Stop laughing! But seriously, it was like I had a certain burst of new life. Like she was taking me by the hand in some way – look, just listen, will you – and helping me up off the floor. I have never met anyone like her. The warmth of her, like a fire burning inside, and the smoothness of her skin and strength of her muscle. I

(MACCLESFIELD, LATE MAY 1642)

could almost believe the rumours you speak of, for she seems more like the child of some faery creature."

Matthew's grin vanished. "Say nothing of the sort. I don't want to hear it and we don't want anyone else hearing it. Did you not hear what I have been saying? She did us a kindness – you more than me, so it seems – so this is no way to repay her. Have you ever seen them hang a woman for witchcraft? Or worse, burn one? Maybe there is something to it, only God knows. But Richard, there are many who do believe we are surrounded by evil hags in league with Satan. You know this."

"I do. Once when we were delivering a shipment – some German duchy or other – we passed through a forest in a mountainous region that seemed to go on forever. Eventually we came upon a village. Deserted. But there must have been more than thirty piles of ashes, in a circle, some with the stake still standing. It looked like all the adults in the village had gone up in smoke and screams. The smell, Matthew, I have never smelt anything like it. We cannot have missed the event but by a day. But that wasn't the end of it. Outside of the ring, past the last hut, we found the children. In a pile, like the last stand of desperate soldiers in a battle they could never win. They had been tied together and clubbed to death. Jesus! If my faith was not already doubtful, that tipped me over. No loving God could want that."

"And yet, by your actions, you risk it."

"Again, my friend, you are right on this. Thank you. I will take more care."

"Think nothing of it. But we should be moving. We must not keep Master Samuel Walker waiting. Apparently, there are many of the godly folk hereabouts that see him as their spiritual leader, so we must not fail to bind him to our cause."

As they made their way to the Walker house, Richard also mulled over their strange discussion of ancient warriors;

beserk pagan Vikings feeding off the energy of the dead. He had dismissed it, but what if she was right? There was some truth in what she described and this thought seemed somehow to connect him to her even more strongly.

*

They were received warmly at the Walker house, a grand affair on the Mill Street, on the slope below the ruins of the old castle. They waited in the front room as the servant went to inform Master Samuel that they had arrived.

As they waited, they became aware that they were being watched from the doorway. Two heads peered cautiously round the frame, one at chest height to Richard, the other nearer his knee. He caught a glimpse of fair hair and two pairs of bright blue eyes before both disappeared.

Moments later Samuel Walker entered, bowing slightly before extending his hand. "Forgive me, sirs, for keeping you waiting, and for my rather cold manner yesterday. I think that at this time we need to be cautious, and I had a fair idea of why you were seeking me out. Now, in mine own home, I can be more gracious. Please, sit. Is it too early for a glass of claret? We need some comfort against this cool and inclement weather."

"Indeed, sir," Matthew responded. "It has scarce stopped raining since we arrived. But, please, no apology is required. If we were not in such a hurry ourselves, we would have courted you with less vigour and more subtlety." He smiled, and Walker nodded in acknowledgement.

"You are emissaries of Sir William, I believe. A fine and godly man, and a friend to Macclesfield. We were so pleased when we heard he was connected with Pym and other fine men of Parliament. He fights for the free speech of some of

(Macclesfield, late May 1642)

the inspiring preachers who spread the true word. He must know he has widespread support in the area."

Matthew proceeded to lay out in more detail Brereton's concerns and at least a glimpse of what he feared was coming from a King under metaphorical siege. "Sir William has full control over the flow of arms and men to Ireland, but has few allies in Chester, where the bishop, in private for now, rants against him. He fears he may need to fall back on more friendly towns in the county, and he seeks to make certain of these allies and identify likely foes. Master Walker, it is not unrealistic to see a country at war with itself within the year. Sir William would wish to know where you, and Macclesfield, stands?"

"Aye, gentlemen. 'Tis a hard time we face. You have heard the most recent news?"

Matthew and Richard exchanged glances, and Matthew shrugged. "There is so much happening, and at such speed, that I am not sure what news you refer to?"

"That is very true. Just yesterday I heard that the King has rejected Parliament's Nineteen Propositions. I am not sure they ever really expected the King to give up control of the militias. Now, perhaps in retaliation for losing the armoury at Hull, he has required Baron Strange… ah, you probably know him as James Stanley, son of the Earl of Derby? Not always a friend to Sir William." Matthew nodded in confirmation; he certainly knew of him. "Well, Baron Strange instructed his men to take the armouries in Liverpool, Warrington and Preston, and he is exerting his grip on the whole of Lancashire, although Manchester and Stockport will never be his, I think. The King has been touring Yorkshire to consolidate his support there. I see no way back now, gentlemen. It will be war. And soon."

The conversation ranged back and forth, but it was clear that Walker was an admirer of Brereton and would do what he could, with the other prominent men and burgesses, to raise the town for Parliament if required.

While the other two were debating and negotiating, Richard again became aware that they were being observed. Perhaps it was his long association with suspicion, King's agents and sneaky bastards like Roger DeLacey, but he could sense a presence just outside the half-opened door. When the opportunity presented itself, he got their attention and spoke quietly. "In the interest of caution, Master Walker, do you have trust in the members of your household?" He looked towards the door and looked back, indicating that they were being overheard.

But instead of a look of concern, Walker sat back and laughed out loud. "Ah, you mean my spy! She is just checking that you mean me no harm for, believe me, gentlemen, if you had lifted a finger or raised a voice against me, you would have had hell to pay. Eliza! Eliza, come in and say hello to these gentlemen."

The fair hair and startlingly blue eyes of Eliza Walker returned to view. She was young, on the brink of womanhood, Richard thought, and immediately reminded him of his sister, Angelica. The determined gaze, in no way daunted, regarded them coolly from the doorway. "Come, Eliza. These gentlemen have come from Chester to talk with me. They are friends of Sir William Brereton. A very important man, as you know. They must be godly indeed to have his trust." Matthew and Richard exchanged a look which Walker did not notice but his daughter did. She narrowed her eyes and advanced cautiously. "Eliza, let me introduce Master Briggs and Master Farrell." They bowed in turn. "Gentlemen, let me introduce my eldest daughter, Eliza Walker, my adviser and protector."

Eliza curtsied elegantly and sat on a chair near the fireplace. She resumed her study of them. "Actually, Father, whilst you are correct that Master Briggs hails from Chester, I believe

(Macclesfield, late May 1642)

Master Farrell has travelled further. I believe you have not long since come from London, sir?"

The three men looked at her astonished. "Why, daughter, you have outdone yourself. How do you know this?"

Richard swallowed nervously. "I too would be interested to know this, Mistress Walker."

"'Tis simple really. I saw you gentlemen in church on Sunday and observed that you were more intent on talking to the great and good of the town, than on the fascinating sermon." She smiled slightly. "I also observed that you seemed to have some kind of signal arranged with Mistress Hume who cleans the church. I thought this a curiosity until you then approached Papa. At that point, it was clearly my duty to find out who you were and what you wanted."

"It is true that strangers do tend to be noticed in a small town such as ours. But, Eliza, from whom did you discover their names and all?" Walker had leaned forward, a slightly concerned look on his face.

"Well, I spoke to Mistress Hume, as she was obviously in on the whole affair." Richard groaned inwardly and tried hard not to catch Matthew's eye. *Rumbled by a thirteen-year-old girl. Another triumph!*

"But Eliza. My love. We have talked about this. You know I do not like you to speak to that woman. She has something of a reputation and whilst I know nothing of what truth may lie behind it, it is not seemly for you to be seen conversing with her, for the sake of your own reputation."

"I know, Papa, but there is no harm in her and she is by far the most interesting woman in this town. She has actual thoughts, and views, and knowledge. Oh, she tries to pretend otherwise, but she is clever, and more travelled I suspect than any of us here. It was she you told me you had come from London, Master Farrell, and that you had been a soldier."

"Mistress Hume appears to be full of information. It is true, and no secret, that I have been working with the Ordnance Office in bringing arms from the Tower up to Chester for the aid of our troops in Ireland. 'Tis there that I met Master Briggs, and Sir William hired me to help him."

Eliza eyed him with interest. "And what, sir, did he hire you for? You do not fit the mould of a gentle follower of the Lord."

"Nothing evades you, I can see," said Richard smiling, impressed but worried where the conversation would go next. "In truth, my job is to make sure nothing bad happens to Master Briggs as he goes about the county. I have certain experience and skills that might be useful in that regard."

"You are paid to kill men? Is that what you mean?"

Before a slightly shocked Richard could respond, Walker leaned across him. "Enough, Eliza! These men are not here for your amusement. They have important work to do and perhaps I have humoured you too much. I think you should apologise to Master Farrell."

Now Eliza swallowed hard. "Indeed, Papa. You are right. My apologies, sir. I forgot myself." Her eyes were moist, and Richard could see that she was close to tears with embarrassment and reminded himself of her age.

He smiled. "Think nothing of it, Miss Walker. I do have that look, I think." And he winked at her on the side of his face her father wouldn't see. "Are you so interested in London then?" He tried to change the subject.

She brightened immediately and opened her mouth to speak, but again Walker cut across his daughter. "You do not realise your danger, sir. For now she could pursue you endlessly until you admitted to having met her heroes such as Master Lilburne, or the other prolific pamphleteers who seem to make up half the population of the City, judging by their output."

(Macclesfield, late May 1642)

The three men laughed, but Eliza looked indignant. "Not so, Father! Certainly they are good men, but I follow no heroes. I aspire to follow my heroines! Oh, sir, Tell me! Did you ever come across word of Katherine Hadley, for it is she who tended to Lilburne in the Fleet prison and freed his words so all could hear him. Or brave Katherine Chidley. Sirs, have you read her pamphlet on 'The Justification of Independent Churches'?" Blank faces looked back at her. She threw her hands up. "Oh, but you should. The way she attacks…"

"Eliza! Eliza. Please. These gentlemen are very unlikely to have read any of her work, let alone have met her. Please, now we must progress our discussion. Would you perhaps see what has happened to your sister? I hear no sounds of exasperation and scolding from elsewhere in the house, and with your sister, silence is a worry to me!"

She took the rebuke in good grace, but as she rose with a smile and a polite nod to the visitors, a thought occurred to Richard. "Actually, Miss Walker, whilst I have not met any of the people you mention, I can tell you that not only is my best friend a close acquaintance of John Lilburne, but he was taught to read and write by Katherine Chidley's daughter. It must be the same woman, there cannot be many of that name in London. If you wish, I will carry your words of support to her via my friend. I am sure it will be appreciated and treasured."

Her maturity and control dissolved before his eyes and she rushed him, flinging her arms around him and burying her head in his chest. "Oh, Master Farrell! How I now regret my earlier words to you." He could hardly hear her muffled words coming from somewhere in his shirtfront. "Thank you, sir. It would be my dearest wish to meet her and this is the next best thing to that unlikely dream."

And without looking up at his face, she rushed from the room.

"Gentlemen. My apologies. Since my dear wife passed over, she has taken it on herself to grow up way before her time. She is a strength to me, but sometimes she tries too hard to be ten years older than she is. I love her dearly, but I worry about her. I am sorry for the inquisition."

Both Matthew and Richard were quick to make light of the conversation. Richard had been enormously impressed by the quickness of her mind and the resolution of her spirit. "Is it you, sir, who has helped her to develop such a sharp wit? She clearly has great intelligence and strength of will."

"Aye, she has that. My wife was a strong woman before illness took her. It was she that tutored Eliza, and her sister. As a result, her education has slowed and she has lost her best friend too. Eliza is almost a woman and I am not sure there is much more anyone could usefully teach her. Her sister, Margaret – we call her Maggie – however, has much to learn."

He sighed and looked to the heavens. "I have interviewed several governesses, but none are suitable. Both Eliza and Maggie would have eaten them alive. And I am so busy, I cannot devote the time to either tutor them myself or search more widely for a good candidate. Someone who could be a companion for Eliza, and a positive influence on Maggie's education. Anyway, friends. Enough of my troubles and on to the great cause. Tell me, please. How does Sir William expect me to help?"

For the rest of the meeting, Richard could let Matthew take the lead. His thoughts kept going back to Eliza and her resemblance to his own sister. Not in looks but in her fierceness. How she attacked life. Both had lost their mothers and had taken on responsibility for other family members early in their lives. But strangely, the other person that kept coming into his mind was Marleigh Hume. He had been struck by her clear intelligence and, as Eliza herself had said, there was a

(Macclesfield, late May 1642)

depth to her which was uncommon in someone of her station. He had no doubt that Marleigh Hume would have no trouble managing Maggie. The issue was her reputation, and of course he had no idea whether she would even be interested in such a post. He would think on it further.

*

Matthew was horrified and wanted nothing to do with it. He began to wonder if Richard was, in some way, bewitched.

Marleigh was at first dismissive, unwilling to risk her existing position. Finally, she accepted that as a companion in a private house, she would be less in the public eye than through her work at church and school. She was prepared to try.

Samuel Walker was shocked and angry, but given his predicament and trust in Richard, prepared to listen and observe. Only Marleigh knew how much effort she put into moulding his mind to be open to the idea.

It was watching Marleigh with Eliza and Maggie that truly convinced Walker that this was a solution that had some potential. The chemistry between the three was immediate and, to Marleigh's surprise, required little intervention from her. She liked Eliza's passion and saw Maggie as an interesting challenge. After all, here was good practice for her own child-to-be. Walker agreed to give it a week, provided Marleigh kept a low profile and understood that the arrangement could come to an abrupt end. Marleigh could think of nothing better. Richard and Matthew rode away from Macclesfield on the road back to Chester two days later, content with the success of their mission.

37

MARLEIGH

(Macclesfield, late July 1642)

She clung on to the bed sheet, knuckles white, eyes staring wildly at the ceiling. Sweat covered her, and strands of drenched hair matted across her forehead and cheeks and stuck to her shoulders.

It felt like every muscle quivered and she felt every tremor like a harp string vibrating in her head. She gulped in air irregularly, with a lack of control that terrified her, although she felt detached from it, like a horrified onlooker. She had no idea if the next heaving spasm would mark the end. She had been like this for days, or was it only hours, or minutes? Time seemed to pass like her breathing, in sudden rushes and periods of absolute stasis.

But it was her mind that was in deep trouble, not her body, because she was losing it. Her grip on sanity, the fortress of her ideas and certainties, honed and reinforced, deep foundations dug and strengthened, was engulfed and battered by an irresistible tide of blinding, uncontrollable light. Even if she jammed her eyes closed, and blocked her ears, and curled foetus-like, there was no escaping the assault.

(MACCLESFIELD, LATE JULY 1642)

As she had done every day of the three weeks since her night with Richard, she had lain quietly on her new bed in the attic of the Walker house and reached into herself to touch the seed of new life she was convinced was there. Forming itself into her daughter. She knew it would be a girl. Wanted that desperately. She searched every muscle twitch, every slight ache or jab of discomfort. *I am here. I will always be here for you. Come to me! Reveal yourself to me. I will protect and teach.*

A growing unease and disappointment had been following her like a wraith, and she had to fight against the dread of a missed opportunity, to be happy, helpful and supportive to Walker and his girls.

Perhaps she could not conceive? This was not uncommon. But she had exerted all her power to ensure success. What if this wasn't enough, would never be enough? Could she survive another dead end?

But this day. This day. As she had lain in the dark before sleep, she had asked her body the usual question, and she had found an answer. Again, her mind had walked the corridors of her body and finally, finally, she had glimpsed something. Something like candlelight seeping under a closed door. She had moved her consciousness carefully towards it, searching for a key to the door she perceived stood between her and her child. Feeling like a performer she had once seen balancing on a single strand of rope, she reached, stretching every joint to popping point, tiptoes and fingers extended. With her mind she brushed the surface of the door like a fingertip. She nudged it with the edge of a thought, straining, but not quite getting the purchase she needed to open it and greet the new life within her. She could feel a tear on her cheek.

But then she felt another presence, like nothing else but a small warm hand in hers. Tiny but strong. It allowed her to lean her mind a little further, anchored by the firm grip that held her safe and stopped her falling. She had reached the door and gently pushed.

Like a shutter which creaks slowly open but is suddenly caught by a gale of wind whipping past, the door was ripped from her fingers and slammed open. It was like an opening onto the surface of the sun. A tide of light and power hit her like a physical force and smashed her flat into the thin mattress. For minutes she was unable to take a breath as her brain was overwhelmed with the rush.

She didn't know how much time had passed. Was passing. She twitched and twisted and gripped, trying to regain control. She felt herself sliding slowly, very slowly, down a slope towards a hole filled with blackness. She knew, somehow, that if she fell within, she would never surface again. She became resigned to it. At least she could rest. *Let go.* Stop fighting the inevitable tide. She closed her eyes, exhaled slowly and swallowed hard as she felt an acceleration towards the brink.

But something was tugging at her. Pulling at her consciousness – something frantic, desperate. Something digging in its heels to slow the descent. She cast around for the source – peering through the massive sensory overload for a sense of its presence. *There. Was it? There!* Two wide eyes peering at her, pleading. Strange eyes – one grey, one hazel – but eyes she immediately recognised. She sensed a hand on her. The same small hand, tiny fingers straining to hold their grip on her. Her child. It couldn't be, not in just a few weeks? Was she already mad? Or was this a glimpse the future? This was the child as she would be? She felt tears in her own eyes. She would only ever find out if she survived this siege on her sanity.

A new determination flowed through her. With her mind, she grabbed the hand. The lifeline. It was like finding a slow eddy in the furious white water of a mountain river. She clung on and

(MACCLESFIELD, LATE JULY 1642)

waded to safer waters, relying entirely on her new anchor. With a new feeling of relative safety and security she tried to make sense of what was happening to her. She assumed the door she had opened in her mind had been a connection to her unborn child, albeit only a few weeks formed. Now she had felt the presence of that person, she understood that the child was also an observer, not the source of the violent, overwhelming flow of information. She also knew, with great clarity, that if she once let go of her connection to the child, she was lost.

She slowly regained a degree of calmness and started to understand that her desperation was merely an inability to process the rush of information bombarding her senses. It was not a flow coming from her child, but rather the presence of the child had helped her open a door in her own mind. The child – she couldn't keep referring to her as 'the child'. She had to give her a name now. If she was the only reason Marleigh was clinging to sanity, then she deserved a name. 'Eva' had been chosen long ago. It meant 'Giver of Life', and how appropriate, for no one else had helped her to see like this before.

Like a thin veil over a window, she realised she had been seeing the world as masked and shaded glimpses. Shadowy, partially hidden, grey and obscured. Somehow, Eva had helped her pull back the veil and now she was confronting the world as it was. In all its glory and complexity. And it was threatening to drive her mad.

She was starting to sense the energy as attached to objects, not as a jumbled mess of light flowing at her. She was starting to be able to recognise sources. A moth in the corner of her room emitted a bright pulsing, which screeched at her senses when it vibrated its wings. She could see a glowing outline slowly stalking it along the angle of the ceiling and made out a spider's form, otherwise invisible behind a strip of flaking plaster.

Even in the walls and floors she detected a faint sheen of

energy, intensifying in the corners and behind objects. *Where my cleaning is not so thorough*, she thought. *There is life on brick and stone and wood, and in the dust on the windowsill. It is there, even if I cannot see it. I am surrounded.*

She was slowly calming, and her breathing was slowing. She was processing her surroundings more rationally as she lay rigid on the bed. She raised one hand in front of her face and the madness threatened to return. A coursing, surging web of light occupied her flesh. It was as if she had kicked a nest of ants as light and energy wove and flowed across her senses. She felt she could see into and through her skin, muscle and bones, but her mind could not take in the complexity in a sensible way. She teetered again on the edge of the abyss, but this time, without her conscious control, her mind seemed to make its own adjustment. It was as if her vision defocused, so that she was still aware of a lightshow, but it was somehow in the distance, and her brain had readjusted to perceive her usual reality.

As time passed, she found she could switch between this reality and the complex view, like a telescope focusing and un-focusing on an object. Calm again, she spent some time experimenting, and finally, nervously, she sat up and moved to the window of the high attic room. She closed her eyes and gripped the windowsill, feeling a faint fluttering under fingertips. Slowly she opened them and looked out at the early morning rendering of the town.

At first, she looked down to the street, trying to concentrate on using her normal vision. When she was ready, she slowly tried to bring forward her new senses, and she almost collapsed at the knees as her view was immediately overlaid with light. As she raised her eyes to the forested hills to the east, uncovered by brick and stone houses or muddy part-paved streets, she saw it was ablaze. Ablaze with life. She finally saw the living world in its glory and understood.

38

RICHARD

(near Huntingdon, 22 August 1642)

He spurred his horse into a canter as he scattered ducks and fat white geese from the lane leading from the whitewashed farm. The rain, which had been lashing down for several hours, had slowed to a drizzle and he was anxious to recover lost time. He was on his way home, chased by the rising tide of impending war and drawn by his promise to himself, made months ago in an inn in Macclesfield, that he would visit his family and consider a future back with his brothers and sister.

After Macclesfield, he had journeyed with Matthew back to Chester to report on their mission to Brereton. Sir William had been delighted with the messages of support but was clearly agitated by the ratcheting up of tension in the country, with every letter and messenger reporting more news of conflict. Street fighting in Manchester where Baron Strange had taken on the mob. Parliamentarian troops defending the Hull arsenal from the King's men as soldiers now openly gathered to either the King or Parliament. Militias being raised. Skirmishes in Somerset, and a siege of

Royalist troops trapped in Portsmouth by Parliamentarian Trained Bands.

Brereton had resolved to try to raise support in Chester, understanding how crucial the city was to the region and control of the sea road to Ireland. He also knew the odds were strongly against him, and so the work done by Richard and Matthew had also opened up a secure path of retreat to loyal friends of the cause, should it be necessary.

He had wished Richard well in his journey home, urging him to think about loyalties and where he would pledge his sword in the fight to come. Richard had considered that question in the days that followed, jogging along quieter country paths, trying to avoid increasingly agitated towns and villages. His home, he knew, would declare solidly for Parliament. Men like Cromwell would see to that, rallying the Puritan folk and others critical of the King's popish leanings and indulgence of Archbishop Laud, now languishing in the Tower. He saw little of merit in either side and the idea of a quiet life in the country around Godmanchester seemed a more attractive option. Maybe he would just try to sit it all out. Surely any conflict could not last long in this country. They only had to look at the misery over the sea to see what war meant to the ordinary folk. *But then again, whenever did the rich and powerful give a fuck about the ordinary folk?* Dogma, ego and avarice made the world's wheel turn and tough luck to those who got ground into the mud beneath it.

He had stopped the previous night at the farm, not far from home on the outskirts of Huntingdon. He had wanted to push on and make it to the family hearth that night, but the driving rain and strong wind, a curse in August, had driven him to seek shelter. He had been allocated the barn, the farmer and his family wary of strangers bearing pistols and sword, but learning he came from but an hour's ride away had softened the

(near Huntingdon, 22 August 1642)

banishment, and a bowl of mutton stew, a heel of fresh bread and one of last year's good apples had seen him off to sleep.

It was in the deepest part of the night that he had fallen back into his recurring nightmare. Somehow, on this occasion, the familiar story seemed so much clearer. It was very strange. He had felt recently, ever since Macclesfield, that he had been seeing and hearing things more clearly. His senses slightly heightened. He was not sure why, but now it seemed as if this had translated into his dream-state. The darkening sky over the black sea was peppered with crows and ravens, flying in from the horizon as if to attend the aftermath of some battle. The figure on the pebbled beach, cloaked and hooded, small and vulnerable against the coming storm. As he tossed and turned in the blanket on the straw, mouth drawn into a rictus grimace of tension and horror, the sea drew back, rattling the fist-sized stones and revealing the faceless forms that rose in unison and started their slow progress up the slope. The hooded figure motionless, rigid, as if nailed to the spot. As always, he shouted for her to run. But this time, when the figure turned and looked back at him over her shoulder, he could see into the darkness of the cowl. It was not Neelie. It was not Marleigh Hume. The face of the girl that looked up at him was his sister, Angelica. Appealing to him, helpless, doomed. Tears welled in her eyes and she was calling out to him. He was rooted to the spot and when the end came it was worse than he could remember. Seeing her face just amplified the horror.

He woke, wrapped in a knot of the blanket. Tears streamed down his face and for several moments he did not know where he was. Pale dawn seeped through the warped wood of the barn door and his horse was looking at him nervously, stamping a front foot in agitation. He knew he had been screaming, as his throat was sore with the effort.

He had packed his roll and dashed cold water from the horse trough into his eyes. He bid the farmer and his family a hasty thanks and farewell, and they seemed happy to see him go, shoving another wedge of bread into his hand. Now he was heading for home, rocketing along the lane and ducking low branches. He cursed himself for dawdling along on the roads south and east from Chester. The hours spent dozing by slow rivers in the summer sun, and the long evenings in taverns, spending the handsome reward he had received from Brereton and dreaming of the night spent with Marleigh. Now all seemed trivial and slothful. There was no one around on whom to take out his frustration, so he kicked his heels harder into his horse and it found an extra ounce of pace to match his mood.

After half an hour, his horse was tiring through the heavy mud. He cleared a small rise and emerged from a copse of birch and willow, dense with flies and small biting midges. The early morning sun, the first he had seen for several days, was raising steam from bark, grass and muddy puddles. As his eyes adjusted back to the sun's glare, he saw he was coming towards the edge of Huntingdon. Godmanchester lay just beyond, over the river.

He spurred on, but within minutes, he saw movement to the east and he squinted into the low sunlight. A column of horsemen, two abreast, were passing through the ripening barley, also heading south, parallel to his own path. They also seemed to be making for the river crossing. He slowed quickly and brought his horse to a standstill. He had seen a few such patrols on his way across the country. The King had been touring the north to build his own support and if everything he had heard from Brereton were true, war was seemingly inevitable. He had thought himself safe in his home county. Here was a stronghold of the godly, staunch supporters of

(NEAR HUNTINGDON, 22 AUGUST 1642)

Parliament. He had many letters and documents on his person that would demonstrate his relationship with Brereton, surely a name that would be known hereabouts. While he had no strong personal loyalties to either side, the evidence in his belongings marked him out as having a clear allegiance.

But what if these were supporters of the King, perhaps returning from the North? Not a confrontation he wanted, especially given the urgency of his quest for home. He ground one gloved fist into the palm of the other and cursed his luck. He couldn't wait, he had to push on. He started to walk his horse quietly due south, thinking to navigate around the western edge of the town and avoid the more direct route.

By now the last pair had left the trees and the whole column, perhaps twenty horsemen, were jogging across the fields to the town. This was no experienced unit. They looked like militia, maybe not even that. They rode raggedly, not maintaining consistent spacings and showing no obvious weapons. But the man at the front of the column caught his eye. Straight back, a good horseman, at home in the saddle. He was surely military, even if the rest were playing at soldiers.

They seemed focused on a distant destination, but just as he thought he had evaded their attention, there was a shout. He looked over; perhaps 200 yards away the leader was standing in his stirrups and waving a gauntleted hand over his head. He shouted again, but Richard could not make out a word. He carried on slowly walking his horse, pretending not to understand he was the object of attention.

He stole a look to his left. The leader and three other horsemen were now galloping in his direction. The rest of the horsemen dismounting, stretching, some relieving themselves. *Shit! Shit, shit, shit!* There was no way to carry on now, it would be obvious he was avoiding them. *Damn them!* He could not afford the delay!

As they drew closer, they dropped into a trot. The leader raised a hand in greeting, but his face betrayed no welcome. Iron-grey short-cropped beard and bald head. Hard as nails, he eyed Richard with wary distrust. "Well met, sir." A deep voice, but flat and emotionless. Richard saw his right hand resting on the butt of a well-used flintlock pistol, holstered on the saddle by his thigh. He was wearing a thick leather coat and a cavalry blade hung on his left hip.

"Good morning to you, sir." From his accent, Richard thought he was a man from the area, and he relaxed marginally, letting the man see his own hands were well away from the Spanish rapier hanging from the baldric over his shoulder. "You lead these men?"

The soldier looked over his shoulder at his three companions who were trying to look threatening and competent but managed only to look unconvincing. "Yes. They are under my command for the time being at least. These are become dangerous times. These men are intent on protecting their families and property from threat. They have appointed me to lead them. And you, sir? That is no toy you carry. You are a soldier perhaps yourself, although you seem young to have been part of any conflict?"

"I was, once. A soldier, that is. Now I am heading for my home. Just beyond the town. I am late and would hurry on. I mean no offence or rudeness."

"I understand, but please forgive me, I would ask you a few questions, sir. I too mean no offence, but as I have said, we face uncertain times and I would know what a man alone, armed as you are, is about. Please humour me and you can be on your way swiftly. Your name would be a good start." The man's eyes belied his calm words and relaxed manner. He watched Richard like a hawk.

"As to that, sir, I am not sure what authority you have to

(near Huntingdon, 22 August 1642)

stop me. I am a free man going about my business and need to press on with my journey." He saw the man stiffen and take a firmer grip of the pistol. His men tried even harder to look intimidating. "I will give you my name and answer your questions, but forgive me if I first ask you *your* business. From whom are you and your companions seeking to protect the local folk?"

Confident in the twenty or so men at his back, the man leaned forward, saddle creaking as he looked Richard in the eye from less than six feet away. "You ask which side I am on?" He smiled, without humour. "I am not sure you are in a position to demand our answer first, but whatever. My name is Wolfe. Captain Thomas Wolfe. I fight papists and those who side with them. I have fought them across Europe for twenty years and now it seems I must do the same here. These men with me know nothing of war, but they are prepared to defy their King to live in a godly way. The Parliament is with us. Many of the Lords are with us. It seems that between us, we must persuade the King to change his ways."

His horse tossed its head and danced sideways, impatient to be moving. *As am I*, thought Richard bitterly. The soldier had not taken his eyes off Richard's. *Superb horseman.* "But there are many who side with the King and his traitorous advisers, and they stream north to join him. They ride through our towns and villages, and mostly they behave. But rumour is that the King is about to declare openly against Parliament, and some of our countrymen take that as an excuse to burn, steal and harass folk. My men and I patrol to deter such behaviour." He paused and intensified his stare, if that were possible. "And we look for spies. Those agents of the King's allies who would agitate, who would report on our strengths and weaknesses. Have you seen such men, sir? And now, I *will* have your name."

Richard had relaxed, convinced that the man's story fitted

with the appearance and demeanour of his men. They looked just as he described them. Villagers, farmers, storekeepers. Wolfe was every inch the hard-edged Puritan soldier he had encountered over the North Sea. "As to my name, I am Richard Farrell. My family's house is by Godmanchester." He saw Wolfe's men exchange looks and words, and Wolfe started too. "And I am very familiar with the King's agents, sir. I have been dodging them for longer than I care to tell you. You may relax, Captain Wolfe. I am no spy. In fact, I have been pursuing your cause in the North. 'Tis why I have been away. I have been working on behalf of Sir William Brereton, lately of Chester. Perhaps you know the name? I have papers on me that prove this, but I beg you, sir, trust me, I need to get home. I have concerns for the safety of my family there and you have done nothing to alleviate my fears."

One of the men behind Wolfe walked his horse forward and whispered something to him. They both looked across at Richard. Wolfe spoke, urgency in his voice. "This man tells me that one of the parties of men we seek were rumoured asking after the whereabouts of your family's house. Apparently, it is a pack of wolves that follow a man named Cobb. His is an evil name in these parts in the last weeks. He is the worst of the scum that have started to plague innocent folks. We were riding this way to investigate this rumour, and when we saw that, we had quickened our pace. Something we are seeing all too often, but we rarely are able to catch the arsonists in the act and extract the price." He pointed out across the field, beyond the town. A tall pillar of smoke rising into the blue. "Does the name Cobb mean anything to you?"

Richard gawped back, horror-struck, mute. He had been in such a rush, eyes first on the road, and then on Wolfe's militia, that he had not even seen the distant smoke. He nodded, unable to speak.

(NEAR HUNTINGDON, 22 AUGUST 1642)

Wolfe nodded. "If your journey was not already urgent, I would certainly ride hard now. You bring the storm with you, I think." Richard looked back over his shoulder, and the pleasant cloud-streaked blue of the early morning was being overwhelmed by a steadily approaching wall of black. Even as he saw the storm approaching, he heard the first rumble of thunder. "We will accompany you, Master Farrell! For surely God has guided our paths to cross. Lead the way, sir! We follow!"

But Richard was already wheeling and spurring his horse, kicking up mud in a flurry of hooves. *Cobb! Surely not the same Cobb? Why would that bastard be here?* The sound of the storm rolled behind him and soon he also picked up the thump of hooves as those behind tried to catch him. The wind was picking up as he clattered through the outskirts of Huntingdon, scattering townsfolk. They streamed past the mound where the remains of the castle stood, guarding the passage of the river, driving on towards Godmanchester.

He glanced over his shoulder and saw Wolfe keeping pace, two of his men a little further back, the remainder of the troop not in sight. He veered left down a lane before they reached Godmanchester, taking him straight to the house. No stopping at the Blue Boar today. And suddenly the face of Montague was back in his mind. The last time he had seen the loathsome King's agent. Could he be in with Cobb? He doubted it. If the King were about to declare war on his people, then Montague had bigger fish to fry than Richard Farrell.

By now he knew with an icy certainty where the smoke was coming from. He also knew that whatever had happened, they were too late. He had seen the aftermath of these types of raids and the burning was usually the last thing done before the culprits left the scene.

They were now but minutes away and he spotted something in the lane ahead. It was hedged in on both sides, and a body lay, legs in the path and torso propped half in and half out of a holly bush. He reined in hard and his horse skidded in the mud, barely keeping its feet. He didn't recognise the man, who seemed to be a labourer from his dress. He looked to have been there some time and there was an ugly bruise up his neck and face. His eyes were closed, but it was obvious he was dead.

"Ridden down," came a voice from behind him. Wolfe and his two men were peering around his horse to see the man. "Looks like a lot of horses came this way." The lane was thick mud from the recent downpours, but it was clearly churned by many hooves.

"That's Bill Ward, that is," said one of the men. "From the farm over yonder," and he pointed slightly east of north. "A good man."

"A dead man," said Wolfe, and he voiced Richard's own fears. "And for some time, I think. Last night perhaps. See, he is drenched, and already stiff as a board."

Richard groaned inwardly and he felt a cold band of tension grip his bowels. "Then we are too late."

"No, sir. There is always hope. In the rage of violence, and probably intoxication, men miss things. They do not search efficiently. People with warning can run. Can hide. Do not give up yet. Come, sir. Ride on!"

Richard spurred again, guiding his mount around the prone figure, and then picking up speed along the last few hundred yards. Now he could see glimpses of the house through the trees. *So at least something is still standing! Perhaps Wolfe is right.* It occurred to Richard that if the boot were on the other foot, Wolfe would make sure his men were 'efficient'. None of his enemies would escape. None would be safe in hiding.

They burst through the gate into the space in front of the house, the whole troop having now caught up. Richard came

(NEAR HUNTINGDON, 22 AUGUST 1642)

to a halt in front of the entrance which gaped open. There were no roaring flames, but the whole of the right-hand side of the building was a charred ruin, and the main barn, twenty yards to the south, was also just a few upright timbers, where the fire had not destroyed the massive oak frame. The more northerly side, to the left of the entrance, was intact, evidence, Richard hoped, of the inefficiency of the raiders. While he sat, scarcely believing the desolation visited on his family home, Wolfe was barking orders to his men, sending half around the back to try to find tracks, and telling others to dismount and start searching. There was a flurry of black wings as crows rose complaining from the barn as a group of men approached.

Wolfe suddenly appeared by the head of Richard's horse and he held the bridle. "Master Farrell? Shall we explore the house?" His voice was quiet, calm.

Richard slipped from the saddle. "You might want to bring your pistol, sir. It would seem they are long gone, but it would be wise to be cautious."

Richard nodded and hefted the flintlock from his saddle holster. Holding it barrel up, he walked slowly to the front door. A black forbidding hole, drawing him in.

Wolfe was shouting again. "C'mon! Hurry, lads! The storm is going to be here in minutes!" It was true. The wind was now bending the trees that surrounded the front and north side of the small estate, and had shredded the column of smoke.

There was an answering shout from the ruins of the barn. Wolfe shot Richard a look and put a hand on his shoulder. "You stay here. I will go." He jogged off, leaving Richard still transfixed by the open maw of the house that had always meant warmth and security.

Two of Wolfe's men stood either side of the door, looking at him enquiringly. He raised a hand to indicate they should wait and he looked across to Wolfe at the barn. He was conferring with several of his men; two more had dashed to the edge of the trees and were retching. Wolfe looked across at Richard and shook his head slowly. He issued more instructions to his charges and sent them off in different directions. No harsh orders now, just gentle commands. Hands on shoulders, gentle pushes to get them moving. He turned and walked back to Richard.

"Seems they herded some into the barn and lit it up. Might be five or six in there, I would guess. I am sorry, there is no way to identify anyone. Smoke would have got them before the flames. Seen it before. I am sorry."

Richard nodded, still unable to speak, and wondering how often Wolfe had seen it before and in what circumstances. Finally, he summoned the will and jerked his head towards the door. "I will search what remains of my home. Will you help me?"

In answer, Wolfe again placed his gauntleted hand on Richard's shoulder and steered him towards the open door. As they covered the last few yards, the last of the blue sky disappeared to the south-east, a shaft of sun blinding them momentarily. Then it was gone, the thunder rolled overhead, and the rain started again, slanting in sideways.

He was first through the door, pistol raised to chest height, barrel pointed to the still-intact high ceiling of the hall. To his right, where once the kitchen and dining room stood, there was a void framed by a few surviving beams and timbers. The rain hissing into still-smouldering wood. Wolfe gestured for one of his men to go and search through the ashes.

In front, the doors onto the small courtyard at the back were open, swinging heavily in the wind, all the glass gone. Although it was nearly black as night outside, there was light to show a prone figure lying at the foot of the main stairs. The man was on his back, a black pool of blood congealed around

(NEAR HUNTINGDON, 22 AUGUST 1642)

his head. Richard slowly approached, his knees weak, heart racing. He felt Wolfe a few paces behind him, watchful, pistol raised and sword gripped in his right fist.

As he approached, he could clearly see that it was the body of his eldest brother, John. He knelt and placed a hand on his brother's chest. He could feel his eyes fill with tears.

Pale, waxy. Eyes closed, thank God! He looked peaceful, even with the neat black hole in the centre of his forehead and powder stains across much of his face. He had fallen as if poleaxed, arms by his side, heels together. Richard noted absently that his boots were gone. His brother had been executed. Good, honest, kind, patient John. Gone in an instant.

Abruptly, the cold, hypnotic state he had inhabited was gone. Molten fury erupted in his heart, and he stood, sweeping out his rapier. Wolfe sent the other militiaman to the sitting room to the left of the stairs.

Richard found his voice. "He was guarding the stairs. Why..." but then it was suddenly clear to him why. Childhood games of hide and seek. He knew why. He leapt the prone body onto the stairs, taking Wolfe by surprise. He cursed as he saw, on alternate wooden stairs, a blackening boot heel print. *The wardrobe! Always the same bloody place!*

He careered around the rail and along the corridor to his parents' old bedroom. He didn't need the blackened trail to tell him where to go, but it led faithfully to the bedroom door. In the seconds it took him to reach it, he wondered why it was closed. Why would you close the door?

He grabbed the handle and flung it inwards.

Halfway across the room, the floor had gone, and the far wall had also either burnt or collapsed as the structure failed. He looked out and across to the ruins of the barn and into the copse beyond. Rain pelted down and he could see some of Wolfe's men sheltering in the treeline. The bed had gone, slid down and consumed in the blackened husk of the southerly wing. Just an armchair by the window, looking out over the barley fields beyond. And the wardrobe. Standing against the wall a few feet from the doorway where he stood.

There was a thick black pool caking the floorboards in front of the double doors. He knelt again, and vomited, helpless for a moment as fear and nausea overwhelmed him. A hand under his arm lifted him to his feet. A soft voice, "Please. Let me do this. Wait downstairs, Farrell."

But he shook it off. "My sister," he said. It was all he could manage. He placed a hand on Wolfe's chest and gently but firmly pushed him back through the door. "My little sister."

In his mind, he saw the sea roll back down the pebbles under the sky of jet.

He saw the boot prints lead past him from the sticky puddle and back out through the door.

The faceless figures slowly rose from the shingle and gathered their rocks.

He walked to the massive oak wardrobe and, placing his weapons on the floor, grasped the twin handles.

The black wave climbed into the sky and towered over him.

The rain lashed down, the wind driving it several feet into the ruined bedroom. He swallowed down the urge to vomit again and pulled the doors open. A small white hand flopped out of the confined space and lay palm up on the rim of the wardrobe, delicate marble from some ancient Roman statue suspended over a pool of black.

The figures reached the hooded woman. Pleading eyes turned to meet his helpless gaze.

He parted the hanging clothes and revealed her hiding place. She was half lying against the side of the interior, legs drawn up in a crouching position. She was in a pale grey gown,

(NEAR HUNTINGDON, 22 AUGUST 1642)

but it was soaked in her blood. Her chest and stomach were a mass of punctures, and more blood and bruises down her naked lower legs told its own story. Her face was shielded by one of his father's old riding capes.

Lightning flashed behind him. The wind raged again and crashed the wardrobe doors back. A flurry of rain drenched his back.

Hands grasping the stones picked from the beach were raised high, poised against the tide.

He gently pushed back the cape. Angelica's dead eyes stared back at him, telling him that he was too late.

Seventy miles to the north, in Nottingham, King Charles the First raised his standard and declared war.

The stones rose and fell. The black wave broke over him and all was dark.

THE END OF BOOK ONE

The story continues in book two – Reap the Whirlwind

AUTHOR'S NOTE AND ACKNOWLEDGEMENTS

This is a period of history that entirely escaped me in my school days. Apart from a few basics such as the beheading of Charles I, and the rise of Oliver Cromwell, I knew very little. Now I know a little more about it, I am amazed that it is not more widely taught, because there is so much happening in terms of social, political and religious ideas, and how these mobilised large parts of the population to actions previously unheard of in England, or indeed large parts of the world.

Starting to read about the period led me to some fascinating sources that helped provide the historical context for my story. I want to pay tribute to some of the more prominent sources of information for the novels in this series.

My starting point was the excellent overview provided by Trevor Royle's *Civil War: The Wars of the Three Kingdoms, 1638–1660*. This, combined with the fabulous resource of the British Civil Wars, Commonwealth and Protectorate website (http://bcw-project.org/about), gave me a roadmap of the times, but also so much valuable detail. Antonia Fraser's *Cromwell: Our Chief of Men* also provided great insight into the political minds of the day, and Cromwell's in particular.

I set much of the narrative of the first two books around my hometown of Macclesfield – not the setting for many novels, I think! Here, C.S. Davies' excellent *A History of Macclesfield* was extremely helpful, along with an archaeological assessment of the town published by Cheshire County Council and English Heritage. My own original research included a few drinks in the historic Bate Hall pub in Chestergate, where the friendly barman told me of sightings of its famous ghosts.

As the character of Sir William Brereton became more important to the story, I discovered a wealth of information about his life and career. Much of this is from books authored by Andrew Abram, John Barratt, R.N. Dore and Joseph McKenna, but also from some of his own diaries which are held in the British Library and describe his colourful journeys through the Low Countries, Scotland and Ireland in his youth.

Dealing in Death: The Arms Trade and the British Civil Wars, 1638–52 is an incredibly detailed piece of work by Peter Edwards, which was absolutely fascinating, and essential, to describe the business that Richard Farrell finds himself engaged in. The radical political debates and confrontations of the time are beautifully captured in John Rees's wonderful book *The Leveller Revolution*, where the revolutionary passion and commitment of freeborn John Lilburne and his heroic wife, Elizabeth, are immortalised. *Witchfinders* by Malcolm Gaskill is an equally detailed and vital source for my attempts to weave this important thread of the period through the story.

However, *At the Edge of Promises* is not a scholarly work but the fictional stories of certain people trying to find purpose for their lives in this tumultuous period of change. I think it is important to emphasise that most of the 'point of view' characters in these stories are entirely fictional. Richard Farrell, Marleigh Hume, Will Fletcher, Roger DeLacey, John Cobb and the Walker family are all fictional characters.

William Brereton is the only real historical character who has a 'point of view' role in the books, but all of his interactions with the fictional characters are, by definition, fictional. From the research into Sir William, I have tried to guess at his character, and how he might react in the circumstances where I have placed him, but the main arc of his story in these books, albeit constructed around the real events he was very much part of, is entirely made up.

Finally, I wanted to pay tribute to the support provided my key critics and advisers, my sons, Michael and Joe, but particularly my wife, Sarah, who has had to endure my periods of excitement and depression as my confidence in what I have written waxed and waned. Thank you.

My thanks as well to Adrian Shuker and Dr Michael Tate for their commitment in reading the drafts of the books and for their kind words of encouragement. Thank you both.